REJOICE

A KNIFE TO THE HEART

A NOVEL OF FIRST CONTACT

STEVEN ERIKSON

This paperback published in Great Britain in 2019 by Gollancz

First published in Great Britain in 2018 by Gollancz
an imprint of the Orion Publishing Group Ltd
Carmelite House, 50 Victoria Embankment
London EC4Y 0DZ

An Hachette UK Company

1 3 5 7 9 10 8 6 4 2

A CIP catalogue record for this book is
available from the British Library.

ISBN (MMP) 978 1 473 22382 0

Typeset by Deltatype Ltd, Birkenhead, Merseyside

Printed and bound in Great Britain by Clays Ltd, Elcograf S.p.A

www.steven-erikson.com
www.gollancz.co.uk

To Mark Karasick, for sharing that first ride on the chariot

CHARACTERS

Fictional:

Samantha (Sam) August – a writer of science fiction
Dr Hamish Drake – her husband
Ronald Carpenter – another science fiction author

Raine Kent – President of the United States
D(iana).K(imberly). Prentice – Vice-President
Dr Ben Mellyk – Science Advisor to the President
Daniel Prester – Security Advisor, Homeland Security
Kenneth J. Esterholm – Director of CIA
Adam Riesling – astronaut

Konstantine Milnikov – President of Federation of Russia
Anatoli Petrov – retired cosmonaut

Xin Pang – Leader of the People's Republic of China
Liu Zhou – Head of Chinese Space Exploration Programme
Hong Li – astronaut on Luna mission
Captain Shen – commander of Luna mission

Lisabet Carboneau – Prime Minister of Canada
Alison Pinborough – Science Advisor to the Prime Minister
Mary Sparrow – Minister for Parks and Recreation
Will Camden – Minister for Natural Resources
Marc Renard – Canadian astronaut

Joey Sink – blogger and conspiracy buff (Kitchen Sink News)
Annie Mouse – whistleblower at JPL
King Con – (alias) conspiracy buff

Joakim Malleat – cardinal in the Vatican, Officer of Public
   Communications

Ira Levy – rabbi based in New York City
Richard Fallow – televangelist
Abdul Irani – imam

Simon Gist – self-made industrialist, Kepler Industries
Jack Butler – chief engineer, Kepler Industries
Mary Lamp – PR Director at Kepler Industries
Douglas Murdo – media tycoon
Chrystal Murdo – his wife
Maxwell Murdo – his son
James Adonis – billionaire
Jonathan Adonis – billionaire
Lois Stanton – personal secretary to the Adonis brothers

Kolo – death-squad commander in the Republic of Congo
Neela – slave girl to Kolo
Ruth Moyen – soldier, IDF
Casper Brunt – an arms dealer
Anthony 'Tony' – a resident of LA

'ADAM' – AI communicant of the Intervention Delegation

Non-Fictional (in their own words):
Robert J. Sawyer

CONTENTS

CONTENTS

There is not and never has been
an extraterrestrial presence on Earth.

It is important for you to keep believing that.

This is why.

Prologue ...

Space was astir. In the scatter of asteroids in orbit between Mars and Jupiter, small objects burst into being, like clouds of gnats rising from an unseen pond. They were small, none larger than an average SUV, but as one moment led to the next, these machine-clouds proliferated. Before long, the swarms numbered in the hundreds, and the objects numbered in the tens of thousands.

The clouds, mostly unlit barring the faint reflection of the distant sun's light, dispersed from their point of origin. At astonishing velocities, they set off among the asteroids. Others winged outward, quickly leaving the relatively crowded space of the asteroid belt's field of rubble. Others raced towards Mars.

Over the next few hours and days, the machine-clouds among the asteroids settled on select chunks of rock, some metal-rich, others more comet-like and heavy with frozen water, methane, ammonia and a carbonaceous skin of space-dust. On each of these asteroids, the objects clustered exclusively on one side. Extending filaments they linked up and then settled in. A dozen other clouds converged on the largest asteroid in the immediate area. These too linked up, only to then disgorge smaller machines. These began devouring rock.

Out beyond the swathe of rubble left behind by over four billion years of planets being born and planets dying, of still-birthed moons, of impacts and collisions, lone machine-clouds sped through the dark, hunting comets.

Inward of the asteroid field, the clouds heading towards Mars converged on the smaller of the planet's two moons, Deimos, and like their kin, they settled upon its dusty, pitted surface, concentrating upon one side of the misshapen moon, and then linked up.

Nothing on Earth, or in Earth orbit, was capable of detecting these events.

That only came later, when the machines began dismantling orbital mechanics, and asteroids and comets broke from their ancient paths, and set off, at considerable velocity, towards the heart of the solar system. And when Deimos shifted orbit, to slowly, incrementally, collide with Phobos.

By then, however, very few on Earth were really paying any attention.

STAGE ONE:

Count to Fifty
(Initiation)

Chapter One

City of Victoria, British Columbia, Canada
May 19th, 2:19 PM

Three smokers were hanging out outside the bar on Cook Street. A woman was carrying a cardboard box filled with old clothes, heading for the consignment shop. Across the street, three house-painters had just climbed the stairs up from the hardware store, burdened with supplies for repairing drywall. A man was walking towards Pandora Avenue and the grocery store on its corner.

The street itself was crowded with traffic, congested despite the suicide turn-lane running down the centre. The pace was a crawl in the lane heading south as the last few vehicles caught up to the line awaiting a change of lights down at Pandora. A UPS delivery van had just turned from Pandora, heading north.

In total, eleven cameras caught the event, as stills and video. There was an exceptional amount of concurrence among the witnesses when later questioned by journalists and police officers. The event had already gone viral when the official inquiry began.

A middle-aged woman had been walking down Cook, on the same side as the consignment store and the bar. She had been well dressed, her stride assured, her hands in the pockets of her charcoal-grey mid-length coat and her fiery red hair long enough to lift in the wind coming up from the south, but not so long as to fantail out behind her. Her face – as the nearest witnesses recalled – was curiously memorable. High cheekbones, flat cheeks, a wide jaw, a face that hadn't seen much sun.

There'd been some clouds overhead, scudding in from the Sooke Hills to the west, so at first no one had paid much attention to the shadow settling across the street.

One of the smokers, a Mister John Allaire, was wheelchair-bound. His angle of repose afforded him the privilege of being the first person to sight the dispersal of the cloud overhead, revealing the slightly curved shape of something solid and huge.

'Like the underside of a plate, a china plate,' John said. In the course of his life up until now, this was his defining event. Things had been pretty shitty for some time. His smoking was killing his legs below the knees. His drinking was pickling his liver. He was sixty-three years old and living on assistance. He'd never won the lottery.

'Like the underside of a plate, a china plate. That then started glowing in the middle. Dead centre. Glowing like you wouldn't believe. I had to shade my eyes, but that didn't stop me seeing the beam of light come down. Right on that woman – who wasn't twenty feet from me. She never knew what hit her.'

Margot Revette agreed. 'She was just walking. And then the light swallowed her up, and then the light was gone and so was she. I was bringing old clothes in, you know? And an old pair of high heels – can't believe I bought those. Not meant for human feet. I must've lost my mind. But consignment, right? There's always the chance, I mean, people will buy anything.'

'The light hit,' said Rick Shultz. 'We were just out from the store, me and Jack and Naadi. Carrying shit to the back of the truck. The fucking light stabbed down from that fucking UFO, and bam! The woman was gone. Then the ship just folded up and vanished.'

'Holy fuck yeah,' added Jack. 'She was, like, incinerated.'

'Folded up and vanished,' Rick repeated. 'Damned thing didn't even fly away.'

Who was she?

No one knew. They would have to await reports of someone gone unexpectedly missing. It might take a day or two, and if the woman lived alone, maybe a lot longer.

None of the video or still shots caught much of her face. Too bad about that, but then, not surprising. Everyone was filming the UFO.

•

Dr Hamish Drake worked too hard. People who knew him agreed on that, especially his wife. For the past five years, Hamish had been one of only three general practitioners in Greater Victoria who was accepting new patients. It was something of a crisis.

He was between patients that afternoon, stealing a few minutes trying to work his way into a stack of test results appended to patient files, when his receptionist, Nurjehan Aziz, entered his office. Startled by the absence of a knock, Hamish looked up over his reading glasses. There was an ashen hue to her face, the kind of look he had seen before, usually when red-flagged results came back on a long-standing patient.

Death had a way of stalking the living, a detail both Nurjehan and Hamish understood all too well. It arrived in a pallor, the blood draining from a living face. In Nurjehan's visage, the shadow was there for him to see, and a cool, dispassionate dread rose in answer from the depths of his gut, even as in his mind he searched his memory for who might be in trouble – someone he'd seen the past week, someone he'd ordered tests on, someone –

'Something's happened,' Nurjehan said.

Hamish frowned. This was different. She was trembling. He'd never seen his receptionist so rattled. Removing his glasses and setting them down on the desktop, he said, 'Close the door. Explain.'

His calm, dulcet tones failed to settle her. Instead, she winced.

'I was online – forgive me—'

'Not again. Nurjehan, if you're not here to tell me that a nuclear war has just erupted, I will be—'

'There was a UFO. Here in Victoria. There are recordings all over Facebook and YouTube. I looked at the CHEK news site. The police have posted a photo of someone … disappearing. Inside a beam of light.'

'A UFO.'

Nurjehan held out her cellphone to show him the image she had called up.

Too close. He could make out little more than a blurry figure on what looked like a street. Hamish retrieved his glasses, put them on and then leaned forward.

'That's Sam.'

As if from some distance, he heard Nurjehan say, 'The beam of light. From the UFO. The whole thing was recorded.'

'This is ridiculous,' Hamish said, reaching for his own phone. He fast-dialled his wife's number. The response was immediate. Connection failed. 'Doesn't mean anything,' he muttered, dialling again. 'Even with her online presence, she hardly ever picks up. Sometimes she forgets to even turn the damned thing on.' Same result. He pocketed the phone and rose. 'Let me see that video. I cannot believe this.'

●

It had been barely three blocks away from the city's police station. John Scholes set the phone down. Ignoring the flashing lights of multiple lines left open and on hold, he rose from his desk and walked over to the window.

Traffic churned past and there seemed to be a new edge to it, although that was likely his own imagination. He looked up. Innocent tufts of cloud scudding past and, much higher, a smear of haze paling the blue of the sky. He watched a float-plane bank to make for a harbour landing.

'That sounded tough,' said a voice behind him.

'Dave,' he said by way of greeting, not turning around. 'Yeah, it was. We've got a positive ID. That was her husband on the line.'

'You sure?'

'Yeah, surprised I didn't see it the first time. Granted, the shot was blurry ... but that red hair ...'

His beat partner moved up to stand beside him. 'Still got to be some kind of hoax.'

John nodded. 'Maybe especially now.'

'What do you mean?'

'The woman. Samantha August. The sci fi writer. You know, *Chasms*, the one they made that movie of. That, and other stuff. Vlogger. Politics. Social justice.'

Dave snorted. 'An SF writer got zapped into dust by a UFO? Man, you can't make that shit up.'

John shot his partner a sour look. 'Like I just explained to her husband, we've got a missing person, not a dead one. No evidence that she got incinerated—'

'Can you hear yourself? Evidence? What evidence? That's the whole point of incineration, isn't it?' He waved a hand at the scene outside. 'A gust of wind. Poof! Gone.'

'No one saw her burn up or anything. Just vanish. The light swallows her and then it's gone, and so is she. Man,' he added, 'I've watched the fucking vid about a thousand times already.'

'More sightings?' Dave asked.

'Sightings, kidnappings, anal probes – they're all coming out of the woodwork.'

'But nothing else on vid.'

John shook his head. And then, as if amending his judgement, he shrugged. 'The web's full of that stuff.'

'Yeah, grainy, blurry crap in the age of HD. Bad photoshop shit.' Dave paused, and then said, 'It all gets debunked sooner or later.'

John shrugged. Truth was, he had no opinion on the subject either way. The days were too damned full as it was, and the darkness growing in his mind made his nights an ordeal. He'd heard an old veteran call it 'The Walk' and now he was on it. The walk ... away from faith, away from any expectation except the worst when it came to humanity. A gathering up of sorrow, like soiled clothes into a bag of laundry, kicked to the corner of the room. In the meantime, you just got on with things.

At the walk's end, he'd stop caring.

Maybe there were other ways through it all. He knew he'd keep looking until ... well, until he gave up.

'Want me to take some of these calls?'

John nodded. 'Appreciate it, Dave.'

'This one's fucked you over.'

It had. It took a leap of faith he didn't have in him. But without it he had nothing. He turned to his partner and said, 'Her husband was pretty messed up.'

But Dave was already on the phone, taking another hysterical call.

She was in the house, no matter which room Hamish wandered into, as if he was tracking her passage, with his wife always just out of sight, just past closing the door or turning the corner. He could smell the rank cigarette smell on the stairs leading up to her garret, but it was an old smell, and the faint cloud above the carpeted steps was nothing more than dust lit by the sun's rays slanting in from the skylight.

Her notes and old coffee cup and overflowing ashtray flanked her home laptop, its lid down, its blue power light slowly pulsing.

But something of the ghost she had become now infected Hamish, and he wandered like a spirit trapped in the house, the house itself trapped inside a memory already growing stale and lifeless.

A marriage of thirty-three years, a practice of twenty-nine. No children. She wasn't the kind of woman to sacrifice personal habits and pleasures. Besides, children took time, energy, youth, a prison cell and a life sentence willingly walked into. She'd say that with the usual challenging glint in her eyes, as if on the edge of a harsh, possibly bitter laugh. For all his sensitivity and training, Hamish always had trouble reading his wife. She had knife-edges and a habit of dancing on them. It was a personal trait made into a professional persona. Her vlog, *Here Now*, was loved and was hated, depending on the political divide. She was fearless and a lot of people in the world didn't like fearless women.

The home phone had been ringing, its antiquated jangle of bells startling Hamish every time, the sound insistent and strangely cold. That would be her agent and maybe yes, he deserved a few words, but Hamish left the answering machine to do its work.

Her genre compatriots would be on her Facebook page, filling her Twitter feed with endless unanswered queries and pleas for more information from somebody, anybody. They'd be frantically knocking on the door of *Here Now*. Hamish left them to talk with each other. Beyond the blunt official statement from the police, and all the recorded interviews from the witnesses, there was really nothing else to be said. She was gone, but gone was now a word with a thousand possible meanings.

It was dusk and with none of the lights on in the house, the gloom pervaded, making grainy every detail in the living room where he had at last found himself, slumped in his leather chair. He had watched the videos of his wife's ... disappearance? Abduction? Annihilation? It could have been a scene from any of a dozen SF films and television series. That shaky handheld stuff had been in vogue a few years back, and now it had made a comeback.

She would've called by now. Touching base was important when it was just the two of them, not the kind with any sort of possessive heat; more a familiar brush of lives well known, the usual sharing of droll understatement, sardonic commentary, a handful of genuine phrases. Their private language.

A language he had no one to share with, not anymore, perhaps never again.

Hamish Drake sat in the living room, in the fading light, unaware of the chaos on the online fan sites, the frantic disbelief and shock among her many writer friends, and then the crowing religious fundamentalists going on about God's wrath and a woman's proper place in the world. A war had begun in the ether, centred on a woman no longer there.

And of course there was the persistent assertion by many that the whole thing was a hoax, a publicity stunt – was she writing a UFO novel?

Her half-dozen advance readers knew nothing about that – she'd been a third of a way into a far-future dystopian-nightmare thriller. It had been slowing down but dribs and drabs were still coming in. They'd agreed (among themselves) that she was tired, possibly even fed up. Thirty published novels, three film adaptations, two television series, one ongoing. A vlog infamous for stirring things up. Her stories were always vicious, the writing cutting like a scalpel, meaning you didn't know you were bleeding until you saw your own skin part, and out tumbled your guts. Her vlogs did the same, all delivered with a sweet smile.

The usual brilliant, furious shit, in other words. Sam August, feminist, humanist, occasional satirist and essayist, not one to be trifled with – no, she wasn't writing a fucking UFO novel.

Gone. Vanished, abducted, incinerated, missing, dead, alive, dead, alive, dead …

The lights stayed off in the house that night. Dawn found a man hunched over in his leather chair, his face in his hands, his body wracked with silent grief.

Chapter Two

'What is there to fear from the future, apart from our impending, utter vulnerability in the face of the unknown?'

Samantha August

When she was a child, she'd slipped when running across a pool deck. She woke up a day later in the hospital with no memory of the event. Consciousness had taken a sidestep. Where it went was a mystery, this stretch of static, white noise or, more accurately, absence. Neurologists would compartmentalise the experience. Consciousness, they'd explain, requires memory, the structure upon which experience is built, and experience is the meat and muscle of our sense of the self. An injury to the brain is like kicking an old-style television. The picture flickers, resets. There may be a gap between the last visible scene and the new one. But, if all is well, continuity resumes.

She wanted a cigarette. A visceral desire, systemic flags flipped up. The humbling reality of addiction was, she believed, a worthwhile investment in humility. Most of the communication between the body and the mind was murky, swimming the subconscious depths of autonomic necessity. The need to breathe defined itself, instant by instant. Hunger spoke in pangs, a spurt of saliva at the thought of a perfect BLT. Bright light or the flashing proximity of an object snapped shut the eyes. A list of the more obvious exchanges. The other exchanges were far subtler.

Beneath notice.

But caffeine withdrawal delivered a headache. Nicotine

withdrawal a not-quite-itch to the throat. General edginess for both, the wordless want awaiting articulation. Humility was useful, especially for a writer. It made it easier and less personally offensive to see – or imagine – the world in other ways.

Contrary opinions on how the way things worked, in all those mercurial mechanisms of human interaction: beliefs, politics, faiths, attitudes, opinions. For the addict, piety was the first self-delusion to go. It yanked the stick out of the arse.

So there was the need. For a cigarette. It was probably what dragged her back into awareness, arriving before she opened her eyes which, for the moment, she kept shut. Her senses, awakening, gave her little else. No sound, no particular smell. The surface beneath her back was neither hard nor soft. It was there, to be sure, but in no way did it impinge upon her body's contours. It simply accommodated them.

A decent mattress, then.

Was there light upon her still closed eyelids? Yes, but not insistent.

'Oh, fuck it,' she muttered, opening her eyes and sitting up.

The room was small and, it seemed, without doors. Its only furnishing was the bed beneath her. The light was muted and pervasive. She couldn't see its source and it threw no shadows.

None of the obvious explanations fit the scene. This wasn't a hospital room. None of the grunginess that came to an under-funded place where suffering people were gathered to be cared for. She wasn't on a drip. There was no crappy television on a metal bracket high on the wall opposite. The bed was without blankets and she was still dressed, although not in her coat. Most of all, it was too quiet.

'Hello?'

'Welcome, Samantha August.' The voice was male, well modulated.

'How do you feel?'

Unable to detect the source of that voice, she scanned the room, looking for a speaker grille. The vague off-white walls revealed nothing; not on the ceiling nor, from what she could see, the floor. 'Where's my laptop bag? Where's my coat?' She was tempted to add '*And I need a fucking cigarette*' but that was a sentiment eliciting little sympathy these days, so she held off on that for the moment.

'Expectation and anticipation of a modest endorphin surge.'

'Excuse me?'

'Your laptop bag and your coat are beneath the bed, and in the coat's right-hand pocket you will find your cigarettes. You are invited to satisfy your desire.'

'I must be in Eastern Europe if I can smoke in a hospital,' Samantha said, slipping down from the bed and then crouching to see her laptop bag and beside it, neatly folded, her coat. 'But your accent's all wrong. In fact,' she added as she found her cigarettes and her lighter, 'I can't read your accent at all.'

'A match to yours, then.'

She allowed a wry smile as she straightened. 'Touché. Got an ashtray?'

'The floor will suffice.'

'It's too clean,' she objected.

'And so it will remain.'

She lit her cigarette, sat back down on the bed. 'Latex rubber? Some kind of gel? The mattress, I mean. I've got hips. They hate most mattresses. But this one's pretty special. I want one.'

'You will of course be obliged. Feeling better?'

'My head's spinning, meaning I've been out for a while. What happened?'

'While walking down a street, on your way to the gym where you work with a trainer twice a week, you were abducted by aliens.'

The ash was building on the end of the cigarette and she was loathe to give it a tap. 'Well, that doesn't happen every day ... or does it?'

'No.'

'If I was heading to the gym, it was early afternoon.'

'Correct.'

'People would've seen it happen.'

'People did.'

'When was this?'

15

'Two days ago.'

She stood. 'And my husband—'

'Yes, we are sorry for his suffering ...'

But she had stopped listening. Standing up suddenly had decided things for her, the ash breaking off and falling to the floor. Which then swallowed it, reforming an instant later. She stared down, blinking rapidly. 'You're not bullshitting me.'

'No, of course not. We do regret the distressful disorder we have caused, for your husband and your many friends. A public abduction, however, was deemed propitious, with respect to what is coming.'

'Are we in orbit?'

'Yes.'

'I want to see.'

'We expected as much.'

'And then I want to call my husband.'

'Your cellphone no longer functions. We apologise. It was insufficiently shielded from the energy source employed in lifting you to the ship. That said, we have an alternative and it is at your disposal.'

Sam had finished her cigarette. Quite deliberately, she dropped it to the floor, watching it vanish. 'Forget the mattress,' she said, 'I want this floor.'

•

She was asked to compose what was in effect a text message to her husband's phone. She kept it short, and then, as the voice informed her the message had been sent, she silently castigated herself for the ease with which her mind slipped away from concerns about Hamish, plunging instead into her present, into the immediacy of this impossible circumstance.

A moment later she found herself staring at her home planet.

She'd never imagined herself a sentimental woman, but the tears blurred her vision and ran down her cheeks, and she just didn't care. Earth, smeared white and blue, occupied a realm of surrounding darkness. The glitter and glint of low-orbit satellites

16

and other objects skimmed the rim of upper atmosphere on the sunward side, like insects buzzing a lamp.

'We're in cislunar orbit,' she said.

'Correct.'

'And no one sees us?'

'Long experience has taught us that it is best to remain unseen.'

'Barring obvious abductions on a busy street.'

'Yes. Barring that.'

She remained in the same room where she had woken up, but now one entire wall was either a window or a video-screen.

'Do you have a name?' Sam asked. 'And when will you show yourself to me?'

'For this iteration I am named Adam. As for revealing myself, there is nothing to reveal. I am a construct, the equivalent of an artificial intelligence as you would understand it. I am presently extended and cognisant of many points of view within this solar system. Lastly, beyond these words I speak, my state of consciousness manifests in a dimension your technology is not yet able to observe. And this is something all sentients share.'

'I know a few neurologists who'd disagree.'

'They would be wrong.'

Sam wiped at her eyes and then her cheeks. She drew a deep breath, still staring at the Earth glowing in its black pool. She nodded towards it. 'I know this may be a simple picture lifted from NASA archives, as part of some elaborate hoax. Or, more likely, a delusion created by some kind of psychotic break. I've seen this shot before, you see. Granted, the real-time effects are impressive.' She fell silent, and then shook her head. 'Do you know how many times I have dreamed of something like this happening to me? With our whole fucking civilisation spiralling into utter imbecility, I would think "what if" ... oh, well, what does it matter what I'd think? Anyway, it was the floor that convinced me.' She nodded again at the planet. 'This is real. I'm here.'

'It was our assessment that you would not unduly resist the evidence of your senses,' Adam replied. 'Imagination is an essential quality of a flexible, adaptable mind.'

'I have questions,' Sam said. 'But I don't know where to start.'

'Begin with the immediate.'

She considered, and then said, 'All right. Why me? No, wait! Am I the only one you've snatched?'

'For our immediate purposes, yes.'

'How big is this ship?'

'Modest.'

'Who else is on board?'

'No one else is on board, Samantha August.'

She could feel her heart pounding. Irritated at this sudden wave of panic, she lit another cigarette. 'Back to my first question, then. Why me?'

'The Intervention Delegation has deemed you suitable for its purposes.'

'Okay. First off, who or what is the Intervention Delegation?'

'A triumvirate of alien civilisations presently engaged in Intervention Protocol.'

'Intervening in what?'

'The continuing evolution of Earth as a viable biome.'

'"Intervention", Adam, could be construed as conquest.'

'It is not.'

'Then what is it? How do you go about "intervening" and more to the point, what relationship do you plan on trying to establish with the dominant species – namely, us? Because, to put it bluntly, we're not good with being told what to do.'

There was a long moment of silence, and then Adam said, 'We are aware of that. There is hubris involved—'

'Whose? Ours or yours?'

'Both. However, only one is subject to challenge in this instance.'

Sam frowned, and then, with an effort, she pulled her attention away from the distant Earth. She began pacing. 'I think I see. By virtue of your immense technological superiority, *your* presumption is not relevant, because when it comes down to it, you can do precisely whatever you choose to do, and there's not a thing we can do about it.'

'This is correct.'

18

'And *our* hubris?'

'You presume that humanity is the primary target of our intervention regarding your planetary biome.'

She sat down on the bed. Her cigarette was done. She flicked it to the floor, watched it vanish. 'You'd rather talk to the whales.'

'There was some debate as to your fate. Either we neutralise your species, or include it as part of the genuine biome and therefore within the parameters of salvation. Inclusion was decided, despite the added burden of managing your transition.'

Sam barked a laugh, leaning back on her hands. 'Burden? You have no idea what you're getting into, Adam.'

'We have done this before.'

'Here? With us? "Ancient astronaut theorists say ..." That sort of thing?'

'With other dominant species, on other worlds. Bear in mind, each planet needed to meet specific critical thresholds. A far greater number of worlds have failed to meet the necessary criteria, and so were exempt from Intervention.'

'And their fate?'

'Most died, or now exist in a severely truncated state. While the machinery of evolution continually operates via innovation, a world with impoverished resources will limit such diversity.'

'But Earth has passed your test.'

'Your world's present extinction event – as precipitated by your species – is nearing a critical threshold. Left unchecked, you will destroy most of the life on Earth, including, of course, your own species. This in itself is insufficient cause for Intervention. But your planet is middle-aged. Depleted of resources, the new forms of life to emerge from your biome collapse will be limited and relegated to the simplest forms. Complexity will not rise again with the vigour which characterised the aftermath of past extinction events. Fortunately, there is still time to effect healing.'

Samantha nodded. An exhausted planet with most of the easily accessible resources gone. James P. Lovelock had said as much in his seminal book, *The Gaia Hypothesis*. But these details were proving distracting. She drew a deep breath, let it out slowly. 'Let's back up, Adam. You abducted me in front of witnesses.

You've begun an "intervention" that will save the Earth, incidentally dragging us into a new world order. And by "dragging us" I mean kicking and screaming.'

'We too have concluded that there will be some resistance.'

She snorted, and then leaned forward and rubbed at her face. 'And where do I fit into all of this? What do you want from me that no one else can provide? Why aren't you talking to, oh, I don't know, the President of the United States?'

'It may come as a surprise to many humans,' Adam said, and there was a new tone to the disembodied voice, 'but the assumption that an alien civilisation is interested in reaffirming the artificial hierarchy you have imposed upon yourselves is invariably the first one requiring readjustment.'

'Hmm, something tells me you're about to put a lot of people out of sorts.'

'This is why we have selected you as our facilitator.'

'I'm sorry, what?'

'There will be no direct contact between us and your species. We wish for you to speak on our behalf, in a venue permitting the broadest dissemination of information, to keep humanity informed of the progress of the Intervention.'

'Wouldn't you rather have a diplomat?'

'Not yet.'

Sam rose again and began pacing. 'Okay, let's trot out the usual suspects. You're not interested in phoning a president, or prime minister, or a committee or politburo. Why? Because you don't care to acknowledge our petty expressions of authority. And the time for the UN isn't now, as you said. Okay. Why not an astronaut?'

'Technical expertise is not relevant.'

'Exobiologist?'

'We are not here to discuss myriad forms of life in the galaxy.'

An arid, droll reply, hinting of disdain. Sam found that curious, but chose for the moment to let it pass. 'Okay. But every government must have some secret agency, a selected team put together for just this eventuality.'

'Really?'

'Well, they'd be crazy not to. You know, Men in Black.'

'And their agenda would be?'

She considered. 'Well, presumably, it would be to protect the interests of humanity.'

'Why would any particular branch of a single government be interested in protecting the interests of all humanity? Would it not, rather, be wholly concerned with protecting *national* interests, specifically in regard to maintaining social order and security?'

'There's no international group out there?'

'And if such a group had been already compromised?'

She halted, looked back at the Earth. 'Meaning?'

'The protection of humanity constitutes what, in particular?'

'All right, I'll bite. Social order is the base line. Prevention of panic in the streets. Economic chaos. But also, basic human rights in the face of an unknown galactic alien presence. Protocols for transition to advanced technology and new ways of doing things.'

'What if your present social and economic structures are incompatible with that galactic presence and, more specifically, all future participation in that community?'

'Ah.'

'In other words, what if that global Contact Team's stated purpose is fundamentally flawed in its moral precepts?'

Sam was silent for a few moments. Then she sighed. 'I get it. They'd probably say, "thanks but no thanks."'

'This option is not available. Accordingly, we have selected a different point of First Contact with the aim of circumventing the potential impasse.'

'In other words, it ain't up for negotiation.'

'Ultimately, this is a question of value systems, Samantha August.'

'Go on.'

'Technology, political structures, cultural and societal traits are constants in the galaxy,' Adam replied. 'There is little variation, and few instances of true innovation. Accordingly, the only value system of any significance between sentient species is found in the art each civilisation produces. Appreciation of said art remains both volatile and ephemeral, and value is highly variable. Among our Triumvirate, Samantha August, humanity's artistic contributions are much appreciated. And that of course includes your own work.'

'Oh, wait until my agent hears about this. Not to mention my publishers' legal departments.'

'Furthermore,' Adam continued, 'you personally have an extensive public presence, which we find propitious.'

'Sorry. Still thinking about the legality of galactic bootlegging.'

'Very soon, Samantha August, wealth – as you humans measure it – will be irrelevant.'

She grunted. 'Well, all right, that's an "out" likely to drop the jaws of every lawyer on the planet.' Sighing, Sam walked closer to the vision of the orbiting Earth. 'I see the Space Station,' she murmured, and then, after a moment, she spoke again. 'Adam, when is this Intervention of yours starting?'

'Samantha August, it has already begun.'

Chapter Three

'In space, no one cares if you smoke.'

Samantha August's first text to her husband

West of Djambala, Republic of Congo, Warlord Camp, May 22nd, 6:18 AM

Kolo had been nine when the bad men came to the village and took him away. Now he was one of the bad men. The deep forest of the Congo was not the forest of his youth. Back then the branches overhead had been full of life. Monkeys, snakes, lizards, bats. Animals made use of the trails, mostly at night, leaving their tracks everywhere to give proof of that other world, the one where people didn't belong. Now the forest was silent, silent and empty.

Hunger was the currency of this new world, guns, bullets and machetes a working man's tools. He had eighteen followers, all well armed, all with blood in their eyes. His camp was six kilometres from the nearest road, seven from the nearest village. Eleven children lived with them, some on their way to becoming warriors, others already slaves ready to do a man's bidding.

The morning began like any other. Kolo disentangled himself from Neela's skinny arms and pushed her to one side of the cot as he sat up.

She'd fixed herself just before their lovemaking the night before and was still dead to the world. He studied her briefly from beneath lowered, sleep-heavy lids, to make sure she was still breathing. She was.

Addicts made for co-operative slaves. So long as the service

23

expected of them was kept simple and required little effort. She'd told him her age when he had first stolen her from her dead mother's arms, two years past. Eleven then, thirteen now. They died young, these slaves, but there was a never-ending supply. Not as easy as it once had been – the nearest villages were now all abandoned, their inhabitants having fled the endless raiding, the random killings. So it was getting harder to scrounge food.

And slaves.

Soon, he told himself as he threw on a ragged Split Endz T-shirt, he'd have to send a runner to the mining camp – the one that had no business being where it was. Some forest people were left, usually getting in the way when it came to digging new pits or felling more trees. A week or so of working for the miners, killing and scaring off the forest people, meant he could feed his camp for a while longer.

He had few memories of the time when his country was not an open wound, and no illusions about the blood-suckers who kept it that way. He was one of them, after all. But the guns came from China and the money came from corporations all over the world. Nobody wasn't dirty.

Pulling on his old army pants and slinging on his web-belt and checking the heavy army-issue .45 in its tattered canvas holster, he collected his Exxon baseball cap and left the hut.

People were up, but not many. The pickets were coming in from the bush as dawn marked the end of their vigil, and the children were already out, ranging the lifeless forest and dreaming of a fat lizard or a monkey, but ready to settle for grubs and insects.

Things that broke down stayed that way. The world wanted this place to stay broken, and nothing was going to change that. But he had his tribe now, and he would do what needed doing to keep it fed. Loyalty was born of necessity and the belly was a wallet and wealth wasn't what you had, but what you'd still have a week from now. Kolo never planned beyond that week.

Manioc was roasting, a blackened pot of coffee was on the boil, and a young naked boy was lying nearby, surgical tubing still wrapped tight around one ashen arm. Kolo walked over and

24

nudged the frail form. 'Joak! You gave this one too much last night, and now it's dead.'

Joak, huge and sitting slumped by the fire, his massive scarred hands cradling a coffee mug, lifted a miserable gaze to Kolo. 'Never would've made a warrior anyway.'

'No. He was a slave.'

Joak shrugged. 'One less mouth. And we're short on powder.'

This last statement elicited a dark glower from Kolo, which made Joak nervously lick his lips.

Kolo walked up to the man and spoke in a low voice. 'Shut your fucking trap. You want trouble in the camp? Letting that news get out.'

Not meeting his eyes, Joak shrugged again. 'Not saying it don't change it, Captain.'

'We're getting in a new supply. Any day now.'

'Yes, Captain.'

'Now drag the body away. To the pit.'

Joak scowled. 'I don't like that place.'

'No one likes that place,' Kolo replied, 'but you killed it, you dump it, that's the rule.'

Sudden motion from the bush to his left made Kolo swing round, one hand smoothly plucking the .45 from its holster.

The young ones were rushing back in, on their faces confusion and fear.

Kolo stepped forward. 'Is it soldiers? You!' He snagged one child by the shoulder and spun her round to face him. 'Soldiers coming?'

She shook her head. 'Forest spirits!'

His warriors were up now and gathering their weapons, drawing close to their captain. Releasing the terrified girl, Kolo pointed. 'You and you, go and see who's coming.'

He'd chosen two of his youngest warriors, still eager, still in the habit of stroking their AK-47s and strutting past the slaves, hoping to catch a girl's eye. They hurried off without a question asked. Glancing over, Kolo saw Joak's jaded regard as the man watched the scouts heading into the bush.

He might have to kill Joak soon. Some things couldn't be

helped. 'The rest of you, load up. Joak, get all the slaves together. Robbie, collect up the drugs. Henry—'

He stopped upon seeing the sudden return of his scouts. One of them had a bloody nose.

'What the fuck, man? You fall? Who's coming?'

'A wall,' said the second scout, rubbing at one swollen knee. 'Invisible wall, Captain!'

The first scout spat blood. 'I run into it. I go down. Then it starts pushing me.'

'Pushing?'

'It's coming, Captain!' said the second scout.

Three warriors who had been standing near the huts to Kolo's left all staggered in unison, turning in alarm and raising their weapons.

Though he squinted, Kolo could see nothing. 'What fucking game you all playing at?'

One of his men reversed his AK-47 and slammed the shoulder-stock against something that rebounded so hard it knocked the weapon from his hands.

'Step away!' Kolo ordered. He fought down his terror. The bush was alive with spirits. He knew enough to know that. But nothing like this. Moving cautiously, he edged forward, pistol held out.

When he reached the place where the three warriors had been, the pistol collided with something. 'Fuck,' he muttered, pushing harder against the invisible barrier, 'there's nothing there!'

He ducked when Joak fired off a quick burst. Kolo heard the slugs impact something to his right, less than an arm's length away. But when he looked, he saw nothing.

The invisible wall was advancing, pushing at the pistol in his hand. He moved back quickly and then said, 'Spread out to either side – find its edges!'

His warriors fanned out in some confusion. They encountered the wall with grunts and curses. One tried to hack it with his machete, but the blade recoiled.

As far as Kolo could make out, the barrier was a straight line, slowly crawling over the camp. It had emerged from the deep forest on the western side. A dozen or so warriors attempted to hold back the wall's advance, and Kolo stared at the absurd scene of men leaning against nothing, their feet being pushed through the dirt.

None of the huts on that side of the camp were accessible now, and two drugged slaves had been pushed out through the flimsy wall of their respective huts, and were now rolling senselessly forward. 'Robbie! Collect them up.' He holstered his .45 and turned back to his own hut. 'Collect everything!'

Behind him, Joak asked, 'Where we going?'

'We're getting the fuck out,' Kolo answered.

'I thought all the forest spirits were dead.'

Kolo halted and turned. He eyed his rival, wondering if the man had been joking. From his closed expression it was impossible to tell. 'This is no fucking spirit. It's a weapon.'

At last, Joak's eyes widened.

'It's a fucking weapon,' Kolo repeated. 'No more hiding in the bush, Joak. No more hiding from anything.'

'No way.'

Kolo wasn't interested in continuing the conversation. He turned his back on Joak and continued on towards his hut. Neela weighed next to nothing. He'd throw her over a shoulder. Barring that, there was nothing else he needed in there. He had taken three strides when he heard a click behind him.

Kolo spun, pistol in his hand.

Joak stood scowling down at his AK-47. 'Fucking jammed,' he said, and then, startled, looked back up at Kolo. After a moment, he managed a lopsided smile. 'You win, Captain.'

'Better start running, Joak,' said Kolo in a calm voice.

Dropping his weapon, Joak bolted.

Kolo raised his pistol and took careful aim. Then he hesitated. Was the man worth the bullet? He doubted he'd see Joak again. Only fools hung around when there was a price on their head.

He slid the pistol back into the holster and made his way into the hut.

Neela hadn't moved. 'Good girl,' he whispered. 'You'll stay loyal. Your kind always do.'

Joey Sink sat in his basement surrounded by monitors. Weird shit going down everywhere, he didn't know which way to look. A tinny voice came though his headphones.

'Joey? You tracking this?'

'Hey, King Con. Tryin'.'

'What do you think? Ecoterrorist Super Weapon?'

'What –' he then leaned forward, eyes darting from one screen to the next. 'Oh shit, see what you mean. Can't believe I missed it. They all started in wilderness areas and then spread out.'

'A "fuck-you-super-weapon",' said King Con, with plenty of nasty satisfaction in his tone. 'And Sat-feeds are going haywire. Fishing fleets right over big schools of fish, and they can't drop their nets!'

'What do you mean?'

'Shit just piles up on the deck. All those fish and they can't touch em! Greenpeace must be dancing and why not? They're probably in on it.'

King of Conspiracy was an old and loyal contact on Joey's Kitchen Sink Vlog. Wherever the man was holed up, he had access to all sorts of esoteric shit. Rode the waves, always attuned to the next whisper. But for the time being, Joey just let him talk. He was too busy to reply, as he studied the monitors. After a long moment, he leaned back and said, 'Take a breath, King Con. The mid-lat places are being hit hard. Central America, Chile, Bolivia, Amazon Basin. North Madagascar, all over Africa. Cambodia, Vietnam, Indonesia's being hammered.'

'National parks in the States, most of Florida and the Everglades and half of fuckin' Alaska—'

'Hey, what did I tell you about profanity?'

'Sorry, Joey. Just, uh, getting carried away. Anyway, I've got reports from some heavily populated areas, too. All that new ranchland in what used to be the Amazon, the mining and logging towns. Shit in the Congo, too—'

'Taiga in Northern Russia,' Joey cut in. 'Inland British Columbia, Northern Alberta – wow, everybody's being pushed off the Tar Sands, equipment and all. Whatever it is, it crushes bulldozers like tin cans.'

'Eco-Fuck-You-Super-Weapon – you recording us?'

'That's what I mean about the profanity, King Con. Now I got to go in and edit and bloop and it's all a pain in the arse so just cut it out, will you?'

'You not getting it yet, Joey? It's all going down, the whole ff— damned mess! And it's impenetrable, that forcefield. And you can't dig under it and drones just crash into it overhead—'

'Wait, what's that about drones? Someone's doing fly-overs?'

'Tried,' King Con replied with a cold, short laugh. 'Oh, and helicopters and other shit all get collision warnings – but they think it's dome-shaped and, oh, get this, birds can fly right through it!'

'Huh?'

'Birds, man! Birds! Ultra-Eco-Terrorist-Doctor-No-Eco-Fuck-You-Super-Weapon!'

'I'll get back to you,' Joey said in a grating tone. 'Go wash out your mouth with soap.' He clicked off.

Official statements were coming on. Nobody knew a thing. Nobody was taking credit, and then suddenly all kinds of wing-nut groups were taking credit. Science teams had been dispatched. The military was on alert. Tourists piled up at the entrance to Yellowstone National Park. How big were these things going to get? No idea. Are they all still growing? So far, yes. What's going to happen to all those displaced people? No idea. Relief agencies have been alerted. Riots in Brazil, but miraculously no one was hurt—

Joey Sink looked back at that last report. Thousands rioting at a mining town … 'And no one got hurt? What the fug?'

Ottawa, Ontario, Canada, May 24th, 3:45 PM

Officiousness had a way of bloating the ego, all that self-importance conjuring an aura of exceptionalism, of secrets held and the fate of millions hanging in the balance. Alison Pinborough had little time for it. The last administration had made overtures, murmuring about an invitation into the PM's inner circle, but the very idea had offended her. A photo of the country's last Prime Minister adorned every office in the science community, studded with darts. That fear-mongering anti-intellectual neo-fascist who had ruled the country, actively shutting down research programmes and muzzling scientists, had set things back by decades.

It was worth something, she supposed, that Canada's new PM didn't seem to be living in a cave. Still, it was early days, and Alison had little faith in politics. Too many vested interests in maintaining the status quo, even when that status quo was a recipe for suicide. These days, worldwide, reason was an endangered species.

Nonetheless, she had finally given in, accepting the appointment as the PMO's Science Advisor. Clearly, credentials in geology well matched the glacial pace of change in government.

The thought elicited a crooked grin as she made her way down the corridor, following the secretary as he led her to the PM's conference room. As far as cities went, Ottawa felt cold and damp. At least she didn't have freshmen to teach, or university administrators to battle. And the apartment was decent, with a lovely view of the Rideau Canal. And as for all the briefs from the field agents who'd managed to report back in time, the folders were blissfully closed and tucked under her left arm. A few more seconds remained before she would have to begin discussing the impossible.

She didn't like being afraid, but afraid she was.

The secretary reached a door, knocked once and then opened it, turning to invite Alison into the room beyond. 'Thank you,' she said, stepping past the young man. Courtesy was one of the few aspects of officiousness that she actually appreciated. In the wake of the last PM's belligerence and bullying, it was a welcome return – or so she'd been told at the meet-and-greet that accompanied her appointment. People had been relieved, the bureaucracy resettling itself with a new zeal for propriety.

The conference room was, of course, well appointed. She was led to her seat and found herself opposite Will Camden, Minister for Natural Resources. On Will's left was Mary Sparrow, Minister for Parks and Recreation. Neither one looked happy, although something glinted in Mary's dark eyes that, upon reflection, didn't surprise Alison.

Some pundits had viewed appointing a Metis to oversee the country's national parks as ironic. Others appreciated the gesture. There was no end to self-ascribed analysts of everything irrelevant yet potentially inflammatory, and their incessant babbling made for a constant background roar to public life. More than a few had crowed with savage glee at Alison's own history working for Big Oil.

Alison and the ministers had not long to wait, as another door at the head of the room opened and in strode the Prime Minister. Lisabet Carboneau, the newest liberal darling of politics, had features sharper in person than they were on-screen. Her regard, which seemed honest to the tracking camera, held a predatory hint when face to face. Until now, there had been only one meeting between Alison and the PM, and that one had been awash with platitudes and the pronouncement of vague expectations.

Not this time.

Swiftly seating herself at the table's head, the Prime Minister fixed Alison with a steady stare and said, 'I have scanned the public statements issued by other countries. I have watched the newsfeed and sat through token experts doing little more than describing what we can all already see. I anticipate much of the same from you, not due to any disrespect for your competence, Doctor Pinborough, but because what we are facing appears to be inexplicable and therefore unanswerable. Am I correct?'

Alison had set her file folders down on the table in front of her when she had first been seated. She glanced down at them now, fighting an urge to open the first one and begin leafing through the summary. She already knew the contents, of this and every other file. 'Madam Prime Minister,' she said, 'there are some highly unusual properties to these forcefields—'

Will Camden grunted sourly, but added no further comment since Carboneau's attention on Alison had not wavered.

After a brief pause, Alison continued. 'Ground penetration radar gave no return signal. In fact, no above-surface radar gives a return signal.'

'How is that possible?' the Prime Minister asked. 'Planes on flight paths taking them towards the forcefields all report collision alarms forewarning the pilots.'

'Yes, madam, and so naturally it was assumed that, since those collision sensors are radar-based, a solid return of the signal was implicit.'

'But now you are saying that's not the case.'

'Correct.'

'Yet another impossibility,' Carboneau said. 'If these forcefields cannot be detected by radar, then some other form of signal must be activating the collision alarms.'

Alison shook her head. 'Madam, the sensors are specifically calibrated. They are not equipped to receive or interpret any other signal. Reinforcing this, on-site examination of the forcefields indicate no energy diffusion or emanation. In fact, application of energy against the forcefields also results in zero return.'

Lisabet Carboneau studied Alison for a moment, and then she said, 'I understand that bullets disappear when fired into the forcefield.'

'Yes. They vanish. Furthermore, the impact zone cannot be measured. In other words, no energy escapes the point of contact. One might as well be shooting holograms at a blackboard.'

The Prime Minister frowned. 'Is that an accurate analogy?'

'Not really, madam. But this effect on hypersonic projectiles is unique. Slower-traversing objects, such a drones, simply break up, in the manner one would expect if they had flown into a wall. In those instances, energy is transmitted outward as a consequence of the impact, following natural laws relating to mass and velocity.'

'This is not your area of expertise, is it?'

'No, Madam Prime Minister. Geologically speaking, the forcefield, when passing through, for example, Precambrian bedrock, effects no structural change in the area of intersection. This too defies all expectation. At least,' she amended, 'no structural alteration that we can detect from outside the field. But visual examination is in no way impeded.'

The Prime Minister sat back in her chair. 'Let's return to the subject of radar and the triggering of collision alarms in aircraft. Speculations?'

Alison hesitated, fighting down a sigh. 'The forcefield is selective. It possesses agency.'

At that, Mary Sparrow broke protocol by speaking. 'The Wall of God.'

The statement was startling enough to draw Carboneau's attention.

'What's that?'

'Pardon my interruption, Madam Prime Minister,' Mary said. 'A new meme. Someone online related the forcefields to a computer firewall, in that they seem to share the ability to discriminate. For example, there has been no confirmed report of any injuries directly related to the field's edge. This isn't Stephen King's *Under the Dome* scenario, cutting people in half. Also, wildlife has been observed passing through it.'

Alison cleared her throat. 'That's confirmed. The exclusion properties seem to be limited. Human access is denied, including human technology.'

'Not entirely true,' Mary cut in again. 'A report from Brazil reached me just an hour ago. As you know, I have been engaged with the Global Indigenous Peoples programme—'

'Yes,' interjected the Prime Minister. 'This report?'

Mary pressed her lips together, revealing a flicker of annoyance. 'The forcefield now covering the pristine regions of the Amazon extends upward for a height of about three hundred metres. Fly-overs are possible, and late yesterday a team of government officials recorded one of the uncontacted indigenous tribes known to exist close to the border with Peru. These are the very tribes being slaughtered by loggers, and we have confirmation that all logging and land-clearing activities inside the forcefield have now ceased, and the camps are abandoned – the invaders have been forced out, but the indigenes have not.'

Alison studied the satisfaction that softened Mary's face with this last statement, and found no cause to condemn it. The 'Wall of God' no longer seemed so absurd. Her own thoughts had been circling the notion for some time, as the data continued to pour in.

'Agency,' said the Prime Minister. 'Intelligence. Intent.' Abruptly she seemed to shift gears. 'William, how badly has our access to natural resources been affected?'

'It's bad, Madam Prime Minister. We've lost half the Tar Sands – every block opened in the past three years is now out of reach. Extraction hardware destroyed – and there were claims that some of the machinery had been singled out—'

'Singled out how?'

'The forcefield jumped ahead, broke its own steady line of growth. The numbers aren't in yet, but the material loss will be in the tens of millions, maybe more. Production is much worse. We're down to a trickle.'

'Vengeance,' stated Mary. 'They were being punished for their stupidity. You cannot wound the Earth and expect to get away with it.'

'Enough of that, please,' the Prime Minister said. The PM was notoriously difficult to offend, and nothing in her expression now indicated anything but mild irritation with Mary's pronouncements, or the pleased tone with which the Minister uttered them. 'Alison, how many zones are still expanding?'

'Very few, madam, and they have slowed down considerably. About a metre a day now, and no longer consistently along the line of advance. There are extensions now, like arms. But a more apt descriptor would be "corridors".'

'As in ... wildlife migration?'

Alison nodded. 'Seasonal rounds: northern woods in the winter, summer on the plains.'

'So, preservation of nature appears to be the emerging theme,' observed the Prime Minister.

Alison nodded again. 'Fisheries confirm this. Hook and line seems to be an acceptable practice. But not drift-nets, bottom-trawlers, or any other non-discriminating means of ocean harvest. And national boundaries are irrelevant, as the zones relate to fish migration, feeding and breeding grounds. Cetacean pods appear to be individually enclosed by forcefields, which travel with those pods and may well send extensions around outliers.'

'Makes me wonder,' said Will Camden.

The PM's gaze flicked to the man. 'William?'

He shrugged. 'If eco-terrorists have hooked up with Satanists and someone, somewhere, is busy throwing virgins into volcanoes.'

There was a long moment of silence, and then Mary Sparrow burst out laughing. 'Oh crap, Will! That's a good one – can I quote you?'

'If you did,' the Minister of Natural Resources replied, 'I doubt anyone would even notice.'

Abruptly the Prime Minister rose to her feet. She was tall, taller than Alison, leaving her with a moment of intimidation. Despite that, there was something to the woman that Alison couldn't help liking. 'Thank you,' she said, meeting the eyes of each of them in turn. 'The general consensus among other nations – the ones prepared to discuss this matter – all concur with the inevitable conclusions you have drawn.' She paused, and then said, 'We're being—'

Washington DC, May 24th, 4:00 PM

'—royally fucked with,' the President of the United States finished.

Ben Mellyk winced. The Science Advisor was old school, and his president's penchant for crass bluntness was beginning to irritate him. He withdrew his thick glasses and began methodically cleaning them with a silk handkerchief.

President Raine Kent, meanwhile, had shifted his considerable bulk in his chair to regard the Chairman of the Joint Chief of Staff, Albert Strom. Raine opened his mouth to say something and then visibly changed his mind, turning his attention instead to his Security Advisor. 'Dan, if there are files you're supposed to crack open right now ...'

'Files, Mister President?'

'Files! X-fucking-files! The effect is global. No one with any credibility is taking credit and even if they did, this technology leaves the rest of us in the dust and research like that we'd know about – Ben! We'd know about it, wouldn't we?'

'I think so, Mister President,' Ben replied, restoring his glasses only to take them back off and rub at his sleep-deprived eyes. 'Energy fields remain in an infant state, and all require massive outputs from a recognisable power source.'

'So,' snapped the President, returning his glower to Daniel Prester, his Security Advisor. 'Bug-eyed aliens. Roswell. Spill it, Daniel.'

'There are no X-files, Mister President.'

'Why am I having a hard time believing that?'

'Sir, you assume a greater capacity for security than is humanly possible. Conspiracies crack. People go rogue. Whistleblowers—'

'And how best to discredit them than by ridiculing everything they say?' Raine Kent leaned forward. 'That's a viable and common tactic, is it not? We've done it before, haven't we? Enthusiastic disinformation – I happen to know you have full-time professional sceptics trolling the UFO sites.'

Daniel reluctantly nodded. 'Experimental aircraft can be hard to hide one hundred per cent of the time, particularly in testing and trials.'

'So that's all they're trolling for?'

Ben saw Daniel's eyes flicker. 'It is, sir.'

'And all the secret moon-bases and secret space fleets and ruins on Mars shit, it's all rubbish, right?'

Daniel glanced at Ben, who sat straighter. 'Mister President, there *are* ruins on Mars. We think. We're pretty sure,' he amended upon seeing Kent's visage darken. 'We've been actively smudging images prior to releasing them to the public.' They had been doing the same for the Moon, but for a long time these had been matters in which need-to-know had not included presidents. For one very good reason. Presidents came and went, and most if not all of them were reluctant to leave the limelight once out of office. Sitting on the biggest reveal of all time would be tempting as hell.

This president was some time in calming down. Eventually he sighed. 'Fuck me. And no one bothered telling me about it?'

'Sir, you have only been in office three months. Your slate has been pretty full, what with all the protests and riots and what-not—'

'That shit takes care of itself,' Kent growled. 'You're side-stepping, Ben. This isn't some climate change discussion we're having here.'

Ben shrugged. 'It was not considered a high priority.'

'Ruins on Mars. Okay. But *ruins*, right? Empty. Dead. Ancient.'

'Yes, sir.'

'So, nothing to make me lose sleep over.'

'No, sir.'

'Which is why you didn't brief me, making me wonder how many other things you're not telling me in the interests of the President getting his beauty rest.'

Ben said nothing. It seemed the wisest option.

Kent's expression twisted to signal his disapproval. He shifted his attention to Albert Strom. 'Al, tried lasers? Big fucking lasers? On the forcefields?'

The Chairman blinked owlishly, and then said, 'Of course, Mister President. As well as microwave, sonic, and depleted uranium projectiles. The forcefields remain impervious and more to the point, entirely unaffected.'

'That's American soil someone's just stolen from us,' Kent said, his florid face deepening a shade. 'Ben, what do the SETI people say?'

'Nothing detected, sir.'

'NASA?'

'Nothing detected, sir.'

'Are you on a fucking loop, Ben? I need more information. Daniel, crack down on the eco-terrorists. Haul 'em in. I want their computers. Their networks. All their contacts. I want the works.'

'We have all that, Mister President,' Daniel Prester replied. 'Homeland's been trawling that data since the first manifestation, as soon as the environmental angle became obvious. Lots of chatter but nothing concrete, sir. Thus far.'

'Thus far,' Kent muttered, as if the words were a personal affront. 'Why now? That's what I want to know? Why on my patch? What the fuck did I do to deserve this?' He sat up straighter. 'Wait. Can we take credit for this?'

The Chairman of the Joint Chief of Staff choked on his coffee and the cup clashed ominously as he set it back down on its saucer. 'Mister President, every country would declare war on us!'

Something gleamed in Raine Kent's eyes. 'And not one country can do fuck all about it.' He pointed at his secretary. 'See how that one plays with the eggheads. Scenarios.'

After a long, tense moment, the Vice-President, D.K. Prentice, cleared her throat. 'Mister President, we cannot take credit for these forcefields.'

'Why not?'

'Because we don't know what they are going to do next. Thus far, miraculously, there have been no definitive losses of life as a consequence of the manifestation. Nowhere worldwide, sir. But that is no guarantee that our luck won't change. It would seem that our pre-eminent concern, at the moment, relates to the economic impact of these forcefields. That, and the already growing wave of displacement as entire populations get forced back into already crowded and desperate urban areas.'

Kent frowned, but said nothing.

Prentice continued, 'An extraordinary session has been called at the UN and I think we should—'

'Yeah,' cut in Kent, 'you do that. Right. You go to that, D.K. See what they're going to do about all those people because they sure as hell aren't coming here. Report back to us on that.' He looked round the crowded Situation Room. 'Meanwhile I've got to address the nation, and I need something to say. I need to tell 'em we're on this, working on this, figuring it out.' He looked to Ben. 'Get your eggheads together, Ben, come up with shit. But not too complicated. Make it plain so the people get it, get what's going on.'

'Mister President,' said Ben Mellyk. 'That's just it. We don't know what's going on.'

'Not good enough.'

'I'm sorry, sir. I wish it were otherwise.'

'I bet you do. So do I. So does everybody. On my fuckin' watch, too. If it gets worse, people are going to panic. Should

38

we wake up the National Guard again? Get planes in the air?' He thumped the table with both fists. 'How the fuck do we respond to this?'

Silver Steading Farm, Utah, May 24th, 5:16 PM

The Range Rover had always been an extravagance, Dave Ketchen's mechanical cage of guilt making a serious dent in his carbon footprint. That and the ATC which he used whenever saddling a horse was just too much bother. In his mind, however, he figured he was still deep into the green, since the virtue of restoring the valley's natural environment and then planting a tiered canopy of productive fruit- and nut-bearing trees and beneath that a whole host of undergrowth plants of varying seasonal yields ... well, that had to count for something, didn't it?

He'd stopped believing that about eight hours ago. Sitting in the Range Rover, parked on the open, unbroken scrubland that flanked their valley, he sat cradling a bottle of bourbon in his lap.

Down below the watercourse glittered between new green leaves. The pond had lost its ice and the family of beavers had been busy all day, thinning the stands of saplings on the banks. Ten years ago, the valley had been bone-dry, the stream a spring occurrence in a good year. The beavers had changed all of that, a poignant reminder that nature could turn a desert into a paradise if people just let it do its thing.

Sure, this list of virtues was as long as his arm. He and Ev had left the city, dragging their kids with them. Bought this valley. The ranch on the west side had been converted to bison, with Jurgen Banks just about breaking even selling the lean meat to top restaurants back east. The other side was reservation land, an isolated parcel of Northern Shoshone remotely connected to the Snake River group. It had been cattle land for some time before that, with a small ghost town connected to some failed mining operation being the first European settlement in the area. When the Shoshone bought the ranch, they'd sold the cattle off and left the buildings to fall into ruin.

Dave had done some research, curious about what the Shoshone wanted to do with the land, and as far as he could tell, the answer was 'nothing'. Which suited him just fine.

So the valley had been perfect. Whatever leachates might creep down from the higher ground to either side were now entirely natural.

Ten years. Quite the transformation. Certification of Organic Produce had finally come and the shift from the Farmers' Markets to high-end speciality food-stores now seemed within reach.

Until it was all taken away.

Some Game and Fisheries guy on the tube had described the migration corridors now taking shape, one of them winding its way down from Alberta, Canada, with another narrower one working southward from some place called Southwest Saskatchewan. The western corridor skirted the east side of the Rockies, but then branched out to follow some minor valleys and flat-land. The other one looked to be heading for Kansas.

'Why not just cut the country in half while you're at it,' Dave muttered. The bourbon had dried his lips. He wet them again with another mouthful. 'Look at me, the cliché.'

That was kind of funny. The locals in town already had him down as one anyway, the hippy organic farmer, the eco-warrior, the guy with the beard and flannel shirt, driving his brand-new Range Rover. Selling bags of pine nuts every Saturday for a god-damn fortune.

The forcefield had obliterated Jurgen's fences. His sixty-three-head herd of bison could now wander at will, down into the valley eager for all that new green growth and leachate was the least of Dave's concerns.

Opening the door, he climbed out of the cab. Too drunk to drive back home, even though he'd be nowhere near a road the whole way. There were sinkholes, big boulders, run-off channels. Wouldn't do to get stuck, roll the thing, or break an axle. Besides, this way he could walk off some of the bourbon. Stumbling in drunk as a skunk in front of his wife and kids wouldn't do.

At least *she'd* understand. They'd just lost everything.

'You'd think doing good in the world would mean something.' Leaning against the Range Rover, he glared up at the cloudless sky. Wishing for a first star but it was still too early in the day for that.

And over at the Wild West, where he'd bought the bottle, that shit-for-brains Hal Smart was probably still laughing, asking one more time if he could come on over to shoot him some beaver, hah hah.

'Well, no, Hal, you can't. That's the whole point of these forcefields. You and your hunting buddies are plumb outa luck, as they say in these here parts.'

But hey, Dave, ain't we all outa luck? I mean, you and me both? Oh man, it's enough to make a man drink, ain't it?

'Just one star, God. Just one.' He pushed himself off the truck and began walking, the bottle held by the neck in one hand. He could ditch it. But then it might break. There were deer, and elk, and pronghorn. Fine then. He'd stash it in the old outhouse since nobody ever went in there.

'Give me a star, Lord. So I can *curse* it.'

When a man does good, it shouldn't be good for nothing.

Boulder, Colorado, May 24th, 9:56 PM

'So what's it all mean?' Joey Sink asked the web cam's blinking light. 'They're calling it the Wall of God. But ... really? Seen any angels lately? Fire and brimstone? Or is this just Gaia saying "guess what, humans, as Stewards of the Earth, you've just been fired". Or is someone else saying that? In no uncertain terms? Someone who's yet to show up, but is about to with a big sign saying "Earth, Under New Management"?'

He left that to hang for a few moments, and then said, 'So if those big saucers come down to hover over Washington DC and every other capital on the planet ... well, we've read the script, and it ain't pretty.' He cocked his head and offered up a twisted grin. 'Anybody hear a clock ticking? Or is that just me?

'This is Joey Sink and the Kitchen Sink Vlog, and hey, wasn't this a heck of a day?'

Chapter Four

'Science and technology are just the clothes we SF
writers wear. But every now and then, some of us
choose to go naked into the future, and that is an
entirely different proposition.'

Samantha August

Cislunar Orbit, May 25th, 3:02 PM (by Samantha August's watch)

'You can't be doing this,' Samantha said. 'You've just hit the
most disadvantaged people in the poorest countries on the
planet.' Before her on the massive screen was a map of the world,
initially startling because it was orientated sideways, with the
North Pole to the left. The Exclusion Zones were marked by a
translucent grey filter overlying the geomorphic details of the
land and the ocean floor. There were a lot of them. She pointed
at North America. 'You're re-establishing the Great Plains. That's
going to cut the United States nearly in half ... all the way down
to Kansas. The heart of America's agricultural bread-basket.'

'The ongoing anthropogenic deterioration of Earth's climate
will render your "bread-basket" uninhabitable within forty
years,' Adam replied. 'The present population displacements are
minor compared to those you will experience within twenty-
five years. Rising sea-levels, drought, desertification, extreme
weather events, will all directly impact your species' preferred
habitats, and at that future time none of your countries will possess the capability to deal with the crisis. In effect, if not for our
intervention, your civilisation will collapse within this century.

Estimated population loss exceeds six billion. Unfortunately, your extinction will take the rest of the biome down with you.'

'I think that's enough good news for one day, don't you? So, you're going to restore the health of our atmosphere?'

'It is necessary in order to best preserve the biome. Atmosphere will be returned to early industrial levels with respect to carbon dioxide, methane and other greenhouse gases.'

'Why early industrial?'

'To prevent recurrence of an ice-age. Atmospheric circulatory patterns need to be calmed, necessitating redressing in order to effect the proper equilibrium—'

'Has all that begun?'

'Not yet.'

'Why didn't you start with that?'

'Because the expansion of your species needed to be stopped immediately, Samantha August.'

Adam had provided a chair. Rather, at her request it had grown out of the floor. She sat in it now, eyes still on the screen and the global map with its grey zones. Dotted lines indicated the full projection of these zones. She could only imagine the chaos afflicting the world below. She lit a cigarette – it seemed there was no end to her supply. 'You know why I said I'd do this for you? Free cigarettes.' Her eyes narrowed. 'Unless I'm running up a bill.'

'Money is an anachronistic concept. While in our care, you incur no debt.'

She settled back, smoked some more. 'I am having second thoughts about being your spokeswoman. It's not that I was naïve, either. But I figured you had a more palatable plan. Not something that would drive poor people from their homes.'

'At present, many nations possess the wherewithal to manage this displacement event. Food is plentiful, transportation capable, labour available. If humans are now suffering, it is due exclusively to lack of will on the part of fellow humans.'

'Because of political complexity,' Samantha retorted. 'Sovereignty, logistics, the cost.'

'Indeed, the cost.'

43

She waited for more from Adam, but instead the silence stretched.

'All right,' she said at last, 'I get it. Societies establish their own value system, and once that system is in place, it becomes that society's own cage. It exists to feed itself, in an endless cycle of reconfirming its own arbitrary worth. Still, Adam, some undeniable truths lie at the core of those value systems. Specifically, we exist in a state of scarcity and imbalance, and most if not all of our mechanisms are devoted to managing both.'

'This is true.'

'So, within that system, displaced populations will suffer – they can't help but suffer. Even aid needs mechanisms to be set in motion, and in the case of a shortage of land, there are no easy solutions.'

'There is no shortage of land,' said Adam.

'Nations get protective about that sort of thing. Cultures feel threatened by a sudden influx of strangers. There are issues of language, expectation, religions and their own legal structures – you can pretty much guarantee that a clash of world views will end up getting messy.'

'You are presenting, Samantha August, the opinion that in the present circumstances, humans will not sufficiently assist other humans to prevent suffering, or indeed, death.'

'I don't doubt aid organisations are scrambling, or that the UN is trying to get a handle on things. But we both know they won't be enough. Look, the first world resists the influx of peoples from the so-called developing world, and their reasons are of course highly suspect. All those labels that get trotted out. Ignorant, uneducated, terrorists, even unclean – racial purity is making a comeback on the political stage. Not just in the major countries, but everywhere. It's the old tribal mentality, kicked awake like a hornet's nest. Fascism's on the rise, no longer hiding in the shadows, but brazenly upfront and in your face. It's a stressed world down there.' She tossed her cigarette butt. 'Your timing sucks.'

'The Exclusion Zones represent an end to terrestrial expansion,' said Adam. 'Your present civilisation, alas, is predicated on the presumption of infinite growth, infinite expansion, and infinite resources. While limited to your single planet, growth, expansion and resources are in fact finite, not infinite. Your collective comprehension of this appears to be singularly abstract, and thus relegated and unable to effect change upon your insatiable momentum.'

'I know,' Sam muttered.

'Therefore, consider the Exclusion Zones as a forward advancement of the deadline – that future moment when you truly run out of, well, everything. But there is a vital distinction here, as I mentioned earlier. If left unchecked, that future deadline will arrive when your civilisation is least capable of accommodating the new paradigm necessary to ensure its survival. But now, with that deadline advanced by virtue of the Exclusion Zones, your civilisation remains robust enough to begin the process of adaptation.'

She sighed and leaned her head back. 'Yes, all very reasonable, Adam. But you slammed the door. You have to expect us to spend some time pounding away at it.'

'Fruitless.'

'And in the meantime, people suffer.'

'This was anticipated.'

'That sounds heartless.'

'As heartless as the unwillingness of the capable nations to help the incapable nations? As heartless as considering *cost* in the face of imminent human suffering?'

'No,' she snapped, 'you're proving a perfect match to us, Adam. And if that's the best you can do, God help the Earth. And as for me speaking on your behalf, forget it.'

'Prior to the initiation of the Exclusion Zones, Samantha August, Earth was seeded with a sensory suite. This sensory suite established a blanket of sensor presence. The matrix integration is now worldwide. Indeed, without this initial placement, the Exclusion Zones would not be possible.'

Frowning, Samantha stood again and approached the global map. 'A blanket of sensor presence. What does that mean, specifically?'

'It means that I am monitoring all activity on the macro scale.'

'Not possible. Too much data.'

'Not at all,' Adam replied. 'Indeed, I am at the same time monitoring other phases of the Intervention at twenty-seven other localities scattered throughout your solar system. Shall I describe for you some of the principles of quantum folding as they relate to Data Immanence in an AI context?'

Samantha's frown shifted to a scowl. 'I'm not one of those hard-science SF writers, Adam. I write what you might call "social science fiction". I'm more interested in what the future holds for humanity's sense of itself than I am in FTL drives and quantum tunnelling, folding, dicing, slicing or whatever else might be theoretically out there.' She considered, and then said, 'Maybe you picked the wrong person.'

'No. We remain confident in our selection. As I said earlier, technical matters are common commodities, and science is a singular language lacking connotative nuance. What is unique is the human perspective, and that perspective is the exclusive realm of the creative arts. Among your world's artists, Samantha August, those of you engaged in your specific genre have devoted your adult lives to speculation regarding extraterrestrial civilisations and life in the galaxy. This alone makes you the most qualified for the initial phases of First Contact.'

'Then any one of us would do.'

'Possibly. You have described yourself as a humanist. Your fiction explores that condition, with great compassion, yet without unrealistic expectation. You have honestly earned your dismay at what the future holds. Or, rather, held. More to the point, you have crafted a public persona, acquiring many followers. We deemed this of vital importance. No, Samantha August, your suitability is not in question.'

'Back to the blanket,' Sam said. 'You called it a matrix.'

'Yes. In effect, I have incorporated the surface of the Earth into my body. Sensory monitoring is conducted at what you might call an autonomic level; however, even in that state there exists situational awareness. Accordingly, I am able to intervene at will.'

'Intervene how, exactly?'

'Samantha August, we are pacifists. Accordingly, we are imposing the equivalent of a ceasefire, worldwide. Aggression and destruction aimed against the environment, the fauna, and between humans, has now ended.'

For a long, terrible moment, Samantha forgot to breathe.

'Concurrent with this,' Adam blithely went on, 'the sensory suite is now addressing the scarcity of food and clean water. Anticipating human resistance to alleviate the suffering of fellow humans, we are extending our Intervention. That said, we remain in Stage One of five. Accordingly, there is much to come.'

She found the capacity to draw a deep breath, and let it out slowly.

'Oh,' she said in a small voice. 'Holy fuck.'

Chapter Five

'Science tries to convince us that the material world is
all there is. But science has an agenda. Surprise!'

Samantha August

Baltimore, Maryland, May 24th, 11:02 PM

When he went quiet, she knew what was coming. Her husband
was two men trapped in a single body. One of them lived in a
state of rage. The other one liked to drink. The drinker smiled
a lot, at least at the beginning of a session. He got sentimental,
loving in his sloppy, pawing way. His plans got big, overblown.
He'd tell her how he'd change the world, especially their own
world, the one in this apartment, with the curtains drawn, and
he'd make his way into their daughter's room to take the sleeping
girl into his arms, whispering how much he loved her until she
woke up and squirmed in his arms until he set her back down
and tucked her in.

The elation would fade later, at the kitchen table, as the drinking got serious, and he'd get all quiet, hunched over, waiting for
her to bring him his supper.

But there wasn't much in the house this evening. She'd had to
work late at the hotel and paying the babysitter overtime wasn't
something they could afford, so she'd skipped the store in her
rush back home.

And then there'd been Sally's homework, which wasn't much,
but Sally was having trouble with spelling, and words, and
reading. They were saying she was developmentally challenged.

Annie didn't believe it. Her daughter was just hiding inside her own head. Annie knew all about that.

When she'd set the plate down in front of Jeff, he'd looked down at the eggs and two strips of bacon, and had muttered something about having been served the same damned thing that morning. But hunger won out and he'd tucked in.

Until he sent the plate flying across the room, shattering the china and spraying food everywhere. 'The eggs were runny,' he said, slowly rising as Annie backed away towards the kitchen entrance.

He moved to block her way, forcing her back towards the stove, where the frying pan still sat with its bacon fat bubbling and popping.

Something about tonight was different. Not with him, since she saw the familiar rage in Jeff's eyes, as the second man inside him stepped over the drunk and rolled up his sleeves. No, what was different was in her. Tired of being hurt by this man. Tired of being on the receiving end.

She turned and with both hands collected up the frying pan.

Jeff halted, with a sudden tight grin on his red face. 'The fuck you will,' he said.

In answer she lifted the pan higher. The weight made her arms tremble, but if he came at her now all she had to do was tip the pan, let it twist in her hands.

Motion caught her attention and she saw Sally in the entrance-way, frail in her faded Little Mermaid pyjamas, the sleep still in her eyes as she struggled to work out what she was seeing.

Jeff swung round, went to his daughter. 'Sallyyyy,' he sang, taking her into his arms and lifting her up in a hug. He then turned to smile at Annie. 'See your mum?' he asked. 'She's got dangerous. We have to do somethin' about that, don't we? So let's you and me walk on up to her and get her t'put that pan down.'

Their daughter still in his arms, held between him and his wife like a shield, Jeff advanced.

Defeated, Annie set the frying pan back down on the stove-top.

'Now.' Jeff smiled. 'Mummy's been bad and we know what we have t'do with bad girls, don't we?'

Sally nodded, her expression severe, her eyes fixed on her mother's.

'Bad people get hit,' she said.

Jeff set her down and with one hand guided her to one side. The other hand he raised.

It always started with backhanded slaps, the knuckles against one side of her face, hard enough to break skin on occasion. From there, once she'd fallen to the floor, he'd use his fists, mostly on her body.

So she waited.

And flinched when he slashed outward with his hand. The crack that came with the impact stunned her and she blinked, bewildered as Jeff recoiled, clutching his fist. He'd not touched her, and yet there he was, doubled over and cradling his hand. She'd heard it hit something, but that something wasn't her.

'Fuck!' he said. 'Fuck fuck fuck − you broke my hand!' He glared up at her, no doubt expecting to see her face splashed with blood, a welt fast rising.

But she stood as before, motionless, outwardly unaffected although her heart hammered in her chest.

'What the −?' He came back up, straight for her, his other hand reaching out to grip her round the throat.

Instead, the fingers all snapped back and Annie heard popping sounds.

'Goddammit!' Jeff staggered back a step, staring down at his left hand and its array of dislocated fingers.

Annie turned to Sally. 'Go to your room, sweetie.'

The girl bolted.

Jeff was now down on one knee, breath coming in harsh gasps, eyes wild in their red sockets.

Annie collected up the frying pan again. She stepped forward and sent the bacon fat slinging towards her husband. The oil splashed up against something she couldn't see, not a drop reaching Jeff. The horror on his face, mottled by the intervening slick of dripping fat, then shifted to confusion.

'Fuck, woman, I'm going to kill you.'

Suddenly exhausted, even as a strange elation burgeoned

within her, Sally set the frying pan back down. The bacon fat was now pooling on the floor. Not a drop remained to slick the invisible barrier between her and her husband. She moved to collect a roll of paper towels. They went through a lot of those paper towels, and the roll was the only soft thing she knew to clutch for comfort after one of Jeff's beatings. Now, she paused, staring down at the roll in her hands. Then she looked up and met her husband's vicious gaze, and shook her head. 'I don't think so, Jeff. I think it's over. At last, it's over.' A wave of pity ran through her as she studied her husband. 'You poor angry man,' she said, 'what are you going to do now?'

Gaza Strip, Israel, May 25th, 2:13 PM

Private Ruth Moyen of the IDF stood at the checkpoint, the bulky M-16 cradled in her arms, belt heavy on her hips, and watched as rocks and bricks sailed towards her and then bounced off nothing, some thrown with enough force to create little puffs of dust in the air. Behind her, the APC's crew had tumbled out and was arguing over the vehicle's crumpled front end. The last order, to advance into the crowd beyond the checkpoint, seemed to have crumbled in the face of its apparent irrelevance.

No one was getting anywhere. Not the screaming mob opposite, not the advance team on the ground. Overhead, drones circled, and somewhere to the north was the sound of jets, still high, still far away. She had a feeling they weren't having much luck either.

Earlier that day, six missiles had left the banked roadside a few hundred metres ahead, arcing up and racing towards Israeli settlements. All six had exploded in mid-air, at the high point of their arc. Radar and drone triangulation had fixed their point of origin and a counterstrike had been immediately initiated, but that missile had suffered the same fate, detonating harmlessly high in the air.

She listened to the excited, frightened chatter in her earbud as teams called in, argued and begged what to do now. She watched, unmoving, unafraid for perhaps the first time in her young life, as the Palestinians gave up throwing rocks and bricks, as they

51

tried to advance en masse only to run face first into one of those forcefields, the foremost line then pressing up against it as the crowd behind it tried surging forward. She watched as the effort finally broke up, as people limped away or wiped blood from broken noses and split lips.

There had been shots fired sometime earlier, about a block away. A group of locals colliding with a scout team, sudden close quarters, plenty of shouting, weapons sighted, the radio chatter terse and then fierce, and then frantic. Bullets flying, bullets hitting nothing.

She turned slightly at the arrival of Captain David Benholm, his face sunburned at usual, the golden hairs of his sparse beard glinting in the sunlight. 'Can't even throw a punch,' he said, fingers combing through his beard. 'Can't force into a home, can't make arrests, can't evict.' He looked at her. 'It's stalled, Ruth. Everything ... stalled.'

'What now?' she asked him.

His weapon was slung over a shoulder. He stood like a man who'd put away his vigilance. It made him seem so much younger than the warrior she was used to seeing, the one who gave orders, the one who never hesitated to pull the trigger. It made him beautiful. He pulled out a pack of Marlies, offered her one. 'What now? I don't know. No one does.'

He paused for a moment, and then, 'I guess ... we talk.'

From the mob across the street, a young boy waved and made smoking motions with one hand. Then, tentatively, he approached. They let him come, watched him pass through the place where the forcefield had been. It was all down to intent, and whatever eye was fixed upon this and every other scene, it never blinked.

The kid was too young to smoke, but then they all were – that was a bitter joke among them all, on both sides. Too young to smoke, but not too young for killing and dying. David tossed the pack to the boy, who took one out and stepped closer.

David's lighter flicked to life between them.

Cigarettes lit, the three of them stood at the checkpoint, smoking, witnesses to the end of an eternal war.

Casper Brunt worked for a lot of people. This time, he worked for the Chinese. He stood to one side, sunglasses cutting the harsh glare, while the three buyers popped the crate's lid and flung padding and bubblewrap aside to get at the guns. The plastic stuffing flew away, skidding across the dirt track to flatten out against the barbed wire fence beyond which stretched desert scrub.

These days, the Chinese were making cheaper AK-47s than the Russians. The steel wasn't as good but there was no point in mentioning that. There were plenty of international agreements and prohibitions against selling arms to known terrorists, warlords and death-squads. But the truth was, everyone mostly looked the other way. War was good business, after all, and good business kept the world machine well lubricated. The gears needed turning in that machine, and blood worked as well as oil.

One of the men slid a full clip into his brand-new weapon. He gestured to his fellow jihadists waiting by the Land Cruisers, and a few moments later two more appeared, dragging a man between them. His face was battered, one eye swollen shut. He moved his legs as if he was having trouble with his equilibrium.

Casper Brunt looked away, stared off into the west. People liked killing each other. They liked the power of life and death, right there in their hands, and they never hesitated paying for the privilege.

Once this deal was done, he was heading by bush-plane south and then west, to another hotspot with its resident insurgents who used whatever ideology they needed to justify a way of life they had come to love. A way of life that was nothing more than bullying, and hallelujah, bullies loved to bully.

Casper had been at this for a long time. He had plenty of competition, but no one took it hard if a rival got in first. There was a never-ending demand, a never-ending supply. Capitalism in its purest, rawest form.

Shots ripped the air behind him, and then angry shouting. Casper turned round.

The kneeling victim was still kneeling, his one working eye blinking rapidly in the glare.

The leader of the jihadists stalked towards Casper. 'Joke? Blanks?'

'Blanks? What? No, of course not.'

The jihadist lifted the gun and fired point-black into Casper's chest.

He stumbled backward, his mirror sunglasses dislodged by his flinch. But there was no pain. Looking down, he saw his silk shirt unmarred. No holes, no bloom of blood. Ears ringing, he took off his sunglasses and looked across to the man who had just tried to kill him.

'What the hell?'

Abruptly, the jihadist drew out a pistol and fired again at Casper.

He saw the muzzle flash, saw the weapon recoil.

The jihadist stared in disbelief at his weapon, and then threw it at Casper. It struck something invisible between them and fell to the dusty ground with a heavy thud.

Behind him the prisoner had pushed to his feet. Two men closed to restrain him, and were rebuffed before they could lay hands on him.

Casper watched as the battered victim staggered back a few steps, and then wheeled and began a shuffling run up the track.

A dozen weapons let loose behind him, to no effect. Another jihadist ran in from one side, a knife in his hand. He too was flung away, the blade never touching the prisoner, who simply continued his wavering, drunken run.

'Oh,' muttered Casper. 'It's those forcefields, isn't it?' It had to be. He'd studied those damned things online, seeing all the sudden barriers to his trade, wondering which eco-terrorist group was responsible. Which government. Wondering who he'd need to contact to find the inevitable work-around. He'd seen the vids showing people shooting into the damned things.

But this new forcefield wasn't some kind of green nut job's wet dream, protecting threatened areas, national preserves and parks and whatnot.

Sweat now soaking his shirt, beading on his face and unaccountably chilling him despite the sun's intense glare, Casper put his sunglasses back on and looked skyward, seeking signs of a drone. The intervention here was too personal, too specific. Someone was watching, fiddling with dials.

But he saw nothing up there, and the more he thought about it, the more he realised how ridiculous it was to think that someone had tracked him all the way out here. Nobody cared, nobody ever cared.

His buyer was shouting at his men now. The crates of weapons were left lying on the ground as the troop started climbing back into their trucks. From the small huddle of buildings that marked this mostly abandoned hamlet on the east side of the road, an old woman had appeared, all wrapped up, face hidden. As the trucks roared to life and backed into three-point turns, the woman lifted a hand and pointed a thick finger at the jihadists. Whatever she then shouted to them was lost amid skidding tyres and spitting gravel, as the trucks pulled out onto the road and roared off into the north.

Casper glanced back at Jamel, his driver, and saw the man leaning casually on the shaded side of the Land Rover. He headed over. 'Let's go,' he said.

Straightening, Jamel nodded towards the crates.

'Leave them,' Casper said, walking round to the passenger side. 'They're useless now.'

Moments later they sat side by side in the Land Rover.

'Where to?' Jamel asked.

'Airstrip,' Casper replied.

'What's happened?'

'Eye in the sky, Jamel.'

'Whose eye?'

Casper shrugged. 'God's. The Archangel Michael's. The fucking Martians' – does it matter? I need to find a new line of work.'

Jamel started the engine, slid on his own sunglasses. 'Good.'

'Not good.'

'Yes, good,' said Jamel, who then looked across at Casper. 'You a professional piece of shit. Too bad they didn't kill you, those

55

bullets.' He put the truck in gear and they lurched forward. 'Go back to Australia. Don't come back.'

'Lacking fear, he said what was in his mind,' said Casper, leaning back in the seat. 'It's a brave new world, Jamel.'

'Professional piece of shit,' said Jamel again, nodding.

'I see an end to respect,' Casper said, sighing. 'The question is, what will take its place?' He glanced at his driver. 'Like you. All that hate. All that anger. What're you going to do with it, Jamel?'

The road was bumpy. Jamel was driving too fast, but there was no other traffic in sight.

'Me?' Jamel asked. He shrugged.

'You could have made me walk,' Casper said. 'I couldn't have stopped you.'

'That's true.'

'But you didn't. I sold nothing. No cash. Nothing in my pockets. I guess you realised that. Realised that I could only pay you the second half of your fee once we got back to base.'

'I know how it works,' Jamel agreed.

'You were happy enough to take this piece of shit's money. Still are, it seems.'

'This last time, yes. Then you go and you don't come back.'

'Then what, for you?'

Jamel suddenly smiled. 'Then, arsehole, I party.'

Los Angeles, May 25th, 11:02 AM

It wasn't easy living a life where nothing went right. The first rule about being pissed off was to stay pissed off. At everything. At the old man who took off when Anthony was seven, who came back when he was seventeen only to take off again a year later and where the fuck was he now? Nowhere. Shacked up with some woman and starting up yet another trail of kids who'd grow up without a dad, because the bastard had leaving in his eyes and that was a look that never went away and the women who fell for him were just dumb fucks.

School had been another mess. Enough said about that. It didn't matter. All he needed to learn was on the streets anyway.

It wasn't his plan and he wasn't the leader, but he knew his job and it was a simple one. First in through the doors, the big old .357 out from under his heavy coat and pointing straight at Stubbs, the bank's lone guard. Jim Sticks in right behind him, heading for the tellers and yelling at everybody to get down on the floor. Paulo next, right over to Stubbs to take the guy's gun away.

They were wearing masks, bulky coats. Their car was around the corner, the closest place they could find a parking spot.

Everything went wrong from the start. Anthony rushed in, couldn't find Stubbs anywhere, so he pointed the gun at everyone, and then, even as Sticks then came in screaming – and none of his words could be understood because the mask didn't have a mouth hole, only nostril holes – out came old Stubbs from the staff bathroom, pulling at his gun—

Paulo's 9 mm barked right behind Anthony, deafening him. And Stubbs skidded to a halt, looked down and then back up again. Then he had his gun out and suddenly everyone was shooting. The recoil of the .357 made Anthony fumble his grip after his first shot. He'd been less than ten feet away from Stubbs but somehow he'd missed the man. Sticks was firing at everyone, hitting no one. The front window shattered.

Through the ringing in his ears, Anthony heard sirens. 'Fuck it!' he shouted. 'Let's go! It's fucked up! Let's go!'

They retreated to the doors.

Stubbs stood watching. He'd emptied his clip and missed with every shot, which wasn't like Stubbs – the guy was a fuckin Vietnam vet. 'Aw shit,' he said even as Anthony reached the doors, with Sticks and Paulo crowding right behind him. 'You guys? You idiots – Sticks, Paulo, Anthony – you all live a block away!'

'Shut the fuck up!' Sticks shrieked, pushing at Anthony.

Moments later they were outside in the bright California sunshine. And cop cars had already blocked both escape routes. Heavy weapons were out, trained on the three boys.

Suddenly, Paulo yelped a laugh. 'Watch me!' he yelled, rushing forward, gun blazing. The roar of fire that answered him came in a wave. And still Paulo ran, laughing as he did so. He darted between two patrol cars. Cops closed on him. Hands reached out, and just like that, Paulo was caught.

Anthony had seen enough. He dropped the .357 and then held his hands up. Swearing, Sticks spun and ran back into the bank.

Anthony heard him arguing with Stubbs, and then there was a scuffle and Sticks yelped. The doors opened again and out came Stubbs with Sticks in an armlock.

It wasn't easy living a life where nothing went right, but Anthony was used to it by now. It made it easy to stay pissed off. As cops closed in on him and forced him to the hot pavement, he railed in his mind at everything and everyone. And then, feeling the gritty heat of the pavement on his left cheek as the cuffs were put on, something broke inside. He suddenly relaxed.

He could see to the corner, and watched, without any feeling at all, a tow truck turn onto the street just beyond the barricade, dragging his car behind it.

A moment later, he began laughing.

Chapter Six

'To see the universe and all reality from a solely intellectual, materialistic perspective, is akin to blinding yourself in one eye. You can still see the surface, but you've lost all sense of depth.'

Samantha August

Victoria, British Columbia, May 24th, 11:36 AM

'Ronnie! It's your phone!'

Ronald Carpenter continued staring at the newsfeed. He'd been watching one impossible thing after another. The newscasters were frantic, stumbling over everything they tried to say, which wasn't too surprising, as what they had to say made no sense.

Though, in a way, it did.

'Ronnie!'

'Right,' he said, straightening from his forward perch in his recliner. He walked over to where he'd left his cell on the dining room table, took a glance into the kitchen where Emily was doing dishes.

The ringtone wasn't immediately familiar though he'd heard it before, but even as he collected up the phone and looked at the caller ID on the screen, he recalled who'd insisted on that ringtone. In disbelief and growing joy, he answered the call. 'Sam? Is that—'

'No, sorry,' came a man's voice. 'It's me, Hamish ... Sam's husband.'

'Oh, yes, of course. I just saw the ID and—'

'One of my wife's other cells,' Hamish explained. 'Listen, I don't – rather, is there any chance you could come by? Do you remember where we live?'

'Of course.' Ronald glanced back the television. 'But things are kind of crazy right now.'

'I know.'

'Is this about Sam?' Ronald asked. 'Some word—'

'Well ... yes. And no. But I need to talk, and I maybe need some answers.'

'From me?' He looked up as Emily entered the dining room, drying her hands on her T-shirt. When things got strange, Emily did housework. When she was ticked off about something, she did housework. When she was bored, she did—

'Well, you write hard SF, Ron. At least that's what Sam tells me.' He hesitated, and then added, 'Everything that's going on right now. Worldwide, I mean.'

'Trust me,' Ron said, 'you couldn't write this. It's impossible.'

'I'm sorry, what do you mean?'

He rubbed at his eyes, shrugged in answer to Emily's silent query. She moved on, heading for the stairs, seeking another room to conquer. 'Hamish. The forcefields – they were manageable. Inconvenient, but still, can be worked around. But this shutting down all violence, slamming the door in the face of our natural aggression ... that's too big, if you see what I mean.'

'No, I'm not sure I do.'

Ron's gaze returned to the television. Someone was reporting from the ruins of Beirut. Behind the journalist, a mob filled the street. Hands reached skyward, fingers spread wide. 'It's civilisation, Hamish, and it's going to go down. Do you see? Shut down our avenues of competitiveness and aggression, the pathways inside us that define what we are, as a species, socially and culturally ... with no outlet ... well, you're a doctor. Think about it.'

'I think it's connected.'

'Connect— oh. *Oh*.' Suddenly, Ronald Carpenter found a need to sit down.

'She's alive. I know that,' Hamish said. 'There have been a few text messages. Ron, can you come over?'

'I'll be right there.'

Ron had known Samantha August for over a decade. They'd met at a convention in Ottawa. Canadian SF writers comprised a small group, all things considered. Some hefty talents in that bunch. Sawyer, Spider Robinson, Watts, Gibson, Samantha August. No point in counting Atwood since she'd refused the membership card and secret handshake. Ronald Carpenter was a relative new-comer – only two novels out so far, with a third one on the way.

Sam had been an intimidating presence at first. A sharp mind, a caustic wit, a smoky look of gravitas in her eyes. But she'd greeted him warmly, complimented him on his debut military hard-SF series. Now they shared the same New York agent, and had met often at a café to talk writing and publishing.

Her disappearance had been a shock. He had watched the video recordings of the abduction. He had deconstructed the clearest feeds and taken screen-shots in order to more closely examine the underbelly of the craft that had come out of the clouds.

The whole thing had seemed too obvious. Digital editing could pull off anything these days. He hadn't known what to think. He still didn't. Sam had a twisted sense of humour to be sure, but he couldn't imagine her being involved in a stunt like that.

Then, as the days passed, other events had overtaken the im-mediacy of the mystery surrounding Sam's disappearance. Things that gave him some ideas about what was happening. And yet, oddly, he had never connected any of it with Sam's abduction. In retrospect, he cursed himself for an idiot.

He parked in the driveway to Sam's house. Hamish had been waiting by the door and now he opened it and invited Ron inside after a quick handshake.

Hamish had been suffering in his wife's absence. Take-out and delivery cartons crowded the island in the kitchen as Hamish led Ron through to the roofed-in deck. The man himself was unshaven, wearing clothes he might have used to work in the garden, and slippers on his feet.

'I've been moving patients,' Hamish said as he sat and ges-tured for Ron to do the same. On the small deck table between them was a bottle of Glenfiddich and two glasses. Hamish poured healthy shots into both glasses. 'It's been hard to concentrate. I wasn't doing my patients any good.'

'You said there's been text messages,' said Ron as he collected up the glass. 'Definitely from Sam?'

'Yes.' The older man sat up in his chair and fumbled in his cardigan pocket, withdrawing a small notepad. 'Things only the two of us know. All that. It's her. She's alive.' He opened the notepad and peered at the first page.

'That's great, Hamish. I'm so relieved. Those UFO videos – well, it's one thing to write about this kind of stuff, it's another to ...' his words fell away as he realised he had nothing more to say.

Hamish pulled out his reading glasses and continued studying the notepad. 'I left out the personal stuff.' He paused and looked up at Ron over his glasses. 'She's up there, Ronald. In a craft. Just her and some kind of artificial intelligence.'

Ron's mouth was dry. His hand shook as he took a sip of the single malt. 'There were reports of other abductions ...'

'Inventions,' said Hamish. 'Hoaxes. She's alone. They picked her.'

'Picked her? Why?'

'Seems they place a high value on artists.'

Ron scowled. 'What do they want, autographs?'

'I think,' ventured Hamish, 'to speak on their behalf.'

'So what are they waiting for? Have you been paying attention to what's been going on, Hamish? To what's happening out there, shutting down all aggression? This is omniscience, omnipotence. Might as well be God as aliens, with one crucial exception.'

Hamish frowned. 'And that exception is?'

'God's into free will. These guys ... not so much.'

The doctor looked away, and then he settled back again into his chair, slowly closing up the small notepad. 'The situation,' he said. 'It's impossible. For her. I try thinking about it, but it's too much.'

'You're not alone in that,' said Ron. 'What's happened seems to have paralysed us. Except for the fundamentalists and all that wailing about the end of the world. Judgement Day.' He took a mouthful of the whisky and let out a heady sigh. 'But it's the governments. They're locked up. Helpless. Meanwhile, refugee camps are overflowing. There's reports of imminent starvation, people getting sick – that's bound to happen. And now, all these spontaneous mobs filling the streets.' He leaned forward. 'Can you text her back, Hamish? If she's going to speak for them, it'd better be damned soon.'

'No,' said Hamish. 'I can't. At least, I don't think so. I try, but she's not responded directly to what I write. It's mostly ... well, personal stuff.'

'Is she being held against her will?'

'She says not. She says this is all on some kind of schedule. She says they've done this before, on other worlds. There is more to come.'

'They must have made official contact by now,' Ron said. 'And all those statements from all the governments are just a smoke-screen.'

'I don't think she's talked to any government,' Hamish said.

Ron considered, trying to make sense of all this. He studied Hamish for a long moment, and then said, 'Should I do something with this information? Is that what you're asking me to do? Because if it is, I doubt anyone would listen. Besides, the net's gone insane. Even some of the big servers are getting overloaded.'

'I think she needs help,' said Hamish.

'What do you mean?'

'Some ... groundwork laid.' He took off his reading glasses and rubbed his eyes. 'Rational people are drawing proper conclusions – I mean, rather, people are discussing the near certainty that an alien presence is now interfering with us.'

Ronald nodded, and then snorted. 'So much for the Prime Directive.' Seeing Hamish's expression, he explained. 'Star Trek, the non-interference protocol the Federation worked under, not that it stopped Kirk from ... never mind, not important. But, you're right. It's being discussed.'

Hamish waited.

'Groundwork ...' Ron mused. 'That would be problematic,

Hamish. We're all waiting for the news networks to start calling on every SF writer who won't wilt in front of a camera. Picking their brains, inviting speculation. It's coming, once the hysteria dies down. But I think what you're suggesting is some kind of consistent statement. I don't think you'll get it.'

'If you let them know, Ronald, about Sam.'

'Okay, she's well respected. And then there's her vlog, but sometimes that's just a giant target painted on her back. Sam never pulled any punches.' He leaned forward. 'Ah, that might be it.'

'I'm sorry, what?'

'Their selecting her, as opposed to anyone else. She's recognisable, even to people outside the nerdo-sphere. Like Stephen King, or Martin. All right, maybe not that big, but still, pretty big.'

Hamish's gaze was level. 'I can't imagine either King or Martin as ideal spokespeople for an alien First Contact.'

After a moment, Ron snorted. 'Yeah, point taken. So, they picked her. Could've been some other SF writer, but it wasn't. Because she's got the high profile, they chose her. And like I said, she's well respected in the field. Still, getting all the other writers on board? Probably not, at least not yet. The problem is, we don't know enough. About their intentions beyond what's already happened. In other words, we don't know enough to decide it'd be anything but, well, treason, if we co-operated with this interference – and whatever's still to come. If we tried to ease people into this.'

Hamish settled a level regard on Ron. 'Treason? Let me ask you this, then. It's coming anyway. It's arrived, in fact, and no one down here has any idea of what's still to come. It's inevitable, and whether you "ease people into this" or not, makes no difference at all, since it is clear that these ... aliens, they're not much interested in asking us about what we might want, or need.' Having said his piece, the doctor sat back once again. He frowned down at his notepad and opened it up, flipping pages. Retrieving his reading glasses he said, 'Here, then ... she wrote: "There are no men in black negotiating with this ET. Nobody on Earth has any control, and that's where the real trouble is going to come from. The power-brokers will panic."' He looked up. 'This is what I've been thinking about, Ronald. I'm not unaware of global events. I saw how savagely the authorities came down on those Occupy protestors a few years back. They perceived that movement — quite rightly — as a fundamental threat to their power structure. They couldn't co-opt it, so they crushed it. And we've all seen what's happened in the States with the last two elections.'

Ron studied Hamish for a long moment and then sighed heavily. 'She's right, Hamish. Never mind the aliens posing a danger. The power-brokers must be shitting bricks right now. No control of the situation, no governments to be bought, no strings to be pulled, no courts to subvert.'

'And yet,' said Hamish, 'all violence has been stopped.'

'And it's a pretty broad definition of "violence",' Ron added. 'Fracking operations have shut down, same for the Tar Sands. And all those other assaults on the environment, the illegal logging and poaching and mining and all the rest.'

'So, what will those in power do now, Ronald?'

'I'm not sure. What with the stock market spiralling down—'

'No,' Hamish cut in. He held up the notepad. 'Here. "Beware the propaganda machine. The One Per Cent own the media. They control the information. Watch for the attacks."'

'Hmm, whipping the public into a frenzy of fear — that's already happening, even without Big Media's help.'

'It needs to be countered,' Hamish said. 'A voice of reason—'

Ronald's laugh was bitter. 'My thinking hasn't changed. We don't have enough to go on.'

'What do you mean?'

'All right, Hamish, let's walk it through. Sam gets abducted, in public and in front of dozens of witnesses. And you're right, it was a huge red flag waving in our faces. Was that UFO tracked on radar? I've seen no official statement to that effect. How about you?'

'No,' Hamish replied. 'Nothing like that. The police ... it's just an open file, that's all.'

'With no one asking the uncomfortable questions. At least, not publicly. I expect our military has been rattled, though. Okay, then. Abduction, but no other communication that we know of—'

'According to Sam, none.'

Ron considered for a time, the whisky glass in his hands and his eyes on the amber liquid as he rolled it in a slow circles. Finally, he nodded and looked back up. 'Okay. So. Abduction. Then their next move is to make whole swathes of land and sea suddenly out of bounds for humans, and the selection criteria seems to be about preservation and restoration of threatened ecosystems. Kicking people out seems almost incidental.' He paused. 'But maybe not. Maybe the two are connected.'

'Of course they are,' Hamish said, with a trace of anger. 'Who has been threatening those ecosystems? Us.'

'We got our hands slapped.'

'More to the point,' Hamish persisted, 'the responsibility for preserving and protecting those ecosystems has been taken away from us.' His blue eyes fixed upon Ronald. 'We must assume, I think, that we've been ... monitored. For quite some time. And that the aliens have elected to act based on evidence gathered—'

'And conclusions drawn,' Ron finished, nodding, as a faint shiver of something awoke inside him. Excitement? 'That opening move, those forcefields, they're announcing a lack of faith. In us. And,' he added quickly, 'they prioritise the planet over humanity.'

Hamish jabbed a finger at Ronald, as if to pin the notion down, and then he began scribbling in his notepad. 'Exactly, Ronald. And then?'

'And then ... they take away our guns. Our knives, our fists.'

'Our nuclear arsenal, tanks, fighter jets, cruise missiles, drones, all useless.'

'Presumably,' Ronald pointed out. 'No one's made any such announcement. But then, they wouldn't, would they?'

'What happens,' Hamish asked as he continued writing, 'when borders can't be enforced? What happens when you can't stop people from, from just *moving*. From there to here?'

'The segregation of settlements in Jerusalem is in shambles,'

Ron said. 'No one can hold anyone back. By the same token, no one can even hurt each other — there were lots of arguments, shouting back and forth. Lots of cursing and waving fists. But it all fell away, since it incited nothing, went nowhere. All just a waste of breath. Even when a mob tries to rush a line of soldiers, they can't get at each other.'

'There is a complexity to these rules,' Hamish said.

'Yes, there is, isn't there? Right, the option of violence has been removed. All over the world, all those warring ideologies ... now asking themselves, *what do we do now? How do we win a battle we're not allowed to fight?*'

'There is one exception to the rule against violence,' Hamish said.

Ronald's eyebrows lifted. 'There is?'

Hamish removed his glasses again. 'Suicide.'

'What? I mean, really? Are you sure?'

'I'm a doctor, remember? I made some calls. I've since confirmed it — what caught my eye was that suicide bomber in Lahore, just yesterday. He was in a crowded mosque, but the explosion annihilated only him — even sound did not penetrate the forcefield that wrapped itself around the man. There was a flash, and then just scraps and bits of meat, bone and hair. So, violence, but self-directed.'

'I missed that report,' said Ronald.

'I called some people I know in the Emergency Response Services. Suicides have continued. It seems that violence against oneself is permitted.'

'But not all suicide attempts are true attempts, are they?'

Hamish shrugged, his expression bleak. 'There have been no successful interventions by any first-responder in the past seventy-two hours — not here, not in Vancouver or Calgary. That was as far as I could inquire, for now.'

'What about accidental overdoses?'

'Too early to tell. The data points are ambiguous. There was one medical intervention with a patient who immediately regretted their overdose — that wasn't prevented or interfered with. At Vancouver General last night.'

Ron rubbed at his face. The whisky was making itself felt – he'd forgotten to eat lunch. 'Let's try to think through the progression. Abduction, forcefields, no violence. We've been ... emasculated. If they landed now and just took things over, worldwide, all we'd have left is passive resistance. A blanket refusal to co-operate.'

'One must hope,' Hamish said, 'that the pacifist edict also applies to the aliens as well.'

'I'm not sure it does, though. Those forcefields pushed people out. Maybe nobody was physically injured by that, but they sure suffered emotionally.'

'Carrot and stick,' Hamish said, his frown deepening.

'The non-violence thing is a pretty bitter carrot.'

'Tough love.'

Ron grunted. 'So, the "stick" of the forcefields, the dubious carrot of non-violence. Logically, we're due for another "stick".'

'Ronald, one could reverse those labels quite easily. The carrot is the preserved environment and all its diversity saved from extinction; the stick is the end of human aggression towards anything but oneself. But that, too, is not an absolute. Slaughterhouses continue processing domestic livestock, after all. But wholesale harvesting from the sea has been stopped. Crops are still being harvested, and we know how destructive that can be, especially when that harvesting is mechanical. Rather, better to consider our aggressive instincts to have been selectively curtailed. It is not an absolute.'

'Curious, that. But you have a point. You could read the carrot and stick metaphor both ways. Which puts us at an impasse regarding what might come next.'

Hamish shrugged. 'If a stick, what? What more can be done to us?'

'Occupation. Landings. Troops – no, what am I saying. They don't need troops. Unless they're prepared to force us into something, or, conversely, coming down in transports – aw, shit, Hamish. See what bad SF does to us? That makes no sense either.' He threw up his hands. 'I have no idea.'

'And if a carrot?'

'Christ, where to start?'

'Precisely, Ronald, where *would* you start?'

'Feed the starving, provide clean water, sanitation, medicine. Shelter.'

'All the things we *could* do, but lack the will in doing so.'

Ronald stared for a long moment, and then he nodded. 'Yes, I see that. I see it. Carrot or stick? We won't know, can't know. Not yet. Because the next move is supposed to be *ours*.'

'And how well has the present power structure handled such acts of salvation?' Hamish asked. 'How generous has the One Per Cent been in redistributing its wealth? Sam warns us of propaganda, of a counter-movement against what is happening. What is the likelihood of the power-brokers wilfully sacrificing the lives of a million starving peasants, in order to enflame the general population against this alien intervention?'

Flinching, Ron sat back. 'Hamish, you're a cynical man.'

'Ronald, I have spent thirty-six years in the medical profession, a profession firmly trapped in the back pocket of Big Pharma. It is no stretch for me to imagine the worst possible scenario. People get used, my friend. Lives expended. The machine's primary function is to feed itself. What is the present statistic? Sixty-four people now own half the world's wealth?'

'If the aliens are waiting for us to do right by those displaced refugees, we're going to disappoint them. Thus, up next, another stick.'

'Or not,' Hamish said. 'Since they must have been monitoring us, they surely know how things will work out. The question is, do they care about the lives that will be lost, especially when those lives serve as a justification for global rejection of their presence?'

'So they'll just sit back and watch us dig an even deeper hole of culpability? That's ... cold.'

'Not nearly as cold as our deliberate exploitation of human suffering.'

'Don't throw me into that crowd! How many writers will you find among those sixty-four gazillionaires?'

Hamish shrugged again, but said nothing.

After a long moment, Ronald said, 'Got any coffee? I shouldn't drive right now.'

'Of course. I can also call you a cab.'

'Great. Okay, Hamish, you've made your point. I'll contact as many writing colleagues as I can. I'll spread the word. No guarantees, but we have one thing going for us – a lot of those writers are fucking smart people. They're probably thought things through a lot further and a lot better than we've managed here today.'

'Good. The world needs them, and it needs them now.'

Chapter Seven

'Every fiction author knows that wish-fulfilment
is a dangerous thing. Being the hero of your own
story sounds great, but in an honest tale, hell is
just around the corner.'

Samantha August

'You washed my clothes.'

'Organic contamination has been removed while you slept,
yes.'

Sam sat up on the bed. 'Sleep's coming way too easily right
now,' she said. 'You must be drugging me somehow. Some kind
of aerosol mist? Something in the food you've been providing?
Come on, Adam, fess up.'

At the far end of the room a chair and the small table that
preceded the arrival of her meals had reappeared, on which
waited an urn of coffee and a plain white cup and saucer and
spoon, along with a sugar bowl and small pitcher of cream. And
her pack of cigarettes and lighter.

There was a slight delay before Adam replied, during which
she arose, naked, and walked over to the table.

'You are nearing an age in which your homeostatic mechanisms
begin to lose their efficacy—'

'Really?' she cut in as she sat and poured some coffee. 'I hadn't
noticed.'

'I believe that to be sarcasm.'

Sam lit a cigarette, then collected up the cup and sipped coffee
as she studied the image of the Earth on the wall to her right.

'In any case,' Adam resumed after a moment, 'I have introduced to your internal system a tailored nanosuite. All major endocrine functions are now optimal, organs restored to various levels of health, and system-wide telomere maintenance and regulation is now in effect.'

Sam slowly set the cup back down, no longer paying any attention to the blue, white and brown world on the screen.

'I am detecting an increase in heart rate and concomitant rise in blood pressure.'

'You should have asked me first,' Sam said. She flicked ash and took a deep drag on the cigarette. Gusted out smoke. '"Various levels of health" you said. Which is why I'm not coughing right now, or feeling sick from the nicotine.'

'Correct. Fortunately, volatiles, free radicals, toxic gases and minerals are all used as fuel by the nanosuite. As are the fillings in your teeth, but this latter effect is gradual as the replacement of enamel is a slow process.'

'Really? Well, tell that nanosuite to leave the nicotine and caffeine alone, or I won't be a happy camper.'

'This was anticipated, particularly since nicotine is an effective cognitive enhancer and presumably this is useful.'

'Adam, have you dosed *just* me?'

'For the moment. We have not reached that stage yet on the planet below.'

'And will you? Reach that stage?'

'There are stages for the Intervention Protocol, but the specifics must be considered protean. We are in the early phase of engagement at the moment. That said, your personal health was deemed essential if you are to act as facilitator between us and humans.'

'Adam, you really call what you're doing to us down there an "engagement"? Pushing us around like puppets is not *engagement*.'

'Shall I reheat the coffee in your cup?'

'No.'

'My reply to your observation will be extensive.'

'Finally!' She stood. 'All right, then, hot it up, darling, while I get dressed. Oh, and I want some toast. Lightly buttered.

Sourdough, but sliced thin — none of that two-inch-thick crap that keeps making my jaw pop.'

'Your mandibular joints will not dislocate anymore.'

She walked over to where her clothes were left neatly folded on a shelf that projected from the wall near her bed. 'Oh, right. And this is why I just realised that I don't need my reading glasses, isn't it?' She began dressing.

'Focal correction is regulated through corrective volume pressure adjustments and restored flexibility to the lenses' associated muscles.'

'Okay, got it. You fixed my vision, but you forgot to add the lasers and internal targeting system.'

'Do you wish to have a cape and close-fitting multicoloured costume as well, Samantha?'

'Ah! The AI's got a sense of humour.' Sam returned to the table and her coffee and, now, breakfast.

Adam began. 'The relationship between your species and other species on your world is also an engagement. The control and regulation of domestic livestock, poultry, and innumerous plants, all invoke a presumptive exchange, wherein your species elevates its own particular needs over that of the aforementioned species. The nature of this engagement extends to virtually all other life-forms on your world, from animals to be hunted, pests to be eradicated, weeds to be poisoned, insects to be exterminated, and bacteria to be expunged.'

'What you're describing all serves our daily sustenance,' Sam replied. 'Basic needs and the organisation required to manage and control them. There's no getting around it.'

'Agreed, to a point. But where is your consideration of these other life-forms, particularly in terms of their attendant suffering?'

'Hold on,' Sam said around a mouthful of toast, 'are you trying to tell me that other civilisations out there don't possess the same basic needs of sustenance?'

'Not at all. For most, successful expansion among naturally predatory species into space is quickly followed by a paradigm shift. This relates, of course, to an end to scarcity, since the technology required for interstellar travel is concomitant with technologies involving atomic and molecular reassembly. In any case,' Adam went on before Sam could get a word in, 'the alteration of the mind-set is without doubt the most profound event in sentient evolution.'

'You said "some" predatory species just then.'

'Yes. Alas, there are other forms of predation, but that topic, while imminent, must await certain impending events. Now, to return to my question and the situation here on Earth. Where is your consideration of these other native life-forms, particularly in terms of their attendant suffering?'

Sam sighed. 'Granted,' she said, 'agribusiness is lagging behind when it comes to humane care. But surely even you can see that the tide has been turning.'

'What delays the turning of that tide, Samantha? If one cannot help but be cognisant that other life-forms do indeed suffer, why have wholesale changes not already occurred?'

'Because efficiency is good for business.'

'And efficiency, in this context, extends to more than just a predictable and bounteous supply of basic necessities, correct? Efficiency, in this context, also requires a cognitive shift in thinking. By reducing domestic life-forms to units for consumption, organised and valued on the basis of weight, quality, variety and so on, the notion of suffering is sidestepped. Not simply the suffering experienced by these domesticated life-forms, but also the suffering experienced by non-domesticated life-forms as a consequence of, say, land clearance, wetland drainage and deforestation.'

'Well, that's capitalism for you,' Sam said, shrugging. 'Economics is the altering of language from the holistic to the specific for the purpose of applying a value system to shit we don't really own, only pretend to. Land, water, animals, plants, each other, our labour, our interests, our likes, wants, needs ...' She selected a second piece of toast and studied it for a moment. 'Any human population reaches a threshold where organising everything into categories is the only way to manage the complexities of civilisation. I bet your three alien species did exactly the same.'

'We were speaking of engagement, were we not?'

'So you're applying the same presumptive relationship with us as we do with cows, sheep and pigs. Given what you've done to Earth, I'd say that's pretty accurate. What disturbs me is, well, you see, we kill and eat cows, sheep and pigs.'

'While endeavouring to not think of their suffering.'

'Making you no better than us.' She let the piece of toast drop back onto its delicate plate. 'I am still undecided, you know. About speaking on your behalf.'

'Yes, and clearly I have not yet provided you with enough information on the nature of our Intervention.'

'Let's just say that you've been coy, Adam, and that I'm having to work for it.'

'There are philosophical underpinnings,' Adam said, 'which lie at the core of engagement. Given that humans are capable of compassion, why has economic efficiency so easily triumphed over it? More to the point for you, perhaps, what is the spiritual effect upon a species and a civilisation that has segregated its sense of compassion?'

'Spiritual?'

'Psychological, then.'

'Well, I suppose, the effect is, we acquire the habit of closing off avenues of compassion, of being selective. But we don't do it collectively; we do it individually, within a general framework defined by cultural mores and taboos.'

'Hence the ethical objection to meat by vegetarians.'

Sam snorted. 'You know, when a vegetarian says she doesn't eat meat because she doesn't like the taste, I'm good with that. Taste is personal, and an inalienable right. But that whole ethical argument rubs me the wrong way. More wild species have been and are being wiped out by agriculture than hunting or the slaughter of domesticated animals ever has and ever will. So the dead animals are just once removed, and in some ways even more egregious since we don't eat them. To then argue against cruelty is just sophistry.'

'The inhumane practices of modern livestock agribusiness notwithstanding?'

'Then you're back to selective compassion,' said Sam. 'Decry the slaughterhouses and factory-farms while scoffing down soya bean paste that came from another massive chunk of Brazilian rainforest cut down.'

'Agreed,' said Adam. 'Shall we consider, once again, this notion of "engagement"?'

'Go on.' Sam sipped more coffee. It was still hot, impossibly so. 'But just so you know, you giving me that — what did you call it — nanosuite? Giving me that without asking me first is making me feel like a steer loaded up on hormones and antibiotics.'

'Indeed, and I don't recall any instance of a human being asking the animal's permission.'

'And you wonder why I'm reluctant to be your spokesperson?'

'Not at all. Paradigm shifts may appear to arrive suddenly, overwhelmingly, while in truth they depend upon a gradual, if inexorable, transformation of basic philosophical precepts.'

'This nanosuite, what else does it do? You mentioned telomeres. Have I stopped ageing, then?'

'In many respects, internally and selectively, your ageing has already been reversed, as each organ is brought to a higher efficiency, which at your age has necessitated DNA repair and what we might call a resetting of the clock.'

'You can't make us immortal, Adam. Well, maybe you can, but don't you dare.'

'Yes we can, or as near as immortal as finite biological entities are capable of being. And of course, no, we won't. That said, if indeed we proceed with a universal application of nanosuites—'

She thumped the tabletop with her fist. 'You will fuck up Earth's biome, Adam! How can you not see that? Are you going to give it just to humans? What about all the other life-forms? Whales, bats, dogs, goldfish? Fire-ants, termites, malaria viruses? I mean, what the hell *is* this nanosuite? What happens when it spills out into the environment? And guaranteed, it will!'

Adam was silent for a few moments, and then the AI said, 'Then you understand the nature of humanity's presence within a specific and defined biome, presently contained on this single planet you call Earth. We suspected as much. For example, and despite the subversive efforts of your pharmaceutical industry, all effective treatments and cures for virtually all diseases afflicting life-forms on your planet are *readily* available within your global biome. And this, of course, is no accident.'

The sudden switch of subject left Sam momentarily confused, and she frowned as she said, 'My husband drops hints every now and then, but even for a man in the profession of healthcare, it's more a suspicion than a certainty. Subverted cures, huh? Well, the reasons why are obvious enough. If you can't make an artificial version of something, you can't patent it, and if you can't patent it, there's no point in spending millions on research. And when a treatment or cure is found in the natural world, most of the effort and delays by the industry relate directly to the search for a manufactured match, or at least an artificial version that will do the same thing.'

'Such subversion is in truth of little consequence,' Adam then said. 'There are greater dangers pending. If you will allow me this brief digression.'

'Sure, go ahead. I doubt you can make my head spin any more than it's already doing.'

'Bear in mind, Samantha, that as with any singular, self-contained organism, there are two sources of risk. One is external. That is to say the space between planets and stars. Life on Earth was seeded from space close to four billion years ago. Cometary ice and debris are in fact rife with basic life-forms, in particular bacteria, algae, viruses and retroviruses. This appears to be the primary source of life's proliferation in the galaxy and likely in the entire universe. Contrary to your belief, the void is not empty, not lifeless. Your planet, therefore, is in constant battle with external infection, but a healthy biome is one that possesses a strong immune system, and the adaptive capacity to accommodate alien viral incursions.'

'Holy crap.'

'The second risk is internal; when the biome sickens itself through excess toxicity. I trust my point is obvious here, Samantha. The sicker you make your world, the greater the risk from space-borne infection.'

'We really have been living in a bubble,' Sam said. 'But there's already plenty of evidence for alien rain, though the scientific consensus has been to ignore it.'

'Do you know why?'

'Maybe.' She considered. 'Okay, it might be like this. There's something comforting in the notion that everything beyond our immediate atmosphere is inimical to life, hostile and deadly and, therefore, utterly empty. That belief builds us a cosy cocoon.'

'Yes,' said Adam, 'I imagine it would. Consider again the principle of the incorporation I described thirty-one hours ago, in which I in effect assimilated your planet into my extended body, subjecting it to both autonomic and directed agency on my part. Your planet has done much the same for itself, and did so billions of years ago, with the first flowering of life, and continues to do so to this day. Indeed, this is a requisite necessity for life itself.'

Sam nodded. 'Right, I'm familiar with Lovelock's Gaia Hypothesis, the planet as a singular life-form. But he also suggested a directed purpose to evolution of complex life, leading to a planet becoming conscious of itself, which it did – with us humans.'

'Yes, and accordingly, it should come as no surprise that, just as with your own body's internal regulation, the planet as a whole operates within a similar system of self-regulation.'

'Then why the hell didn't you just leave us to come to our own realisation? To figure all this out for ourselves? Sure, I get it. That cocoon. All the delusions we cherish about our implicit isolation. I mean, despite everything that might be raining down on us, our medical system still manages to keep us alive. Well, most of us, anyway.'

'Is the Gaia Hypothesis universally understood and ascribed to, in the self-maintenance of your planet's body and all the necessary components within it?'

'No, obviously not.'

'Then can it not be said that your planet's consciousness is not yet mature? That in its old habits of self-destruction – characterised by the unrealistic attitude of the very young who believe themselves to be immortal despite all evidence to the contrary – humanity does not yet comprehend the responsibility that attends adulthood? Samantha, in all life, more offspring are produced than can be expected to reach maturity. The position of immaturity in all life-forms is risk-laden, subject to predation, to fatal errors in judgement, to sibling competition, to the attrition of the environment's harsh truths, to biological unviability itself.'

'Continue,' said Sam in a near whisper, as comprehension began to dawn in her.

'Now,' Adam said, 'extend the notion of risk-laden juvenile life-forms. Increase the scale, so that individual biomes – as defined by single life-bearing planets – are viewed as immature individuals within a litter, an array of related offspring in any given region of the galaxy. Some will survive; many will not. Most complex life-forms are characterised by care for the young, by direct parents and by community—'

'And which are you, Adam? I mean, your three alien civilisations? Parents or community?'

'The analogy is not intended to be that precise,' the AI replied. 'But I comprehend your need for a specific – if loose – category of behaviour. Accordingly, consider us as community.'

'I see. As members in this region of the galaxy.'

'Yes, although the origin planets of the three alien civilisations all share the characteristic of being well inward, nearer the galactic core and therefore on the very edge of your region. Nonetheless, we possess a parental prerogative, or at least that of potential care-giver, for this region of the galaxy. Accordingly, we are governed by considerations of viability, and this is central in determining whether or not we intervene in the development of any individual planetary life-form.'

'And we barely made the grade.'

'Your biome made the grade with ease, Samantha. Its consciousness, as characterised by humanity, did not fare as well.'

'So you considered giving Earth a lobotomy.'

'Yes, we did.'

'But Earth is just slightly too old, reducing the chances of a new consciousness emerging in time.'

'Correct, particularly given the level of resource-depletion already present.'

'You could have intervened much earlier, though. Say in, oh, I don't know, the fifth century BC. Unless, of course, you weren't paying any attention to us back then, or you weren't yet technologically advanced enough to intervene.'

'Not the latter, I assure you. But this is the dilemma of Intervention, Samantha. We must adhere to some measure of faith in the child. Although your choice of the fifth century BC is interesting.'

Sam grunted, reaching for her cigarettes. 'It's when we first cut off our head – humanity – from the rest of the body – nature.'

'Yes. In retrospect, we should have identified the ultimate fate of that self-directed decapitation.'

'So you watched us fucking it up for centuries. And still did nothing.'

'There were many times, Samantha, when a paradigm shift could have occurred. It has only been since mass industrialisation that certain economic principles achieved ascendancy, shaping all that followed.'

She nodded, now regarding the planet on the screen again. 'So, your nanosuite won't cure me of all diseases.'

'To the contrary, but not in the way you might think. Like a planet's biome, the human body is self-regulatory and self-contained. Your nanosuite is maintaining internal conditions that are optimal for that regulation. For conditions such as cancer, for example, your body regularly identifies and eliminates such flawed transcriptions within dividing cells. Only when the body is stressed can cancer take hold, and the sources of stress are myriad and, alas, burgeoning in your modern civilisation.'

'Yes I know,' Sam said. 'Hamish calls it the six-headed elephant in the room. In lifestyle choice people are healthier than ever, and yet cancer is now an epidemic in the modern age, showing no signs of abating. The opposite, in fact. It's getting worse.'

'You have stressed your biome, yes, and polluted it with toxins. You are progressively eliminating its self-regulating capabilities. Your collective attack against personal habits is misdirection at best, hypocrisy at worst, since it is your *civilisation's* habits that are killing you – and the entire biome with it.'

'But now you have intervened.'

'Yes, now we have intervened.'

'The child gets her hand slapped.'

'It is a common form of engagement under the circumstances.'

'Oh, fuck you, Adam,' Sam sighed, but there was no heat in the curse. She finished off her cigarette with one last drag and then dropped it to the floor. 'Better be careful now. That child below is about to have one hell of a tantrum.'

STAGE TWO:

Warning Shot
(Contemplation)

Chapter Eight

'There is a question that comes with every thought
experiment: just how far are you willing to take it?'
Samantha August

Tiny mangroves filled the narrow cut between the main island and its smaller companion. To Douglas Murdo, from where he sat in the shade beneath the awning on the deck of his house, they had the look of small multi-legged creatures emerging from the turquoise waters, strangely ominous and unnerving. He'd wanted them all cut down, but the grounds manager had refused, saying they were needed for protecting smaller, younger fish, and besides, mangroves diminished the damage from hurricanes.

Douglas had fired the man and was now looking to hire a new grounds manager. When he wanted something done, he expected it to be done. No questions, no complaints. He paid people for their obedience.

He shifted in his chair, considered pouring himself another glass of iced tea, and then decided against it. He glanced at his cell where it rested on the linen-draped coffee table.

'Oh, do relax, Dougie,' sighed Chrystal from her lounger. She was lying naked in the full sun. There weren't any boats out on the water. The Belizean Maritime Patrol was doing its job, steering nosy people away from Murdo's Island. 'He'll call when he calls.' Her sunglasses were on and she faced the sun instead of him. 'Go for a swim.'

'Sure,' he snapped. 'Go for a swim, so when he *does* call, I won't be here to answer it. Right, that makes sense.' He drew a deep breath to calm himself down. He'd not married this twenty-nine-year-old model for her brains, after all.

Once again, it seemed that his irritation simply ran off her, and she repeated her sigh. 'Oh fine, then. Sit and stew why don't you?'

'I should've left you behind,' he said.

'It was cold and wet in London, darling. You know how I love this place.'

He was under no illusions about her. She'd married his wealth and the lifestyle it bought. His seventy-three-year-old body and his media empire were little more than the contract's unpleasant fine print. Still, there was some measure of satisfaction for him, knowing how he could buy people as easily as he bought companies. *And with this butt-ugly face, too.*

'Bernard's handling it,' she continued.

Douglas wondered, idly, if she'd lined up his son for when the old man was gone, or was there enough in her inheritance to keep her content? Money didn't always buy power, he knew. Sometimes it bought uselessness.

Models didn't age well. It had nothing to do with the body or face or anything personal. It had to do with the profession and the way it kept alive those perfected images from every model's prime. There was no matching up to that shit. But now here she was, with him, the California girl on his arm, barely taking a shoot anymore, and the calls were getting few and far between.

He could buy another magazine. Tell the editor to line Chrystal up, or else. He'd even spring for the coke.

Anyway, she might want her hooks into Bernard, because Bernard had learned well his father's talent with power and how to wield it. Unlike the useless wreck—

The French door behind him slid open and his other son, Maxwell, sauntered out onto the deck. He was getting fat – that came from his mother, as did the permanent smirk on his thick lips. He was holding a pad in one hand and in the other a bowl of pineapple chunks already drowning in melting ice cream. 'So,' he said, 'when are you all going to leave?'

'You get to stay here,' said Douglas, 'because I'm indulgent.

Last I looked, the island still belonged to me. Same for this house.' He gestured. 'And that lagoon, and the yacht and the chopper and all the rest.'

Chrystal had lifted up her glasses at Maxwell's arrival. 'Ooh, is that ice cream?'

'Don't even think it,' Douglas said. 'You'll get fat. Like Max here. Fat and useless.'

Pouting, Chrystal slid the sunglasses back down.

Maxwell tossed the pad onto the coffee table and sat. He began slurping from the bowl. 'Jorgen's spraying the toilet brown again,' he said, then snorted.

'Oh, Max, that's gross.'

Jorgen Pilby, Douglas's fixer, never fared well in the tropics. 'Oh for fuck sake,' Douglas snarled. 'It's been two days now. I need him up and at it.'

'Right,' Max said, setting the empty bowl down and reaching for the pad, 'I'll go and tell him, then. Hey, Jorgen, get better and do it now. Your master insists. That should do it.'

But Max didn't get up and head inside. Instead, he began surfing the net.

'Stay away from that bullshit,' Douglas told him. He poured himself some more iced tea.

'Why?' Max looked up, smiling. 'Because you don't control all of it yet? You don't own every single media outlet? Or the servers? Or even the search engines? But hey, don't worry, they're all just like you. In your camp, your bed or whatever. Managing the news. What happened, what didn't happen. What they're all talking about, what no one is talking about – well, that's not true. They *are* talking about shit, but those conversations, they don't get past the filters. So, Pops, all in all, what's your problem?'

'Fuck me,' said Douglas, 'a speech.'

'Oh dear,' murmured Maxwell as he peered at the pad's screen, 'market's a mess. Shares plunging. Currencies shaky, futures non-existent. Well, guess there's no hiding all of that, is there?'

'You idiot, why would I?'

'Fear is good, is it? Even with your personal worth doing a

crash and burn. You'll take the hit to make sure people are terrified.'

Chrystal lifted her sunglasses up and turned her head to squint at Douglas. 'Is that true, Dougie?'

The few surviving critics he had left who could still successfully attack or mock him often described his death's head smile, a stretching of thin lips peeling back parched, lifeless skin to show a man-eater's teeth. The description had stung at first, but Douglas had since learned how useful that smile could be, so he gave it to his wife now, and was pleased as she suddenly withdrew, quickly pushing her sunglasses back down and turning her face sunward again.

'So,' Maxwell said a few minutes later, 'you buying what all the science fiction writers are saying? We're not alone, and whatever's up there isn't interested in talking, but so far, it's been a velvet glove? Hey, Pops? You liking this velvet glove?'

'You fool,' said Douglas. 'If I go down, you go down with me.'

Maxwell laughed, leaning back to stretch out his legs. The underside of one his flip-flops had the crushed remnants of a cockroach still clinging to it. Fucking bugs, impossible to get rid of them – how many times did he have to fumigate the whole damned island? Then in came the next food shipment and it was roaches all over again.

'You think that's funny?'

'Oh not again, you two,' sighed Chrystal.

He turned on her. 'Just go back to London, will you? Since I know how much you hate that place.' To his son, he said, 'All this amuses you?'

'You're not getting it, are you?'

Douglas's tone levelled. 'Not getting what?'

Chrystal knew that tone. She was up in an instant, gathering her towel, bikini and blouse, then padding quickly inside, closing the sliding door behind her.

Max knew the tone, too, but he'd never run from it. This was why Douglas hated his youngest son.

'Just what's staring you in the face, Pops,' Max now said. 'You, and the other jerks controlling the media, you all still think you can manage what's happening. Still think you can keep running things – running what people know and what they don't know. Deciding public opinion, getting the great unwashed believing what you want them to believe.' He laughed again and wagged the pad back and forth. 'No violence. Anywhere. Guess what, the people don't need you to tell them about it, or not tell them about it. They're living it.'

'Irrelevant,' said Douglas. 'All you're showing me, son, is that you haven't thought it all the way through – not like I have. Bernard, too. We're leaps ahead of you. As usual.'

'Oh? Well then, Pops, do enlighten me.'

'Do you think this no-violence shit is making people happy?'

'Safe is what it's making them. Everyone. Safe.'

'Safe from who? Safe from what?'

'Each other, of course.'

Douglas jerked a thumb skyward. 'But not them. Not safe from them, are we? Guns can't hit anyone. Tactical nukes? Useless. Don't work.'

'Don't work? Someone tried?'

'Of course someone tried! Listen, even ICBMs won't fire. You see my point? Against the bug-eyed aliens, we're helpless. We can't fight back. So, what's next? Turning us all into slaves?'

Max sneered. 'Well, you'd know all about that. And that's where you're wrong. If they wanted to do that, it would have started already. Right on the heels of the no-violence thing.'

'Why?' Douglas demanded.

Max tapped the pad's screen. 'You should be reading these sci fi writers. They've sussed it, at least that far. This isn't a conquest, Pops.'

'You haven't answered my question. Why?'

'Why would they have started enslaving us right after the no-violence thing came down? Because we'd have been in too much shock to resist. That would have made us compliant. More to the point, these writers say, there'd be no time to get organised, to form any kind of serious resistance.'

Douglas waved dismissively. 'They're wrong. Resistance is exactly what's going to happen. So just sit back, Max, and watch your pop and his allies do their shit. We'll have a global rebellion in no time. No enslavement for us. We'd rather die instead.'

'That's the line you're going to sell?' Max stared at his father in obvious disbelief.

'Resist. Refuse. Never bow, never kneel.'

'Catchy.'

'Always keep it simple. Complex ideas make people nervous. Complex ideas ask people to think, and people don't want to think. That's why we do their thinking for them.'

'All very fine, Pops. For as long as your game was the only game in town. Or, should I say, "planet"? Those aliens? You can't pretend to know what they think, and you sure as hell can't tell *them* what to think, can you?'

'Can't I? When all of humanity is on the streets and waving fists at the sky? More trouble than we're worth, they'll decide.'

'Or the opposite. "Oh fuck em, use the death-ray."'

Douglas shrugged. 'Like you said, they could've done that right at the start. They didn't.'

'You're gambling all of humanity on the aliens blinking first?'

Douglas leaned forward and showed Max his smile. 'I'm telling the fuckers it's freedom or nothing. Simple enough, wouldn't you say, that even bug-eyed aliens can get it?'

Max studied his father in silence.

Satisfied, Douglas finally sat back. 'Think I'll go for a swim.'

'Go for it, Pops,' Max replied. 'Oh, one last thing.'

Douglas stood, turned to the sliding doors. 'What?'

'If you're the best of humanity,' Max said, now offering up his own smile, 'I hope they use the death-ray.'

Inside, Douglas found Chrystal standing in front of the closed bathroom door. She turned, nose wrinkling. 'He's using this one, Dougie! I wanted to take a shower.'

'So use the other bathroom.'

'I don't want to use the other bathroom. The staff use the other one. I want this one!'

'Then wait,' Douglas replied. 'If you can stand the smell.'

'Oh, I can't believe this. I'm going for a nap.'

He watched her head off towards the bedroom. Naps these

days were euphemistic for two or three spliffs, and then she'd be out, unless he got there in time, in which case they'd make the bed bounce for a bit first. He reminded himself to pop a blue pill, once Jorgen got out of the—

The bathroom door opened and out staggered the pasty-faced man. The stench wafting after him made Douglas take a step back.

Jorgen looked up with puppy eyes circled in dark rings. 'I need to lie down. I don't know if I can make it.'

'You don't know if you can make it? What, you think you're about to die?'

'The sofa.'

'You know, there was a reporter once, some *Guardian* piss-head, who said you had shit for brains, Jorgen. That better not be the case.'

Jorgen didn't have the guts to glare.

Douglas watched him head off for the living room. If he took a deep breath and held it, he could probably be in and out with the blue pill.

•

Outside on the veranda, the cell buzzed and shimmied its way across the coffee table. Irritated, Maxwell set down his pad and collected up the phone. 'Bernie, what the fuck's up with you?'

There was a long pause on the other side of the connection that had nothing to do with distance. 'Max. It's before noon over there, isn't it? What are you doing up?'

'Just had breakfast. So, eat any start-ups lately?'

'There are no start-ups,' Bernard replied with a protracted sigh. 'Deer in the headlights, everywhere. You bastard, Max. Getting laid? I'm not. Oh, unless I pay for it. Where's Pops?'

'Went for a swim.'

'Said he'd be waiting for my call, fuck sake.'

'Yeah well, you haven't noticed? His short-term memory's not so good anymore.'

'I've noticed. Makes him meaner.'

'And that's the road you're on, brother. You got his sociopath gene, remember? You're stuck with it. Me, I'll just keep getting laid. By real women.'

'I'll probably cut you out when he's gone.'

It was an old threat, as was his reply, 'I'm sure you will. So, what was so important? I can pass the message on.'

'Op-eds across the board. Except for the *Sun*, which is leading with some more leaked BBC shit on paedophiles and let's face it, the BBC deserves it.'

'Well, you would say that. Op-eds on what?'

'No way you've been keeping your head in the sand, Max. Planet Earth has been conquered. We won't stand for it.'

Maxwell laughed. 'No,' he managed, 'you're right. Don't stand for it. Given how long it's taking, you're better off sitting.'

'Ha ha.'

'You and Pops think you can stir up six billion people, do you? Fucking megalomaniacs, both of you. But you're deluded, did you know that? It won't work.'

'Like hell it won't.'

Max looked out into the bay. He saw their old man who'd gone through the house and down onto the beach, now wading into the pellucid turquoise waters. 'Okay, say you get 'em all standing in the streets, shaking fists heavenward.'

'That's it precisely.'

'Fine. Then what?'

'What do you mean?'

'I mean, brother, *then what*? Those fists? They can't punch anything. Those angry shouts? Equally useless. I'll tell you what happens then and you can chew on this. They all go home. Six billion people, standing around, hoarse and with aching arms, they go quiet, look around, at each other. Then they shrug and, well, they fuckin' go home.'

'Once those aliens finally land—'

'They probably won't.'

'What?'

Max picked up his pad again, studied the essay a sci fi writer had written for io9. 'Why bother? They've already shown that they can do what they want to us remotely. From somewhere in space – and US Space Command can't even find their ship. So, why bother coming down?'

'But that's ... fuck, that makes no sense.'

'We're stuck with *us*,' Max said. 'Get it, yet? Might as well get mad at God and see where that takes you. People get mad at God all the time, but God never shows up, hat in hand and looking shamefaced, does He? So, you and Pop, you need to get this. Your supposed bug-eyed ET isn't playing along. Oh yeah, people will start looking for someone to blame, but even that's getting them nowhere. But' – and he picked up the pad to quote the writer, '"the only face humanity is staring at is its own".'

'Where the fuck are you getting this?'

'I'm getting it from people who made a career imagining "what if's" and you know what the real kicker is? So far, not one government agency has thought to ask them. They bring in scientists, sociologists, economists, the military. Experts, they call them. But they're not experts.' He linked the article and sent his brother a quick email. 'Check your inbox, brother.'

'Tell Pops I'll get back to him.'

'Sure,' Maxwell replied. 'And I'll let him know about all those useless op-eds that will by tomorrow make you look like idiots. Mind you, riots may not end up injuring anyone, but it seems property can still get damaged. Wonder if the world will send Pops the bill?'

'Where's Jorgen?'

'Shit for brains, meet Montezuma.'

'What, again? Well fine, if a head needs to roll. It was his idea.'

They both knew it wasn't. It was Pop's idea. 'There you go, brother, the sociopath gene kicking into gear.'

Bernard sighed. 'What's the point of a high-paid fixer who can't fix anything?'

'The poor guy's got the trots pretty bad,' Max said. 'Happens every time, yet Pops insists on bringing him down. He likes to see people suffer.' He watched his old man swimming in the shallow waters of the lagoon. 'But hey,' he added, 'the cook tells me there's been a tiger shark on the prowl, a big one, probably came out of the Blue Hole. Anyway, it's been circling the island.'

'Does Pops know? He doesn't, does he? You know how scared he is of sharks. Max, you're such a bastard.'

'Yeah, I forgot to mention it.'

'And you call us sociopaths.'

'Oh I'll feel plenty if Pops gets chomped, bitten in half, chewed up. If he ends up in the middle of a feeding frenzy, why, I'll feel something all right. I'll look up at the sky, up at God, and smile at such a fitting end to Douglas Murdo. Poetic justice and all that. You see, that's the difference between us, brother. I feel. You and Pops don't. Man, you've no idea what you're missing.'

'Whatever. Pass on the news. Tell him I'll call again tonight.'

'If I'm around.'

'What? Where are you going? You never go anywhere.'

'Thought I'd take out the cook's skiff, maybe chum the local waters for a bit.'

'Ha ha. All right, Max. Love you.'

'Love you too, bye.'

'Bye.'

•

The sun was down on lower Manhattan, drowning the city below in gloom, and the lights coming on had a murky cast to them, as if seen through nicotine-smeared glass. Lois Stanton stood with her back to the empty boardroom, luxuriating in the moment's respite, this brief instant of being alone. Vague memories of an old story she'd heard as a child, about the twins who founded Rome, had since morphed into a new story, at least in her mind. Romulus and Remus, the orphaned children raised by wolves, were now the wolves, surrounded by children. The children were nervous but were hoping for the best. The wolves, after all, weren't *always* hungry. So, she had her private nicknames for her two employers, the brothers who were the icons of the new neoliberal world order, the one where corporations ran the planet, feeding heaps of bullshit to the poorly educated, anti-intellectual, great unwashed. The fox crowd, being spoon-fed what they all wanted to hear and never mind the facts.

She'd come far from her Indiana small town. The road to hell, it turned out, went east.

The doors behind her opened and she quickly turned to greet James and Jonathan, the sibling masters of appalling wealth and, one presumed, equally appalling power.

They were getting on, into their sixties now, showing hints of dissolution despite the ten-grand suits. That jadedness came from their eyes, leaching out to make sallow the flagging skin of their cheeks. The skulls beneath the meat were becoming visible. Despite the wealth she'd earned as their private secretary and as head of Adonis Enterprises PR Division, she longed to see them both laid out in caskets, eyelids blissfully glued shut.

James waved her over to the table as both men sat.

Lois joined them, seating herself opposite the brothers. Being old-fashioned, she pulled out a notepad and ballpoint pen, and then waited patiently.

They'd eaten. She had not, having been ordered here to await their pleasure. She could smell the food on them, the sour hint of wine. One glass each, never more. These men didn't do boozing. She tried to imagine them as teenagers at some high school, but no, that didn't work. It would have been a private school, boys in uniforms, unlined faces emanating auras of privilege.

As always, James was the first to speak. 'Forty-seven per cent and climbing,' he said. He wasn't addressing her directly, not yet. He was just laying out the groundwork, describing the playing field. 'All defence contracts on hold. MIC's in free-fall.'

MIC was James's only mildly ironic acronym for the Military Industrial Complex, or maybe it was Consortium, or even Conspiracy, for all she knew. He never used anything else and had never bothered spelling it out for her. She'd figured it out from context.

Jonathan now chimed in. 'The boys at the Think Tank, Lois, they're in free-fall, too.' And he smiled at her.

Boys indeed. Not a woman in the lot, unless she was serving drinks. The Freedom Institute was old school in the way that only old money could pull off. Its membership required nine figures plus in actual worth. Its primary task was to keep the machine running. Into it at one end went everything not nailed down and out the other end came ever more wealth. She imagined mechanical fangs going up and down, up and down, without pause, indifferent and remorseless the way machines were. Last century's historians wrote about industrialisation in the same terms, and the fact that the word 'industry' once had a human component to it was now long forgotten.

Idly, she wondered if historians still existed.

'We're losing net worth,' James resumed.

Yes, well, she wanted to tell him, that's what happens when you invest in war and suddenly peace breaks out everywhere. And, it seemed, little chance of things ever going back to the good old days of strife, mayhem and suffering.

'We're fighting back,' said Jonathan. 'And we'll win this, Lois.'

'Public statement or backroom assurances?' Lois asked, ignoring James's sudden frown.

'Backroom to start,' Jonathan said. 'Most calls we've already made. Take it to the lobby teams.'

'Then we go public,' said James. 'Some bright sides. Real estate's going up. Populations heading into cities, adds pressure on housing, prices go up and we're already positioned for that windfall.'

She nodded. Get rich enough and diversifying your interests and investments only made good sense. You can survive getting a rug pulled out from underfoot when you're standing on fifty rugs.

'Distribution, transportation,' James went on. 'Hungry people and feeding them. Logistics. Surpluses too valuable to dump.'

'Finally,' Jonathan said, 'and isn't that a good thing, Lois?'

'Worth emphasising,' she agreed, making a note.

'Tech's shaky,' said James. 'Not sure what's coming, what's going to get dumped in their laps. R&D, all that money invested.'

She eyed him. 'You think more is coming?'

'Think Tank does,' James said, nodding. 'We need to position ourselves for the landing, the negotiations. We have the infrastructure to manage what they'll give us.'

Which ET seemed to be not only ignoring, but also not needing.

'Atmospheric analysis.'

Lois sat up, studying James. 'I'm sorry, what?'

Jonathan explained. 'Some egghead took some readings. Electromagnetic skeins.'

'Skeins?'

'We're caught in a web,' James said. 'Seems we've found out how it's all being done.' He glanced at his brother, who had more technical savvy.

Jonathan nodded. 'Still can't be blocked or cut off. This web, it's probably a natural phenomenon; it's what the planet does, being a planet. But ET can manipulate it, make it bulge or tighten up, or stretch out. Its power source is the planet's magnetosphere. Clever, damned clever.'

'And then there's the quantum angle,' added James, as if quoting scripture, or speaking in tongues.

'It's a *fine* net,' Jonathan said. 'Subatomic level.'

'I've not seen this discovery reported anywhere,' said Lois, somewhat bewildered to be hearing this from these two men.

'No,' said James. 'And you won't. Not for a while yet, maybe not at all. This is intel. Detection precedes intervention, we feel our way through, observe and analyse. Our best people are on it, and once we crack it, we own it.'

'For now,' Jonathan said, 'we ride this out.'

'Confidence,' James said to Lois. 'That's your bottom line.'

They were done with her. She stood up, looked down at her notepad, and read what she'd written: *Orchestra leader smiles, band plays, Titanic sinks.* 'Got it,' she told them, and then made her way out of the room.

•

A scale model of the Infinity-3 on a brushed aluminum stand dominated the sideboard above the sleek black filing cabinet. A smaller model of the first electric car, bearing the company's flag name, Kepler, served as a rubber-wheeled paperweight on the desk.

It was late afternoon. Simon Gist, founder of Kepler Industries, sat with one hand resting on the beautifully recreated model car, slowly rolling it back and forth.

Seated opposite him were two of his favourite people. Mary Lamp, the VP of Operations here at the Roswell Kepler Centre, was diminutive, spidery, her black hair a bit of a mess, her face extraordinarily pale given this New Mexico setting, her blue eyes fixed upon him with unwavering intensity. It was a stare that many found unnerving, but not Simon. He liked that promise of no bullshit.

Beside her was a man who looked startlingly similar to the actor Fred Ward, who'd played Gus Grissom in *The Right Stuff*, and then went on to show his comedic chops in *Tremors*. Simon's chief engineer, Jack Butler, had large battered hands, a mechanic's hands, grease included. He was restoring a '71 Datsun 510 in his spare time, something of a bird-flip to Kepler's electric-car-in-every-driveway's aspirations, a detail that amused Simon no end.

His gaze settled again on his hand atop the model car. Chocolate brown, a descriptive unwisely employed by a magazine journalist a few years back. But not Cadbury's chocolate. More like Lindt's. Dark, 97% pure. The man from Nigeria, who'd fled in fear of his life, had made good in America. The American Dream made real and all that. This detail now operated as the opening banner, waved almost stridently in every exposé and interview he'd done the past few years, standing as the solitary proof that the Dream was still real, that it actually still meant something.

Strident. Yes indeed. Perhaps even desperate.

'So,' he finally said, 'what are we looking at?'

Jack cleared his throat. The air in this state was dry, and the man cleared his throat a lot. 'All the virus scans bounced, Simon. Alice tells me it's impregnable. Normally, it would have been dumped as a matter of course, but it showed up on every IT address, including the internal ones.'

Simon frowned. 'So it was made in-house? If this is a practical joke, I'm not amused.'

The file in question had a curious name: *Scalable Power Unit*

Design and Specifications, with Appendices for Conversion, No Patent Permitted. It now sat like a time-bomb on every computer in three departments, still ticking.

'Alice says no,' Mary said. 'It's on our servers and it arrived there at seven this morning, but left no back-trail.'

'How is that possible?' Simon asked. 'Never mind. It isn't.'

'Spontaneous generation,' muttered Jack.

Beyond the office, the plant was quiet. Simon had sent most people home and that had been a solemn procession back out to the parking lot. He'd kept a dozen engineers and all the IT people at their desks.

The risk to ambition was the fatal misstep. Almost impossible to predict. Infinity-2 had crashed in the desert, taking the test pilot with it. All down to a cable snagging on a mangled rivet. But that sort of tragedy was a burden that came with the territory. Earth was possessive of its children. Leaving its embrace was never easy. But ambition in the broader sense, ambition as a life's commitment, well ... the future was uncertain, but in a way it had never been as uncertain as it was now. His backers were locked up, unwilling to commit. Alien technology could kill Kepler Industrial.

Of course, it would kill everyone else too, in business and technological terms. Resilient as the global economy was, Simon was not sure if it would survive such a fundamental resetting of principles, not to mention its most basic assumptions of value, exchange and worth. Simon had spent more than a few nights lying awake, thinking things through. Enough science fiction authors had explored the disruptive aspects to benign First Contact, usually in terms of the threat to the status quo – which, for all its faults, was still home-grown, still human. But invariably in these tales, things had turned out if not rosy, then manageable.

But here and now, in this reality, Simon was not too sure about that. Still, civilisation had managed to survive new technologies, revolutionary technologies, absorbing the changes into the great machine of progress. The landscape might indeed change, but the people in it adapted.

Or died.

Abruptly he shook his head and leaned forward. 'Jack. Pull up your laptop. Take it offline.'

Jack grinned. 'There's forty-three people downstairs waiting for this, you know.'

'Because they think it's a gift.'

'Yes.'

Simon looked to Mary. 'Do you think it is, Mary?'

'I don't know. Why us?'

'That's just it,' Simon said, 'we don't know that, do we? We don't know if every high-tech engineering firm isn't holed up right now, staring at the same unknown executable file.'

Jack paused, clearly startled by the notion. 'Shit,' he said. 'And here I thought ... well ...'

'That we're something special?' Simon smiled. 'I appreciate the sentiment, Jack.' He held up both hands as he leaned back. 'I certainly thought we were!'

The two men laughed. Mary's frown deepened.

'I'm ready,' said Jack.

'Open the file.'

A click on the laptop resting on Jack's thighs.

Simon watched his engineer squinting at the screen, watched as the man slowly sat forward, now hunching over the laptop, watched the man's eyes tracking, darting. 'Aw, cripes,' he breathed, 'they dumbed it down so far even a cretin like me can follow.'

'And?' Simon asked.

'And ... shit, Simon. It is what it says it is. A scalable power source.'

'Fuel?'

'No fuel.'

'I'm sorry, what do you mean, no fuel?'

'It's powered by the planet's natural electromagnetism, which it uses, but doesn't use up. You borrow the power and then hand it back, instantly renewable, no emissions, no waste. It focuses, shunts through and then releases. Its primary transmission matrix is graphene. Simon, there's even an adapter assembly unit, to swap out our batteries for the Kepler, and that's specific engineering, using proprietary specs no one else knows about.' He finally looked up. 'Say good-bye to the oil industry.'

Simon Gist abruptly stood, unable to remain motionless. He turned to the window and stared out at the scrubland in all its magnificent muted tones of ochre, tan and dusty green. He felt like running across that desert. 'Conversion timeline?' he asked, without facing Jack.

'A month, two, tops. We can do our own machining for most – no, probably all of it. That's assuming our backers don't pull out.'

'They won't,' said Simon. 'Not now.'

'Simon, if our rivals all have something like this ...'

'Then we're in a race and we'd better get moving.'

Mary Lamp said, 'This needs thinking through. Simon, why do I feel like the ground's about to open up in front of us?'

He faced her with a tentative smile. 'Because it is, Mary. Not just for us. For civilisation. For humanity. Dominoes are going to tumble. We need to position ourselves to avoid most of that fall-out. Our backers need to understand where it's safe to put their money, and we're it.'

She stood. 'I'll start making the calls.'

'Jack, how soon for a prototype?'

'Give me a week.'

'That fast?'

'The file's full of work-arounds, using what we already have. It's damn near assembly instructions for a model kit. The theory is touched on, but details are in appendices. It's laid out as "build it first, worry about how it works later". I love it.'

'Assemble a team. When do you want to start? Is tomorrow morning too soon?'

'Excuse me, boss,' said Jack, 'but we're starting tonight.'

Simon felt his eyes well up. He stared at them both. 'This morning I woke up thinking we were dead in the water. That all my ambitions, my dreams, were turning into ashes in front of my eyes.' He laughed and waved a hand, suddenly embarrassed. 'Go on, you two. I've always been too sentimental.'

'Maybe,' said Mary. 'And maybe that's why we're all here, working for you, believing in you.'

Mercifully, both then hastened out of the room, to give Simon time for a good old-fashioned cry.

Chapter Nine

'Exaltation is ephemeral. Any philosophy suggesting
that such an experiential state is both natural and
sustainable has a serious disconnect with reality and
human nature. Every high comes with a crash.'

Samantha August

'So it was kinda hard to miss,' said Joey Sink, unable to keep the
mocking smile from his lips as he stared at the webcam's steady
green LED, 'mainstream media going wild, stirring up a frenzy
of fear and paranoia. God help us all, the aliens are poised to
land, in giant fleets, mech-warriors trooping out, blasters cocked.
Hey, bro, it's a call to arms all right. Resist! Refuse! We won't
be slaves to nobody!' He paused, and then sat back, only to sit
forward again. 'Oops, still here. Got to stop doing that, don't I?
Oh I know, you all make fun of it, ole Joey showing only his
forehead. It's just I get animated, right?'

He tapped his headphones. 'Got Annie Mouse from JPL or
maybe it's NASA on the line, the one who's been keeping us
informed of the fact that the country's best scientists are still uninformed. It's confirmed: they can't find any UFOs in orbit. But
they have to be there. Unless they've already landed and who
knows, maybe your neighbour only *looks* like your neighbour.'

Annie Mouse cut in with a muted strangled sound, and then
a very male voice said, 'Hold on, Joey, that kind of paranoia we
don't need, especially from you.'

'Hey, just following the headlines, boyo.'

'Well, don't. That joke of yours about us being uninformed. Funny, but not quite right.'

'Really?' Joey asked. 'Do tell.'

'The forcefields and shutting down all violence, it's all being powered by the Earth's own magnetosphere.'

'You mean the thing that keeps away all the nasty UV from the sun?'

'More or less. How technical do you want me to be here?'

'It's that protective thing, that field — I've seen graphics, how it absorbs the radiation and energy from solar storms. Comes from the planet's core being, uh, molten metal. Mars doesn't have one, because its core has gone cold, maybe even solid. Will that do?'

'It's your show, Joey. But you've described it well enough, I suppose. In any case, the aliens are able to somehow manipulate the field on both the micro and macro scale, but the real kicker is the fact that they're doing it everywhere, specific to instances, meaning they are intervening in real time, and that real time is virtually instant.'

Nodding, Joey said, 'I've heard about this. Shooting someone point-blank — accidentally so far, not deliberately. At least, as far as I know. But the bullet never touches the target — no matter how close it is.'

'We don't think it operates that way,' Annie Mouse replied. 'There are too many examples of hidden intentions, not involving guns, but kitchen knives, fists, even — for example: an embrace that begins friendly and then turns nasty. The attacker is simply thrown away from the intended victim. You have to understand, electromagnetism permeates everything. Our brains work on electric impulses, right? Now, imagine a sensor system linked to a supercomputer that can read those electric signals as they fire, like a super-fast ticker tape. Read, interpret, react, all fast enough to prevent.'

'Wow,' said Joey. 'That's ... God-like.'

'It can only work with a quantum component, Joey. That's what's got us all so excited. We're seeing a quantum interface based on contingency, operating out of normal time constraints, meaning entangled. So, our guess is, there really *is* an alien supercomputer out there. And we can't find it because it's sitting in a parallel universe, maybe even in a nil state.'

'A what state? You're losing me here.'

'Schrödinger's cat, Joey. The supercomputer is inside the box. Hiding in that liminal state of either/or, here/not-here, yes/no.'

'So open the box!'

'We can't. That's the whole point. The nil state can only exist so long as we're not knowing.'

'Oh man. But wait, if that's the case, then how can the aliens stick a supercomputer inside a nil state? Don't they have to be "not knowing," too?'

'Probably.'

'So? I don't get it!'

'The only answer we can come up with is, they built the supercomputer and made it a true AI, a true artificial intelligence. Then they told the AI to think itself into the box.'

'And what? Plop! Gone?'

'Plop. I like that. Plop theory. Yeah, we can use that. Thanks, Joey.'

'Hold on! If a supercomputer AI can think itself into that nil state, then we could, too, right? I mean, theoretically.'

Annie Mouse laughed, and laughed some more. 'Nice one, Joey. "Theoretically." Awesome.'

'What are you going on about? I asked a legitimate question.'

'Oh, thought you were making a pun. Right. Well, yes, we could, only we don't know how. In fact, it may not be in the realm of Western, rational thinking, Cartesian thinking, I mean. Maybe esoteric philosophy, or religion. Meditation. Nirvana, you know?'

'The ETs are Buddhists?'

'What? No. I mean, who knows? Why, are the Buddhists building a supercomputer? Wasn't there an Arthur C. Clarke story – or was it Asimov? You know, all the names of God, calculated.'

'We're in lala-land now, bro. Let's get back to where we started. So you guys think you've worked out how these forcefields are powered. Same for the non-violence shtick. But you can't figure out a way of shutting it all down, or pulling the plug or something.'

'No, of course not. It's so far out of our league we might as well be amoebas.'

'So we're stuck.'

'Oh, I wouldn't put it that way. You can walk home now without fear of getting mugged. Is that so bad? Besides, big changes are coming. I haven't even told you the latest – though it should be out on the feeds by now, coming in from the east.'

'From the east? What are you talking about?'

'You're on Mountain time, right? Sun's almost down? Head outside, Joey, and look for Venus. It should be in the southern sky.'

'Okay, I'll do that. What should I be looking for with Venus?'

'You got that slightly wrong, Joey. You won't be able to see anything on Venus. You won't be able to see Venus at all.'

'What?'

'The planet's disappeared.'

'No way. They stole the planet from us?'

'Nah. It's still there. That's been confirmed. Only it's now in shade. We think a sun-blind's been built, maybe out near the Lagrange point.'

'Okayyy,' said Joey. 'So, what are they doing?'

'Cooling it, Joey. And that's not all. There's anomalous bodies coming in from out-system, lots of them. We're thinking asteroids, frozen water, lots of frozen water.'

'Terraforming! But hold it, bro, why not Mars? I always thought Mars was the best choice.'

'Not really. Venus is a closer sister, Joey, in terms of mass and even orbit. Thing is, the energy expenditure to terraform Venus is huge. Only, if that's not a limiting factor, well, Venus over Mars every time.'

'What do you think about this, then?' Joey asked. There was sweat dribbling down his brow. His chest ached. It was all too much. 'Are they moving into the neighbourhood or something?'

'I hope not! I mean, it'd be nice to believe that they'll respect our sovereign claim to our native solar system. But then, who knows? It's not like we planted a flag there ... or maybe we did. Those Russian landers ... well, the thing is, we can only speculate.'

'And isn't that the part that sucks?' Joey said, recovering. 'It's all out of our hands – all of it!'

'Yeah. But strangely enough, I'm not scared. Are you?'

Joey hesitated, and then said, 'I don't know. Haven't decided yet. There's plenty of fear going on right now.'

'Achieving what, exactly?'

'I heard tranquilliser sales are through the roof.'

'Whatever, Joey. Me, I'm going to sit back and enjoy the ride.'

'Not joining the freedom marches, then? Well, me neither. Talk to ya later, Annie Mouse.' He cut the connection and grinned again at the camera. 'That's what I was opening this session with. Was going to talk about the freedom marches. A waste of time. Pointless. Silly, in fact. So we lost our freedom to kill and destroy – that's kinda existed all along. We call them laws. You can't kill your neighbour or anyone else, or you'll go to jail. As for nations going to war, which is like sanctifying killing on a bigger scale, well, I'm not missing an end to that shit. I mean, I served three tours in Afghanistan, right? Been there, don't wanna do that ever again. Good riddance is what I say on that stuff.

'And the destroying bit, all those rainforests going up in smoke and all that. The orangutans with nowhere to live. Even those gold prospectors up in the Yukon – you're poisoning the rivers, man! What were you thinking? Well, time to find another line of work, bros. Gates closed and padlocked, all shut down.

'So sure, march about that. That lost freedom to dredge beautiful rivers and cut down trees. But I don't think those marches will do anything. Face it, it's been a while since marches did anything, even before the aliens arrived. And here's the real kicker. For years now mainstream media's been deliberately under-reporting on protest marches, at least in the West and especially since you-know-who became President. In fact, nine times out of ten they just ignore them, as if they never happened at all. So now they're getting all frothy and calling on people to get out into the streets with banners and stuff? That, my friends, is a joke.

'A joke. And you can take that to the sink and dump it.'

A muted click in his ear told him one of his regulars was coming through. He read the tag and smiled. 'And now here's King Con.

Hey, bud, how's it going? And remember, no profanity.'

'Forget Venus, man! Deimos just lit up like a spaceship – attitude thrusters firing all over its surface – and it's moved down behind Phobos and is slowly catching up to it!'

'What? Deimos? Phobos?'

'The two moons of Mars! They're gonna go crunch, buddy! Only slowly, like. No mess, no explosion, just grinding together. Mars is about to get one bigger moon!'

'But, what for?'

'Planets need moons, bud! Tidal forces! Get the tectonics moving, right? Only, that core's going to need heating up, but I figure they've got that sussed, too. Don't you get it, Joey? They're giving us two new planets to live on!'

'Maybe. Maybe,' said Joey. 'Oh man, this is too much. My head's spinning. Wait! Venus doesn't even have a moon!'

'Not yet it don't, hah! But guaranteed, it will!'

'Look, I'm no astronomer, but you can't just wing big rocks around the solar system like so many billiard balls, can you? I mean, isn't it all finely balanced? Everything sits where it is because of everything else, isn't that right?'

'Yeah, that's kind of true, Joey. Will Venus getting a big ole moon affect Earth's rotation dynamics? I hope not! But they must've worked that all out. All within acceptable parameters or something.'

'I hope you're right, King Con.'

'Anyway, there's over a hundred big asteroids and comets and shit on the move out there, Joey, all heading inward. Towards Venus and Mars. And closer to home, our own moon's acquired a ring – it's faint, you can barely make it out with binoculars, but it's there. Dust, they figure. Something's being built on the Moon? Maybe. It's UFO mayhem out there.'

'Whoah! UFOs? What's that about UFOs?'

'Speeding out from the Moon, right? There's pics all over the net, Joey. Not from NASA, of course. It's squawk from NASA, as usual.'

'Are these the aliens then?'

'Well, who knows? I mean, most of 'em look like they're

bugging out, to be honest. Besides, we're talking unidentified flying objects. Could be asteroids or meteors or flocks of geese.'

'Flocks of geese on the Moon?'

'No! In our skies! You know, those shots of the Moon with something flying across the face of it, right? A UFO could be anything, is what I'm saying.'

'So you've got asteroids and meteors flying *out* from the Moon.'

'Yeah. Weird, huh? Spooky weird.'

'Oh man, I've got a headache.'

'Gotta go, Joey. Gotta go on a march.'

'You? No way!'

King Con laughed. 'Made up a big banner, me and a buddy of mine. Know what it says? It says RELAX! Hah hah!'

•

The air was bad this morning in Beijing. What was the statistic? At these levels, every man, woman and child out in the city was breathing the equivalent of smoking two packs of cigarettes a day? That seemed to be a lot of cigarettes for Liu Zhou's four-year-old daughter to be smoking. Of course, most of the high commissioners and officials in the government lived in airy enclaves well outside the city's sprawling limits. Liu Zhou had ambitions of joining them soon, of getting his family out of the city. He wondered if, alas, such dreams were dead.

The gym buried deep in the government complex had been emptied of other officials. Even the staff had been led away. China's Party Leader was not one to alter his exercise session no matter how terrible the crisis, and given the present circumstances, it was probably a wise response, as the disasters were mounting daily.

There was talk of the United States reneging on its debts. The rumour alone had the yuan tumbling in value. But such matters were not in Liu Zhou's remit, thankfully. He was not one for diplomatic niceties, and as the Leader's personal Science Advisor, decorum was less important than the succinct presentation of facts, no matter how unpalatable they might prove to be.

The security teams were the first to arrive, ignoring him as they swept the room and then took station at the two sets of doors. A few moments later the Leader arrived, dressed in Adidas sweat-pants, sneakers and a sleeveless Chicago Bulls T-shirt. Clearly, such indulgences would never be seen by the people. This gym was located at the heart of the Party Central Command Centre, shielded from all prying eyes.

Xin Pang seated himself on a stationary bicycle and began pedalling. He gestured Liu Zhou closer. 'Begin,' he said.

'Leader,' Liu Zhou said, bowing briefly, before continuing. 'The old lunar sites are being ignored for the most part, although not in every instance. It does suggest, however, that the previous tenants have indeed departed.'

'Fled?'

'Perhaps, Leader. The new presence appears to be mechanistic. The construction at Site 71 is already powered and, we believe, producing an oxygenated atmosphere.'

Xin Pang was pedalling harder now. 'For nothing but machines? That makes no sense.'

'No, Leader, it does not. The atmosphere generation is, we believe, for us.'

China National Space Administration's long-term plans for Luna involved an extensive national presence, with at least three major, interconnected settlement domes. The first assembly modules were already well past the blueprint stage. The challenge, as ever, was getting them off the surface of Earth. Now, it seemed, such plans were in complete disarray.

'You are certain,' the Leader said, now breathing hard, 'that the Americans are not behind this?'

'As certain as you are,' Liu Zhou replied.

At the faint challenge, Xin Pang smiled slightly. 'Point taken. True, Intelligence Services assures me. Indeed, the Americans continue to repress general knowledge of alien lunar mining, despite pictorial evidence to the contrary.' He shook his head. 'The extraordinary capacity of the American people to humbly acquiesce when invited to ignore irrefutable evidence continues to astonish me.'

Liu Zhou shrugged. 'When it is clear, even to a regime as corrupt and incompetent as the Americans', that the impudent exploitation by aliens of Helium 3 and other resources on our moon is something no one on Earth has the wherewithal to do anything about, its decision to stick its head in the sand is not perhaps so surprising.'

The planned Chinese occupation of Luna had not been a naïve stratagem, and indeed had included a strong military component. Given the American and Russian lack of will in this effrontery, the Chinese people would have taken the lead in ousting the intruders, site by site, room by room if necessary.

Room by room. The notion still chilled the Science Advisor. Orbital seismic mapping had indicated the Moon's subsurface to be rife with tunnels and occupation nodes.

But now, it seemed, the interlopers were gone, and this new presence, so vast and so powerful, had begun its own reshaping of the Moon, and against these new strangers, weapons were useless.

'Tell me,' Xin Pang said, slowing his pedalling and leaning back, now folding his hands on his belly. 'Have you faith in these newcomers?'

'Faith, Leader?'

'Faith. They present a certain calm, it seems to me, at the core.'

'Leader, have you read the reports on the activities in space? The blinding of Venus, the moons of Mars and the swarm of asteroids and comets now being individually powered and converging on the Inner System? This seems anything but calm.'

'We cannot agree, then,' Xin Pang replied. 'There is order at work. Deliberation. It has the feel of a Chinese plan. Extensive, methodical, inexorable. I feel a certain ... kinship, with this unknown newcomer.'

Liu Zhou hesitated, knowing his next statement was slightly out of his area of responsibility, but economics were always relevant when it came to scientific ambition. He cleared his throat and said, 'I understand that the export of armaments has ceased, Leader.'

Xin Pang shrugged, now picking up the pace again on the pedals. 'We will adjust.'

In other words, *you'll get your funding*. Liu Zhou was relieved. 'Leader, one other thing I must bring to you, and it is, perhaps, wondrous news.'

The Leader's smile was wry. 'That would be pleasant.'

'A file has appeared, at Shanghai's 2nd Bureau of Mechanic-Electrical Industry, and elsewhere. We conclude that it originated from the newcomer.'

'A file, and it contains what? One presumes all caution was employed in opening it.'

'Of course. Leader, the file contains the schematics for constructing an emission-free, eternally renewable power source. An engine that can be constructed at any scale one desires.'

Xin Pang stopped pedalling so fast he was almost thrown from the seat. He twisted to face Liu Zhou, blinking rapidly for a moment. 'I begin to comprehend the intricacies of their plan.'

'Leader?'

'Initiate the conversion process immediately. All factories, all power plants.' He held up a hand and an aide appeared as if from nowhere. 'I want the Deputy of Energy here at once. We must ready ourselves to shut down our coal production, and all nuclear energy production.' He paused, hand still raised. 'But continue the solar projects.' The aide rushed off. Xin Pang regarded Liu Zhou. 'We must be poised to act, old friend. No hesitation. We are being guided and we will not resist.'

'Understood, Leader.'

'I think not quite, but enough for now. Inform the Lunar Occupation Committee that the present suspension of activities does not include ground-based preparations for Project 937. If anything, they are to make haste. We will still reach the Moon first among all humans, if such is permitted us. We will occupy the bases and the plants and the settlement nodes. Leave the Americans and Russians to their wilful inactivity. Now,' he concluded, resuming his pedalling, 'you may go.'

•

'The Rus, yes,' said Konstantine Milnikov. 'I know that nonsense. Swedish Vikings as the original founders of the Russian state. In Kiev, was it? Thus justifying the conceit that Aryans were born to rule and Slavs were born to be ruled. They say Russian history is the history of oppression. That my people have been on their knees for so long they know no other way to live.' The President of the Russian Federation paused, eyeing the man standing opposite him.

They stood in the countryside, away from the groomed gardens, away from everything. The grey winter had given way to the brown spring, and soon the green of summer would arrive. But not yet. At least the sun was out, almost warm. Milnikov turned from his guest and fixed his gaze once more on the four horses gathered round the heaps of fresh hay at the far end of the paddock. A foal was not long in coming for the mare. He loved this place, the open land, the untouched forest of aspen, alder, birch and spruce forming a skeletal line beyond the grazing fields, and at their backs, beyond the ranch-house, the rolling steppes. The blackflies were out, but not yet the mosquitoes. 'Tell me again,' he said.

His guest, Anatoli Petrov, had been a cosmonaut. He had spent time on the ISS, cheek by jowl with Americans, Canadians and one miserable Frenchman. More importantly, to Konstantine's thinking, Anatoli had known the privilege of looking down upon the Earth. Konstantine envied that.

Anatoli had been a pilot, was a physicist, linguist and now head of the Russian Space Programme. The man looked fit, with something of the Cossack in the tilt of his eyes. His head was shaved and spotted after decades in the sun. His eyes were the palest grey, like old bones bleaching on the steppes. Women found him irresistible. Despite this, Konstantine liked the man.

'President,' Anatoli began, 'a number of proposals have been presented on the potential of terraforming Venus. Given the sunshade now being employed by the alien threat, we believe that we will be witness to a method described by an Englishman named Paul Birch, which involves a rapid cooling of the planet through sunshades, the impact of ice-rich asteroids, a polar soletta

113

to effect a twenty-four hour day/night cycle, and the sequestering of carbon dioxide.' The cosmonaut paused, and then smiled. 'Birch's proposal is a five-year plan.'

Konstantine swung round, brows lifting. 'Oh,' he laughed, 'how delightful! And at the end of the five years, a habitable planet?'

'Domed settlements that are initially suspended high in the atmosphere, riding an ocean of carbon dioxide, and thereafter slowly settling to the surface as the CO_2 is gradually captured.'

'Ingenious.'

'Yes, elegant,' Anatoli agreed. 'You could say, quintessentially English.'

Konstantine scowled. 'After my last conversation with their Prime Minister, "elegant" is not a word I would use. The pompous ass.' He shook his head. 'I will never understand English voters, again and again choosing a privileged ... oh, what would he be called?'

'Twat?'

'Yes! Precisely. Perhaps, however, the common Englishman is, shall we say, used to being ruled by privileged twats, hmm?'

Anatoli grunted. 'Return to *Downton Abbey*.'

'Yes! Ghastly. If Russia did a version of that show, it would end with all their heads on pitchforks.'

Smiling, Anatoli said nothing, waiting as the President did some thinking.

'And now, Mars, too,' Konstantine finally said, sighing. 'And the Moon. Surely they cannot be thinking of terraforming the Moon!'

'Not immediately,' Anatoli agreed. 'And we have confirmed that the Moon's present occupants have departed.'

'You are certain?'

'We have an old satellite, sir, still orbiting the Moon. It's small with a limited sensor package, not enough to incite yet another unfortunate accident. The exodus was caught in a series of still-shots.'

'Exodus – where to?'

'Uncertain, sir. It is theorised that the ships, being so modest, will rendezvous with a mother ship, likely at their Phobos Station.'

Konstatine's expression soured. 'Phobos,' he muttered. There had been two "unfortunate accidents" on the Russian missions to Phobos. 'Do we know if they were chased away from there as well?'

'Unknown, sir. Personally, I view it as likely.'

'You do? Why?'

'I believe the Greys fled our newcomers. I believe they want nothing to do with them. I believe they are hopelessly outclassed.'

'Sometimes,' Konstatine sighed, 'I do regret our financial collapse. Had the Soviet Union remained strong, by this time all of humanity would have laid claim to the inner solar system, out to Mars at the very least, with us even now venturing out to the Jovians. More to the point, we would have been in a better position to confront the Greys.'

'That is certainly possible, sir,' said Anatoli. 'Competition was healthy, despite the tensions, and the public revelation of the Greys would have changed the world. Perhaps even united us all.'

'Yes, just so. Oh well, what's done is done.' Konstatine hesitated, and then faced Anatoli squarely. 'Do you realise, for the first time in the history of the Motherland, we need not live in fear of our neighbours? No, not even China.'

'I do, sir. I have.'

Konstantine studied the cosmonaut. 'Ah, I think I see. You are thinking of our many acts of aggression, which each time found justification as acts of self-defence.'

'And before that,' Anatoli said, 'we acted in the name of communism, in our zeal to spread the rejection of unfettered capitalism.'

'Mostly to get under the skin of the Americans,' Konstantine muttered. 'My father's time. I'm sure it was fun, if only slightly terrifying.'

'And now, sir, we must suspend our fear.'

'Yes. The alien threat. And yet, we stand here now, finally unafraid of our fellow human beings. What an extraordinary thing!'

'Until the first citizen refuses to pay his taxes, or do his duty.'

'If only Russians could be as obedient as the Chinese, eh? What has gifted them such powers of co-operation? Of such collective patience?'

Anatoli shrugged. 'Seven thousand years of uninterrupted civilisation, perhaps.'

The President grunted. 'Even their Mongol conquerors in the end succumbed to the civilisation they'd believed under their heels. In that, no different from the Rus. You may be right, Anatoli Petrov. Well, no matter. We can be sure the Chinese will now accelerate their plans for the Moon.'

'Yes. If they are permitted.'

'So,' Konstantine said, turning back to look at the horses, 'when that first citizen refuses to pay his taxes, what will I do?' His attention on the horses, he did not see the cosmonaut's brows rise.

'I do not know, sir, and I do not envy you on that day.'

'I'm sure you don't,' Konstantine murmured. 'How does one rule a nation when the threat of violence becomes an empty one? How does one maintain the borders, police its citizens, impose law and order? This is what the Westerners never understood about us. We toil in silence, we drink hard, and we survive. In the glory and comfort of family, we survive. Yet, beneath it all ...'

Anatoli nodded. There was no need to finish the thought. Russians understood this in a language without words, burned upon their souls. The Nazis had discovered it the hard way.

'If chaos comes,' Konstantine continued, 'will the aliens do anything to stop it?'

'If chaos comes,' Anatoli said, 'it will come first in the West. Or perhaps in the Islamic states. It will come somewhere else first, sir. And we will watch, and wait, and then decide. It is what we do.'

'When we are at our best, yes, it is what we do. But recall the debacle of Afghanistan. Chechnya. Now the Ukraine. Our days of being bold and belligerent have passed. What people will, will be.'

'Perhaps,' Anatoli ventured, 'the ghost of Karl Marx at last begins to smile.'

'Or,' Konstantine retorted, 'it is Ayn Rand's ghost who's now smiling.'

Anatoli, well versed in the writings of both, shook his head. 'I doubt it. That woman made internal misery an act of defiance, and then had the nerve to call it a philosophy. Her arrogance was bluster. That and nothing more.'

'The Americans love her.'

'There has always been a hint of anarchy in the heart of Americans,' Anatoli said. 'But I don't think the aliens desire anarchy. Consider this first loss we must now all adjust to: we have lost the right to be bastards to each other.' He halted then, wondering if he had gone too far.

Instead, Konstantine turned and drew closer, one hand settling on Anatoli's broad shoulder. 'Let's saddle up and ride out, Anatoli Petrov, onto the steppes again, like warriors of old. Would you like that?'

'Sir, I would. I have been practising hard, with horses, of late.'

'Indeed? Inspired by your old Cossack blood?'

Anatoli shook his head. 'No, oddly enough. The trail of my inspiration is a crooked one.'

'How so?'

'*Star Trek*. Captain Kirk, a cosmonaut I would follow anywhere.' Konstantine's laugh was surprised and genuine, and then he frowned. 'But what has that to do with horses?'

'William Shatner, sir. A superb equestrian.'

'Ah, I see. Well then, let us ride out onto the steppes like Hollywood actors!'

Anatoli laughed, and they headed towards the stables. After a moment, the cosmonaut sobered and said, 'Sir, in the time ahead, I think Russia will do just fine.'

'So do I, but I expect our reasons differ for our optimism. What are yours, then?'

'You, sir.'

'Ah. Then yes, our reasons do differ.'

'Sir, I apologise for my comment about being bastards to each other.'

'No need. You are correct. But it leads me to wonder, if we cannot be bastards to each other, what can we be?'

'Ideologies differ, and in that context arguments rarely if ever persuade. And yet, when we have words and only words left, what choice remains, except compromise, conciliation and, perhaps, co-operation?'

'What a world awaits us.'

'It has been said before,' Anatoli began as they moved into the shade of the stables and a dozen figures were stirred into motion by the President's sudden arrival, grooms and aides and bodyguards quickly resuming their posts – the scurrying about startled Anatoli for a moment.

'What has, Anatoli Petrov? What has been said before?'

'Oh, ah, that the Earth when seen from space shows no borders.'

'Hmm, yes, a different perspective, then.'

'One that must be second nature for the aliens, making our distinctions here on the surface seem if not quaint, then irrelevant.'

'Good point,' the President of the Russian Federation said. He paused in thought, and then nodded. 'A good point and, I think, an important one. Come,' he added as two horses were brought up, 'let's ride, Captain Kirk!'

The bodyguards exchanged curious glances at that, but wisely said nothing.

Chapter Ten

'Scepticism is habit-forming and many will see that as a
healthy virtue. Thus, I risk intense approbation when
I say that sometimes the habit of scepticism can be so
ingrained that it becomes wilful denial attached to an air
of smug superiority, signifying the worst flaw a person
can possess: a closed mind.'

Samantha August

'Aliens mining on the Moon?' President Raine Kent's face was red
and getting redder, and the two men seated opposite him in the
Oval Office were both sweating. 'Our fucking Moon? And this – this
was above my security clearance? I'm the goddamned president!'

Security Advisor Daniel Prester glanced across at Ben Mellyk,
but found no help there. The poor man looked to be melting
down, his clothes damp and rumpled, his brow glistening. 'Mister
President, of course this is not above your security clearance.
You have not been in office long and—'

'And didn't I get a clear answer from you the last time? "No,
Mister President, there is no alien conspiracy! Sure, there may be
some weird ruins on Mars but that's all dead and probably mil-
lions of years old!"' He leaned forward. 'But the Moon? Greys?
Fucking *X-File Greys* with those giant eyes and light-bulb heads?
You lied to me!'

'We are not and have never been in contact with the Greys,'
Mellyk said. 'Hence, no conspiracy. The brutal truth is, Mister
President, we do not possess the technical prowess to do any-
thing about the Greys mining on our moon.'

'Why the hell not?'

Mellyk seemed at a sudden loss.

From a chair close to the wall to the right of the President's desk, Vice-President D. K. Prentice cleared her throat. 'Raine, space has been a low priority for a long, long time. The budgets are always being cut, usually in favour of defence contracts, military prototypes and classified interdiction projects now being led by Homeland Security. The simple fact is, the United States government has not been prioritising space exploration since the early seventies.'

'Why the hell not?' the President demanded again.

The Vice-President smiled and said, 'Tax cuts. Administration after administration, selling the American people on tax cuts. Space exploration isn't the only area where we have suffered. Infrastructure is the most obvious victim of reduced budgets. There are parts of our country that look like the third world – if one can even use that phrase anymore. We both know that all that austerity crap was just that. It's not like money just disappeared, went up in smoke, is it? No, it's all out there, more now than ever before. It's just now mostly in the hands of the few, the very few, and we can't touch them, or that money.'

Raine Kent stared at her for a moment, and then rubbed at his face with both hands. 'So,' he said with a sigh, 'when did we find out about the bug-eyed bastards stealing shit from our moon?'

Mellyk cleared his throat. 'Well, there were suspicions with the landings, and the close fly-overs. Vehicle tracks, odd shadows, towers and pipes . . .' His words trailed off as the President slowly stood, fists planted on the desk.

'Are you fucking kidding me?' Kent whispered.

'They thought it was the Russians,' Mellyk explained. 'At least at first. Those were paranoid times, Mister President. Cold War fears dominated everything. People weren't thinking very clearly. By the late seventies, however, the consensus was that something odd was going on up there. But even then, the matter was being discussed only at the highest levels. There were multiple efforts to contact the Greys. These failed.'

'Do *any* ETs ever pick up the effing phone?' the President demanded.

'And subsequent ventures,' Mellyk continued, 'made it clear that further lunar exploration was forbidden. The Greys were thorough and succinct in showing us that the Moon was now off-limits.'

'They blew stuff up? Our stuff?'

'Not just ours, Mister President. Russian stuff, Chinese stuff, Indian stuff.' He shrugged.

'And not one blackbook project in the works to get the bastards out of there? Not in all those years? Those … *decades*? I can't believe this.'

'I think,' ventured Mellyk, 'that president after president just wished the aliens would, well, finish up and leave. Instead, operations continued to expand. The problem was too big—'

'And,' cut in Diana Prentice, 'we kept distracting ourselves with all the usual jockeying around here on Earth.'

Kent slowly sat, gaze now fixing on Prester. 'And it never occurred to … anyone … not even once, that keeping this stuff secret might actually be counterproductive? Allowing us – all of us, every effing country and every effing government – to go on fighting the old battles, getting ever more divisive and parochial, when instead – if they'd come clean – we could possibly have actually united all of humanity?'

'Like in that old film?' Prester asked. '*Independence Day*? But sir, that was just a film.'

'You small-brained navel-wanking idiot, I know it was just a film! But the message was simple enough – even for you, I'd think? Give us an external threat and we get together! Duh!'

'Sir, a panicked population would have toppled governments, crashed the market—'

'And this is why politicians are the worst people to be running anything! They have no faith in humanity! None! Get people together and you get things done!'

Both Prester and Mellyk had recoiled in their chairs at their president's tirade.

Diana Prentice said, 'There was clearly another fear at work here, Raine. Those Greys possess technology we can't match. That much is obvious by virtue of the fact that they came here from another planet, from another solar system. Sure, we could maybe have built something and loaded it up with Marines or whatever, and tried to make a beachhead on the Moon, but honestly, that sounds like a scenario that ends with bits of dead Marines floating around in space. And then, what about the potential for retaliation? Eating holes in the Moon is one thing, eating holes down here is another.'

'Those Greys, they're fucking thieves.'

Mellyk straightened. 'And now, Mister President, they're all gone. Chased away.'

'Because something nastier is in the neighbourhood? Oh, that's just great.'

'It's not exploitative, so far,' Mellyk said. 'That is a significant detail, we think.'

'Even more encouraging,' Prester chimed in, 'the Greys ran away, no shots fired. Probably just a wag of ET's finger. The Greys outclassed us but these newcomers outclass the Greys, probably by a long shot.'

'Turns out,' said Mellyk, 'the galaxy is a lot more crowded than any of us believed.'

'So why did SETI come up with diddily-squat?' Kent demanded.

'That, sir, is a mystery.'

Raine Kent slowly sat back again, looking drained. 'Our entire nation's police forces are reduced to saving kittens from trees. The rioting's done. There's no crime anywhere, not even burglary. What happened to all the drug pushers? The addicts are going crazy. We've got a methadone shortage nationwide and in the meantime, a million Mexicans are crossing our border and there's dick-all we can do about it. You all talk about budget crunches – what happens when the citizens decide not to pay their taxes? Oh sure, garnish their wages, but now you're talking tripling the size of the IRS trying to administer that, hell, who am I kidding? Tripling? More like gazzippling, and servers are already crashing everywhere. We can't maintain any control over this. The only people in control are aliens and all they care about is protecting pandas and trees and whales and horn-rimmed owls or whatever. Oh, and keeping recess friendly. But every recess ends. With a buzzer. Where's the buzzer? When's it coming? What the hell happens then?'

'The illegal drug trade seems to be a curious development,' the Vice-President said after Kent had run out of breath and, it seemed, the will to live. 'A very subtle application of the no-violence-against-others principle, particularly when the addicts themselves want their fixes. After all, self-harm seems to be allowed—'

'What's your point?' Kent asked.

'Well, my point is just that, Raine. This is a strong ethical statement being made here. It probably doesn't relate to drug abuse per se, but to the criminal element behind it. Criminal activities have been shut down, worldwide. Supplies are processed, prepared, warehoused, and then it all just vanishes. Except for hospital-grade heroin and other related opiates.'

'Wait a minute. There's hospital-grade heroin?'

Diana Prentice shrugged. 'Pot seems acceptable, at least insofar as we can tell in those states and countries where it's legal.'

'The buzzer,' said Raine. 'Recess is over. Out comes Jesus, waving a big bell.' He pointed a finger at his Science Advisor. 'Enough of this waiting around shit, Ben. Tell NASA we need to launch someone. We need an effing astronaut in a capsule or something, heading out looking to make contact with these new hidey-hole aliens. We make it a public spectacle. We say we're expecting an actual contact with the aliens. Whatever it costs, Ben, am I understood?' He stood. 'Something for the people to get behind, right?'

'Well,' said Diana in a flat tone, 'better than freedom marches.'

Kent snorted. 'Murdo always was an idiot. A rich, powerful idiot, but still an idiot. Glad that backfired on him. But that's a point – let's make sure this launch thing doesn't backfire on us.'

'Mister President,' said Ben Mellyk, 'that's up to the aliens, isn't it?'

'Call their bluff.'

'It's a gamble,' said Prester.

'And exactly when did that make Americans flinch?'

'We think,' said Prester, 'the Chinese are accelerating their Luna Colony programme.'

'While we just sit here with our thumbs up our arses. This country's gone off the rails. I said it during my campaign and I'm saying it now. We've lost our balls – sorry, D.K. But dammit, we have. All this thin-skinned wimpy mamby pamby oh my feelings are hurt crap, good grief, we're a nation of crybabies! Listen, all of you, it's time to take the lead.'

'A snap mission into space will still take some time,' Ben Mellyk said.

'We'll need congressional approval—' began Prentice.

'They'll approve what I tell them to approve,' said the President.

'You're not popular there, Raine. They'll jump all over you with this.'

'Oh really? Tell 'em I'll veto every one of their pet projects. I'll empty the pork barrel. Listen! I need to address the people. I'll lay it out. The rest of the world can cower, Americans won't. Dammit, that's *our* solar system out there!'

'To be honest sir,' Mellyk said, 'this may not even be our *planet* anymore.'

Raine Kent slowly sat back down. 'Is that why they're ignoring us? We've ceased to be relevant?'

'Governing remains necessary,' his Vice-President said, pushing off from her chair to stand, arms crossed under her breasts. 'The fact that we have not been contacted in any official way suggests at least two levels of engagement from these new aliens.'

'What do you mean?' Raine asked.

'Well, there's the global – no, call it *macro* engagement. The forcefields showing up all over the planet and then ET enforcing non-violence on human behaviour. And, of course, the things going on with Venus and Mars. And no doubt the non-violence aspect is affecting human actions, but only insofar as backing up our legal institutions, worldwide, since it seems we can still arrest and incarcerate people. And the forcefields have halted expansion and access to additional resources, necessitating population readjustments, especially among the poorer nations.' She paused, noting at last that she had everyone's attention. 'But actual *governing* – the potential *micro-management* side to all of this, they're still leaving to us. Us humans.'

'So far,' said Daniel Prester.

She nodded. 'So far. But those macro effects they've imposed, they do seem to be pointing us towards a specific attitude readjustment in our thinking, and by that I mean our thinking as it pertains not just to governing, but also our economics.'

Raine Kent thumped a fist on the desk. 'They're fuckin' socialists!'

'They're reining us in in the name of preserving the planet and managing its dwindling resources,' Diana said. She shrugged. 'Is that socialist?'

'Maybe not,' the President retorted, 'but it sure as hell isn't capitalist!'

'The space mission aside,' Diana said after a moment, 'we do have pressing issues here on the ground, namely, the need for foreign aid—'

'Screw 'em,' said Raine in a low growl.

'That might be dangerous,' Diana observed.

'Why? Is Burundi about to invade?'

'No sir, by "dangerous" I meant the aliens. Consider this, sir – in fact, all of you – the non-violence interventions are all instantaneous. What does that imply?' She fixed the Science Advisor with her gaze. 'Ben?'

'I said it before. It applies agency.'

'Yes. An omnipresent ... presence. Observing, monitoring, comprehending what it sees in real-time.' She paused. 'Are none of you getting it yet? We are being observed. Watched, and probably recorded. And what we decide may well determine what they do next.' She turned to the President. 'Show a cold, cruel heart, sir, and they might well decide to do the same.'

Slowly, the colour left Raine Kent's face.

'Neither socialist nor capitalist,' Diana went on. 'More like ... our *conscience*.'

The word hung there in the now-silent Oval Office, like a judgement from God.

•

Fame was fleeting, but it had yet to leave Marc Renard. As a Canadian astronaut he had been only the fifth from his country to spend time at the International Space Station, and like his predecessors there had been speaking engagements, radio and television interviews, and a book with its attendant cross-country signing tour. It helped that he was affable and comfortable in front of a crowd, or a camera. Most of these virtues seemed far away at the moment, as he sat opposite the Prime Minister and did his best to explain. 'Secrecy is a big part of the package,' he said. 'If you don't sign on you don't go, as simple as that.'

Lisabet Carboneau's eyes were hard. 'And this supersedes the oaths you took in service to your own country?'

'Madam, when I agreed to non-disclosure prior to my stay at the ISS, I had no idea that it would create a conflict of interest with respect to my oath as a military officer.'

She leaned forward in her chair. The office seemed stifling and the vase full of lilacs from the Prime Minister's garden yielded a scent pungent enough to make the astronaut's eyes water. 'Just tell me what's going on up there. What did you see?'

'We had company,' he replied. 'Irritating company. They were, well, remotes. Not big. They did a lot of hovering. They got curious, especially when anyone was on a walk. For all that, no one ever felt they were friendly. More like wasps at a picnic.'

'And the Moon?'

He sighed. 'A busy place. Half our job was making sure our external shots didn't catch anything too overt. Positioning for public shots was so damned complicated we needed Mission Control to guide us.'

'So the book, the tours and the speeches, all bullshit.'

He winced.

'Yesterday,' the Prime Minister said, 'I had a long conversation with the British Prime Minister, Jeffry Kemp, where we discussed our "special" relationship with the United States. Of course, this also involved matters relating to the European Space Agency and the recent revelations about the Moon. Our moon.'

Jeffry Kemp. That wanker. Marc glanced away.

'No, sorry, back here please.'

Marc's head snapped back. 'Apologies, madam. Allergies.' He nodded towards the lilacs. 'Making my eyes water.'

'Will you get hives?'

'Pardon? Oh. No.'

'Then suck it up,' she said. 'You know, everyone in power thinks the same thing. The privilege of keeping secrets, it's like ambrosia. It's heady stuff. When people say someone is drunk on power, this is what they mean, whether they realise it or not. The idea of people knowing too much – of the citizens actually finding out what governments and corporations are really up to – that's what scares them the most.'

Abruptly she stood, collecting up the vase to carry over to a side-table. 'And then there's some people who were born to it, born *in* it, thinking their power is a birthright, a product of blue blood or some such thing.' She walked back to reseat herself. 'That's Kemp. Even on the phone and thousands of kilometres away, I found myself wanting to throttle the man.' She blinked. 'Needless to say, you can't quote me.'

Marc nodded. 'I've met him, madam. Proof that power corrupts, I suppose.'

'Well, I'm not yet corrupted,' Lisabet said. 'At least, I don't think so. You understand, I want to see full disclosure, and I want to be the one to lead the way. With an address to all Canadians.'

Frowning, Marc asked, 'Why? They've left, the Moon, I mean. And, from what I've learned, all the remotes are gone. Nothing in orbit.'

'That's not the point. The point, Marc, is the principle. The assumption that the general population consists mostly of idiots who, as the film once said, can't handle the truth.'

'If disclosure is that important,' Marc said, 'why have the newly arrived ETs not made a public appearance?'

'You think they're hiding what they're up to? That hardly seems the case.'

'No, at least on one level, you're right. So, two very public, worldwide gestures: the forcefields and the ending of all violence. But what if there's more going on, things that we've not yet noticed? Those two acts couldn't be disguised or hidden away. They were explicitly public. But not everything is, Madam Prime Minister. We both know that.'

'What have you heard?'

'High-tech schematics, files containing instructions on building an emission-free energy source. An engine. You can make it so small it'll run an electric toothbrush, or big enough to lift an Atlas rocket. Those files arrived at every tech and engineering firm, everywhere.'

She waved a hand. 'Yes, I'm aware of that. And how is that any less public, Marc? It's pointedly non-proprietary. No one can patent the technology. The automotive companies have just seen decades of electric-car research go down the tubes, not to mention the hydrogen-fuel prototypes and the improvements on bio-diesel. As for the oil sector, let's not even go there. These new ETs aren't hiding anything, despite the potential chaos of their revelations. And you know what? I find that refreshing.'

'But we still don't know that they're not hiding anything, apart from themselves, that is.'

'In their place, I wouldn't make an appearance either. No alien visage to focus our resentment on.' She slid into view a file folder. 'But it may be that we're going to be surprised again.' She opened the file and pushed it across the desk towards Marc.

He leaned forward, spun the file around and began reading, only to stop. 'I remember this,' he said. 'The abduction event in Victoria, all those videos—'

'And what were the conclusions from your Don't Tell Anyone crowd?'

'You make that sound so ...'

'Juvenile?'

After a moment he returned his attention to the file. 'Well, it didn't really match past abductions, which tended to be more ...

private. There was worry that the Greys were ramping things up.'

'Did you see the video recordings?'

'Yes.'

'Was that flying saucer recognisably a Grey ship?'

'Impossible to say, madam. They reconfigure, or there are multiple styles. The initial thinking was that the Greys wanted us to believe that they weren't the only ones up there, travelling through and occupying our sovereign space. A multitude of vessel styles meant to intimidate us.'

'I would think it worked.'

'Yes. It did. Kept us in our corner, for certain, looking out at the big boys playing the real game.' He glanced back up from the file. 'You are thinking that these new ETs took Samantha August?'

'What do you think?'

After a moment, he sat back. 'You know, you might be right. Still ...'

'Why didn't they snatch up someone like you, you're thinking. An astronaut, someone's who been up there. Or maybe a major mover and shaker, a very public figure. An actor or a president or even a prime minister. Or a scientist, someone like Tyson. Hell, why not Jodie Foster?'

'Well, it's a good question, isn't it?'

'Surely you're a fan of science fiction, Marc?'

'Of course. But at the same time, they do, well, they make things up. Warp drives, singularity drives, hyperspace. They're not necessarily ... grounded.'

'Hmm. Very well. Let's assume they took her. And just her, no one else.'

He offered up a sheepish smile. 'At least she's Canadian.'

'Yes, and so are you, when not bound by some other country's non-disclosure agreements.' She retrieved the file folder and closed it up. 'Maybe you're the wrong person to bring in on this, when it comes to trying to figure out why they abducted Samantha August and not some modern Carl Sagan, or Jeff

Goldblum. What I need is an expert on alien sociology – any idea where I can find such a person?'

Marc Renaud felt himself sinking deeper into his chair. He shrugged helplessly, and then said, 'Well, find another science fiction writer, I suppose.'

The gleam of triumph in Lisabet Carboneau's eyes was only slightly marred by a hint of malice as she smiled at Marc.

'Madam,' he said, 'Sam August's abduction – I don't know if anyone else has connected it to this First Contact event – do you plan on making that public, too?'

'Not yet,' she replied.

'So it stays, uh, secret?'

'Touché.' She was silent for a moment, and then she said, 'Kemp tried to talk me out of it.'

Marc nodded. 'Of course he did.'

'Is it telling, do you think, that the ETs didn't snatch an Etonian?'

He hesitated, and then said, 'I hope so.'

'So do I, Marc. So do I.'

Chapter Eleven

'The best solutions usually suck.'

Samantha August

One wall of her room had been transformed into a multitude of screens, showing feeds from television stations as well as webcasts. The news networks were a riot of reports on how the end of violence was shaking human culture to its core, driving civilisation to its knees. Philosophers were never so popular as they were now, as journalists floundered and stumbled through their questions, only to gaze with bemused confusion at the answers.

Not that answers were readily forthcoming. At least most of the philosophers, dusted off and brushed up in their academic tweeds, were pushing to the heart of the issue, which had nothing to do with alien technology, and everything to do with how humans related with each other.

On other stations, the sitcoms and reality shows continued. Sports were played, crowds cheered and jeered, hotdogs and nachos all around, and it seemed the pretence of civilisation was more important than ever. Even there, however, it felt like everything was sitting on a powder keg, and the fuse smouldered on.

'This is overwhelming,' Samantha August said, reaching for her pack of cigarettes and lighting up. 'The economy's in tatters and they're predicting shortages soon, and it seems that while you're good at what not to do, you're not so good at what we need to do to replace the things we've always done.'

'You do comprehend, Samantha August, that dictates delivered now would be counterproductive.'

Sam pointed her cigarette at one screen. 'There, what that guy's talking about. This is a crisis of authority. What you've done is strike at the heart of human society.'

'Would you care to elaborate?' Adam asked.

She sighed, rose and walked over to her bed, where she settled back and stared up at the white ceiling. 'Authority is fragile. Even the smallest groups establish a set of rules governing behaviour. Rituals and taboos, ways of dealing properly with one another. A lot of this relates to identity, to how a group chooses to define itself. But it's also about keeping the peace.'

'Understood.'

'I'm not sure you do. The *fist* is implicit. Sure, small hunter-gatherer groups didn't go for that threat of violence as a means of coercing civil behaviour within the band or tribe. Their final threat was banishment, often tantamount to a death sentence, but once removed. The banished often just withered and died, possibly because they lost the most important thing to them: their identity. Isolate the criminal. It's an ancient practice and of course we still use it, only now, in modern societies, banishment is not a death sentence anymore.'

'Why not?' Adam asked, interrupting her train of thought.

She blew smoke upward. 'Increase your population and you get anonymity. You also get sub-cultures, sub-groups, so the outliers are now more able to find one another and thus reassert identity, even if that consists of a secret online cabal of child pornographers, or molesters, or Nazis or whatever. These days, anonymity is often desired.'

'Because a particular behaviour is deemed heinous.'

'Yes.'

'Accordingly,' Adam resumed, 'anonymity permits the perpetuation of these heinous behaviours, even within a context of self-identification. Outside the law, as it were.'

'Hence criminal organisations, yes. But the thing is, both sides of the law require that fist, that ultimate threat of violence, and the fear that such a threat engenders. Because fear makes people obedient. The converse of that is just as important, Adam: the absence of fear, or threat of violence, can make people monsters.'

'Apprehension of criminals is not being prevented,' Adam said. 'I apply full discriminatory judgement in each instance. However, the distinction between intention and action is one that is central to your collective human legal systems.'

'Don't you need to make the same distinction?' Sam asked.

'No. In order to prevent a crime, I must act upon intention.'

'So your blanket presence down there can read minds?'

'Unnecessary. Intention is rarely difficult to assess, based on numerous physiological indicators.'

'You can read us like a book.'

'But with more than typical comprehension. As we understand it, with respect to your species' relationship with the written word, both entertainment and pleasure is possible even with minimal comprehension.'

'Ha ha, very funny, Adam. But let's get back to the point. Among humans, it's not a crime to think bad thoughts. It's only a crime if you act on them. And that is a valid recognition of human nature, since we're not all sweetness and light.' She gestured towards the screens on the far wall. 'What you've done is stepped in as the ultimate arbiter on human behaviour. You've taken it out of our hands and that's where the flaw in your thinking comes in.'

'In what way is our thinking flawed, Samantha August?'

'We define adulthood as a solemn recognition of responsibility. We make the distinction when considering the acts of children, and will argue that they were not responsible, because their brains have not yet matured to make the proper connection between an act and its consequences.'

'Those adults who subsequently commit crimes are those who failed to comprehend that connection, then?'

'Some, yes. Others don't give a shit. They deliberately choose to commit a crime and bank on not getting caught. At this point, in kicks our belief systems, which is where you find the ultimate arbiter to our lives: that unblinking eye that saw everything, knew every thought, witnessed every sin. And thou shall be judged.'

'But only after you die.'

'Setting that judge outside of mortal constraints is the only guarantee of its incorruptibility.'

'Yet few choose to believe in the manner they once did,' observed Adam.

Sam pursed her lips. 'Historians insist we were more God-fearing once, yes. Personally, I'm not convinced. Sure, there have always been fanatics, but here's the thing. Every fanatic I've ever met shares one thing: the unswerving conviction that they're right. They may speak out in the name of this god or that god, but what they really are is egomaniacal control freaks. They don't speak for God, they think they *are* God.' She flicked her cigarette to the floor. 'So, for everyone else, in those so-called God-fearing ages, it was more likely a case of being terrified of the fanatics — who often held positions of power, and who always presumed to speak on God's behalf. As an appeal to authority, you can't get much better than that.'

'So,' said Adam, 'even in the recognition of a god outside of corrupt influence, that god was nevertheless corrupted.'

'The sacred succumbs to the secular. We can't manipulate what goes on after death, so we manipulate the hell out of everything else. And if you don't agree, we kill you, burn you, torture you, get you to confess your crimes. But none of that has much to do with God. It's all about control, and by extension, authority, which brings us back to the threat of violence. The fist behind the veil.'

'Which in turn relates back to a notion of identity,' said Adam, 'but one where to belong is to live and to not belong is to die. Where believers are allies and non-believers are the enemy.'

'And from there it's not a far step to protest groups demanding rights over a woman's own body. Speaking of which, what's your take on abortion?'

'Do you eat eggs?'

'Excuse me?'

'The unborn embryos of chickens, Samantha.'

'But we humans make a distinction between the value of human life and all other lives, and yes, I know, it's a pretty self-serving

134

one. The scientific types define that distinction on the basis of sentience. The religious types on the basis of the immortal soul, which apparently only us humans possess, since we were made in God's image and are unique in containing His spark.'

'But did not God create all life? Is life itself not defined by virtue of that spark? Furthermore, the distinction of sentience is not valid. There are many forms of sentience, and a sentience that defines sentience based exclusively on itself has not only imposed false parameters on sentience, it is in fact not yet fully sentient. In other words, Samantha, there are many sentient species here on Earth.'

'I suspected as much. But we can't help but anthropomorphise what we observe in the behaviour of other animals, so that we can call it cute. Like you say, ours is the only definition of sentience we possess.'

'One's body is sovereign,' said Adam. 'None can impose their will upon it.'

'And the unborn embryo? What of an external will imposed upon it?'

'All life is potential, Samantha August. Within life, sentience is a contingency. An embryo is not sentient. It is a life set forth as potential. Not all potentials are realised.'

'So ETs are not going to be carrying a sign outside any abortion clinic in the foreseeable future.'

'More to the point, Samantha August, those protestors are no longer able to impose their will upon women seeking abortions.'

'Well, they took to recording women who enter the clinics and then posting the video online. Even before you arrived. Presumably as an act of shaming.'

'It was understood early on,' replied Adam, 'that humans were capable of reprehensible acts, particularly when proceeding from a position of self-righteousness. Such video recordings will not survive online, as I am in complete control of your web.'

'You are? And you're what, censoring us?'

'I am removing the spiritual violence being committed behind anonymity. I am refusing the more despicable examples of false courage, bullying, hate-mongering and intimidation. Violence, as we both know, need not be physical. Your society displays cycles of pernicious judgmentalism, and you are in one such peak period at the moment.'

'Our education system no longer teaches empathy,' Sam said. 'Now, if everybody in college had to take a minor in Literature, the world would be a better place.'

'The future will demand such empathy, Samantha August.'

'Then we'll have to learn it the hard way. Which is, I suppose, what you're doing.' She sat up, walked back to face all the screens. 'So, what's next, Adam?'

'The Intervention Protocol's second stage is proceeding. Selective advances in technology have been provided under terms of universal access. Disclosure elements are pending.'

'Uh huh. Now, tell me more about the Greys.'

'A parasitic species that will no longer plague you. They are already exiting the solar system.'

'Why? You being pacifists and all, why should they fear you?'

'Those whom you call the Greys are what you might call psychic-feeders. The more powerful the emotion, the more addictive it becomes to them. They force terror upon their victims and feed on the biochemical reaction.'

'Great, a spacefaring civilisation of junkies.'

'This means of feeding is violent and constitutes a fundamental assault upon the sanctity of individual consciousness. We impose our denial. They have moved on.'

'That's it?'

'I detect an increase in blood pressure.'

'They fucking mind-rape humans and you just brush them away? So they can do what? Find the next planet of victims?'

'We are not their primary reason for their flight from your solar system, Samantha August. You are. But we venture into latter-state Protocol elements and it would be premature to discuss them now.'

'If these mind-rape details get out, Adam, we'll go after them.'
'Yes.'

She considered that for some time, eyes on the screens but not quite seeing the endless images flashing upon them. 'Adam, are there other potential victims out there?'

'Yes.'

'Close by?'

'Yes.'

'And you want us to do something about it?'

'Yes, and you will, I'm sure. Intervention Protocol is a complicated undertaking. There are immense responsibilities involved. Your species well understands righteousness, and will adhere to it with admirable ferocity.'

'For the first time,' Sam said quietly, 'you highlight a human virtue.'

'Awakening it requires patience, and a subtle process of disclosure.'

'The day you tell humanity that it's a rape victim is a day those Greys will remember.' She hesitated, and then said, 'I think I've decided.'

'You will speak on our behalf?'

'You've finally given me the ammunition to consider the possibility that we can actually make this work.'

'Our faith in you was absolute.'

'Right. Only now I need to convince you to have faith in humanity, and for me to do that, I need to think of a way to convince humanity to have faith in itself. No small task, Adam.'

'We will help.'

'You mentioned "disclosure elements" as proceeding. What did you mean?'

'The universe is fractal, Samantha August. For this reason, it is reasonable to assume that things scale up just as they scale down. We have skirted the concept of God in our discussions, and much of what is being discussed in the media below has now come to address this fundamental issue of religious belief. After all, where does ET fit into your human concept of God? What do we believe? Do we believe at all?'

'I was skirting all of that for a damned good reason.'

'Understood. Samantha, consider our present level of omnipotence on your planet. From your scale of measure, it certainly may seem godlike. Religious people are expressing this unease. We have been called God and we have been called Satan. We have been cited as proof that God does not exist.'

'And?'

'True omnipotence is neither scalable nor relative. Accordingly, we are not omnipotent. Our area of influence is limited. Does there exist an entity or consciousness capable of perceiving the universe in its entirety, capable of similar omnipotence but on a much grander scale? If so, we cannot determine one way or the other. To date, our activities have not triggered any observable response from such an entity. But absence of proof is not proof of absence. If I may, I will return to the notion of sentience. The highest form of sentience is to ask "why?" Reducing your mind to the pursuit of "what is" without ever asking "why?" is to deny the greatest gift of sentience.'

'Ah. I like that. Most atheists won't.'

'We share with humanity this curiosity and this questioning. It is, perhaps, the only truly universal trait among all sentient species. It is directly a product of our imagination, our capacity to wonder, and to recognise that in order for an inner world of the mind to exist, an outer world must also exist, and as much as we may seek – even need – to impose a fundamental distinction between the two, we remain forever trapped within our realm of perception and, indeed, nothing exists beyond it. Nothing at all.'

'So what I think you're saying is that perception defines the universe. Well, we humans have ventured onto that ground. But like so many ideas, it struggles to find an anchor, because it begs the question: if so, what's the point?'

'Samantha, it may be that sentience imposes the ethical framework upon the universe. That the attribution of meaning is not only our primary purpose, it is also sacred.'

'I think we'll need to revisit this discussion about God sometime soon. But … are ethics homogenous among all sentient species?'

'Within a certain range of expression, yes. With but one exception that we are aware of, all advanced civilisations understand the concept of right and wrong. The challenge is, as always, finding mutual recognition of this simple truth. Xenophobia exists and must be overcome before such recognition is possible.'

'Adam, is our galaxy a free-for-all battle for resources? So many of my fellow SF writers write it as if it was. Only a few offer any other kind of vision. Iain M. Banks comes to mind – oh, why didn't you show up ten years ago, abduct him, cure him and ... aw, shit, never mind.'

'You are experiencing grief. I am sorry.'

She shook her head, and then sighed.

'To answer your question, Samantha, no, there are resources aplenty. Worlds with biomes are rarer, but colonisation of such worlds is rarely attempted.'

'Really? Why not?'

'Biomes are self-contained. Complex life-forms are fundamentally adapted to their home world and its biota. Most biomes are not conducive to extraterrestrial invasion. Native food sources are not compatible and the native biome will resist the introduction of foreign biota. Enforced "terraforming" usually fails.'

'So where do all the aliens live? Giant generation ships? I suppose the gravity well of worlds isn't always desirable.'

'Gravity poses no obstacle, Samantha. Large artificial biomes, such as your "generation ships" can function and are often employed, but one fact remains and it is an important one. All species arose within a natural, planet-bound biome. We are genetically predisposed to not only favour it, we also *require* it. Species that abandon their natural biomes over successive generations often sicken and die.'

'So, back to my question, then.'

'Terraforming lifeless worlds through the alteration of orbital mechanics, atmosphere, water supply, the presence of moons and so on, are the principal means of colonisation. Such candidate planets exist in numbers uncountable.'

'That's what you're doing with Venus?'

'Yes. We are preparing for humanity a sister world that will be home to a biota brought to it from Earth.'

'And Mars?'

'Details on the Mars Reclamation Process will be forthcoming as the Protocol proceeds.'

'Uh huh. Right.' She crossed her arms, studying the newsfeeds. 'So, a post-scarcity galaxy out there.'

'Yes, Samantha.'

'Ah, Iain, you were right after all.'

'A brilliant writer whose death was mourned by many,' Adam said. 'I should point out, his innate optimism has done much to support our belief in your species' potential.'

She barked a laugh. 'Oh man, billions and billions of readers?'

'Hundreds of billions,' Adam replied. 'The human imagination is a most valuable currency.'

'And not a dime in royalties. So, you could write me a nice cheque too, couldn't you? With my billion or so bootlegging readers, right?'

'Billions. And yes.'

Momentarily stunned, she had nothing to say. On the newsfeed, a drone camera was showing a mass of mostly unclothed refugees in some denuded African landscape. They were pouring out of a relief camp, burdened with foodstuffs. There was dancing, and dark faces laughing, teeth like pearls. 'You said they wouldn't starve, didn't you?'

'I did. They won't.'

'All right, Adam. I'll do it. I'll speak for you. But first, you need to do something for me.'

'Of course.'

'A big thing.'

'I am at your disposal.'

'Hmm. Since bootlegging stories and novels is fine with you, what's your take on copyright, intellectual property and trademarks?'

Chapter Twelve

'The Big Bang, what a sweet theory.'
Samantha August

Washington Post Editorial, June 1st

The End of the World (as we know it)

Jacob P., an itinerant heroin addict in Milwaukee, never felt so helpless. He had been getting by. He wasn't looking to change his life. The hole he'd found himself in was dark, cramped, and, when he was high, as comforting as a womb.

And then the drugs stopped working. That elusive kick, the one he had experienced that very first time, the one every addict chases, was no longer there – not in his head, not in his body. The hunger was gone. So was the need. It was as if he'd forgotten his first love. These days, his only love. He didn't want it anymore, wasn't even interested in it. How did that happen?

More pointedly, now what?

Government leaders of the G7 met yesterday in Ottawa, in a cordoned-off block just up from the banks of the Rideau Canal. The usual mob of protestors crowded the barriers, but something had changed. No one quite knew what they were protesting, and the police presence was minimal, with none of the usual riot gear and crowd-suppressant paraphernalia. Many of the banners and signs being held up showed nothing more than question marks, and this muted plea could not have been more poignant.

In the banquet hall of the Hotel Frontenac, seven of the world's most powerful leaders met in sessions closed to the media, but even this nod to security had a hollow feel. What was being discussed? Easy answer: our unseen but surely felt overseers. What was being decided? Probably nothing.

Or is that being too facile, in the face of such fundamental changes to who we are and what we do? Day by day, moment by moment, we are all being confronted with how things have changed. That sudden road rage on the beltway? Pointless. Take a deep breath and settle down. Whatever you were thinking to do won't happen, and your foot flooring the pedal, your eyes seeing the car ahead in a red haze, all of it achieves nothing. The damned car doesn't speed up. The engine doesn't even rev higher. You are shut down. Instantly. Definitively. Just one more driver in the line.

How's that blow to the ego feeling?

Or when the buzzer sounds and the school day is finally at an end. The sixth-grade bully, the one usually waiting for you down a block and at the mouth of the alley you take to get home, well, he's still there. But the cold look in his eyes is gone. His old man can't beat him up anymore, so he has nothing to pass on to you. And as you walk by, he surprises you with a nod.

Back in Milwaukee, Jacob P. isn't thinking about the Exclusion Zones (it seems that's what they're called, though who coined the term is unknown). He isn't thinking about the G7 and those helpless world leaders reduced to discussing the volatile market and its imminent crash and burn, with all matters pertaining to security, military co-operation or the lack thereof, peacekeeping and trade embargoes, all out the window. Jacob P. isn't thinking about the sudden over-abundance of food and fresh water miraculously appearing in refugee camps all over the world. He isn't thinking about the strange absences of infectious diseases, or answering the question: when was the last time anyone had a cold? Jacob isn't thinking about his next fix, either.

A thirty-nine-year-old ex-addict for whom the label doesn't even carry the usual trepidation and distrust anymore, Jacob P. is climbing out of the hole. Turns out it wasn't such a nice place after all.

There comes to us all a time when we need to leave the womb, our world of private comforts, whether those involve intimidating another driver on the beltway, or beating up a little kid after school. And that father who used his son as a punching bag? He's got a real punching bag now, hanging on a hook in the garage. He drives his fists into it with metronome precision and a lifetime's worth of frustration and anger, but all that fuel inside is fast burning up, and his eyes are wide, looking at a future both unknown and unknowable. Just one big ... question mark.

There were about eight thousand protestors to the G7 emergency session. They stood at the barricades, until a light rain sent most of them home.

The G7 leaders departed, not one of them inviting comment, or even so much as appearing in front of cameras. Their entourages of officious-looking aides, secretaries and minders still scurried about, but there wasn't anything to show for it. Bodyguards stood around with nothing to do and no reason to be watchful. The whole event had all the self-importance of a pantomime. What now? What next?

Daily Mail Editorial, June 3rd

PRISON EARTH!

So this is how it ends, not with a bang but with a whimper. Cowed into submission by aliens lacking the courage to even show their bug-eyed faces (or what passes for faces for these galactic communists), we might as well start lining up for our manacles and tattoos, shuffling up the ramps into the bellies of cattle-car transporters that will wing us into space to mine gold on the Moon.

But it's likely nobody will complain much. Better taking a pick to moon-rocks that living in the gilded cage Earth has become. If you can call it living. Free market capitalism is being snuffed out, like one last flickering candle, and what's coming promises to be dark, interminable and miserable.

Our spirit is being crushed. We have been made meek, but alas, we shall not inherit the Earth.

Resist. Refuse. Never bow. Never kneel. Plant your feet. Make them come down here and drag us up those ramps. And while they're doing it, spit in their bug-eyed faces.

Financial Post Editorial, June 7th

When Sweating the Small Stuff Is All That's Left

Overseeing a financial apocalypse must make for entertaining viewing on the monitors of the alien spaceship hovering unseen over our heads. If they're a betting species of extraterrestrial, the wagers must be heating up as we totter ever nearer the precipice of global meltdown.

The military industries have virtually shut down worldwide, sending tens of thousands of skilled workers to the unemployment line. The end of oil exploration and the closing of the Tar Sands and all fracking operations are finally impacting the global oil reserves, and this rumoured new power system isn't doing much to allay fears as universal dread of oil scarcity ripples through the markets.

Compounding the volatility, the very question of national sovereignty is now at risk, as borders become porous in the wake of an end to all forms of coercion. Locked gates can be climbed over. Barbed wire fences can be cut. The mass movement of populations has risen to a flood that threatens to engulf the developed nations, further burdening infrastructure in countries already struggling to emerge from the last market crash.

Under any other circumstances, wars would be erupting everywhere, hotspots flaring up in a cascade of death and destruction. Instead, we have all become witnesses to a collective repositioning of our entire species, as might come after a natural catastrophe of global proportions, with not a skinned knee to show for it.

Now the species waits, pensive, desperate for the first sign that order is coming, that whatever lies ahead will be better than how things are now. For decades, free market capitalism has been the dominant driving force of human civilisation. The old battles between the collective and the individual were consigned to history, a footnote to the triumph of freedom. But how much of our hard-won freedom meant the freedom to do wrong?

More, it seems, than we had imagined.

The signs are there for those willing to see it. The monetary economic model is in its death throes. Whatever wagers are being thrown back and forth in that orbiting spaceship, they don't match our value system, and make no mistake: it's our value system that is being rejected here.

The history of humanity has never before experienced anything like this. And should we succeed in emerging on the other side, we may well find ourselves unrecognisable to ourselves. Indeed, we shall have become the aliens in our own world.

Guardian Editorial (guest writer), June 7th

Barbarians At The Gate
By H. L. Toynbee (PhD, Classics, Cambridge University, OBE)

In the third and fourth centuries the borders of the Roman Empire were crumbling. In the deep forests of Northern Europe, on the wind-swept wilds of the Balkans and in the mountain ranges of the Caucasus, entire peoples were on the move. Pushed by Attila and his ever-expanding Hunnic Empire, the many tribes that would one day make up the cultural identities of modern Europe began flooding into Roman territory, seeking protection, seeking new homelands.

Many of their tribal names remain with us: Franks (France),

Lombards (Lombardy), Angles (England), Saxons (Saxony), while others have morphed over time (Goths, Vandals) into what some might call modern sub-cultures, characterised more by behaviour than filial identification.

Rome could not hold them back. The Empire's internal infrastructure, already stressed by political chaos, environmental degradation, religious upheaval and regional uprisings, simply broke apart. In the West the collapse was sudden. In the East it was more drawn out, ending with the fall of Constantinople to the Turks in 1453.

History offers us many lessons. Mass migration of populations is nothing new. The privilege of hindsight allows us to focus on the long-term revivification of culture and civilisation that resulted from such vast shifts in peoples and their places, the renaissance of new blood and new ways of living. Civilisation only rarely vanishes; more often it simply transforms, evolves. The English deem themselves British, quintessential inhabitants and natives of the British Isles. Of course, the original Angles came from Denmark, Germany and Saxony. And genetic studies now point towards an even earlier and far more eastern origin – somewhere on the steppes of modern-day Georgia and Khazakstan.

How we define ourselves is an ongoing process, and the notion of nativity is essential to that self-identification. Headlines and front pages of other newspapers proclaim, strident with panic, the onset of barbarians at the gate, interlopers landing on the shores of our fair isle. If Roman Britain had its tabloids in the fifth century, they would have cried much the same thing.

All over the world, in country after country, borders crumble, and populations on the move seek out new lives in foreign places. Cultures clash, but these drumbeats of fear and xenophobia no longer lead to bloodshed, and this fact alone stands stalwart and bold, announcing unambiguously that a new age is upon us.

From one empire's fall, many others rose in its place. What lies ahead? No one can know, but whatever comes, we shall live it, day by day, moment by moment. History's tide is our companion, and neither politics nor wishful thinking can change that. Sixteen hundred years ago, we were the barbarians at the gate, and how did that turn out?

National Enquirer, June 7th

OSWALD WAS AN ALIEN!
John Wilkes Booth the First Alien Assassin?
Scientists want to clone Abraham Lincoln to find out!

Doctor John Milkos of J. VanderMeer University has formally requested that the Smithsonian Institute make available a cellular sample extracted from the body of Abraham Lincoln, which he will then clone so that he can interrogate the American President on the alien conspiracy of assassinations of American presidents.

'The secrecy has gone on long enough,' Milkos said. 'We need full disclosure. Those aliens must be brought to justice.'

Evidence is still pending on the alien nature of Harvey Oswald, but Dr Milkos believes the genetic proof is forthcoming. 'It's widely surmised,' he went on, 'that this new evidence of alien occupation on the Moon is where we'll find the vault containing the secret archives detailing all that they've done to manipulate us Americans, all the way back to the *Mayflower* landing.'

The Smithsonian Institute had thus far refused comment on the scientist's request.

The McKenzie Gantry Show (Fox News)
Interview Transcript with guest
Barbara Backlow, Moreland Institute of Global Strategy.

GANTRY: Welcome, Dr Backlow. Now, for those viewers who don't know much about the Moreland Institute, can you give us a quick breakdown on what you do?

BACKLOW: Thank you, McKenzie, and of course. Our institute is an economic think tank specialising in identifying global economic trends and then devising strategies for positioning the United States to benefit and thereby capitalise on those trends. We have advised the past four administrations and continue to work closely with both Democrats and Republicans.

GANTRY: When you talk about 'trends', you're meaning what's coming, what's waiting for us. I guess that's turned into a bit of a dog's breakfast these days, hasn't it?

BACKLOW: There's been a dramatic, even fundamental, shift in the paradigm, that's true. Not just in economics, although that is naturally where we're concentrating on at the moment. We can talk about specific markets that have been impacted—

GANTRY: Impacted? You mean trashed, don't you?

BACKLOW: We prefer the term 'Externally Deviated'.

GANTRY: 'Externally.' By that you mean the aliens.

BACKLOW: An outside agency, yes, a force beyond our ability to control or predict.

GANTRY: And by 'deviated' you mean what, exactly?

BACKLOW: Well, deviated from normal operations would be a simple way of putting it.

GANTRY: In other words, trashed. Got it. So there's the obvious markets or industries we're talking about here, right? Oil, for example. Fracking. Oilsands. But now there's reports that even coal mining has been shut down. We're looking at an energy crunch, aren't we?

BACKLOW: That seemed the immediate conclusion, yes. Now, with news of this new energy source, this emissionless, fuel-free engine, we at our institute are taking a step back from our original dire projections—

GANTRY: You're backpedalling. Well, that's hardly surprising. I mean, if that engine actually works, and can do, well, everything that a regular oil-burning combustion engine does, it's a game-changer, isn't it?

BACKLOW: Well, yes and no. By that I mean, the entire manufacturing industry needs to retool in order to ramp up production, and secondary and tertiary – I mean, related industries – ones that make use of oil, such as plastics, and oil-based equipment, well, they have to get in line now. Which makes for a lot of jostling in terms of which industries take precedence over others. To be honest, it's a bit of a free-for-all at the moment. We don't yet know how this will play out. The challenge for many industries at the moment is in keeping afloat, in, uh, managing the transition while still staying viable.

GANTRY: So you believe the EFFE is real, then? The emission-less fuel-free engine.

BACKLOW: Oh yes it's real, and since the specifications are open source, it's all down to which companies are first to get the things built. That will decide who becomes the front-runner in terms of manufacturing.

GANTRY: There's news now that the Chinese government is already past the prototype stage and into real manufacturing. But what about us in the free world? What's going on here in America? Why aren't we already pumping the damned things out?

BACKLOW: Well, first off, there's really no such thing as a proto-type version. The only challenge with this new energy source is in engineering the interface between the engine and what it needs to do. The Chinese reports are unconfirmed, by the way. As for here in America, the first engines off the line will probably come from the aerospace engineering sector. Boeing, Lockheed, or maybe even one of the outliers, like Kepler.

GANTRY: If the Chinese get a jump on us with this one, they'll flood the market – we'll all be driving good old American cars with Chinese engines in them.

BACKLOW: Unlikely, McKenzie. Even if the Chinese are the first to go into mass production of the EFFE, those engines will be earmarked for internal distribution first and foremost.

GANTRY: They'd be smarter heading straight to export though.

BACKLOW: You mean in terms of economic strategy?

GANTRY: Well, either way, I mean. Say they ramp up everything internally, with these new engines. That means they get a jump on the rest of us globally – by the time we're ready with a, say, Boeing version, there won't be any markets left to sell it to. The Chinese will have sewn it all up. Or say they go straight to export. Same result. We've got to get going on this, don't we? Problem is, we don't have slaves chained to the machines, do we?

BACKLOW: I am unaware of slaves being used in China—

GANTRY: Guaranteed, Doctor. It's a communist country for crying out loud!

BACKLOW: Excuse me, McKenzie, but you're still thinking old school on this—

GANTRY: Old school? What do you mean by that?

BACKLOW: Well, you're looking at this as if it was simply one more new product on a traditional market scaffold, slotting in like, oh, I don't know, a new iPhone or MS Office-VR. Unfortunately, that scaffold is pretty much in pieces – this is what has become brutally clear to us at the Institute. Free market competition – the very basis of our capitalist economics – is based on aggression. But our natural acts of competition – for example, outbidding other companies for, say, mining exploration rights, oil prospecting, logging – well, that's all been impacted. It's not as obvious as not being able to punch someone, or shoot them, or drop bombs, for that matter. But the ethics of the new paradigm are clearly pointing us towards a broader theme of—

GANTRY: Now you're just complicating things, Doctor. Using big words to cloud the issue. The simple fact is, the Chinese are beating Americans to the punch. The President needs to step in – did you hear his last press conference? He's like a chicken without a head! Sending an astronaut up there – for what? Forget the damned astronaut! What we need is those magic engines put in attack ships and those ships – a whole fleet of them – blazing into the sky, to hunt down and wipe out these aliens. We need America to win back our planet! Let the Chinese chew on that for a bit!

BACKLOW: You think that will work?

GANTRY: We'll damn well make it work! Aggression you said? Well, we know all about aggression. Just get us riled and we'll show 'em all about aggression!

BACKLOW: Yes, and how well has that worked thus far?

GANTRY: It's our scientists who've let us down. We should

fire the lot of them. And now it turns out they were probably all working for the Greys on the Moon. Charges should be brought against them—

BACKLOW: I'm sorry, who?

GANTRY: What? The scientists, of course! Hiding in their labs working on baby embryos or whatever it is they do when we're not looking. Now thank you, Doctor, this has been a real eye-opener. You just go on advising the President or whatever. After the break, folks, we'll be here with Reverend Richard Fallow, who has made a call upon our great nation for a national day of prayer – with God's help maybe we can drive the alien communists right off the planet, maybe right out of the universe. We'll be right back.

Chapter Thirteen

'Go back to the beginning of everything and you must face a choice. Mind before matter or matter before mind. Which one for you? The spiritualists will say the former; the materialists will say the latter. And neither one has an answer for what came before the beginning of everything. Before the singularity. Before the Word. Curiously, between the two, we don't know what precedes a singularity, but we do know what precedes the Word. A single, drawn breath.'

Samantha August

UN Refugee Camp outside of Gambola, Republic of Congo, June 8th

The smoke from countless cook-fires was thin but pervasive, suspended like humanity's own breath. It spanned the camp for as far as Kolo could see, from where he perched on a rickety stool beneath the awning of the temporary bar. Hunched over his lukewarm beer, he kept his head turned, eyes on the bright sunlit world and all the people passing back and forth on the lane, many singing as they carried food-packs and bundles of artificial wood.

His own tribe was somewhere out there, now broken up, now nothing but memories of a brutal time, when everything was a struggle and death stalked them all like a bush-ghost from the forest. He'd long since abandoned his weapons, and the heavy knife at his belt was getting dull from shaving kindling from the odd blocks of wood that came from no tree he knew.

Huddled in the shade at his feet, amid rotting lemon peel and spilled beer, was Neela, as silent as ever. When the heroin had run out he'd plied her with gin, but now the gin wasn't working either, although there'd been none of the usual convulsions and fever, the wild panicked eyes and the shivering. Even so, she stayed with him, and he didn't know why.

His thoughts had journeyed far. They had gone into the bush, where the spirits of old still remained. His thoughts were like children, lost and frightened in the deep forest. And in their wanderings, in the cold, damnable sobriety of his nights, they had come upon the ghosts of the men, women and children he had slain, revisiting the moments of their deaths that stood so bleakly in contrast to his life. Each instant was punctuated by a gunshot, or the spattering rain of blood as he plunged or slid his knife through flesh.

A child's thoughts struggled with words. A child's thoughts remained formless things, and he could not help but think of his own thoughts as young, fragile things, for they had led him to a new place, one he had never known before now. The faces of his slain looked upon those thoughts with pity, and that stung. For as with any child, shame was the deadliest enemy.

He had never before felt shame. There had only been need. When the soul is starving, every meal becomes a bounteous feast, and it mattered not if the taste was bitter, if it was dirt and sweat, or blood and the tears of people on their knees begging for their lives. Each morsel was savoured, and this, he now realised, made starvation itself an addiction. A soul that knew hunger knew hunger forever. Or so he had believed.

His tribe was gone. His thoughts were lost. And now his shame huddled at his feet and refused to go away.

Kolo could barely look at her. But looking inward was worse. Something clung to him on the inside, and it stank of recrimination. He wondered if this was what he had never before felt. He wondered if this was guilt.

The beers couldn't get him drunk. The weed stole the rest from his sleep. But his belly was full with real food, and that old *other* starvation – the one to do with power – had withered into dust and blown away, like a spinning spirit racing down the road. He'd lost his tribe only to find himself in another, in this camp filled with people who used to be his victims, who now laughed and sang and danced and spoke of God's unblinking eye and sure hand.

The sprawling camp itself was changing. Longer pieces of the artificial wood were now being used to build more permanent shelters – since the rains were coming. Heaps of perfectly shaped slate had appeared and roofs were being assembled, in a style Kolo had never seen before.

No murders, no gangs, no drugs, no thieving. Even money seemed pointless. He couldn't recall the last time he'd heard an argument.

Was it all as simple as this? Food and shelter in abundance, and from these two simple, basic things, peace?

Neela stirred at his feet and he looked down. She had sat up, her huge eyes fixed upon the street scene in the sunlight. Absently, she reached up to curl one hand over his left wrist, and then she spoke in her tiny voice. 'We need to walk.'

'We don't,' said Kolo. 'We're safe. You're safe. There are schools here now. I think—'

She pulled herself upright, still gripping his wrist. 'We need to walk.'

'Walk where?'

'Malawi.'

'What?'

'We need to walk to Malawi.'

'Why? It's the same there. Here and there, all the same.'

'Buy a cart. For food and water, and blankets,' said Neela. 'Then we walk.'

'Why?' Kolo demanded again, some of his old anger stirring awake.

She looked up at him. 'To save you,' she said.

He laughed bitterly. 'Girl, I'm no man to be saved.'

'You are.'

'Who are you going to save me from then?'

'From me.'

A child's thoughts often struggled with words. But sometimes they cut to the heart.

Baltimore, Maryland, June 9th

Jeff worked for the power company five days a week. He used to be on call as well but too often he'd showed up drunk on call-outs after six p.m., and his boss, who could have fired Jeff, had instead cut him out of the emergency response unit. A man with a mild case of the shakes was a man made weak and not one to cause a fuss, so Jeff had got the shit jobs.

But at least it was work. Besides, he'd been in the habit of swallowing his anger and humiliation and bringing it home, which kept things well out of the spotlight as far as his employers were concerned.

These days, when he came home from work, he hardly spoke, ate whatever she'd made for him without complaint, and then retired to the bedroom once Sally was put to bed, where he'd weep himself into sleep.

Annie felt pity, but they were slow drips, softly sizzling on the heat of a decade's worth of rage. She had lived with fear and confusion for as long as she could remember, and while the fear was gone the confusion remained, caged like an animal awaiting slaughter. Cornered, it hissed and snarled, bared sharp teeth and lashed out with long claws to slice empty air. At other times it simply curled up as if wanting to die.

Back and forth in her mind she went, and in the wake of Jeff's inability to hurt her anymore, what should have been a growing strength within her instead left her feeling, if anything, even more helpless.

Did she want to leave him? Take Sally and flee? But where would she go? Her mother was dead, her father in a hurry to join her and besides, he'd done his own share of beating on his children, and worse. Her older sister had run off and Annie had no idea where she'd gone, and that betrayal remained unforgivable.

Besides, Jeff loved her. Or at least what passed for love for her husband: a thing full of control, domination and possession.

155

Loved her like a master his slave, maybe. But that hardly mattered, did it, for the slave? Once the chains were snapped. What slave would stick around, when every memory was the razor slash of a loving whip?

She didn't know what kept her here. She could still recall, vividly, that sheet of spitting bacon fat she'd slung from the frying pan. How she'd wanted that burning liquid to reach his face. In that instant, she'd wanted so much pain from him, a single moment to answer every bruise, cracked rib, puffed up eye and jaw, the yanks on her hair, the fingernails digging into her arms. The kicks.

She would have gone to jail for that, her only regret losing Sally. And that was the most frightening thing about that instant. She would have thrown her daughter away, just to get even.

Meanwhile, Jeff huddled on the bed and bawled his eyes out, making as little noise as possible so as not to wake Sally. Annie would stand in the doorway, looking down on him, trying to work out what she was feeling.

The television said this was happening everywhere. Divorces were through the roof, as women took their children and ran away from the bastards they'd married, and those bastards couldn't hunt them down, couldn't stalk them, couldn't get near them. All the fear was gone but its legacy remained, with nowhere to go. People, it turned out, weren't as forgiving as might have been expected.

She wasn't ready to forgive her husband. She wasn't ready to comfort him, either. For now, she'd let him bleed, no different from what he used to do to her after a night's beating. It wasn't a frying pan full of bacon fat, but as far as getting her own back, it would have to do.

Besides, she already had one child. She didn't need another. Too many husbands were red-faced little children inside, turning wives into mothers they could beat up. Now they were orphans.

All those people on Fox wringing their hands and talking about the breakdown of the American family because of abortion rights or gay marriages or whatever – well, none of those things stood a chance in the face of what truth could do. The ugly truth of men who'd never grown up. And now they'd lost their private playgrounds and there was no one left to bully.

Was she now supposed to offer up a comforting arm?

Fat chance, and Fox and its crybabies could boo hoo all the way to the bank for all the good it would do.

Jeff. Poor Jeff. Time to grow up.

Los Angeles, June 9th, 1:26 PM

Anthony was out on bail. The bail had been one dollar, the judge's eyes blinking like an owl's and a small smile curving his bloodless lips. Anthony remembered looks like that, from teachers and other arseholes. It always arrived when the bastard knew that Anthony was helpless, that he couldn't do anything to hurt them.

So he was out and the public defender, who looked a lot like his buddy Paulo's sister, with that black hair like silk and those dark, dark eyes – she just shrugged and said it was getting like that on everything. Just Anthony's bad luck that the shutdown had come when it did, right in the middle of hitting a bank. If they'd delayed the attempt, she said, even one day, they would've seen what was going down everywhere. They wouldn't have bothered.

A day earlier, and they'd all be dead. He was lucky, she said. But he didn't feel lucky. He felt like a fool. Old Stubbs the bank guard had been right. The whole plan had been stupid. Those masks didn't even have holes for their mouths. Nobody understood a fucking word they said.

Okay, maybe that was funny. The cops thought so. The judge thought so. And that glint in the PD's dark, dark eyes, probably showed that she'd thought so, too. Paulo's sister never had time for Anthony. But this public defender – he thought he might have fallen in love.

The world was full of jokes. It fucked with the head. It fucked with the heart. It fucked with good luck and it fucked with bad luck. The charges weren't going away. They'd scared a lot of innocent people that day. He was starting to feel bad about that.

The day was hot but, fucking miracle, it had rained last night.

So it wasn't as hot as it could have been. And somehow the air was cleaner. It didn't have that half-dead smell that came up off the pavement like those shimmering waves that he supposed was heat.

He knew he was going to jail. But that didn't sound so bad now. Paulo had told him that all the shit that used to go on inside wasn't going on anymore. No rapes, no shivs in the back. But no drugs either. That sucked. Good and bad, then. Now prison was just a fucking boarding house, roof over the head, decent bed, three meals, and plenty of people talking shit about shit. He could hit the weights in there, put on some muscle. He could get disciplined. That was a good thing, people said. Getting disciplined.

Then he'd come out and look up Angelina Estevez, heaven's own public defender. He'd be all cleaned and cut sharp and looking good, not heading down a bad path because all those bad paths were gone.

So now he walked, on his little vacation before going up, and the pavement didn't stink and the hot was not brutal hot, and there were no wildfires in the hills so the sky wasn't hazy. There'd been rain – who could believe that? Amazing. He walked, and he felt kinda ... good. Relaxed, not bothered by fuck all. Those aliens – it was an amazing world, dammit. Even the cops couldn't beat the shit out of people anymore.

And that was a point, what Paulo kept harping on about. The 'Man' was fucked. Anthony couldn't believe Paulo used that old name for them, but he did. Probably got it from his upstate ten-to-thirty old man. Anyway, fucked and fucked up, Paulo said. The Man couldn't do shit.

And now the Mexicans were coming, only they weren't coming as much as they'd been at first, when the fences went down and that whole giant wall thing turned out to be a joke. They weren't coming so much, said Paulo, because the shit wasn't so bad anymore south of the border. The drugs were gone, the gangs were gone, the killers, too. And all those car plants that went down there for cheap labour, well, they were now making those new engines, and suddenly there was work.

He missed Paulo. His buddy had skipped bail and gone down to Mexico to get a job. How fucked up was that? People were just going back and forth and the Man couldn't do a thing about it.

Freedom, that's what this was. The aliens were fucking with the President's head, with all the presidents all over the world and all their fucking heads, too. Fucking up the cops. Armies, terrorists, dealers, fucking them all up. Hah.

Freedom, yeah, that's what he was feeling. And here was Sticks, sitting on the bus stop bench. Fucking one dollar bail.

'Hey, bro.'

Sticks glanced over. 'Bony Tony!'

'Don't call me that. I'm hitting the weights when I go in. Gonna pack some muscle.'

'Beats brains, don't it?'

'You should talk. Stubbs nailed us all in like, ten seconds.'

'They'll hit the prisons first.'

'Who?'

'The bug-eyed Martians, fool. They'll sweep us up and stick us into the mines. Weights, bro? Hah. You'll be swinging a pick.'

'If I am, bro, you'll be right there beside me.'

'Fuck that. I'm no slave. I got my way out.'

'You going to run, man? Where? Mexico? Paulo—'

'Paulo's a fool, as bad as you, bro. Nothing but fools. I'm drinking the kool-aid.'

'Kool-aid? What the fuck you talking about?'

'They ain't getting me. They ain't fucking with me. There's a bunch of us. It's freedom or death. You want to grovel you go right ahead. Have fun in the mines on the Moon, bro. Once they got you, they won't let you kill yourself. They'll just work you to the bone, Bony Tony. Weights, huh? Joke.'

'You're gonna kill yourself?'

'I'm gonna die free, bro. There'll be hundreds of us, maybe thousands. Plenty of kool-aid. You got any brains you join in, bro, for the big day.'

'Nah,' said Anthony. 'Think I'll do my time. Met a girl.'

'Bony Tony finds a girl, yeah right. Whatever. Get out of my face.' Anthony shrugged, and then walked on. Okay, Sticks

159

kinda clouded his day. Kinda pissed on it, in fact. But then, freedom couldn't stay down for long. He still felt good, and he didn't think he'd miss Sticks.

There was a lot of talk about suiciding these days. Lot of people doing it. Drunks who couldn't get drunk anymore. Addicts who couldn't get high. Take that shit away from some people, and they got nothing else to live for. He'd heard a whole town in fucking religious-freaking Utah went and did themselves in. Tried to take their kids with 'em only that part didn't work. Now the kids were orphans, but maybe that was better than having wingnuts for parents. Hard to say on that one. But lots of grief going around.

Which made it weird how good he was feeling.

Angelina was hot. He'd seen something in Sticks's eyes when he'd told him about her. Some kind of flicker. Like it hurt to hear.

Anthony's steps slowed, and then he halted. Watched the traffic rolling past, listened to the wind in the palms. 'Aw, shit,' he muttered, turning around. Talk Sticks out of it. Or try, anyway. It's what bros did, wasn't it? If it worked, fine. If it didn't, well, he bet Angelina would get all tender hearing about it, and that couldn't hurt.

'You back, bro? Changed your mind?'

'No,' said Anthony. 'But I just thought I'd tell you, before you off yourself, I mean. Paulo's sister, she thinks you're kinda hot.'

'Like fuck she does.'

'No, really, I seen her looking at you plenty of times.'

'No way. You fuckin with me?'

'No, for real.'

'Fuck, bro, and she's all right.'

'All right? You kidding me?'

Sticks half-grinned. 'Well, yeah. I mean, she's no Queen of the Tacos, is she? Steps pretty high, though, all that college shit.'

Anthony shrugged again, turning away. 'Just thought you should know, bro. She might shed some tears when you're dead, I guess. That's something, right?'

He felt Sticks staring after him as he resumed his walk.

Might have been enough. Or maybe that last bit, about her

bawling, was the wrong thing to say. Not that it was true, anyway. Julia couldn't stand Jimmy Sticks. Most people couldn't stand Jimmy Sticks. And nobody'd probably miss him once he was gone.

But none of that was reason to want him dead.

Besides, he'd been thinking about Sticks spotting him with the bench presses and shit. Assuming they ended up in the same place.

Fuck, this air smelled good!

Tel Aviv, Israel, June 9th, 10:15 PM

Ruth Moyen had a taste for Turkish coffee, sipping it through a sugar cube. Bad for the teeth, no doubt. She imagined herself in her sixties, a wrinkle-faced old woman, toothless and probably fat. Something about thinking like that, something about that old woman she'd one day become, left her feeling elated.

She was out of uniform. Wearing sneakers, for crying out loud. Dressed in a white linen blouse that showed off her sun-darkened skin. Faded jeans. She'd got used to all the heavy gear, the belt riding her hips and the way it changed how she walked, and the way the M-16 hooked over one shoulder changed the look on her face. Amazing the things a girl could get used to. Checking out David Benholm on the sly, wondering when his ticket was up. Wondering when hers was up, and was there time to get him into bed? Just one serious, scintillating fuck. Not much to ask for in a life.

That old woman, sucking coffee through a sugar cube, she didn't exist a month ago, and that was the truth of it, the truth at the core of pretty much everything. Ruth never expected to live that long. The fear had burned away and what was left was the dull expectation of it all coming down. Bullet, brick, rocket, plastic explosive, some fertiliser car flipper on the street. Or five years down the road, after her service was up, the old barrel in the mouth. The list was long, and one of them was going to take her down. Or David. Or Bennie or Sarah.

She had a cousin, five years older. Old memories painted a picture of a round-faced girl, smart and tough to make laugh

– people had to work for it. A bit of an athlete, too, was Rebecca, light on her feet.

After her stint of compulsory service, Rebecca was a different person. Fucked up in the head. Depressed. No more reluctant laughs for her. Just a chain-smoking, fucked-up mess.

Ruth wanted to look her up. Last she heard her cousin was living in a flat in the Old City, with about six others from her old unit. How did it feel, turning your life inside out all for what turned out to be nothing?

Sitting at the kerb-side café beside the bumper-to-bumper traffic, her eyes roving restlessly behind her aviator sunglasses – the old paranoia difficult to shake – she gestured for a second cup of coffee and then shook out a Marlie from the pack on the table.

At the other tables there were a few couples, eyes only for each other. And old men hunched over a backgammon game. And some guy who looked like a journalist, probably French, squinting into his phone.

Strangely, she'd lost interest in David. Just in the past day or two. As if some vital need had been snuffed out. Even stranger, she'd found a deep pleasure in sitting alone. The unit had been tight. That was a necessity. People had your back and you had theirs and that was a given, a fact, an anchor to sanity. But she didn't need that anymore, so cutting loose had just more or less happened when no one was paying attention. The whole IDF was melting, coming apart. All that mobile armour so much junk – oh, they were mothballing the works, including the personal weapons and gear. Packing up the drones, the helicopters, the jets. Just in case things went back to how they'd been before the aliens.

There was history in that caution, and she respected it. Understood it. But the thought of going back, into uniform, onto patrol, now terrified her. She'd had nightmares about it, in fact.

The coffee arrived, delivered by a young smooth-faced gawky Palestinian, the son of the café's new owner, she supposed. She smiled up at him her thanks and the blessed boy actually blushed before hurrying off.

Old women could afford to be indulgent, being toothless and all.

She wondered how Rebecca was dealing with all this. Then she wondered, with a faint start, whether she was any different from her cousin.

Well, of course she was. Not depressed, not fucked up. Sitting here on the edge of who she'd once been − before the service − that teenaged girl with the knobbly knees always dropping things. A girl who would have maybe sneered at the Palestinian kid's blush. On the edge of that, then, wondering if she'd end up going back − but no, that was impossible. Not once she'd seen and done the things they'd all had to do. No going back from that. Besides, the teenaged girl she'd been was, let's face it, something of a snob.

Life now felt more real. Still bitter-tasting every now and then. But she was breathing easier. No more tension.

After all, one day she'd be an old woman. What a thought. She fished out another Marlie and settled in for her second cup of sweet, thick coffee.

Above her, swallows wheeled and darted among the buildings with their opened shutters and billowing curtains, each flitting bird like a thought cut loose and plucked away by the warm wind.

Dar es Salaam, Tanzania, June 10th, 11:15 AM

Skirted by fishing dhows, a big tanker was making its way up the strait, likely headed for Zanzibar. The red sails of the dhows looked like the past catching up to the present, all scudding northward into the future. Casper Brunt had heard about an imam on the island, a man named Abdul Irani, from some venerable Iranian family if the name was any indication. They called him the Laughing Imam, a true child of God. He'd made Zanzibar his home. He was talking about a new Golden Age, which made him something of a rare beast. If Casper Brunt could be bothered, he could head to the rail and lean far over and squint into the north-east, and maybe see the island with that mystical, exotic name. Zanzibar.

Instead, he remained sitting in the lone chair on the spacious balcony of his ground-floor flat overlooking the muddy waters of the strait. It was paid for, a worthy investment with all that blood-money he'd earned. He shared it with lizards, bats in the joiners and four dancing butterflies circling an overgrown lavender shrub in a cracked pot beneath the air-conditioning unit.

The air-con was on full blast, keeping the room behind him nice and cool. Water dripped from the unit onto the plant. Better than a cruddy pool of goo on the linoleum. He sat with a cold beer cradled in his hands, still in shade despite the climbing sun.

It was an odd thing, feeling utterly safe. Not a target for anything. He'd been an infidel with guns on offer, making for a curious détente when dealing with warlords and Muslim militants. Now that he had nothing to sell, he should have become a target for third world wrath. Instead, he was just ignored, and that, too, was an odd feeling.

Even shaking fists got tired eventually.

Aliens. Still hard to believe, but then, he'd witnessed their capacity to interfere. The unseen hand that slapped down, tsk tsk, time to be a better man, son. Time to shuck off the old ways, the business as usual, the playground antics of brokering war. Sure, the causes remained. People were still aggrieved, still pissed off, still feeling cut out and dumped on. But even poverty had lost its teeth.

He'd been hearing things, hanging out down at the almost-attached Firefly Bar with the half-dozen ex-pats and arseholes on the run who inhabited this eyesore block of condos. Food like manna, water that purified itself, diseases that just went away. Eyesight to the blind, the works. The Serengeti off-limits and more animals than ever ranging the vast park. Elephants keeping their tusks, gorillas their hands and feet.

And now some kind of construction project was happening in Malawi. That bit of news was a cause for alarm, to be honest. Were the aliens finally assembling their strongholds? If so, there was nothing anyone could do about it. The edifice was going up, building itself. The whole thing surrounded by one of those forcefields. Word was, it was going to be huge.

Casper was curious, curious enough to maybe head down there

to see it for himself. Still, why Malawi of all places? Mysterious doings indeed.

He had no money coming in. His accounts were dwindling, his investments damn near worthless. He should be panicking.

But that was the least of his problems. No, what was bothering him the most had nothing to do with money, or even a future in which his skills were irrelevant and unwanted.

The endless gaggle of prostitutes and beauties for hire was getting stale. The misery of it was, he was lonely. Chasing the deal had been one of those all-consuming distractions, and it had been one that carved cold edges on a man's soul. Being heartless had been a necessity, with a conscience nowhere in sight.

But now it seemed that the landscape of his mind had changed. The bleak, airless wastes were in upheaval. He saw mountains ahead, monstrous and looming, and he knew he'd have to climb them sooner or later. Each step a slog through unfamiliar emotions. Guilt. Shame.

Regret.

These details told him the aliens had done more than just fucked with ecological preserves, food and clean water, diseases cured. They had somehow got into his head, tinkering with the cold machine of his self-interest.

Or was it just a philosophical thing? The sudden shock of realising that you were no longer the centre of the universe, not even your own universe – that little sphere of ego that consisted of – mostly – the fucking voice in your head talking to itself day and night. A whole life of internal blathering away that probably ate up more energy than anything else you ever did.

He had a vault packed full of precious excuses and rationalisations for everything he had done or would do. His own private hoard of justification. Worthless. Fucking worthless.

The beer had gone warm in his hands. The butterflies were chasing each other, the same thing they'd done yesterday, the same thing they'd do tomorrow. Until they laid eggs or mated or some shit like that, and then died. If there'd still been a puddle under the air-conditioner he'd find them in it one morning, floating like dead flower petals.

In the strait the tanker was angling out of sight, losing itself in the heat haze of midday. The dhows had found a school of fish to chase with their lines and hooks. The big Portuguese trawlers that had been looting this coast for European dinner plates had all left, sans nets and all the other stuff that didn't work anymore.

The local catch was showing up in the better restaurants, and then in the neighbourhood dives and on market stalls. Bounty dropped the prices. Everyone was eating better. The whole she-bang reeked of paradise.

Supply was controlled by the market and the market was a global game. It mostly took from the have-nots and then gave it back to them at inflated prices, then hoarded the money earned to create a standard of living bubble that made rich people into gods. Need had proved a fertile field for extortion. He'd lived on the rich side of all that, or, rather, he'd planned on living on the rich side, after one more deal, one more windfall.

He'd had his target. He'd been almost there.

But the aliens were stepping around the market, ignoring the old rules of civil extortion (not that it was ever actually civil at all). All the guns and threats that kept people down didn't work anymore. Seven billion restless souls were now shaking awake.

He wasn't sure that was a good thing. Most people were un-educated, ignorant, and at least half of them below the mean in intelligence – an obvious observation that still offended people.

Casper had been happy enough preying on stupid people, profiting from them. He'd sold weapons to idiots who had little or no chance of ever winning. Whatever it was they wanted to win, and a lot of them didn't even know what the fuck that was. Most of them just ended up liking all that firepower, warlords or warlords in the making. People who even if they had a religious cause were in truth more interested in the high that came with terrorising other people than they were in making life better for anyone except themselves.

The need to control others was probably at the core of it all, and that need came from insecurity, and the world was full of insecure people who'd defaulted to the delusion that making everyone think like them would quell that insecurity. It wouldn't. Couldn't. The shit inside never went away.

He'd sucked them all dry. Made a career of it.

Casper set the beer down. It'd gone flat anyway. He'd pack up his grab-all this evening. Tomorrow morning he'd book a flight to Lilongwe. Rent a car and head down to Zomba. Check out that alien construct.

The Laughing Imam had announced a pilgrimage to the site. Casper wanted to beat that crowd, and be long gone by the time they arrived.

By tomorrow that tanker would come back down the coast. Crammed full of pilgrims.

Meanwhile, the butterflies could keep on dancing. The fishermen could keep on fishing. And all the wankers down at Firefly could keep grousing. The world had ended, but something was coming.

Still, the lavender smelled good. A sprig of it to slip into the long hair of a beautiful smiling woman would be rather nice, too.

He should be feeling worse, but he couldn't do it. Just couldn't and damn, wasn't that a thing?

Silver Steading Farm, Utah, June 14th, 8:35 AM

It sounded simple, logical even. This planet was for sharing. It wasn't a grab-all, wasn't a global land-rush, wasn't that horizon beyond which waited the promised land. Promised? Well, maybe that was where all the trouble started.

The kitchen looked normal enough. The usual appliances and countertops. Dave sat in it no different from what a normal man would do, this time last year or the year before. Or even a decade ago. He was in a scene that Rockwell might have painted if he'd been still alive here in the bright twenty-whatevers, and he'd fit right in, too.

Nostalgia was god when the scene inside a man's head showed a house on fire, bodies in the yard, and a sky full of smoke. But none of that internal world of strife bled out into this room, with its dripping tap, ticking clock, and all that stunning sunlight pouring in through the window above the sink.

Then again, Dave considered, who knew what hid beneath those sweet brushstrokes of paint? Entire realms of regret, all the wounds of youth, all that innocence and wonder crushed underfoot by the grisly advance of years. So, even nostalgia ended up being nothing more than a cute mask hiding the brutality of the past.

He needed to get out of his head, but all the ways of doing that didn't work anymore. Well, maybe that wasn't true. Evelyn was in the White Room upstairs, its house-spanning length fronted by glass offering up a scenic view of the backyard and the valley and the hills beyond, but she wasn't paying any attention to that. No, her eyes were on the screen of her laptop as it filled her head with an entire world's worth of panic, pointless speculation, fear-mongering and rumour.

Crowd the skull with stuff and who needs drugs or booze? Information had no intrinsic value. Sufficient quantity made quality irrelevant. Information, Dave now knew, was its own drug, and the brain was an addict that could never get enough. So it could be then that Ev had found her own way out, so that their own story – here with their lost land and crushed ambitions – blended with all the other stories out there, until it sank from sight, taking the pain with it.

They'd talked it out. They'd brought Mark and Susan in so it was a family thing. Explanations to put that look of fear into their children's faces, because dread news always came from grown-ups and the helplessness of a parent was the last lesson a child would ever need.

How much of a life was consumed by the sheer effort of coping? Day in, day out, doing all it took, whatever it took, just to get by. Claw your way through, like a drowning man fighting a riptide. Reach the beach if you can, there on that island called sleep. So the mind can run away for a while. Getting ready to tackle the next day.

He was drinking coffee. He hated coffee. Their nest-egg was gone and foreclosure's fatal blow was next. But even that wasn't cut and dried. It wasn't like the bank could turn around and sell the land, could it? Either way, the investment was a write-off, and if any compensation ever arrived, it would be for the bank, not David and Evelyn Ketchen. Because that was how the world worked.

Or used to.

Now? Who knew?

Last night, Ev had been excited. She'd been saying things that Dave thought had more to do with reassuring the kids than being possible, even though all the technical terms were clearly way over their heads. It had to do with financial structures and what some economist was calling market disarticulation, the plucking and prising apart of all those things once interconnected. The dismantling of the entire global economy, and what it meant for investment strategies and asset relocation. Of course, the bitter pill at the very end was the one investment deemed safe in terms of value: real estate.

But Ev had simply laughed, waving away that advice. 'No! It's idiotic. It's one last grasp at the straw. Value? What's that even mean now?' Her face had been flushed, offsetting her golden blonde hair in a way that had reminded Dave of that one skiing holiday in Banff all those years ago, before they'd sworn off planes and started up their ledger of carbon-heavy frivolities that they could do without. 'Dave, are you listening to me? We have to stop thinking in the old way. That's all going away.'

'And are we?' Mark had then asked. Twelve-year-olds had a knack of getting back to the point. The things that needed doing. It was a whole other side to his son, one that Dave had never seen before. The dreamer suddenly pragmatic, like throwing a switch. But it wasn't a switch Mark should have felt the need to make. He'd done it because his dad was too broken to utter a single damned word. The boy took over from the father, but Dave had been too numb to feel any pride. Too self-pitying, to be honest.

'We don't have to go anywhere at all,' Ev had said, smiling down at her son, and then at Susan, whose teenaged misery had just found new heights of despair at the prospect of a different school, a different town or city or, as her desperation went over the edge, a refugee camp on the Canadian border. 'Don't you see?

The bank can't kick us out unless we decide they can. They can't evict us.'

'So what do we eat?' Susan demanded. 'How do I buy clothes? Make-up? Get my hair done?'

Ev had blinked. 'Suze, you've never bought make-up in your entire life. And anyone can cut your hair in that style – it's a brush-cut for crying out loud. You wear second-hand jeans and—'

'*That's not the point!*'

'Look, darling, we still have the garden and the greenhouse. And besides, you've seen it online. No one goes hungry. No one at all.' She'd paused, to take them all in with incredulous eyes. 'Are any of you getting it? It's all changed! All of it!'

All right, then, Dave had wanted to say. *All right, then.*

But what do we do? With our lives. What the fuck do we do with our lives?

Too numb to talk, too past caring to feel, too pathetically eager for sleep's blessed oblivion.

Her enthusiasm sputtered and died on the dining room table. In sudden anger, she'd thrown up her hands and stood. 'Fine. You'll figure it out sooner or later. I'm going to bed.'

But she hadn't gone to bed. She'd gone back to her laptop.

How would she take it, he wondered, when the internet service went down due to unpaid bills? When all that information stopped tapping her dopamine? When the howling silence filled her skull?

It was a normal kitchen. All the usual appliances, the dripping tap, the ticking clock, the sunlight pouring in. Yet it was packed solid, so solid with its invisible truth that Dave could barely move.

Destitution. Like concrete settling, still settling. You couldn't see it from this angle, but a single nudge of the chair, and you couldn't see anything else. He had a reason for not moving. This was it.

Chapter Fourteen

'Ah yes, the search for consciousness by dismantling the
brain. I'm not the first to pose the question this way,
but when was the last time you dismantled your radio
looking for the little guy doing all the singing?'

Samantha August

'Beliefs provide the unseen, rarely examined scaffolding upon
which attitudes, opinions and certainties are founded,' said
Adam. 'They are held to be self-evident and unassailable. Most
conflicts, no matter the scale, are essentially a clash of such belief
systems. Does this seem obvious, Samantha August?'

'Yes,' she murmured, eyes on the screen where ER and ambu-
lance attendants were wheeling out covered corpses amid flashing lights and a blustery wind, with the banner beneath the live
feed scrolling past announcing the total number of dead at eleven
hundred and twenty-six.

'The manipulation of power is an ancient force among human
cultures,' Adam went on, 'and from these early battles of will, a
tribe comes to define itself, its range of acceptable behaviours,
its taboos, its daily rules of conduct. These are the foundations
of belief systems. Conformity becomes a pressure invoked with
every passing moment. Rarely is it recognised that the most
insidious element of this system is to be found in the earliest
triumphs of power. All that follows is thereby tainted. Samantha
August, you seem to have disengaged with us.'

'Eight hundred and seventy-three orphans,' she said.

'When selfishness becomes a pathology there will be many

innocent victims,' said Adam. 'Religious conviction can, if unchecked, lead to a form of ego-centrism that dehumanises everyone else, and would make of them little more than symbols, each one sacrificed to a single ego. In this sense, you return once more to the many reprehensible expressions of unconstrained power. In the case of these mass cult suicides, such power is denied in the only manner available to you.'

'Children don't understand any of that,' Samantha said. She pulled her attention away from the screen, rose and began pacing. 'To them, it's just Mummy and Daddy going away forever. Abandoning them. And now strangers surround them, offering blankets and sweets.'

'I cannot refute your observations, Samantha August. Nor can I reasonably defend the necessary limits of my intervention with regard to voluntary suicide. Such acts are the supreme expression of free will, after all. As to the human wreckage left in the wake of these acts, I have no defence.'

After a long moment, she shook her head. 'I need to talk to my husband. I need to sit down with him, late into the night, talking until the silence finds us. Then I'd go outside and watch the sun rise.'

'Your husband is being electronically monitored.'

'Of course he is. Canadian government?'

'Curiously, no. American.'

'Oh, right. Sovereignty is a one-way street when you've got the biggest gun.' She paused. 'Can't you block them?'

'I can. This will of course escalate their panic.'

'And in the old times, they'd then abduct him. But they can't do that anymore, can they? So block them, Adam. Leave them to their panic.'

'Very well. A physical visit between you and your husband, however, could prove difficult.'

She shook her head. 'I know. Never mind that. But enough of these text messages. I want to hear his voice. I want him to hear mine.'

'Understood. Preparations have begun to enable this. In the

meantime, Samantha, shall we resume our discussion of religious crises in the wake of my arrival?'

She sat back down on the bed, rubbed at her eyes. 'Good grief, how can faiths so strongly held prove so fragile?'

'They hold up the entire house of cards in which one lives, Samantha,' Adam replied. 'The fragility is more pervasive than it might at first seem to be. The fiercer the certainty the more vulnerable it is. Our arrival and Intervention has shattered that certainty for many of your kind. One must then examine the details of those convictions. To begin: humanity stands alone between God and the beasts of the wild. Two: God's grace of the awakened soul is a gift given exclusively to humanity. Three: the defined institutions of human religion each purport to be the singular legitimate path to God. Four: your planet is the sole home of God's chosen children. Five: human domination and superiority are both by the will and desire of God.'

'Right,' Sam interjected, nodding behind her hands. 'One: humanity does not stand alone between God and the beasts of the wild. Two: the divine spark has scattered far wider than is believed, thus diminishing our sense of being special. Three: there are myriad paths to God. Four: we're not unique and God's children occupy countless planets in this universe. And five: this one is the real kicker, because it knocks us off that pedestal from which we justified our every act of domination as being righteous in the eyes of God. Because you show up, change the rules, and make it clear in no uncertain terms that we're not in charge anymore.' She looked up. 'Is that about it, then?'

'Too often the virtue of humility is confused with shame,' said Adam. 'That said, there is plenty to be ashamed about.'

'Ouch.' Then she managed a dry laugh. 'Don't you get it yet? The shameful things are the first things swept under the rug. History is constantly revised. Truths pared down, crimes whittled away.' She shrugged. 'But how much of that is a survival mechanism? How much of that keeps us sane?'

'How much of it permits the continuation of crimes, the repetition of atrocity, the persistence of patently destructive behaviour?'

'Careful,' she murmured, 'you're showing the fangs behind that benign smile.'

'Imposing denial seems to have elicited the fiercest responses, Samantha. More so than any other form of intervention. The Exclusion Zones are already being accommodated. The ending of all wars and military conflicts has already begun redefining diplomacy, compromise and negotiation. Even the global market is adjusting, as best it can, to the closure of numerous industries. Governments are redefining their roles as bastions of stability, triggering unprecedented examples of co-operation. The core value systems of political parties continue to evolve.'

'And yet.'

Adam was silent for a moment, and then the AI said, 'Indeed.'

She returned her attention to the scenes on the screen. 'Freedom or death. The number of suicides is growing at an exponential rate—'

'Not universally, Samantha.'

'No.'

'Cultures in which collective precepts successfully counterbalance individualism are proving more adaptable to the Intervention.'

'Some people just don't like being told what they can and can't do.'

'Some people use that line to rationalise being arseholes.'

Samantha barked a surprised laugh, and then shook her head. 'Those people don't like being called out. Used to be, the media would do just that. But then the media got co-opted, bought up and now toes the party line. About the same time we lost our collective ability to be so outraged by things that we actually did something about them.'

'Individual freedom among humans was lost a long time ago, Samantha. What remains is but an illusion, a cherished one to be sure, but nonetheless an illusion. Now, may I ask, what is the primary factor responsible for ending human freedom?'

'Economics.'

'Yes. Capitalism is founded on the selective application of freedom among the few at the expense of everyone else.'

'But every time it's dragged down, Adam, what takes its place is just as ugly, if not uglier.'

'Not this time,' the AI replied.

'Promise?'

'In economic terms, Samantha, what happens when there is too much of something?'

'It loses value.'

'Yes. What would happen when there is too much of everything?'

'The economy collapses. But ... too much of everything except freedom.'

'The value of freedom has never been truly expressed in economic terms, for the simple reason that freedom as an absolute has never existed,' Adam said. 'But let us set freedom aside for the moment and return to notions of scarcity and post-scarcity. As you stated, when there is too much of everything, the economy collapses and a value system based on exchange must find a new paradigm. Now then, in place of the economy as humans recognise it, what arises within a post-scarcity scenario?'

'I don't know.'

'Why, Samantha, the answer is simple. Freedom. Freedom arises, in a manner not yet experienced by humanity. What remains to be seen, of course, is what you will do with it.'

She considered that. In her world, in her time, words had lost so much power that despair ever threatened to overwhelm her, although even in that instance, there was an imbalance, as hurtful words retained their ability to savage a human soul. But those of compassion seemed pretty much dead, buried beneath layers of well-earned cynicism. Virtues were readily adopted and corrupted, making a mockery of such things as fairness, integrity and compassion. As Adam had just intimated, the arseholes were winning the battle, souring the world for everyone.

Yet, beneath it all, there were unspoken words. Those beliefs, core assumptions, unchallenged convictions, that collectively asserted the veracity of being self-evident.

When they weren't.

The Intervention was challenging humanity at that base level, dismantling those unspoken assumptions, proving their false-hood. The notion that *it doesn't have to be that way* would need to gain ground on *that's just how it is*. She wondered if that was even possible.

'Your husband's television has been engaged to permit the two of you to see one another and speak in a less constrained manner.'

'The television? Hamish never watches television.'

'He has taken to doing so in your absence, and given the extra-ordinary events being reported on a daily basis.'

'He's watching the news? Good grief, he's really in a bad way.'

'Again, my apologies.'

'Oh, and our television doesn't have a camera, so how exactly are you pulling this off?'

'Blanket agency.'

'Ah. Right.' She stood, faced the nearest screen, and then paused to straighten and smooth down her clothes. 'How do I look? Never mind. Oh, and is there anything like privacy here, Adam?'

'Of course. Once the link is established, I will block out this room. When you are ready to resume our fascinating discussions, Samantha, simply call my name and this will re-establish connection.'

She watched the images of the suicide event flicker and then fade. 'Don't hold your breath,' she muttered.

A moment later she was looking at her husband's shocked expression.

•

'. . . and I said I'd do it. But now I'm not so sure.'

The expression on her husband's face was solemn. It was, she suspected, the same expression so many of his patients saw. He was listening, not saying much, but listening. That first rush of delight, relief and pleasure in this contact was now past, and Samantha found herself working through a litany of feelings, confessing in ways she had rarely done before. She was a com-petent, confident woman, after all. She didn't do flustered. She didn't do flailing around, either.

'Those children, Hamish. Those orphans.'

He slowly nodded.

She scowled in return. 'For crying out loud, say something!'

He took his time to gather his thoughts. His hands, cradling a glass of whisky, looked sculpted by Madame Tussaud. They hadn't moved at all which was something of a relief, since drinking was not her husband's forte. Of course, these days, the prospect of abuse was no longer an option. Even so, the psychological lure could still exist, the one that simply used whatever was at hand, be it alcohol or morphine or whatever.

'I've sat with enough families,' he finally said, 'telling children that they would soon lose a father, or a mother. And if only one parent was left, then I was telling them that they would be orphans.' He paused, and then sighed. 'The generational turnover. It comes at those precise moments, Sam, when the child takes the place of the parent. When the line is drawn anew. One moment still in front of you, the next right behind you. Just like that.'

She thought about it. 'Okay. But usually those children are already grown up.'

He shook his head. 'Age makes no difference, really. Oh, true, if they're very young, there's the question of whether they even comprehend the notion of death. But someone "going away forever", well, they do get that. And so they run the idea through their heads and you see that passage in their eyes, their faces. Loss, Sam, it's universal.'

'Parents getting sick. That's not quite the same as parents killing themselves. And what happens when those orphans finally find out that their parents tried killing them, too?'

'Yes. That will be hard.'

Sam felt a surge of anger, of resistance, flaring up inside. It wasn't the first time. 'This First Contact has blood on its hands. Driving people to extremes, ruining lives, crushing hopes and dreams. Hamish, how can I be party to any of that? What happens to my conscience?'

He sat back with a heavy release of breath. 'Conscience, yes. Well, let me tell you about conscience. To be in the medical

177

profession, Sam, is to be constrained by things we should never be constrained by, not if we want to make our Hippocratic Oath actually mean something. Even here in Canada, we have a hierarchy of response. The most expensive is invariably the rarest, and often the last resort. That applies to pharmaceuticals, diagnosis, treatment – the works.' Those hands finally moved, finally broke their waxen immobility as he set down the glass, and then held them up in a helpless gesture. 'I listen to a bunch of symptoms from a patient and is my first thought to schedule an MRI? Well, no. If I did, and if every other GP did, how long the lag time? And what of the cost? Those units don't come cheap, and they wear out.'

'So the system sucks.'

'The system is what we made it, Sam. Everything dependent on cost and availability. Even as we're all stuck inside it, we continue to sanctify it, and we break the hidden rules at our peril.'

'But you don't lose sleep over it.'

His brows lifted. 'Don't I?'

Samantha didn't say anything for a few moments, and then she sighed. 'Hamish, I didn't know.'

'You weren't meant to.'

'Men!'

His answering smile was wry, the one she loved so much. 'Women! Conscience can't be relieved by talking about it.'

'Tell that to the Catholic Church!'

'Oh no, darling.' He was shaking his head. 'I seek neither forgiveness nor absolution. Instead, day by day, I work to redress the imbalance. Besides, I care for my patients. Every one of them. And those families I sit with, telling them the bad news ... I'm not indifferent to their grief, because I feel it, too. That loss hurts. And more than once, after they've all shuffled out, I've sat behind my desk and cried. That, Sam, is my penance. It's not much. It's private, probably selfish, but it's what I've got.'

'I don't know what to do.'

His smile returned. 'Think fiction, darling.'

'What do you mean?'

'It's your required dark night of the soul.'

'Hah hah. Only this isn't fiction and I'm not a protagonist. This is me, Hamish, a batty crone with an acid tongue. Or so I've been described, more than once.'

'From you shall wisdom come forth.'

'That's a fake quote if I ever heard one.'

He shrugged.

'I still don't know what to do.'

'Are you asking me?'

'I don't know. Maybe.'

'Are you asking what I'd do in your place?'

Her gaze narrowed on him. 'You know I hate the subtext of that.'

He answered with an expression of mock innocence. 'Would that be the subtext referring to asking a man for advice?'

'Good thing I love you for the bastard you sometimes are.'

'Ouch. Grammar, darling.'

'Fine, I withdraw all requests in that area. Besides, you're right. Whatever you'd do in my place is your business.'

'And what you do now is yours.'

'It just goes to show how unsteady I am right now, to fall into that kind of thinking. I know, habits of preconditioning in a patriarchy and all that.'

'Uncertain is the way ahead.'

'Thanks, Yoda. Can I quote you on that?'

Their gazes locked, and after a long moment, he held up a hand, palm towards her, as if to reach through the television screen. Samantha's eyes welled up. She reached back towards him.

Her dark night lay ahead, and she knew – by the look in his eyes – that he would sit with her through it, and nothing more needed saying.

STAGE THREE:

The Elegance of Ennui (Rejection)

Chapter Fifteen

'There was a time in our deep past when materialism and spiritualism were one. One day we'll return to that, and the idea of a bleak, empty, mechanistic universe will seem both quaint and woefully naïve.'

Samantha August

Irony was not a strong point in the American psyche. These days, it was generally met with outright hostility or the recoil of the honestly wounded. As a Nigerian, it had taken Simon Gist a few years living in America to move away from the very British legacy of exquisite irony as a way of life, and to understand that the most powerfully ironic elements in his new home were, one and all, unintentional.

The American Dream was one such concept. Born of genuine truth and an article of faith, a cornerstone, in fact, of the great American experiment, it had in fact become ironic, probably as early as the mid-sixties. A dream in the true meaning of the word: never to be reached, never to be realised by the majority of Americans, whether native-born or newly arrived.

He had set about stripping away that bitter irony, because he refused to reject his belief in that dream. Books had been written about his meteoric rise into the realm of wealth and fame, serving up as articles of faith that dreams need not die. But more often than not, such unauthorised exposés missed the point. Somewhere along the line, not yet tainted with irony, the American Dream had lost its moral compass. Wealth became the goal, the means to it irrelevant. A grab-all fuelled by cold ambition and avarice. And what was celebrated was hollow and lifeless.

Simon sought to resurrect the ethics that gave birth to the American Dream. The desire to make the world a better place, a freer place, not held on to selfishly but for the good of all. To take a firm grip on the heavy rope of humanity and drag it forward into civilisation, making that civilisation a place for emancipation, equality and enlightenment.

He'd begun to believe he was achieving such a thing, despite the tide's resistance – that upswell of embittered dream-killers who clawed and tugged and yearned to drag him down into the mediocre swill, who hunted for weakness and followed every scent of blood offered up in the dark currents.

The machine of capitalism was, in his mind, the only one that worked, and so he used it – better than most – to make his dreams real, striving to elevate first the country, and then the world, into that sublime city on the hill.

Now, as he stood on the floor on Warehouse Seven, with his chief engineer at his side and his personal aide, Mary Lamp, on the other, he began to have doubts.

The mostly featureless unit before them was box-like, barring one side where a recognisable gear mechanism hummed with virtually no vibration, the gears a shimmering blur of efficiency. It stood on a metal trestle that normally would have been bolted to the floor against an engine's combustive hammering, but for this new creation there was no need for bolts. The trestle was utterly motionless.

They stood barely three feet away. Apart from the air convulsing around the whirring gear, there was no other indication of the prototype's vast power. No heat, no smell barring that of lubricant and metal. Yet this single unit had the output capacity to run the entire plant.

It was, in short, incredible.

Yet he stood unmoving and unmoved, his mind mired in confusion.

The aliens' gift was moral perfection. Clean, cheap to construct, emission-free, seemingly without the need for fuel. Its presence shattered the world. It would cleanse the air, silence the low roar on every freeway. It would slow the derricks to a desultory throb. It would close petrol stations, send cashiers and attendants to the unemployment line, shut down all the fuel industries, the makers of coolants, spark plugs, water pumps, radiators, engine blocks, pistons. It obliterated the clout and power of OPEC, wiped clean the political and economic expedience of countless conflicts over energy sources (not that they hadn't already been shut down). An end to oil spills and contaminated ground-water, black tarry beaches lined with dead and dying birds, bloated fish a rotting carpet on the waves. An end to filthy, carcinogen-laden air, to the free radicals and organic volatiles being spewed out from exhaust pipes every moment of every day across the entire world.

How one gift could take so much down left Simon feeling numb, punch-drunk.

There would be resistance. Just like those idiots who altered the exhaust systems of their pickups to belch out black smoke in defiance of climate change, there would be cults of combustion, hold-outs insisting on their petrol and diesel vehicles. Convoys of Hummers on the highway, American flags waving from their antennae. People might even expect the price of a barrel of oil to drop through the floor, allowing a return to the petrol-guzzling muscle cars of yesteryear. But the price of oil wouldn't collapse at all. Oil was still needed, to make plastics, lubricants, pesticides, though Simon suspected that subsequent gifts from the aliens would do away with those in time. No, the oil industry would persist, gasping, staggering, for a while yet, and the price of their product – now hoarded with a vengeance – would sky-rocket in a self-destructive flare to light the sky before darkness finally closed in on an industry that had been fuelling progress for over a century.

He could see this future, laid out, a drunken stumble, a wavering of hands seeking purchase.

And, buried beneath it all, a sonorous bell announcing the death-toll of capitalism. Because its tenets were no longer true, no longer self-evident or deemed inviolate.

He stood before a product that could not be patented. If what Jack Butler had told him was true, the engine could be built in a garage. Or it could be scaled up, replacing nuclear power plants, hydroelectric dams, coal-burning plants. It could be used to replace solar panels, wind and wave generators, nickel-cadmium batteries, pacemakers. Cheap with the potential to be ubiquitous, it was the definition of capitalism's poison apple. No profit could accrue from this creation. What it offered it offered for free.

True freedom was the enemy of capitalism. Because scarcity meant restriction. Scarcity was the bedrock. And now they were witness to the beginning of the end of scarcity. Here, in America as much as the rest of the world, freedom was now the enemy. How to reconcile such a thing? How could America, that self-proclaimed bastion of liberty, come to terms with itself? When real freedom arrived to sweep away the false freedom it had lived with since the nation's birth?

He had no answer, but he suspected that that reconciliation would prove messy. The American psyche was about to be cut to the core. The rest of the world to greater or lesser degrees would suffer the same, a tumbling of dominoes seemingly without end.

And yet, if he squinted, he could still see that house on the hill. Civilisation's shining beacon of hope. They just needed to find a new path to take them there.

Jack Butler rested his hands on his hips, cleared his throat and said, 'Well?'

Simon Gist nodded. 'Okay. Roll them out.'

'For the Kepler?'

'For everything.'

Jack's thick brows lifted. 'The Infinity-3?'

'Everything.'

After a moment, Mary Lamp said, 'NASA wants to get someone up there as soon as possible. They're looking for a rocket.'

'Forget the rocket. We'll take them up using the emissionless fuel-free Engine. Make the call, let them know.'

She nodded as if she'd already known what he'd say.

'It's something, isn't it?' Jack said.

'Something,' Simon murmured. 'Yes, that.'

186

The machine hummed, a steady, relentless sound. He felt its pressure, like a wall remorselessly pushing forward. Be crushed or move with it, stay a step ahead, always a step ahead. He longed for the optimism and excitement that had begun this whole thing, the burgeoning fires of possibility. These things had not vanished, but they seemed out of reach right now.

'We'll have to massively scale up,' Jack said, 'for the Infinity.' He rubbed at the short bristle on his head. 'Still can't tell you exactly how it works, though. EM fields for sure, but also some kind of quantum shit going on.' He shrugged. 'We can in-house all the components now, so that should speed things up. We won't beat the Chinese, though. They're sticking with conventional fuel rockets for their lift.' He paused to clear his throat again. 'There are application folders in the file, for propulsion in vacuum and high-end output regulators, but we haven't cracked those open yet. Our low orbit plans only needed thrusters, after all.' He glanced at his boss. 'You're sure about this with NASA? It's a publicity stunt and it's probably going to end with a flop. Some astronaut floating around up there with nothing to do and no one to talk to except the boys on the ground.'

'I know, but that's not the point. Not for us, anyway. We use this as a proving ground. Take a peek into those application folders, see how complicated it's going to be. A highly manoeuvrable, full space-flight-capable Orbiter could push us past everyone else. Back in the lead.'

'You want that?'

Simon nodded. 'It's something to strive for.'

Jack frowned, exchanged a look with Mary, who then spoke, 'Simon, what's this about?'

He sighed. 'Money was the means, not the goal. You all knew that. Making it gave us what we needed to keep pushing. To make the world a better, cleaner place. To get us off this damned planet. I know we had to shelve our Mars project. But that was because we weren't ready.'

'No serious investors, either,' Jack said, grimacing.

'We weren't ready,' Simon insisted. 'We would have found the investors. The point is: profit was never the bottom line. Never *my* bottom line. Means to an end, that's all.'

'So what's changed?' Jack asked. He gestured. 'This baby will cut costs on – on everything. For the Infinity-3, our payload potential has just gone through the roof. No fuel tanks, no fuel – that's eighty-three per cent of total weight. The EFFE won't have to mass more than a metric tonne to give the necessary thrust to escape orbit, and that's with a packed cargo bay. The only thing that needs proof is the power-distribution nodes, and that's basic mechanics and simple programming. We can do a lift at a fraction of the cost we've been aiming for.' He threw up his hands in evident frustration, clearly still not comprehending Simon's angst.

'The Chinese think they are heading for a technological windfall,' Simon said, wondering himself what it was he was trying to explain. 'Those bases on the Moon. Now, maybe the Greys' stuff is not fully compatible, or it's a nightmare to reverse-engineer. But I'm beginning to suspect it's all a red herring.'

'Why?' Jack demanded.

'Because our new friends up there leave the Greys in the dust when it comes to technology. And I don't think they're done with their gifts to us.' He shook his head. 'These are momentum killers. Do we just sit back and wait for the next mind-blowing package to show up on our computers?'

His chief engineer said nothing, but Simon could see the man's finely honed mind suddenly at work.

Mary Lamp slumped slightly beside him. 'Fuck,' she said.

After a long moment, Simon sighed and then said, 'Okay. We do it like this. We convert the fuel tanks to a habitat module. It stays on the ship. No separation procedure. Sure, we can prove our concept by giving NASA a ride, but we prove it with a new aim in mind. We're taking the fucker to Mars. Well, Phobos first. Then Mars.' He looked to his companions. 'And I'm on that crew.'

Mary's brows arched. 'First human to set foot on Mars, Simon?'

'You're looking at him.'

'Back up a step,' Jack said. 'We're rolling out EFFEs for the Kepler car too, right?'

Suddenly, Simon's mind was racing. He could see a way

through, if only ET would let him get there. 'Sure, but it can't be a priority anymore. Our ground vehicle can't offer people anything different from what they're going to get from big auto in a year or two. That said, we can use the battery technology as back-up aboard the Infinity – oh, we need to modify the project's name to reflect the new direction, I think. Any suggestions?'

'No direct reference to Mars,' said Mary. 'Not if we want to get a jump on everyone else.' She eyed Simon. 'You mean to win this race, don't you?'

'If I can. If ET doesn't drop a fully functional FTL flying saucer on the front lawn of every house before we even get off the ground, that is.'

'Infinity A-1,' said Jack. 'Ares One. But no one's gonna ask what the "A" stands for in something as generic and obvious as A-1. We pitch it as a prototype spaceflight-capable lifter and lander. A baby step project. A logical progression but also ambitious enough to suit our reputation.'

'Go with that, then,' said Simon. 'Set up the parameters, Jack. Pick your people. In the meantime, we run the blind that is the Kepler, knock out EFFEs and look for related applications.' He smiled. 'Just like everyone else.'

'There's a Grey station on Phobos,' said Mary, who then shrugged at their surprised expressions. 'I surf a lot. The Russians confirmed that two of their probes headed for Phobos were deliberately knocked out a few years back. Stands to reason ...'

'If it's abandoned we'll take it over,' said Simon.

'Christ,' said Jack, 'how big a crew are you looking for?'

'That depends on how long it takes us to fly to Mars, and you won't know that until you crack open those files and we get some idea of thrust, velocity, mass and all the rest. Ideally, I think we can fit eight.'

'Eight? Holy crap. You're talking a tight squeeze even with the expanded habitat.'

'I know. So get us there as fast as possible.'

Mary began taking notes. 'I'll mock up the pitch to our investors. Spaceflight-capable lifter and lander. The Infinity A-1.'

She paused and looked up. 'We could lose them all after this, you know.'

'To be honest,' Simon said, turning away, 'I don't see money mattering for much longer.'

•

The vast financial empire of James and Jonathan Adonis was in free-fall, and Lois Stanton found herself in the peculiar position of being an orchestra leader conducting a symphony with the entire orchestra sinking beneath the waves. The horns were blowing bubbles. The violins were a chorus of drowning cats. Yet she delivered her every gesture with flair, her baton (a simple ballpoint pen) a dancing metronome of disaster. She was, she realised, having the time of her life.

They sat before her in the high-rise boardroom overlooking the grey city, backs to the deepening sky as the day went down. The two men who had deliberately chosen the surname 'Adonis' to mark their intended ascension into godhood ('Dunsall' resisted elevation) now had the bearing of mortal pretenders, clawing and scrabbling at the foot of Olympus. Dust and sweat now defined the limits of their realm and the rising tide of their advancing years had finally crashed over them. They looked old, getting older by the minute, sallow into decrepit, too many hammer-blows to their world – the world with them positioned at its centre. If their children hadn't turned out to be such wastrels, they'd be jostling each other right now for position come the inevitable inheritance.

Well, this legacy had just been cut off at the knees.

Pity was a strange emotion to be feeling, when looking upon these two men. Not only strange, she amended, but also minuscule. If she was being honest.

The staccato style of their typical and definitive duet monologue was struggling to get started. Now it was James's turn to try again. 'Positioning is still key.'

Lois nodded and made a note.

'Anticipatory,' Jonathan snapped, jabbing a finger to underscore his point.

'Predictive qualities,' James said, frowning. 'Think Tank's at a loss. Got the best eggheads on the science, getting nowhere. No plug to pull.'

'Fuck the Think Tank,' Jonathan said in a growl. 'Fools. Invalid algorithms. The alien tech pay-over is tiered. Very clever. They'll only ever give us what's a step below their own. It's a classic strategy, maintains control.' He paused and cracked a brittle smile at Lois. 'We're abandoning that angle. No purchase, no foothold we can find that puts us at an advantage.'

'Loss leader,' James agreed. 'We play the old angle. Financial backing behind the curtain. Pushing who and what we want to the front of the stage. Politics still belongs to us.'

Lois assumed that James's 'us' referred to him and his brother rather than humanity. They didn't think in those terms.

'Puppets,' Jonathan said. 'Dancing to our strings.'

'Always been that way.'

'Always will. The old fallback.' He smiled again at Lois. 'Read much history? It's there, or not there, since most of it stayed behind the scenes. Kings, queens, empires, popes, caliphs, holy emperors. Front pieces. Financiers ran the world. From the very beginning. Our kind. Making the big decisions. War, peace, both profitable, all down to positioning before, during and after.'

'No reason,' added James, 'for any of that to change. It's biological. Built in. Genetic. ET can't change our natures. Someone always needs to be on top or nothing gets done. Civilisations fall to dust. People vanish. Like the Mayans.'

Lois refrained from pointing out that the Yucatan and a lot more of Central America was in fact still full of Mayans. The civilisation might have fallen, but the people who'd built it remained. Curse of the History Channel and its dumbed-down mandate.

Then again, the wild-haired Greek guy was having a field day.

The brothers were nodding at their own assertions, both finding more solid ground in their thinking. James felt so emboldened as to actually lean forward, elbows propped, lacing fingers together. 'We're divesting all the loss leaders. Moving wholesale into real estate.'

'Real estate,' agreed Jonathan. 'Physical ground, real buildings, infrastructure, more solid than money. Even the run on gold and silver: doubtful. Real estate.'

'We buy it up,' said James. 'Everywhere. Buy it up. Industrial parks. Mothballed factories, manufacturing, assembly plants, distribution centres.'

'Transport facilities,' added Jonathan. 'EFFEs in the tankers, people-movers, the migrations. Charge low and pack them in. For the good of humanity.'

'Nice sell,' James said, with a sharp nod. 'For the good of humanity. Unproductive deserts, abandoned refugee camps.'

'Buy it up, all of it. Vacated land, dirt cheap.'

'Leverage with scrap, non-monetary exchanges, government agreements, taking it off their hands. We'll do the clean up.'

'We say that. We don't do it. Why bother?'

'ET does it, the cleaning up. Nano-shit, stepping in and cleaning it all the fuck up. Happening right now. Spills. Settling pits. Contaminants. We're the new leaseholders. We're the new rug for countries to sweep the shit under.' James unlaced his fingers and pointed at Lois. 'Getting this?'

'Of course,' said Lois.

'Play the helping out angle,' Jonathan said. 'Sell it through stability. People are crying for stability. Here, the old rules still in play. No change there.'

'Reassurances,' added James. 'By the time this shakes out we'll own half the fucking planet.' His smile to her was far less pleasant than his brother's.

Jonathan now stood, announcing a shift in topic. He turned to the window and stepped close to look down on Manhattan. 'Rumours,' he said. 'Magical cures. Healing. Maybe even youth pills. Eternal youth.' He faced her. 'Find those pills. We want them.'

'The pills,' she repeated, not making it a question, but just to be sure.

'Pills,' James echoed from where he sat across from her, inadvertently licking his wrinkled lips. 'Eternal youth. Access should be prioritised.'

'Worthy people,' Jonathan elaborated.

Lois glanced down at her notepad. She wrote: youth pills wtf?

Fuck you ET if you let these guys live 4 fucking ever. Time for you to turn into the psycho kid stalking ants on a sidewalk. *DIE! DIE! DIE!* And she underlined the last *'DIE!'* with a flourish of her pen before folding up her notepad.

'All covered?' James asked.

'All covered,' she replied, smiling.

•

This was too good to believe, Douglas Murdo told himself as he watched the feed from the latest mass suicide. Yet another fucked-up religious cult in some arse-end town in Oklahoma deciding to go all in. Bodies in orange bags, children with the thousand-yard stare in their oversized eyes.

He was running this shit everywhere across his media empire. Asking the killer questions. Who's next? Seen your neighbour lately? Seeing any kids alone in a playground with the sun going down? Whiff of gas from next door's kitchen window? Cars gathering dust in underground car parks?

ET was killing people in the thousands. Sure, it was all self-inflicted, but who led those people there? Who stole all their choices? Who crushed their freedom, their rights, their hope? Who led them into such soul-destroying despair?

See what happens when the last freedom left to you is taking your own life?

Maybe the resist campaign had been a mistake. Bad timing. Even passive resistance went nowhere when there was nothing to resist. About as effective as trying to stop time by breaking all the clocks. No, it just went on, and on, tick by tock by tick. Forcefields and new engines that needed no fuel. Food and clean water seemingly conjured up from nowhere. Not a shot fired, not a fist let fly. And still the damned aliens had yet to land in their giant ships, turning the waiting itself into a kind of weapon.

'While we kill ourselves,' he muttered.

'What's that, love?' Chrystal asked, pulling out an earbud and looking at him inquisitively.

If only that expression didn't look so gormless. Ignoring her, he closed the lid on his laptop and leaned back to study the emerald waters of the Caribbean. Women who made the same faces little girls made started palling after a while. Could be time for a divorce. The prenuptials would keep it pretty painless, and he'd be generous with the maintenance package, since being an arsehole after the fact was tactically unwise. Pissed-off exes had secrets they could sell, or let fly in vengeance. Sure, he could shut the taps on most outlets, but it'd go viral anyway. And he was getting too old to have to shovel through that crap.

Maybe he'd just turn to her now and say it plain. *Just grow up, will you?* But in the end it wasn't really her fault. People learned to use what worked, and they learned most of it while still kids. And when it stopped working, why, they didn't know what to do.

Growing up meant finding other things that worked. Smart people figured that out. Dumb people never did, and never would. He'd seen shrivelled old women wearing the same outfits as their granddaughters, for fuck sake, same hairstyles, same high-heels, same make-up. The female version of the mullet, baggy shorts and flip-flops.

Buddy Joe with his beer cases and sports on the big screen with the junk food all laid out and his old high-school chums on the way over for another belching belly-heaving weekend, pick-ups parked in a row on the driveway, yeah, it was a fucking commercial for getting nowhere and not caring if you never did. And this was the world. At least in America, Australia, the UK and probably Canada, the lifestyle power-houses of the Western world. At least in their own minds, anyway.

His customers. His audience, his eager people ready to lap up whatever swill he offered them. That granny, those beer-guzzling bros.

What ET was going to change all that? Hell, even God couldn't change all that. Maybe he was panicking over nothing, after all. He could keep relying on humanity's natural laziness, its unquenchable thirst for entertainment and not much else. No reason to expect any of that to change.

'I want to go to LA,' said Chrystal.

He grunted and then said, 'Sure. Do you good. People. Parties.'

'Maybe another photo shoot,' she said, nodding. 'It's boring doing nothing all the time.'

He glanced at her. 'No, you're right. It is, isn't it?'

'I said so, didn't I? Are we arguing?'

'No, babe. I'm agreeing with you. But it makes me wonder, if it's boring doing nothing all the time, what's with all the people doing just that?'

'Huh?'

'Maxwell,' he said. His son was out on the deck, fat arse splatted on the chair as he surfed the net. The boy only moved to get another bowl of fucking ice cream. Oh, and for the occasional shit, presumably. 'Streaming sitcoms and formulaic cop shows, watching YouTube and checking the latest Facebook trend or Twitter feed — it's all a fucking black hole.'

'So give him something to do.'

'No.'

'Why not?'

'I'm waiting for him to give himself something to do. Whatever happened to ambition? Desire? Hunger? Where's the fucking *drive*?'

'But, honey, you took it all away.'

'The fuck I did. Not up to me. It's what's inside.' He waved. 'All this shit, it's just window dressing. Proof of success. It's not a fucking free pass to doing piss all with your life! Look at you, wanting to go to LA, wanting to find some work. It's not for money, is it?'

'Honey, I do it because it's the only thing I'm good at. And I know it won't last, either. That makes me anxious, but you don't want to hear all about that, do you? You've got your own stuff. I'm just your window dressing, right?' And she smiled.

He studied her with an increasingly narrowed gaze. 'Like you say, darling, a trophy wife.'

Still smiling, she replaced her earbud and resumed doing whatever it was she did on her phone day in, day out.

Douglas returned his gaze to the Caribbean, feeling, for a brief, startling moment, unaccountably proud of his wife.

Out on the deck of this lone spacious house on its own little island among the cays of Belize, Maxwell tracked the world via the internet. His old man's fixer, Jorgen Pilby, had been flown out yesterday, too sick to keep working and possibly wasted enough for it to be life-threatening. Dad's last words to the man had been an unsubtle rumination on firing people who let him down. There was no virtue in being crass even though the terrifying Douglas Murdo had made a career of it. Maxwell was always astonished that his father had not taken a fist to the face, not once, in all these years.

Maxwell had considered doing it himself, on occasion, only to conclude that it was too much effort. Dad was getting old. Time's fist was adding its own scars, and poor old Pops was stumbling into the tenth round and on his battered face the bleak realisation that no champion lasted forever. Death hadn't lost a fight yet, no matter how long it took.

Still, it wasn't pleasant seeing his father's memory starting to fracture. His brother Bernard was seriously worried, especially with the media empire tottering along with every other industry as the market floundered for purchase.

Of course, what used to follow a financial crash – the destitution, soaring inflation, shortages, people losing their homes and all the rest – wasn't really happening yet, or at least not playing out the way it used to. All those other times, people felt pushed off the escalator, free-falling to be sure, but always aware that the great big machine still churned, the gears still spun, and eventually everything would settle, the market would right itself, and the climb could begin all over again. The escalator never stopped, in other words, *because this is how it works*.

Now ... maybe not. Maybe never again, and wasn't that a mind-blowing thought?

Unlike his father's obsessive trolling of his own news sites and all the suicide stuff going on, Maxwell had been watching scenes of chaos in a Florida courtroom, as fundamental precepts of jurisprudence slowly imploded. It had begun as a simple appeal following a minor conviction that had also been a third strike for one Marshall Giminez, and the life sentence slapped down on the man by a judge with no real leeway given the state law.

Society recognised a need for punishing a criminal act. Firstly, as a punitive isolation of the convicted criminal, away from the common benefits of living freely in that society. Secondly, as a public deterrent, the necessity of harsh consequences being seen by all. And thirdly, as an affirmation of social order and propriety. Break the lives of people who break the law.

Lurking behind all of that, of course, was the lust for vengeance — in whatever form was permissible, and sometimes in forms less permissible. *If I'm struggling and doing right by the law, it's got to mean something. Try cheating that struggle, then you fucking pay. Got it?*

All of this made sense. The bitter joke was, back before ET, few people even believed in it anymore. There was no crime if you didn't get caught, or if when you did get caught, you were rich or important or a white college student with a great future ahead of you. The whole thing was corrupt, a sham, and everybody knew it.

His father's news empire's army of anonymous editorialists loved the lust angle, the whole vengeance thing, but they played it as farce (not that the majority of viewers and readers even realised that); in fact, Pop's media gamed it with all the brutal judgement of the truly sanctimonious and all the cynicism of the untouchable. Hypocrisy was water off a duck's back for all those braying, frothing pundits of outrage.

And the readers and viewers lapped it all up.

But where was vengeance now? It seemed that incarceration was still possible, yes, so ET apparently recognised the punitive aspect of criminal transgression. Sure, the death penalty was gone. Couldn't be done anymore, and no one on death row seemed much interested in committing suicide for the good of society, which left a lot of horrible human beings in limbo, though presumably being out from under the shadow of the executioner was its own kind of salvation.

Still, humanity needed its belief that people got what they

deserved. Well, certain people, for certain things. There weren't any generals on death row, were there? No presidents, no spymasters or drone operators either. But those murderers in their isolation cells in state after state, country after country, they'd one and all slipped the noose.

Leaving what?

Poor Marshall Giminez of 1824 Lipton Way, Fort Lauderdale, and his lone public defender, with their argument for a dismissal of the life sentence on the grounds that he could never again commit a crime (no one could!) and had already served time eight months in excess of the maximum sentence allowed for driving an uninsured vehicle while under the influence of alcohol, had inadvertently kicked open a can of worms that could bring down the entire justice system.

The state Supreme Court had just handed the ball off to the Federal Supreme Court. Lawyers – already divesting themselves from the practice of criminal law – were now circling like sharks and dusting off long-lost appeals, pleas for clemency and outright releases of convicts serving time. Prisons had turned into dinosaurs overnight, with the comet bright in the night sky.

Suicide had lost its moral framework of right and wrong. It was the last act of violence allowed to humanity, a singular and final gesture of self-harm. What did that do to the law? A collapsing star, one rather poetic legal analyst had noted, that could either become a black hole or go supernova. Either way, what would follow was anyone's guess.

So Maxwell sat in the refreshing sea breeze of a Caribbean swathed in vast stretches of Exclusion Zones, musing on prison, that sprawling industry of inhumanity. There was another current swirling beneath everything else, and that was *fear*. Violent criminals got sent away because they were feared, or, rather, because society feared their freedom. But now the fear was gone.

Pops would have people fearing ET and the truth was, there was plenty of reasons to fear an entity that could shut down every act of violence, including what was needed for self-defence. Humanity was like a beaten whelp of a dog lying on its back, throat exposed to a possibly capricious alpha male. For the moment, it seemed ET was content with that submissive pose, but a single wrong move could see the whelp's throat torn out. After all, Pop's media outlets screamed, who knew the mind of ET?

But this kind of fear felt as remote as the aliens themselves, unseen somewhere in the dark of space. Maxwell did not think all the suicides had anything to do with fear, except perhaps in the context of a visceral terror of all those old behavioural outlets suddenly shut down. When you had nothing inside except the need to dominate, subjugate, show off your swagger or even shovel heaps of hate online, and then in a flash domination ended, bullying vanished, swagger became a cause for derision, and all that hate went nowhere and threatened no one, what then?

What then? Where do I go from here?

Killer questions, and if no answers arrived, despair could take hold of a soul and crush the life from it.

People were killing themselves because they saw no place for them in the world to come, no future that looked anything like the past, and the end of that comfort made suicide the only response.

The curious thing was, most of these victims were doing it in groups, in cults of rejection, refusal, resistance – Pop's catchy media chant turned on itself, becoming a mantra for giving up on everything. Seemed these people needed company for that final gesture.

The solo offings were, to Maxwell's mind, more disturbing. There weren't many of them, and these loners went quietly, without fuss. In their old lives they weren't bullies, or arseholes. They weren't filled with all the hate that comes with the private fear of personal inadequacy. So, what were they seeing that drove them to the blade, the pills, the hose in the tailpipe?

Aggression was innate, genetically programmed into the struggle for survival and success. So said the sociobiologists. Whatever forms human society took – through all of history and back into prehistory – it all boiled down to competition, to succeeding over others, often at their expense. People fought to make room for themselves and that had been going on forever.

Animals did the same. Insects, too.

Is it typical human hubris to think we're different?

Problem was (or so he'd been reading, getting ever deeper into the philosophical discussions online), that sociobiological tact had been employed as an excuse for virtually every reprehensible act ever committed by one human over another, not to mention the human war against the environment. All genetically programmed, built-in absolution. Apparently, the much-vaunted human mind was little more than a slave to reptilian impulses carved into the DNA.

Now, if ET believed that, then it was in the process of conducting a protracted invitation to universal suicide and, ultimately, the extinction of the human species. All without a single alien appendage being raised. A clever, almost poetic proof of humanity's deterministic, self-destructive fate.

And then, with the world expunged of its dominant, most vicious species, ET could finally land its colony ships, to set up in the fecund garden of humanity's absence.

There was a chilling logic to that.

Maybe the solo suicides were people who'd seen too clearly the future awaiting this planet. People who didn't want to stick around to witness the grisly demise. Or maybe they simply understood that without aggression, and all its outlets, humanity was doomed anyway. Like pulling wires out of the magneto coil, the engine couldn't run. All progress halted, all ambition nullified, an end to dreaming itself.

The optimist needed aggression as much as the pessimist. Both engaged with reality as if it was an adversary. Faith decided the outcome. For the pessimist, it was the faith that nothing would – or could – succeed, which in turn sought to drag reality down to confirm the veracity of that belief. For the optimist there was the faith that things could be better, that life could be improved, that no one need lose in the future's game. And so they pushed against reality, seeking to raise it ever higher.

Fight, struggle, defy, refuse to surrender: all definitive traits of life. Refuse to yield those faiths: it seemed history was the tale of that push and pull, and yet, how often had optimism led to calamity? How often had pessimism fed cynicism and thereby guaranteed that the worst that could happen, did happen?

What the hell is ET up to? Shutting us down like this?

Everyone was asking, but no answers seemed forthcoming. Was humanity meant to work it out for itself? Just what kind of fucking First Contact was this, anyway?

Frustration and anger had the internet boiling over.

Idly, Maxwell wondered if people who believed in God spent their whole lives asking these same damned questions, and just like ET, God wasn't offering up any answers.

He sighed and straightened to stretch his aching back.

Time for another bowl of ice cream.

●

'Don't know about any of you out there,' said Joey Sink, 'but I thought getting out of jail would feel great, so why doesn't it?' He paused, winked at the steady red light of the webcam. 'Hey what, Joey? Did you get sent up for something? That's what you're asking, right? Nah, I only been living in the same world as the rest of you. You know, the prison of fear. And now ET's gone and unlocked the door and out we stumble, blinking in the sunlight. So, you tell me, how does it feel for you?'

He then moved to lean forward, only to pull back again to keep his visage centred in the camera's eye. 'Now you're saying "oh yeah, Joey? What about ET? That's something to fear! So we're out of one prison and into another one, Joey!" Well, maybe so, and maybe that's why I'm not dancing on this desk-top.' He shrugged. 'Hey, got some callers ... hold on, here's my old foul-mouthed buddy, King Con. Hey there, bro, let's hear the latest miracle, just keep it PG – whatcha got?'

'Venus is getting hammered!'

'Sorry, what's that?'

'Impacts, man. Icy comets. Wham wham wham! And there might be a big old asteroid now orbiting the planet—'

'Hang a sec, bro, got Annie Mouse rapping on the window here. Bet he's got something to say about your claims—'

'Claims?' King Con said. 'It's happening, man!'

'Annie Mouse, how you all doing at JPL or wherever it is you are?'

'Hi, Joey, and hi there, King Con. You had it right, mostly. We've already had a rain of rubble from broken-up asteroids, presumably helping to blanket the frozen carbon dioxide covering the planet's surface. Now, these icy asteroids aren't full impacts. They're grazing the atmosphere, being busted up into snow and hail and making multiple passes. Which makes sense. You don't want heavy kinetic impacts on the surface of the planet – not if you can help it. The challenge, beyond just cooling Venus down by shading it, is the runaway greenhouse condition of the atmosphere. The shade turned the carbon dioxide into snow, which was the start of things. But what's left up in the atmosphere still needs settling down. You need water – rain and snow – to start taking out the suspended corrosives – the sulphuric acid. The whole thing is pretty amazing.'

'Wow,' said Joey before King Con could cut in, 'unbelievable. We gonna have ET as our new neighbours? Solar system's getting a bit crowded, ain't it? I mean, that's like, *our backyard*.'

'We don't know why Venus is being terraformed, or who it's meant for,' said Annie Mouse. 'Not to say even us techies aren't panicking every now and then. But well, it's all out of our hands, isn't it? Maybe it does feel like someone's setting up digs in our backyard, it's not like we planted a flag there—'

'The Russians did!' King Con interrupted. 'Only it burned up. Still, they fu– frickin landed there like, *decades* ago!'

'Hardly relevant,' Annie Mouse replied. 'It's all out now anyway, but we were facing serious prohibitions when it came to our space programme, and I don't mean just the funding cuts. Getting multimillion-dollar technology swatted out of the Lunar and Martian skies put a damper on our plans, you know. So, what I'm saying is, it's not all our fault, know what I mean?'

'Sure sure,' King Con said. 'That really sucked. Still, you'd think ET would cut us some slack precisely because of that. Out of our hands, right?'

'We don't know if Venus is being terraformed for them or for us,' Annie Mouse said again.

'For us?' Joey managed to interject, tapping the mute temporarily on King Con's feed. 'Wow, you really think it might be for us? A whole new planet to mob and mess up?'

'It's like this,' explained Annie Mouse. 'Overpopulation is driving climate change here on Earth. The one primary cause that no one talks about, instead going on about air pollution or whatever – don't get me wrong, that stuff was bad in its own right. But overpopulation, Joey, that's your elephant in the room. So, if you're really going to bring down global warming, you need to address the fact that there's too many people on this planet. The fix? Give us another planet, an empty one. One about as Earth-like as we can get. And we won't be able to screw it up like we did the Earth. You honestly think there won't be Exclusion Zones on Venus?'

'Oh man,' laughed Joey, 'that's a brain-trip, Annie. But what's got you thinking ET's going all soft on us? Haven't you been reading the news out there? We're killing ourselves everywhere and ET's not doing a damned thing about it!'

'Actually,' said Annie Mouse, 'most of those cult suicides are going on here in the States, and one small one in Alberta that may have had more to do with the jobs lost with the end of the Tar Sands. Sucks to admit it, but it's *our* country's that losing it. Most of the others are managing just fine.'

Joey released the mute on King Con. 'Hey, King Con, what you think?'

'Hey, bro, if I'm gonna rail I'd appreciate it if you didn't gag me.'

'Sorry, bud, but this is my show, ain't it? But you're clear now. What have you got to say?'

'Aw, it don't matter. Maybe Annie's got it down. Let's frickin hope so. Otherwise, it could be Day of the Triffids from Venus. Hey, Annie, I was gonna ask – what's going on around Mars?'

'Not sure,' Annie Mouse replied. 'Deimos and Phobos went crunch, softly. Barely a cloud in their wake. May have picked up a few more chunks of rock, too. But we're not seeing any wholesale climate tinkering going on with Mars—'

King Con's interruption sounded smug. 'Try IR, buddy.'

'I'm sorry – IR? Infrared?'

'Planet's heating up,' King Con said. 'Just slip some IR film into your telescope, man, and take a pic. Got that news from some amateur, beating you all to the punch. Planet's getting hot, Annie. My pal's guess is the core's heating up, going molten again, and when that happens there's gonna be a new electromagnetic field around Mars, something strong enough to hold an atmosphere. It's baby steps on Mars, but it's happening!'

Annie said, 'Uh, signing off, Joey. Thanks, King Con, we'll get on that – too much obsessing on Venus going on over here. Later!'

'Well,' said Joey as Annie's feed went dark, 'how about that, folks? Stuff's happening out there, for sure. Whew! What next, I wonder? This is it for me right now. Later, King Con, and thanks as always, bro.'

'Anytime, Joey.'

'Put a plug in for Joey's Kitchen Sink, folks, and see you next time!'

Chapter Sixteen

'The belief that all you need to do to create sentient
artificial intelligence is to keep piling on the processors,
is dependent on a belief in a mechanistic universe, a
universe without God. But if the quantum folks are right,
consciousness lies at the heart of the discriminatory
definitions that make the universe work the way it does.
And once consciousness is recognised as a necessary
component to the creation of reality, we are facing one of
two choices: either the universe didn't even exist until
the arrival of humans with the capacity of perceiving it.
Or, our consciousness is not the only consciousness in the
universe. In which case ... hello, God.'

Samantha August

The President of the United States sat glowering at his Science
Advisor. He'd never much liked scientists, with their superior
airs and that technical gobbledygook they were spouting all the
time. And even worse than the ones with verbal diarrhoea, he
now amended, were scientists who talked straight. 'What do you
mean, we haven't got a rocket?'

'The Russians said no, Mister President,' Ben Mellyk replied.
'And we've never had any luck dealing with the Chinese. Besides,
they're launching their own in two weeks.'

Raine Kent turned to Daniel Prester. 'This is ridiculous. We're
the technological leaders of the whole damned world, and we
don't have a rocket?'

The Director of Homeland Security shrugged, making it clear that this wasn't his bailiwick.

Ben Mellyk laced his hands together on the table before him, drew a deep breath, and then said, 'Mister President, the United States no longer leads the world in technology, not in its production nor in innovation. We haven't in some time, to be honest.'

'Really.' Raine Kent's tone was flat. 'And how did that happen?'

'Our education system sucks. At all levels, sir.'

'Passing the buck, huh? Fine, do that. So what's wrong with our education system, Mister Scientist?'

'Dropping standards, underfunding, the transformation of universities into businesses, lack of job security for university professors, a burgeoning sense of entitlement among attendees who used to be students but are now customers ... shall I go on?'

'No,' the President replied. 'I want it fixed. Who's my education weenie?'

'Harcourt,' Albert Strom replied from the other end of the table, where he was now in the habit of taking refuge. 'John Harcourt. One of your first appointments, Mister President.'

'Oh, him. Well, what's he done so far? ... Anyone? Nothing? He's done nothing?'

'The Democrats keep filibustering—'

'The Democrats are all over education! Every third damn quote from their caucus is about education!'

'Yes, sir, but their policies run counter to Republican principles.'

'Republican principles? What, a whole nation of stupid people? Is that a Republican principle?'

'Besides,' added Strom, 'it's primarily a state matter. Education, I mean. Our party typically gets in on the promise of tax cuts, mostly. I think—'

'I want a fucking rocket!' Raine Kent shouted, slamming a fist on the tabletop. 'An American rocket! Not a Russian rocket, not a Chinese rocket, not Indian, not French, an *American* rocket!'

Ben Mellyk cleared his throat. 'Well, there's Simon Gist—'

'What, that black guy with the English accent?'

'Nigerian, originally.'

'He lives here in America, right? So he's American now, isn't he? Shit, don't tell me he's a Muslim.'

Ben shifted uncomfortably in his chair. 'Not that I'm aware of, sir. In any case, he has his Infinity project, low-orbit, low-cost lifter. I think they're working on the third iteration at the moment, though I can't tell you what their schedule for the next launch looks like. Still, sir, that may be our best hope now that Lockheed's overhauled their whole programme to make use of the EFFE.' He let his words trail away, seeing a slightly glazed look in his president's eyes.

'Low orbit, low cost? That sounds like something you buy in Walmart! The guy's Nigerian? You really think it's going to work? Didn't he crash one? Didn't the crew die? We don't need another disaster on the launch pad. Look, I've got my astronaut! All I need now is one simple ... goddamned ... *rocket*!'

'Kepler Industrial may be our best bet,' Ben Mellyk said again.

'Kepler? Wasn't he American?'

•

The conference room was well soundproofed, so all Colonel Adam Riesling could hear from where he sat in the antechamber was the occasional wordless bray from the President.

The air-conditioner was doing its best to keep him cool in his uniform and his dress lid rested lightly on his thighs. His three-year stint flying missions over Afghanistan was beginning to feel like a cake-walk given the utter snafu of this mission. NASA had been trying to angle away from plucking fighter-jocks for its astronaut programme, and lacking a PhD in anything remotely useful, Adam had always considered himself a low bet.

There was a nasty rumour out there that the President had picked him out from a stack of PR photographs – the same package sent off to the rare elementary school that gave a flying fuck about the US Space Agency – and that it had been his All-American Midwestern chisel-jawed, sandy-haired good looks that had decided the President.

Adam had made a habit of being honest with himself, and he

suspected the rumour was probably pretty much dead on. The flying side of things he had down. Same for the engineering expertise, a necessity for anyone entering the programme. But crash courses from ambushed anthropologists and exobiologists in frumpy clothes seemed less than ideal for what could be the first human to alien face-to-face contact in history.

Well, the first contact not involving cave men or tribal priests or pharaohs or Incans or people named Ezekiel.

And now they were bringing in linguists and psychologists and sociologists and priests and the whole thing was turning into an unholy mess.

Whatever argument was going on in the conference room continued, and Adam worked hard to keep his hands from tracking the rim of his hat. He was here with a mission of his own, after all. One last pitch for a co-pilot. He didn't relish the insane prospect of doing all this solo, flying up there alone – really, who did that anymore? Not since the first slew of Gemini astronauts back in the 1960s.

There were about a dozen candidates to choose from – space station veterans one and all, although the run of protracted stays in micro-gravity made most of them high-risk options for another high-g ascent into orbit (a detail kept mostly quiet for PR purposes). And if there wasn't another qualified newbie in the pipeline because of the last round of funding cuts, then grab someone from another country! A friendly. Some Brit or Aussie or Canuck.

Now, Adam considered himself a brave man, and he'd do his duty, and if Gordon Cooper did it solo then by God he could, too. But Gordo wasn't heading up to talk to ET, wasn't heading up to knock on the door like an unwelcome insurance salesman, wasn't on his way uninvited and not knowing if he'd get a wave on in or a proton beam through the forehead.

Unfortunately the man running the country wasn't good with taking advice, and just how scary was that?

So, it turned out that one chump was expendable, but not two. Adam knew he had all of NASA on his side, and Mellyk as well, but maybe it was Mellyk getting the dress-down in there right now.

These days, the voice of reason was down to a whimper. A million people were on the march to DC at the moment, a million bemused, bewildered, frightened people. They wanted something from the leader of their country. Exactly what, no one could say. At least, not coherently. If it all got boiled down, Adam thought, it might come out as 'we want to go back to how it used to be. Please?'

Alas, the President didn't have that power. No one did.

Somewhere up there were the representatives of a civilisation from another planet, a distant planet, who had conquered the cold depths of space, figured out a way around the limits of light-speed, the physical damage of zero-g and radiation, the psychological stress of living in a tin can surrounded by the merciless vacuum of space.

And dear God, how he wanted to meet them.

Hopefully, that counted for something. Up there, down here.

As a last gasp chance, there were about a thousand fighter pilots with shit-all to do. All Adam needed from the President was the go-ahead to make some calls.

It was either that or Tom Hanks.

•

The Director of the CIA was ushered into the conference room through another entrance. Kenneth J. Esterholm was seventy-four years old, a bookish company-man bureaucrat who had been recruited at Stanford in his graduate year of a Master's degree in what was then known as Communications. His finest skill was in patronage. These days, the lure of retirement had become a deafening siren call, one he was ready to heed, possibly within the next hour.

Even as he slowly lowered himself into a chair, the President jabbed a finger at him and said, 'What's with these ET buildings popping up all over the world, Ken? And more to the point, why not here in the United States? What have all those foreigners got that we don't?'

'At the moment, Mister President,' Kenneth began as he laid

out his binder and carefully opened it to reveal hand-written notes, 'what they have that we don't are those strange buildings.'

Raine Kent blinked at him. 'Is that supposed to be a joke?'

'No, sir. We've done an analysis, seeking commonalities among the target countries. There is none. Malawi, Kazakhstan, Egypt, Greece, Haiti, Argentina, Korea, Norway, Canada. In each instance, the constructs are rising in relatively remote areas, often on contaminated ground—'

Ben Mellyk leaned forward. 'Excuse me, Ken, you said "contaminated ground". Can you describe the nature of the contamination?'

The Director glanced at the President, seeking guidance, but the man's famous television glower remained unchanged. Kenneth referred to his notes. 'Post-industrial for the most part. Heavy metals, oil by-products, various leachates. Or over-fertilised farmland. Or denuded scrubland. Basically, dead or dying ground.'

'And the construction material?' the Science Advisor asked, pulling off his glasses to wipe the lenses.

'Some form of concrete, I believe, but otherwise basic. They're going up in recognisable fashion, or so our engineers tell us, just without the need for workers. Any additional determinations are impossible due to the forcefields.'

'Hmm,' mused Mellyk, 'curious.'

'That's it?' Kent demanded. 'That's all you got?'

'Well,' the Science Advisor began, squinting through the lenses before resuming wiping them, 'self-assembly requires raw materials, one presumes. All over the world we're witnessing the breaking down of contaminants, accelerated clean-up and rehabilitation. Even nuclear waste. There has already been a measurable decline in carbon dioxide in the atmosphere, as well as other greenhouse gas parts per million. Some of this material can indeed be broken down, but not all of it.' He paused and squinted at Kenneth Esterholm. 'If I had to guess, the contaminants are being recycled, and that concrete mix is mostly sequestered carbon dioxide.'

'They're building these things out of thin air?' Kent demanded.

'Why yes, literally.'

'Now isn't that exciting?' the President said in a half-snarl, and then he thumped the tabletop. 'No. It isn't. Who cares how they're being built?' He pointed again at Kenneth. 'What are they? Prisons? Killer robot assembly plants?'

'We don't know, Mister President, because we can't get inside them. All we can tell you is that they're big, they're full complexes, suggesting multifunctionality. They're ergonomic in the sense of human scale – entrances and whatnot. And they all seem to possess a very large enclosed compound, with massively thick twenty-metre-high walls and a seamless concrete base or floor. Whether these plazas remain open-aired or will be subsequently roofed over, we don't know. The engineers don't think so, however.'

'Prisons,' said Raine Kent. 'Good thing we're not getting one. Or is it? Maybe they've written Americans off? Slotted for extermination?'

'Sir,' ventured the Director, 'we don't think they're prisons.'

'Why not?'

'For one thing, there are not enough of them. Unless, of course, the aliens just want a representative sample of humanity, in manageable numbers.'

'A fucking zoo?'

Kenneth shifted uneasily in the chair. His voice was dry as he replied. 'One hopes not.' He referred to his notes again. 'Each site shares certain similarities. The variations seem minor. There is a main building, with a footprint equivalent to ten or so football fields. Outer buildings, each one about a football field's worth of floor-space, are connected by solid, broad concourses. In many ways the complexes have the appearance of university campuses crossed with assembly plants.'

'Brainwashing centres,' said Raine Kent, both hands curled into small, white fists on the table. 'And killer robots.'

'Ken,' said Ben, glasses finally back on, 'back to these compounds. Are those high walls completely enclosing them?'

'Uh ... no, one side is made up of multistory buildings, each

211

one linked by walls at the same height as the purpose-built walls on the three remaining sides. In other words, no gaps.'

'Are there windows on the buildings facing onto the compound?'

'Apparently not.'

Ben Mellyk sat back, nodding.

'I swear,' said the President to his Science Advisor, 'I will personally rip your head off in the next ten seconds if you don't explain yourself.'

'Launch pads,' Ben said. 'We really need a sample of that concrete.' He sighed. 'Never mind. These complexes are, in my opinion, space centres.'

No one spoke.

Kenneth Esterholm had looked at more satellite images of missile launch sites than he could remember. Now he pulled out the drone shots from directly over the building sites. Then he sat back. 'Damn, I think he's right, Mister President. There are outbuildings here that could be barracks. And these ... mission control? Over here ... training centres, with classrooms? The manufacturing buildings could relate to hands-on training and familiarisation. The main building? Administration, perhaps?'

'No fucking rockets!' Raine Kent bellowed, rising from his chair and planting both fists on the table. 'And now, no fucking alien space centre!'

'Well, sir,' Ben said, 'we have our own.' He glanced at the Director of the CIA. 'There's your commonality, Ken. Those countries – they either have no space programme infrastructure or those that do – like Canada – use *our* launch sites.'

'But these alien centres are massive,' Kenneth objected. 'Nothing we have comes even close.' He tapped the pictures before him. 'These things, if they're indeed what you say they are, they're designed for thousands of ... of ...'

'Students? Candidates?'

'Barely literate candidates?' the President said incredulously. 'Malawi? Kazakhstan?'

Ben Mellyk shrugged. 'We return, once again, to the unknown alien value system. Who qualifies, who doesn't? We have no idea.

I have only a hypothesis here, gentlemen. Space centres, training complexes. Not for aliens – they don't need any of that – but for us.'

'Not *us*,' Kent said in a growl. 'Not *Americans*.'

'Perhaps we're expected to make use of our existing infrastructure, Mister President. Our own centres, plus our universities, our military academies, air force bases, proving grounds. We will, of course, have to adapt, and quickly, since we're not getting any obvious jump-start from ET.'

At the far end of the table, Albert Strom said, 'Imagine, Mister President, making that announcement – the largest national construction programme our country has seen since the New Deal. Millions of Americans don't know what to do with themselves right now. One announcement, sir, and we could be looking at zero unemployment.'

Slowly, Raine Kent settled back into his chair. 'A national programme,' he said, 'building giant, *empty* buildings.'

Ben Mellyk cleared his throat and said, 'If we don't prepare, Mister President—'

'A hypothesis you said? That's like half a fucking theory, right? On that we put millions of people to work?'

'It's a gamble,' Ben admitted. 'But if we design these to be high-tech training centres, adjunctive to the nearest universities and colleges, we then put a high demand on instructors, teachers, technicians – expertise at all levels. We'll start seriously short in that high-level manpower, so we have to open the doors – wide open, sir. Any American with a hankering to learn more, any skilled foreigner wanting a green card. Crash courses, intense training, steep learning curves – when you pitch this, sir, hit them with the Kennedy angle. Tell them it's going to be hard. Challenge them, sir. It's time.'

'Who needs a speech writer?' Kent asked rhetorically. 'Slow down, bud, you're closer to a heart attack than I've ever seen you.'

'Am I excited, sir? You have no idea. And what has me so fired up? One word: *hope*.'

Kenneth spoke. 'What if those alien space centres are exclusive to their respective nationals, Ben? What if those forcefields don't let anyone else in? More to the point, what if alien technology starts filling up those buildings, along with alien computers and some kind of instant-education technology imprinting on brains or whatever? With us sitting on the sidelines, with all those empty buildings?'

'Precisely why I said we need to use them for the high tech we *do* have, Kenneth. Because if you're right, we'll have to race to catch up.'

'Against alien technology?'

'It's that or we resign our nation to an Earth-bound backwater, while the rest of the world heads out into space, out to colonise Venus, Mars, the moons of Jupiter and beyond.'

The silence in the wake in these pronouncements lasted for nearly half a minute, and then Raine Kent said, 'Get that fucking astronaut in here.'

'He wants a co-pilot—'

'Fine, whatever.'

'I have one in mind,' Ben Mellyk went on.

The President scowled across at him. 'Is this even relevant? You got one in mind? Good! Job done.'

'Well, sir, the one I had in mind is Canadian.'

'What? What the fuck are you saying? We don't have anyone—'

'Of course we do, Mister President.' Ben now looked at Kenneth.

'But now we have an added incentive to step over the border.'

The Director comprehended in a flash. He leafed through his collection of photos and drew one out, which he slid across to Kent. 'Mister President, the alien construct in Canada, near the small town of Swift Current, Saskatchewan.' He shot Mellyk a look of sincere admiration. 'We wanted a chance to get in through the door to one of these sites? If it's Canadians only, well, problem solved.'

'What? I don't . . .'

Ben said, 'We've co-operated with the Canadian Space Agency – in fact, we gave this astronaut a lift up to the ISS. We have a history of working together. More to the point, they *owe* us.'

Raine Kent grunted. 'Should've annexed that country fifty years ago.'

'Then there'd be no alien space centre going up there,' Mellyk pointed out.

'Sure. I got that. I was just saying.' He pointed a finger at his Science Advisor. 'You work with my speech-writers. Programme details. Not too many, though. Make it simple. And then we need to assemble a working committee.'

'Bi-partisan,' added Strom from the far end of the table. At the President's glare, he said, 'It'll have to be, to get this off the ground. We all pull together or we all go down together – our whole country.'

Kent barked a bitter laugh. 'When has that line ever worked. And from you, Strom, of all people. Last administration – nothing but roadblocks you and your buddies threw up – one thing I'll take from the last man in this chair. I will veto the fuck out of people who get in my way. I trust we're understood.'

'Tell that to the Demo—'

'Who learned how to stonewall from the Republicans!' Raine Kent stood. 'I was never anybody's puppet. You knew that – I forced you to see that in the run for the presidential nomination. So now, I don't care if you're a Republican or a Democrat, either you get on board or I crush you. No more games, not anymore. We do this or we're toast.' He pinned Ben Mellyk one last time with a stubby finger. 'If you turn out to be wrong, you're gone.'

'Of course, Mister President.'

'Because,' Raine went on remorselessly, 'launching pads are also *landing* pads. And barracks and manufacturing plants could be for alien death-squads and weapons. All these sites could be processing centres, winnowing through what's left of humanity once the big ray guns start blasting down from orbit. And we don't have one because we'll be one giant pile of ash, just like the Russians and the Chinese and the Indians and the North Koreans.' He paused then to stab a finger at Strom. 'Of course they'll trash North Korea. Everyone wants to trash North Korea.' His level gaze then returned to Mellyk. 'How did you vote last election, anyway?'

'Green.'

Raine Kent continued staring down at the man for a long moment, and then he smiled and said, 'Good man. You see, I already knew. If you'd lied just now ...'

'I am here to be objective, Mister President,' Mellyk replied, somewhat frostily, 'not to tell you only what you want to hear.'

'I know. Like I said: good man, until you screw up. Landing pads. Now, get that astronaut in here, the one who looks like Scott Bakula, but with a smaller nose.'

•

Thus far, conversations at the United Nations were confined to private meeting chambers, as representatives of various nations – mostly ones sharing a border – met to establish a common language of compromise given what few true powers remained in human hands. Populations were on the move everywhere, defiant of prohibitions as refugees fled drought, poverty or religious persecution. The latter, of course, was toothless now, and yet psychological repression still found ways through the cracks of non-violence.

That said, a formal announcement from the UN was long overdue, at least as far as US Vice-President D. K. Prentice was concerned. The roadblock, however, was substantive. What could be said? No one, it seemed, could agree on a statement, one that could be said to be representative of all humanity.

She sat awaiting the Secretary General of the UN, Adeleh Bagneri, in a well-appointed conference room on the sixth floor of the United Nations headquarters. A silver tray bearing a teapot and porcelain cup and saucer was before her, the tea itself piping hot. She had acquired her preference for tea as a Rhodes scholar at Oxford, studying International Law, and yet, thanks to a roommate from rural Yorkshire, that taste tended towards what Brits called 'bog standard', or 'builder's tea', meaning strong enough to be a Class A narcotic. Alas, this tea was a delicate Earl Grey. A single sip left her feeling she'd just drunk hot water flavoured by flower petals. Worse yet, the sugar was raw, not white.

The tea was from India, blended in the UK. The silver tea set was from Pakistan, the sugar from Jamaica, the napkin from China. The conference table was some dark hardwood from Indonesia, the chairs from Denmark. The carpeting was Afghani and the array of paintings on the walls – part of a travelling exhibit – was a privately owned collection of Frida Kahlo paintings and etchings. This room, like so many others in this building, was a demonstration of the cultural and economic fusion that underpinned the very purpose of the United Nations. She could appreciate the demonstration, despite the insipid tea.

She was being kept waiting, indicative of the chaos that had descended upon this bastion of confrontation, compromise and, more often than not, outright cynicism, where nation-states played the game of history in the making, where posturing was a way of life, where politics succumbed to bureaucracy and vice versa, depending on the crisis *du jour*.

She wondered, not for the first time, if in the near future there would be an alien representative's seat and Office of Operations here at the UN. If so, both seat and office would be under perpetual siege.

In the meantime, her species stumbled in circles, made virtually powerless in the old game of nations. One would have thought that an end to the stoking of conflicts, the violence of old enmities and past crimes, where remonstration was an empty threat and arguments no longer possessed the final option of physical force, would have led to something akin to euphoria among the nations of humanity. Instead, the helplessness had simply laid bare the absurdity of clashing opinions, attitudes, beliefs and convictions.

People could not agree.

So what?

People failed to comprehend an opposing point of view.

What of it?

People got frustrated, irritated, insulted, offended, indignant.

And?

Even words died in the wake of such simple, devastating responses. The awful truth was, this imposition of non-violence had exposed the almost infinite differences within this single,

217

beleaguered species, a global civilisation incapable of reconciliation and at a loss to take that first step into a new paradigm.

No one could even agree on what the paradigm would look like. In the most essential ways, of course, defining that new paradigm would be guided by the extraterrestrials, for whom it seemed direct communication was not a priority. Thus far, humanity had been reacting to events and then struggling to accommodate them when it became increasingly obvious that opinions were not being invited. In one way, this manner of imposed change echoed that of nature itself. Earthquakes, volcanic eruptions, floods, cyclones and hurricanes all struck with the same blanket indifference to the desires of humanity.

And yet, Diana knew, ET was not quite as cruel as nature. There was an ethos at work, a subtle one that few paid attention to while in the grip of their fury and frustration. Miraculous supplies of food and clean water to hungry, downtrodden people, a silent but solemn promise that no one would starve. And now, according to the latest WHO reports, there had been a marked drop-off in endemic diseases, particularly in the tropical and subtropical regions of the world. The manner of this health intervention was still unknown, but physicists continued to talk about some kind of energy lattice, wrapped about the planet like a vast spider's web, and instances (so many instances!) of agency in keeping people safe. Diana suspected the two elements were intimately bound together.

But examples pointing to salvation were not enough to diminish the global confusion and fear afflicting her species. Despite the fact the only things being victimised were, one and all, the worst vices of human nature. The rallying cry of freedom lost its clarion purity when it meant the freedom to kill, harm, and make others suffer.

The door clicked open and in strode the Secretary General and her ever-present assistant, Agnes Livy. Dr Adeleh Bagneri held an Iranian passport although most of her career as a surgeon had taken place in London before, in her latter years as a university lecturer, she had returned to Tehran. Her election to the post of Secretary General had followed a labyrinthine path, not least of

218

which was the Islamic Republic of Iran's astonishing nomination of a progressive Islamic woman to the prospective candidacy pool.

Adeleh had poise and then some. Tall, straight-backed, her unbound hair the hue of iron, she had a gaze that could – and often did – make world leaders quail. She carried with her an ever-present Vape, defiant of admonishments and prohibitions and, if challenged, would ask which was preferable: this Vape or her usual Turkish cigarettes? Given those choices, most objections quickly died away.

Then again, outside the sovereign territory of the United Nations building, she might find the average American not so easy to brush off, especially here in Manhattan.

D. K. Prentice had never been a smoker and disliked the smell of burning tobacco almost as much as she disliked the smell of weed, and yet she found herself secretly admiring the Secretary General's bold defiance of propriety. This was not a woman to be bullied. Of course, many would retort that Adeleh's insistence on using her Vape indoors was its own form of bullying. Diana had heard as much, more than once, but as these complaints came mostly from men rather than women, she suspected that more was at work with those complaints than the occasional cloud of vanilla-scented water vapour. And this suspicion in turn awakened her old feminist instincts when a woman's behaviour triggered male desires to put that woman in her place.

In either case, the US Vice-President admitted to some ambivalence regarding this new Secretary General. She had been a ferocious political force as the spokesperson of the United Nations, often speaking against US interests.

Curious, then, how that adversarial history seemed to vanish the instant Adeleh smiled at Diana. 'So glad you made yourself comfortable, Diana. The damned lift broke down, if you can believe it, but as Agnes pointed out in her usual droll manner, we've had so many ups and downs of late that a forty-minute pause in an overheating lift may have been just the thing. For us at least,' she added as she sat down opposite.

Her assistant sat to the Secretary General's right. Agnes Lois was Cardiff-born, her slave ancestors likely from West Africa according to the CIA dossier. While most slaves coming through the British Empire had been shunted through Bristol or Cardiff, only a small proportion had actually remained in those cities, and as the British were among the first to outlaw slavery, the trafficking had been relatively short-lived. As Adeleh on occasion had pointed out, Agnes was more British than the Royal Family, and certainly more Welsh than the Prince of Wales.

'We're still nowhere in the General Assembly,' the Secretary General resumed. 'Even our president is at loggerheads with his VP and most of his advisors. Right now, the smaller committees are managing more practical solutions. As for the Security Council, well, how long is the unemployment line?' Smiling again with something like triumph glittering in her dark eyes, she lifted up her Vape and moments later virtually disappeared behind a thick, billowing cloud of water vapour. That then vanished, still revealing her Cheshire cat smile.

D. K. Prentice shrugged. 'The Security Council continues to reassess the new landscape.'

'Ah yes, the desert of their future. Now then, Diana, this notion of your president's, to send up an astronaut in an effort to establish contact with the extraterrestrials, is very much being taken ... shall we say ... with umbrage by the majority of other nations. More precisely, they're affronted that the US presumes to speak for all of humanity ... again.'

'Again? I don't understand, madam—'

'Oh you know, every damn movie about First Contact invariably puts America in the front line.' She tilted her head behind another cloud, pausing until it cleared before resuming, 'Why is that, anyway?'

'Well,' Diana drawled, 'far be it for me to speak in defence of Hollywood, but you must bear in mind that for those filmmakers, the "front line" audience is American. I'm sure Russian First Contact, uh, films, would assert the same role for Russia and Russians.'

'Couldn't say,' Adeleh said breezily, 'as I've never seen a Russian First Contact film. Are there any?'

'I do seem to recall,' Diana said, 'the *Independence Day* franchise of films expanded to include other parts of the world.'

'As did *Close Encounters*, although only at the film's start. Then it was Devil's Mountain, Wyoming, and a line-up of white military types in sunglasses all ready to board the alien ship.'

'Which, rather pointedly, were ignored.'

'Yes, preferring Richard Dreyfuss and who could blame them?' The Secretary General now leaned forward. 'And wasn't there a Frenchman? Some sort of exo-linguist?'

'That was the film-maker, Francois Truffault.'

'Yes, but not in the film!'

Diana frowned. 'Madam, are we truly going to discuss old films today?'

'Why not? I could use the break from reality. You?'

After a moment, Diana smiled. 'Well, you have a point there.'

'I'm thinking Spielberg was uncannily prescient.'

'Oh, was that where we were going with this?'

Adeleh nodded, then leaned back and pulled on her oversized Vape.

A moment later, Agnes spoke. 'The extraterrestrials in that film, *Close Encounters*, and in *E.T.*, both rejected the governmental authority seeking to impose its will on the situation, seeking, in effect, to control the outcome. And the audience of those films? Why, they cheered the rejection of that control.'

Diana looked to each woman in turn, and then settled somewhat, crossing her legs and folding her hands on her lap. 'Oh. I see.'

'While in the *Independence Day* films,' Agnes went on, 'the authorities were simply ignored until they were destroyed. The course of the stories from that point onward led to a reassertion of central authority and, ultimately, governmental control. Only a couple of decades between the two visions, and yet, how vast the change.'

'History spoke to new needs in the audience, one supposes,' Diana said.

Agnes nodded. 'A retraction towards stability and security, evoked in the very words that founded the nation of the United

States of America.' She paused then and half-smiled. 'I did film studies at uni.'

I know, Diana almost said. Instead, she glanced down at the tea set. 'Tell me, Agnes, do you by any chance have some builder's tea on hand?'

'Excellent idea!' Adeleh said. 'Do be Mum, Agnes darling? Let's get rid of this posh crap. Diana, let's take this afternoon to discuss our present irrelevance. Because, I now strongly suspect, that won't last.'

While Agnes briefly left the room to scrounge up some decent tea, Diana studied the Secretary General for a moment before saying, 'Madam Secretary, in what manner do you think the United Nations will acquire newfound relevance?'

'Why, as the central governing representative of our species, Diana. Oh don't look at me like that. I well know that every nation is ruled by power-blocks desperate to defend their turf.'

'Strictly speaking,' Diana pointed out, 'the General Assembly is not precisely democratic. The means by which member state representatives are appointed will have to change – at least to satisfy our desire for true democratic representation. And that, of course, assumes that nations will obligingly relinquish their sovereign rights to oversee the lives of their citizens. Which, to be honest, seems unlikely.'

'Yes indeed. And yet' – Adeleh sucked at her Vape, frowned and began unscrewing it – 'it appears, does it not, that ET is defining our future for us?' She drew out a small plastic bottle filled with amber liquid and set about refilling her Vape.

'As a surgeon surely you know that nicotine is bad for the heart,' said Diana as she watched.

'But stress is even badder,' Adeleh replied, glancing up to smile. 'Good thing Agnes wasn't here to hear that, she's a terror when it comes to grammar. Besides, I have a heart of stone, and a brain in dire need of jumpstarting. Such as that provided by nicotine. Now then.' She sat back and took an experimental pull. 'There we go. Just think, with a tiny EFFE in this there won't be any batteries to recharge – how the world is changing!'

'ET appears to be indifferent to our governments.'

'Oh I disagree!'

At that moment Agnes returned with a tray bearing a ceramic teapot and three mugs. 'Staff room,' she said.

'Lovely,' said Diana with a grateful smile.

'I feel it necessary,' Agnes went on, 'to point out that I sent an aide to find all of this. Accordingly, this tea may be steeped. In the meantime, I received a report confirming that the Chinese launch remains on schedule. Tomorrow, nine a.m. their time.' She glanced at her watch. 'Which is coming up fast.'

Adeleh sighed. 'And of course they will occupy the abandoned Lunar bases, effectively laying claim to the technology to be found there, not to mention the infrastructure.' She paused and frowned. 'One wonders what they will find there.'

'It's not likely they will be forthcoming on details,' Agnes added as she poured tea for the three of them.

Diana felt her own tension rise a notch. 'Needless to say, we're not happy about this.'

Adeleh's thin brows lifted. 'Security concerns? The old power-brokering of who has what and who knows what and who hasn't and who doesn't? Well, I wonder if ET will indulge such anti-quated posturing.'

'I wish there was an answer to that,' Diana admitted, grate-fully collecting up her mug. 'So far, we've not had much in the way of direct responses to our individual in-camera decisions and gestures.' She met Adeleh's eyes. 'Presumably the same for you?'

'Solemn silence, darling. This notion of secrecy, so human, certainly seems to feed ET's own agenda, given the absence of disclosure. What are we to make of that?'

Diana snorted. 'Only the obvious. We can't hope to win a game when the rules are being kept from us, can we? This is the ultimate power-brokering going on here.'

'Do you think? Rather,' the Secretary General amended, 'do you believe that is the purpose behind ET's coyness?'

'Well, what else would it be?'

'You are assuming ET thinks like us, and sees things the way we do. Consider the alternative: we are being given room to decide how to proceed, not nation by nation, but as a species.'

Agnes said, 'Consider all those First Contact films, Madam Vice-President. Each scenario demanded, in terms of story and setting, a focal point for the ET's attention upon us. National capitals, military installations, the functioning head of government and organised response. So much for the belligerent aliens. The nice ones? Oh, space programmes, secret First Contact men-in-black teams – once again, one particular nation's organised response. Both reaffirm our notions of authority, our structures of knowledge and control. Elite people on the inside, everyone else on the outside.'

'I don't think ET likes that,' Adeleh said. She waved a hand. 'Oh I know, I have no proof of my suspicions. Only what my gut tells me. Look, Security has always existed to protect national interests, the defending of sovereign rights, the protection of a nation's citizens and their way of life and all the rights their native land deems acceptable. And of course secrecy has been Security's first weapon of control, in both peace and war-time. But look at us now – you could lay bare all your secrets and what could anyone else do about them?'

Diana only just managed to keep from flinching.

As if in response to an unspoken accusation, Adeleh said, 'No, I'm not naïve, darling. We've been long enough in this murky world to know that more often than not, the keeping of secrets by governments and its intelligence agencies has as much to do with unethical or even unconstitutional violation of citizen rights, both home and abroad, all committed in the name of patriotism, as it does its officially sanctioned function. Furthermore, we both know that Security as an institution behaves in the same manner as any entrenched bureaucracy: it will defend itself and will employ secrecy to maintain its power, regardless of ethics or even legality.'

'You are describing human nature,' said Diana.

'Am I?'

'Insofar as historical legacy is concerned, yes, absolutely. How have we ever done anything differently? Complex society demands it.'

'Does it truly? Or has that immovable assumption been drilled so deeply into our psyches that we only *believe* it's inevitable, intrinsic to human nature?'

Diana set her mug down and then threw up her hands. 'How can we even answer that?'

'That is just my point, Diana,' said the Secretary General. 'There lies our immediate task. Determining, individually and collectively, what *has* to be over what we *think* has to be. We are being invited to seek a new definition of human nature, no more, no less, and surely you can see that this determination now poses the greatest challenge our species has ever faced.'

Diana Prentice sat back in her chair. 'Good God,' she muttered. 'Where to start?'

'We start here,' Adeleh said. 'With my first formal speech in the General Assembly. In seven days' time.'

Diana's eyes narrowed on the Secretary General. 'Have you had this conversation with other heads of state? Other represent- atives?'

Adeleh smiled. 'We know how important certain things are. You and the United States, Diana, are the first. My next six days will be crowded ones.'

'Well, I don't envy you.'

'Of course you don't but you know, maybe one day soon, you will.'

The smile was there for a moment, broad as ever, and then gone behind a white cloud.

Chapter Seventeen

'I haven't made my mind up regarding global
conspiracies. But it strikes me that the most successful
conspiracy is the one in which the majority of its
participants aren't even aware they're part of the
conspiracy. That may sound contradictory, until you
look at one of the most obvious global conspiracies still
going strong: monetarism.'

Samantha August

'Eleven women have been selected to accompany the mission,
Leader.' Liu Zhou paused only briefly and then continued, 'Of
course this necessitated the removal of nine marines in Captain
Shin's command.'

'Yes,' murmured the Leader from where he sat on the leather
sofa, eyes on the bank of television monitors, 'the captain made
his protests most fervent, but I remain resolved. There is no time
to waste and the invitation could not be clearer.' He glanced up
to fix his Science Advisor with an unblinking regard. 'Highly
intelligent, skilled, talented, fertile women of child-bearing age.
And suitably attractive, yes?' He sniffed. 'One would think our
marines delighted at the prospect.'

'Leader, this initial team – our colonial batch – includes the
finest scientists and technicians available to our glorious homeland. I believe the marines consider their chances to be limited.'

'Ha! Well, perhaps they have a point. Still, the laws of at-
traction are mysterious.' He then waved the hand that held the
remote control. 'No matter. Captain Shen understands his duty,

and well comprehends the mission's new protocols. In any case, it now seems obvious that the marines have little to fear. Empty chambers, echoing corridors.'

'Initial exploration of Luna Site 71 will remain their responsibility,' Liu Zhou affirmed. 'Some risks remain. Even deployment and movement in lunar gravity is an unknown complication. In any case, Major Shin's concerns are perhaps not as trivial as they may seem. The science team has brought to me its considered observation that these women, being such late additions to the mission, lack even the most basic training and familiarisation with shipboard and mission responsibilities.'

'I know, I know, old friend. All of your objections have been noted. But I desire this mission to be a most emphatic announcement of our intention not only to occupy Site 71, but to establish the beginning of a permanent settlement of that base. The first human child born on Luna will be Chinese.'

'And the medical risks of foetal development in low gravity, not to mention the risk of radiation?'

'We shall see, won't we? Oh, I know how cruel I sound, and while you may be thinking it callous of me to gamble with the lives of children, I do not believe the gamble to be as great as you believe.' He gestured at the screens. 'Our silent benefactors have displayed their value for human life, all over the world. Do you think they would not do the same with our first off-planet human colonists?'

Liu Zhou fought off a chill. 'Leader, you are reliant upon the mercy of an unknown alien species.'

'I am.' He began shutting down monitors until only one remained alight, showing a fixed-station live feed from the launch site. 'Now, do sit down with me, so that we may witness the boldest adventure humanity has ever taken.'

As much as Liu Zhou felt he should have been in attendance at mission control at the Beijing Aerospace Command and Control Centre, politics had demanded his presence here at Party Central Command. Of course, if things went wrong, his arrest and incarceration could more easily be achieved away from public view. But surely such days were behind them now?

He gingerly took a seat on the sofa, felt himself sinking deeply into its plush confines, the Premier to his left.

'History,' said Xin Pang, 'belongs to the bold.'

On the screen the countdown had begun.

•

Following their remote mapping by an ancillary mission conducted covertly during the *Chang'e* soft-landing on the lunar surface in 2013, Project 931 had begun as a top-secret mission to occupy the Grey moon-bases. Based on an exhaustive survey of close-encounter and abduction reports worldwide, the Bureau of Psychology had determined that the psychic assault capability of the Greys was limited by range, roughly estimated at one hundred metres.

Under the command of Captain Shen, the marine contingent accompanying the second landing intended to strike, employing an array of specially designed weaponry discharged at a distance of one hundred and twenty metres, to penetrate outer building walls and trigger – hopefully – explosive decompression. They would then advance and, following the doctrine of decompressing chambers via hardened-RPG fusillades, proceed to clear the innermost rooms of the enemy base. Accordingly, even in the event of complete success, the assault team would have advanced with the expectation that all of their potential Grey assailants were already dead. Or at least dying.

Additional defences to the little-understood psychic capability of the Greys included armoured helmets constructed from laminated layers of tungsten and ceramic, every second layer with its molecular polarity reversed. Privately, Shen had expected these precautions to be as effective as tinfoil hats. He had hoped that the loss of atmosphere within the alien constructs would prove as fatal to the Greys as to anyone else. Failing that, he had anticipated what an American counterpart might call a clusterfuck.

News of the flight of the Greys had been a relief, and what had begun in Shen's mind as a suicide mission now seemed achievable as far as mission protocols went. Now, however, new challenges presented themselves. It was unlikely the Greys had left the door open. Three combat engineers were attached to his team, each one loaded down with a collection of machinery that might prove useful, but without a proper vacuum chamber or airlock, the risk of damaging delicate technology in the base, even making it entirely uninhabitable, was very real.

The Long March 15 CZ-7 heavy lift rocket that propelled into space the three modules of the Lunar Occupation mission had been the world's largest, and as with any rocket containing thousands of litres of volatile fuel, failure would have meant the deaths of everyone on board. Despite the rapid scaling up of the EFFE already under way, the risk was deemed acceptable in the name of arriving first and thereby laying claim to all that the Greys had left behind.

At each moment of phase completion, when all aboard were at the mercy of technology – breaths held at tank separation, module disengagement, booster-rockets fired, trajectory input and if necessary correction – the sense of sudden vulnerability afflicted everyone, including Shen and his team of combat veterans.

Space was inhospitable, unwelcoming. It reduced each human form to a fragile sack of precious fluids. Shen had begun to imagine the inky blackness outside as something both alive and hungry. At other times, especially during the sleep cycle in the crew quarters, he could think of it only as a vast graveyard, eager for one more frozen lump of matter. If each planet was an island of life, then space was indeed its lifeless counterpart.

On the fourth morning of the mission, the final module separation freed the massive lander for its descent to the lunar surface at Site 71. Shen and his team were fully kitted, although still breathing ship air. They held bulky weapons resting on laps, thick gloves gripping oversized stocks. Tripod attachments bulked out the back of their life-support packs, since firing a weapon on the lunar surface could send a solider off his feet, spinning through space. In the original mission, the tripods would have been deployed behind each soldier prior to firing.

Shen was fairly certain that such a precaution was unnecessary, but given the immense list of unknowns defining the original mission parameters, he appreciated over-compensation where the lives of his soldiers were concerned.

There were no windows in the lander's main hold, so Shen could only assume that even now they were drawing ever closer to the Moon's dusty surface. The infrequent bursts of chatter from the pilot crew ranged from highly technical instructions to monosyllabic grunts.

He felt very far from home.

'Contact ten seconds.' This directed comment came through startlingly clear in Shen's earbuds.

'Copy.' The captain double-clicked on team coms to wake up his soldiers.

The Greys were gone. This seemed to have been confirmed by innumerable sources. But what if they weren't? Shen had read the reports of abductions. The terror afflicting the human victims was described as soul-crushing, as effective as a paralysis ray. Abject, utterly helpless. Weak as a newborn baby. Under this terrible spell, there was no resisting the Greys. They did whatever they pleased, and often afterward they psychically repressed the memories in their human victims.

As someone online had described it: as pernicious and inherently evil as a date-rape drug.

He would have liked the Greys still huddled in their moonbase. He would have liked to see their flimsy forms spinning through space, dying in the agony of icy-cold vacuum, dying in gasps as the last of the air rushed from the rooms where they hid. But most of all, he realised, he would have liked to put a bullet between the oversized black eyes of a Grey. Just one would do. One chance for pay-back. Standing immune to their psychic terrors, looking down as helplessness spun round to afflict the alien, not the human.

There was a soft thump, then a settling sensation as the faint gravity took hold.

Vocal instructions weren't necessary. Everyone knew their tasks. The chamber decompressed, lights blinked the all-clear, the side door nudged outward, and then began its slow pivot to form an angled platform.

Disengaging from the ship-board air feed and then moving as quickly as seemed possible, two point-men exited the craft. In quick order the rest followed. Shen was the last of his team to leave the lander, last to set foot on the lunar surface.

The low gravity was uncanny. In his mind – after three days of zero-g – all his instincts seemed to be groping for the more familiar pull of Earth's own gravity. Instead, the Moon seemed unselfish about their presence. He could imagine himself launching his body upward – and possibly leaving this white and grey world forever. Not likely, he told himself, but still the unease remained in his mind, dogged in its fearful whispering.

He watched as his team spread out in awkward bounds, watched as the tripods automatically extended behind each man, like the legs of a spider unfolding in the harsh light.

The two scouts were already thirty metres away, hopping in bounds towards the crater's rim, beyond which – buried in shadow – awaited the alien moon-base.

'Advance,' Shen commanded.

They set out, following the scuffed tracks of the point-men.

•

'Joey Sink here again, folks, and it looks like we got the bug fixed. That feed you're seeing is from an amateur astronomer based somewhere in Texas – although you'd be hard-pressed to call anything in that picture amateurish. This is serious state-of-the-art tech going on here. Rock steady, and the lander's clear as day, just to the right of the crater's edge. Looks like a grain of rice, hah hah – oh, listen, wasn't being racist there or anything. Honest. It really does look like a grain of rice! Anyway, those thin lines are maybe tracks – looked like a whole bunch of people left the lander – not that we could make that out, of course. Okay, we got Annie Mouse wanting to chime in here and being the expert and all, maybe he can give us some idea of what's happening right – whoah! Was that flashes? From the crater? Hey, can we run this back – hold on, yeah ... there! Holy crap! Three flashes, and bits of crap flying, and dust – plumes of moon-dust. Wow! Annie Mouse? You there? What did we just see?'

There was a long pause, and then Annie Mouse's feed kicked in. 'Sorry, that got us bouncing around a bit ... around here it's looking like that television series, 24. You know, that top-secret installation with everybody whispering into their cellphones and looking suspicious. Anyway, those flashes. We're thinking they had to set charges to open a breach in the alien construct—'

'You people got a better view than us, Annie?'

'Not much – your buddy on the ground in Texas has serious stuff. I've got it up on a monitor here and it's tracking smooth as ours does with nary a wobble. Great res, too. Nice find, Joey.'

'So you figure they got in?'

'Don't know. Sure, they blew stuff up, but did that manage a breach? And those plumes could've been just blow-back rather than escaping atmosphere. We're analysing those frames right now, trying to decide. If it was atmosphere, then the chamber beyond was relatively small and able to seal itself. Otherwise we'd still be watching jets of air freezing up in big clouds.'

'And we're not. Got it. Anything else you want to tell us before Jack Bauer finds you?'

'That lander is huge. The Chinese aren't being forthcoming on the size of the crew. The thinking is they might be intending on actually occupying the base, as in "permanently". Hang on ...'

Joey squinted at the telescope image of the landing site – something had caught his eye. 'Hey, Annie, that rice grain just did something. Four, uh, pebbles? Separating out from it, two to each side. You seeing this? Annie?'

'Sorry! Yeah, we're tracking that. They're lunar rovers and they're big. I'd say the breach got them in. They're in the Grey base! Shit! And here we are, still looking for a damned rocket! Look, Joey, gotta run here. I'm catching wind that our building's about to go dark – bigwigs coming in—'

'Going dark? What's that mean?'

'Means they're going to cut off signal any moment now—'

'What, as in cellphone signal? Annie? Annie Mouse? Well, huh. There it is, folks, Big Government playing with secrets again – you'd think they'd have given up that stuff by now. Habit, I suppose.

'Never mind, let's keep watching, shall we? Those rovers are making tracks. If they're full of people ... well, that's a lot of people.

'But think of it this way. Up until today the only people managing to live not on this planet were in a cruddy space station, going all brittle in the zero-gee. Now, as of today, humanity has claimed the Moon as the new chic residence *du jour*. Sure, not Americans, and that sucks. Well, try thinking about it like this, folks. Armstrong took that first step all right, but the Chinese brought suitcases.

'This is history in the making, friends, and here we are on Joey's Vlog, sharing it. Could it get any better than that?

'Oh man, my chat-box is going wild. Okay okay, the not-Americans thing has you all howling. Don't blame me! Or, put it another way, yeah, blame me, and then blame yourselves while you're at it, and your daddies and mummies and *their* daddies and mummies. We couldn't be bothered, remember? We dropped the ball in the race to space. Oh, I know, the Greys kept us down, but only because almost nobody knew the truth! If it had all spilled out in, say, the eighties, well, man, we'd have got *fired* up, don't you think? Not in *my* backyard, you bug-eyed interlopers! And I'll tell you this, I survived Afghanistan and the Moon's got nothing on that – it's no wonder the Greys never stuck a hidden base in old Stan. The mujahedin would've kicked their butts! So that's what I'm saying. Hey, all you old retired presidents, listen up! We could've taken 'em, if only you had the guts to tell us the truth. We could've taken them down!

'All right, I'll go all zen now. Someone kicked my toolbox, right? Secrets, man, you know. They suck. Secrets, the hidey-hole of cowards. If I was a swearing man, like King Con, I'd say ... well, you can guess what I'd say, can't you? There's an "F" in it, and a "U" and the rest you don't even need, do you?

'So there it is, the Chinese beat us to the punch. Up there on the Moon, making history. We dropped the ball, us Yanks. Dropped it big time. But suck it up, my fellow Americans. Let's just sit back, kick our feet up, pop a beer and grab a handful of popcorn, and just watch the show. It's pretty much all we do these days, right?'

•

Evidently, the base's automated emergency counter-breach measures still worked. When the outer wall of the base blew apart, the elongated corridor inside expelled its atmosphere, while large locks slammed shut on three hatches on the opposite wall and to either side of the breached section.

Shen and the two scouts led the way into the corridor. He looked around as best he could. There was nothing overtly alien about what he found. Directly ahead, on the three now-closed doors, the mechanisms for deeper ingress into the base were more or less recognisable, with wheeled handles suggesting redundancy and what looked like a function panel displaying nine rows of three round buttons. Selecting the central door, the engineers moved past Shen and set to work figuring out how to manage the evacuation of atmosphere in the chamber beyond to effect an airlock.

His heart was pounding in his chest. He watched as one of the engineers began pressing various buttons. This went on for some time. It was possible, Shen thought, that they would have to knock holes into every room they wanted to explore, meaning they would all need to stay suited, at least until certain breaches were repaired and sealed back up, allowing the portable air tanks to be installed and the valves opened wide. Maybe then, finally, the next set of doors would open of their own accord. It seemed far from ideal, not that he'd been expecting any favours from the Greys.

Then the engineer at the panel stepped back as the door silently opened. The man turned to Shen and the captain saw a perplexed expression through the face-shield. A moment later the engineer lifted his hands in the suited version of a shrug.

Weapons out, the two scouts edged into the new chamber.

•

The surface level of the Grey Base at Site 71 consisted mostly of empty chambers. In some of them, brackets in the walls were the only evidence of machinery and equipment. Everything had been stripped away. Near the centre of the complex, however, Shen's engineers found what they thought to be an atmosphere-processing plant, although its configuration made it seem discordant with the rest of the room. It stood on four stubby legs in the middle of an otherwise featureless chamber. A cluster of tubing rose from its top surface, disappearing into the ceiling.

Biologists set up tests of the atmosphere, filtering for contaminants and biosigns, and after an hour's muted discussion they pronounced it safe to breathe. In fact, the lead biologist revealed to Shen, the nitrogen-oxygen ratio was identical to that of Earth.

By this time, the rest of the occupation team was safely ensconced and a crew was at work sealing up the original breaches in the outer wall of the complex. Gear had been brought in, crowding the rooms closest to the point of ingress. Once heaters had been set out and turned on and the all-clear was given, everyone climbed out of their suits and excited conversation filled the still-icy air. A communications station was assembled in what was now designated Room 5, and contact via lander and then satellite uplink was established with Mission Control down in Jiuquan's Satellite Launch Centre, including video-feed.

In the meantime, Shen's marines completed their mapping of this level, finding in one of the last chambers to be explored a robust and oversized hatch in the floor. A control stand stood beside it, resembling a speaker's podium although at perhaps half the height. Its tilted panel had been shattered, rendering it useless.

Shen now gathered a half-dozen of his marines in this chamber, while his engineers continued examining the control panel. The captain was relieved to be out of the exo-suit. The low gravity still proved unsettling at times, particularly when he made any rapid motions. He could hear chatter from adjacent chambers as teams began setting up cots, including the higher pitched voices of the women discussing sanitation protocols.

Second in command Lieutenant Hong Li moved to stand beside

him. They both studied the massive hatch. 'We may have to drill,' he said. 'The vacuum units should keep particulates down, but I would still advise we cordon off and seal this chamber while the drilling takes place.'

Hong Li held a PhD from Simon Fraser University, in mechanical engineering. He always conveyed the impression that he knew what he was doing, and this Shen found both useful and somewhat heartening. A startling contrast remained, however, given the man's appearance – the over-muscled body, the sloping shoulders and the cabbage ears of a wrestler. His eyes were small in a broad, battered face, and he rarely spoke in anything above a whisper – except when barking orders to his soldiers, when the register of his voice dropped to a basso rumble.

In the wake of Hong Li's suggestions, Shen nodded. It was certainly possible that what awaited them in the levels below was simply more of the same. Gutted rooms, smashed control panels. The Greys didn't seem big on overt expressions of technology. He wondered if their psychic abilities extended to controlling machinery, thus minimising the need for elaborate electronics. He glanced over at the huddle of engineers examining the pedestal. 'Zhou Wei! What have you found?'

The lead engineer looked up, blinking rapidly behind his glasses. 'There is evidence of repair.'

'What?'

Both Shen and Wong Li strode over.

Wei waved the other engineers back a step and gestured the officers closer. He pointed with a narrow metal stylus at the facing beneath the broken shards of glass. 'Here. This is some kind of circuit board. Not complex.'

'Non-Euclidian,' muttered Hong Li.

Wei grunted agreement. 'And here, and here, processing units.'

'They look like M&Ms,' Shen said, and then paused and squinted at the expressions on the faces of Wei and Li. 'Candies.'

Wei grunted again. 'Processing units. You see, though, that the object that impacted the circuit board dismembered the latex – this sensory membrane. Only now ... do you see? These new ... silvery threads?'

The threads Wei spoke of were thin as strands of hair, and yet they formed patterns in their distribution.

'They are not consistent with the original design,' Hong Li observed.

'Precisely,' Wei agreed. 'Two different technologies?' And then he was nodding, eyes bright. 'This new manifestation, it is nanite-based, or so we believe. The underlying Grey technology is not. There are orders of magnitude between the two sets.'

'Power?' Li asked.

'Yes! Returning us to the command package—' He pointed the stylus at the cracked buttons still attached to the web that had been beneath the glass fascia. 'Of course, we can only guess at specific functions, and the necessary sequences are entirely lost to us – but none of that may matter.'

'What do you mean?' Shen asked.

'We think, as with all the other chambers, any button will do.'

The captain considered the notion for a moment, and then he reached out and pressed the nearest button.

Behind him the hatch clunked loudly and then lifted clear, revealing a vertical tunnel.

Shen held up one hand to halt the rush of personnel towards the hatch. 'Remain where you are. We pause here. I need to speak to Command.'

Frowning, Wei said, 'Why, Captain? Were we not intending to explore the entire complex?'

Shen nodded. 'And we will. But this ... new technology. This repairing of the mechanism.'

'Our Benefactors,' said Hong Li. 'The ones who chased away the Greys. They are aiding us here.'

Shen had reached the same conclusion. But it added a new complication to their mission, and though not likely one that would in any way alter their progress, Mission Control needed to be apprised of the development.

'Ah,' murmured Lieutenant Hong Li, 'I see. We may not be alone here.'

'As a setting for First Contact,' Shen said, looking around, seeing the faces of the engineers, his soldiers, 'is not this base ideal?' He met Hong Li's gaze. 'Close off this chamber and set a guard. No one approaches the hatch. I will confer with Mission Control on this unforeseen ... possibility. For now—'

His words fell away as a faint moaning cry drifted up from the hatchway's gaping mouth. And then a wail, the words coming in a rush of some language Shen did not comprehend. Hand reaching towards the 9 mm at his hip, the captain slowly approached the hatchway. 'Did anyone understand that?'

Behind him, Hong Li said, 'It was English, sir.'

Shen turned to frown at his lieutenant. 'Are you certain?'

Li nodded.

'Well, what did it say?'

'Sir, it said, "for the love of God someone help me".'

•

The floor below was visible at a depth of about ten metres. There were no ladder rungs or any other means of descent. Among the platoon's gear were two sets of climbing harnesses and three pay-out spools. After a quick and somewhat terse dispatch back to Mission Control, Shen and his medic, Quang Feng, donned the harnesses. A spool was anchored to the rim of the hatch and Shen took the lead in descending to the level below.

As soon as he edged out over the opening, however, he found himself flailing.

Hong Li, crouched nearby, quickly pulled the captain clear. 'Sir?'

'No gravity!' Shen scrabbled at his harness and managed to unbuckle it. Kicking free of it he moved to the edge again and pushed his boots over, watching as they seemed to float. Gingerly, like a man settling into a hot bath, Shen worked his way out over the hole. Both hands still gripping the edge, he shifted until his boots were pointed downwards. Then he used his hands to softly propel himself down.

He landed in an alcove and took hold of a nearby rail to keep from rebounding back upward. Facing him was a corridor, utterly dark beyond the light spilling down from directly above. As he straightened, reaching for the flashlight on his belt, the walls and ceiling suddenly lit up with a pale, pellucid glow, revealing the corridor's full extent.

It was long and curving. On the outside wall of the curve there were narrow doors for as far as he could see, each one spaced at an interval of a little less than three metres. The inside wall of the curve – which had held the alcove for the anti-gravity pad – was smooth and blank, like milky glass or coconut water. It was icy cold to the touch. The floor –

Shen stepped back, drifting back upward in the column of zero-g.

'Captain?'

He looked up, and then said, 'Quang and my scouts – all of you, come down. Have your cameras recording.' He edged back into the corridor.

There was blood on the floor. Smears of it, crusted brown and sparkling with tiny ice crystals. A lot of blood, staining the floor for as far as he could see in both directions, some of the stains looking very old. In many of the smears he saw strange small, duck-like footprints. Here and there were frozen pieces of what looked like flesh.

Quang arrived, stumbling out of the zero-g column. The breath hissed in a plume from the man as he saw the bloodstains.

Since that first wail they had heard nothing and now the silence held a new flavour, poignant and grim. Mouth dry, Shen turned to watch the arrival of his two scouts. Motioning for quiet, he hand-signalled ten metres and then waved the first soldier down the corridor and the second soldier up the other way. With a gesture for Quang to stay a step behind him, the captain approached the nearest door.

No latch or doorknob, but the panel could be pushed to one side.

The chamber inside lit up.

A raised platform dominated the room and on it was a naked body. Human, male, Caucasian, the pallid form frozen and dusted with frost. There were no immediate signs of the cause but the man was most definitely dead, the flesh bruised and mottled where it contacted the tabletop.

Quang slipped past Shen and began a closer examination. A moment later he waved Shen forward, and then pointed.

There were holes in the side of the man's head, each the circumference of a small Gold Panda coin. Neatly drilled and rimmed with old blood.

And then, as Shen's gaze tracked wherever Quang pointed, he saw more holes. In the side of the neck. To either side of the belly button and down in the groin area. In the penis and the testicles. Each wound was accompanied by a small amount of spilled blood and other fluids.

The frozen expression on the dead man's face was a rictus of terror and pain, yet he was lying on the table without restraints.

Shen backed away.

Emerging into the corridor, he paused for a long moment, counting all the doors he could see along this side of the curved corridor. Thirty-three, until the curvature took the walls out of his range of vision. Unbidden, a shiver took him.

A faint moan came from somewhere, possibly further up the corridor although it was difficult to be certain.

The scout nearest the sound glanced back at Shen.

He nodded, and then, as the scout hurried towards the next door, the captain and his medic followed.

•

Liu Zhou sat beside a silent Xin Pang. All of the monitors on the wall before them were showing the same shaky feed from the shoulder-mounted camera of one of the scouts. Even with the slight lag, the immediacy of the live feed was palpable, and more than once the Science Advisor brought his hands to his mouth as one mutilated body after another was discovered, each to a room, each left lying abandoned. In a number of chambers, the victim had been eviscerated, organs removed, the cavities gaping and black. Among the dead there were children, far too many children.

Forty-seven rooms in all. Captain Shen and his team found the still living man in the fortieth chamber. The camera feed revealed him still on the operating table, but lying on his side and curled up into a foetal position. He had soiled himself and was shivering in the cold.

Liu Zhou and China's Leader watched as Shen's medic approached, but it was Lieutenant Hong Li's deep voice that came from the speakers.

'You are safe, now,' he said in English.

The stranger flinched and then curled further round to squint at the newcomers. He was Caucasian, rounded eyes staring out from within deep bruises, his lips cracked with dehydration, cheeks and chin covered in greying stubble.

Hong Li joined the medic, while the scout with the camera moved to take a position in one corner of the room, so that the feed encompassed the entire scene. 'We are a Chinese exploratory mission,' the lieutenant said. 'The Greys are gone.'

'Gone?'

'Our medic wishes to examine you, so that we can make you feel better.'

In the monitor room of the Premier's residence, Liu Zhou was momentarily distracted by a buzzing cellphone on the table before them. But Xin Pang made no move towards it, eyes fixed on the scene being played out on the Moon.

'I want to go home,' the man suddenly sobbed, even as the medic helped him to sit up.

'And where is that?' Hong Li asked.

'F-Fairbanks, Alaska, USA. Three miles out of town, the Old Spruce back road just past the ... the ...' and once again the man sobbed.

Shen called the second scout close and muttered some commands, and the scout nodded and left the room. The captain now spoke to his lieutenant. 'Tell him we're bringing him some clothes, and the means to clean himself. Tell him' – and here Shen's voice caught slightly, before he continued – 'tell him it's over.'

Back on Earth, Xin Pang hissed as the cellphone began buzzing again. 'Get that!' he snapped.

Liu Zhou collected the phone and took the call. He listened for a moment at the frantic report coming through from Communications, and then ended the call and set the phone down. 'Leader.'

'What? What is it? Can you not see—'

'Our feed from the Moon is being seen worldwide.'

This revelation snapped the Premiere round. 'What?'

'Everywhere, sir. The world watches as we watch.'

Xin Pang blinked, and then he pointed at the cellphone. 'Get Mission Control. Pass a message to Captain Shen at once! He must be told that all security has been compromised. That he now stands before all of humanity. Quickly, before he does something to embarrass us!'

•

Joey Sink had heard enough horror stories when serving in Afghanistan, of Americans taken prisoner by the Taliban. He now sat as close to blubbering as he'd ever been, watching the viral feed that had taken over the entire internet, showing the Chinese team as it proceeded, with infinite gentility, to do all it could with the broken man they had found.

The trail of corpses that had come before this had arrived without audio, the camera shaky as its wielder flinched and trembled with what could have been horror or, just as likely, rage. It did not matter the colour of the skin or the shape of the eyes; it did not matter where these people had originally come from. They were all human, and Joey could feel his own anger rattled awake over what had been done to them.

Tony Newton. That was the man's name. He didn't know how long he had been there – he hadn't even known he was on the Moon. His memories were a mess. He'd come to alone, the door refusing to open. He'd slept once, maybe twice. He was hungry and cold, severely dehydrated and seemed to be suffering from some form of dysentery. He remembered the Greys, but not all that they had done to him.

On Joey's monitor a small window popped up from King Con.

Anthony Newton had been reported missing in February, 2015. His ex-wife had insisted he wasn't a man to wander off. She'd said he was too boring to do anything like that, especially in the middle of winter. There'd been no leads and the file had remained open.

Joey wiped at his eyes. He realised that he'd left his camera on, but he suspected that no one was watching him in any case. The world's attention was on Tony Newton and the solicitous medic in military uniform, and the officer standing a few paces back, who seemed to be on a radio of some sort. He saw the officer stiffen suddenly, and then step towards the one Chinese soldier who could speak English.

Words were exchanged, too low to register, and then the soldier deliberately turned to face the lone camera. 'There is more,' he said in English. 'Four other corridors have been found. The survivors are seven, so far. Two are critical and may not survive. None of the survivors are children. At the moment, the number of confirmed dead is one hundred and thirty-six.' He paused, and then added, 'On behalf of the People's Republic of China, Captain Shen and the rest of us will do all we can to help the victims of this terrible ... crime. You are welcome to continue to watch, but we ask that you respect the dignity of this man.' And he barked something in Chinese. The camera shifted its point of view, a gesture respecting Tony Newton's modesty.

Of all that Joey had seen thus far, it was this one small act that got the tears truly gushing from his eyes and had him scrabbling to disconnect the eye-cam on his monitor.

Chapter Eighteen

'What makes a better human being? Is it just a question of faster, stronger, smarter? But smarter in what way? Computationally? This idea of augmenting our species through technology, adding new RAM to the old hard drive as it were, seems to miss the point. And that is what we can be better right now, without technology. Augmentation is pointless if we keep repeating the same old mistakes. And efficiency is not the same as better, not even close. You want to be a better human being? Start today.'

Samantha August

'Why did you do that? No, never mind. I know why you did that.' Sam's hand shook as she lit a cigarette and then rose from the chair to begin pacing. 'I'm finally beginning to feel like a hostage. This ship is my cell – this room, in fact. All these screens showing our rapid descent into chaos, down there, everywhere.' She paused. 'These damned clothes I've had to wear for weeks now, every damned day. I don't care if you magically clean them every night. Tell me the time has come, Adam, before I start losing it for real up here.'

'Soon, Samantha August. Your unique request is being expedited as quickly as safety allows. The corollary technologies are challenging, although I admit to some pleasure in meeting such challenges.'

Her soul's dark night still awaited the dawn. Her depression was deepening, and depression was not a trait she was in the habit of experiencing. Sadness and grief earned a good cry, and denying or suppressing the value of such feelings had always struck her as one of the more risible consequences of a repressed society. Tears were not cause for shame. They were, in fact, healthy and more to the point, necessary.

But depression, arriving like an all-encompassing, smothering blanket of despair, was not a world she regularly inhabited. For perhaps the first time in her life, she had serious doubts about humanity, and whether or not it deserved any future at all.

At this moment, however, all she could feel was anger. Was that a good sign?

Arms crossed, she glanced at the screens. 'Is this level of global outrage enough for you, Adam? We're out for blood now. You know that, right? Out for blood, and yet not one of us can even so much as kick a television. That's a powder keg you've just lit.'

'The issue of national security was deemed an unnecessary complication.'

'So you hijacked China's live feed. This is one instance where a limited viewership – at least to begin with – might have been the wiser option.'

'Why?'

She took a drag and then gusted out the smoke, waving at the screens. 'To prevent this. The people out on the streets, the marches, the demands that governments disclose everything they have on the Greys – and some of those governments are going to topple when everything finally comes out. Meaning even more chaos.'

'Would the Chinese have released the feed, Samantha August?'

She grunted. 'Traditionally, probably not. But now, who knows? If they did, it would have been edited first—'

'Thus inviting yet another level of distrust and paranoia, with respect to all that was edited out. Accusations of complete fabrication would follow—'

She pointed at one screen. 'They already have. Claims that the whole scene was shot in some studio. On some things we're a pretty sceptical lot. On others, of course, we're as compliant as sheep.'

'It has been my observation that, following the obvious conclusion that an alien presence had arrived – namely me – many UFO-conspiracy experts found themselves not only vindicated, but also elevated in social status. Particularly when the governments released what they knew about the long-term Grey predation of your species and their exploitation of lunar resources.'

'Until we shook the tree a little bit harder and all the wingnuts fell out.'

'Nonetheless, Samantha, one would think that scepticism as a general attitude has lost some of its value.'

She barked a bitter laugh. 'Oh, Adam, you still have a lot to learn about humanity. Sceptics disproved just pick themselves back up, dust off, and find another target to habitually disabuse. Some might argue it's healthy and rational. Some might even use it as a stick to beat up anti-intellectualism and anti-science, as if suspicion of government cover-ups was synonymous with Creationism. Of course, that tactic of equivalence is a common one among debunkers, which makes their position far less rational than they tell themselves.' She resumed her pacing since, all things considered, there wasn't much else to do. 'No, Adam. You just showed humanity that it's a prey species. That's one serious knock to our predatory pre-eminence.'

'Your entertainment media exploits this notion – of human as prey – rather often.'

'But we always win out in the end,' she retorted. 'Besides, the most common prey story in films and television has to do with humans preying on humans. Have you noticed the spike in sales of First Person Shooter games? If we can't do it for real, we'll do it virtually. Now the Grey-modded versions are showing up and how's that for perfect timing? You've got us on the warpath, Adam.'

'Accordingly,' Adam replied, 'now would not be a good time for your species to do anything precipitous.'

'Oh, you mean like a couple astronauts blasting off from Cape Canaveral on an unproven EFFE rocket?' She cocked her head. 'You planning on saying hi to them, by the way?'

'No.'

'So ... they're just going to head out into space and hang around? Do you have any idea how embarrassing that will be for America and Canada?'

'My present time-line for the completion of your contact-specific project, Samantha, has you initiating proceedings two days before the scheduled launch of the handshake mission.'

'Oh. Crap, that soon?'

'Samantha, only a few moments ago you were expressing your impatience. Now you are—'

'I know what I am! Listen, I need a wardrobe upgrade. Do you know what I mean by that?'

'Yes. Any item of apparel you find online can be replicated—'

'Really? But I like trying things on.'

'Understood.'

She snorted. 'You say that like a man, meaning no, you don't understand at all.'

'Strictly speaking, I am neither male nor female.'

'Do you still stand by your decision to hijack that feed?'

'I do, but I don't see why—'

'You're more man than woman, Adam, trust me on that one. Back down from a bad decision? Lose face? Not a chance.'

'I assure you, Samantha, that I am quite capable of backing down from a bad decision, as you will see as soon as I make one. With respect to this notion of "saving face", I well comprehend its significance for your species. Indeed, based on that very notion, I concluded that China would not have released their recordings of the lunar-base landing and occupation, without first severely editing its content. Instead, we saw heroism that was not doctored, but entirely natural. We saw empathy that no doubt surprised China's rivals. We saw the first scene embodying humanity as a single, united species. Perhaps these examples remain subtextual, for the moment, but in my assessment they will prove to be among the more powerful consequences to the lunar landing event.'

She said nothing following that, as she mulled on Adam's assessment. And then, with a shake of her head, she said, 'I keep forgetting. You play this like a chess-master, always multiple steps ahead, and with supreme patience.'

'I would also point out that once the Chinese authorities realised that the hijack had taken place, they made no effort to shut down either the live feed or the hijacking itself.'

'Hmm, I admit, the way that English-speaking soldier acknowledged his new audience was ... remarkable. He just took it in stride.'

'The Chinese government has been instructed by the Premier to embrace my intervention rather than resist it.'

'Really? Interesting. What about Russia?'

'The same. And in many other countries as well. Resistance, of course, proceeds from a position that is almost uniquely Western, barring those more volatile regions of religious conflict elsewhere in the world.'

'Western? Last word from the Scandinavian block is about dissolving their respective borders. And the rest of Europe seems pretty calm about it all, especially now that their resident fascists have been laughed out of contention.' She returned to her seat. 'Western. You mean American, don't you?'

'The United States is indeed the centre of resistance.'

'There are cultural reasons for that.'

'Yes, their collective sense of global pre-eminence has not only been challenged, but also negated. My selection of Space Training Centres in other nations and regions no doubt contributes to this sense of being specifically excluded.'

'And are they? Are they being specifically excluded, Adam?'

'Yes and no. America's potential is vast, but that potential requires a subtle modification of certain precepts the citizens of that country take as self-evident. That said, my optimism for the future of that nation and its people is very high. A historical front-runner never likes to lose its lead and will do all it can to regain its position. I feel that I should point out at this moment, Samantha, that America's loss of that lead *preceded* my Intervention.'

She nodded. 'The odds were stacked against it, to be sure.'

'Corporate globalism is now the dominant power in your civilisation,' Adam said. 'Once corporations won the right to be treated as if they were people, the common citizen was disenfranchised, because the law then became the official control system for corporate interests over human interests, and corporations treat citizens as units of economy, thus stripping them of their essential humanity. There's nothing more inhuman than a corporation and its interests.'

'I know,' she said.

'Corporate globalism certainly represents a fatal path,' Adam said, 'and not just for America, but all nations. Fortunately, my Intervention Protocol is aimed at elevating both humanity and the planet's biome above that of antiquated corporation-based economies. It is no accident that the present fate of corporations seems to dominate the media's obsession, couched of course in terms of economic loss and unemployment, when neither of these consequences is inherently negative in a post-scarcity civilisation. They *are* negative, of course, from the corporate point of view, which your media would make synonymous with everyone's point of view.'

'People can't see what's ahead. They can't imagine an alternative to our most basic economic rules.'

'Yes, and your choice of the word "rules" is most appropriate, Samantha. They are not natural laws, not the inevitable consequences of physics or biology. They are *invented* and depend entirely on everyone agreeing upon their precepts. My dismantling of those precepts has your civilisation floundering.'

'Putting it mildly,' she muttered, eyes on the myriad images and news reports on the screens before her. 'But I do have one thing to say, and it's only now starting to play out below.' She hesitated, decided on another cigarette and lit it with a flourish. 'Women, Adam.'

'Yes.'

'We have existed – probably since the very beginning – under the very real threat of superior male strength. We have, accordingly, learned to live with a deep-seated fear. In the right circumstances, we can push it down so that we barely register it. But it's always there.' She stretched out her legs and leaned back in the seat, feeling it morph to accommodate her new position. 'Fear affects the course of our lives. Everyday decisions – that alley short cut, the underground car park, the elevator or the stairs? This dark street, that stretch of woods. You talk about humanity as a prey species, but over half of humanity has lived as prey for a very long time.'

'It will be interesting to observe the alteration the new paradigm will have upon your gender, Samantha.'

'Hmm. Will we rise to the aggression levels of men? Or will we abandon the patriarchy's business-as-usual ways of domination and bluster? Will we find new paths to achieving control, to political and social power and to forcing others to our will and bidding?' She fell silent, thinking on it, and then shrugged and said, 'Or will we reset our entire value system? Elevate the value of being a mother, the importance of childcare? Will we collectively demand that teachers of our children be accorded the importance and respect they deserve – instead of elevating useless twats like bankers, brokers and everyone else riding the financial sector? Will we expand our notions of what's possible as a woman in modern society? Will we, in fact, take the lead in abandoning the nine-to-five forty-hour working week where we're all trapped in a system that rewards the rich with indolence? Will women be the first to see a future opening wide with possibilities?' She tapped ash to the floor. 'What happens when fear goes away? When prey becomes predator, but in a world where most forms of predation are no longer available?'

'To date,' ventured Adam, 'psychological breakdowns as a consequence of the new paradigm predominantly affect the male gender of your species.'

'Well, yeah. No kidding. They've got their own baggage, especially when it comes to being the breadwinner and protector, not to mention all that testosterone-fuelled one-upmanshit.'

'Is it not "ship?" As in one-upman*ship*?'

'No it's "shit". Trust me. But still, if you're a man who's five foot one, or a hundred and ten pounds soaking wet, the male role can be a bitch. Men are as stuck in a world of poses as are women, with self-esteem the quicksand under all our feet.' She snorted. 'So what was your first move, Adam? If anger is a gun, you stole all our bullets. Is it any wonder people are mentally breaking down?'

'Because anger is a universal language for your species.'

'As is love, and grief.'

'And fear.'

She pointed at one of the screens. 'Those Greys. Fear is all about a sense of helplessness. They stole people, made them helpless, and then dined like vampires on the terror they felt.'

'Yes.'

'You know, pacifism has its drawbacks.'

'Yes, it does.'

'We aren't the only victims of the Greys, are we?'

'No, you are not. There are three sentient worlds relatively close to yours, each one of which has been effectively blockaded from space exploration of their own systems, essentially truncated in their development as global civilisations.'

'That's a nice trick. Exploit the system's natural resources while preying on the inhabitants. Work and pleasure all rolled up in one neat little package. And by using up all the system's resources, the Greys pretty much ensure that the sentient species will never get far even should they manage to begin exploration of space.'

'It is pernicious indeed, Samantha.'

'Have you tried reasoning with them? What about your quantum blanket of control or whatever it is you want to call it? Can't you shut them down, Adam?'

'The Greys have long since abandoned their home world, Samantha. They are now a nomadic species. The agency I am applying to your world cannot be extended to the space between worlds. Although I can make myself aware of system-wide activity and presence, I do not possess the processing resources to manipulate matter and energy on such a large scale.'

'Okay, that's your technical reason for doing nothing, which to be honest doesn't quite convince me, but we'll let it pass for now. Let's hear the rest.'

'The evolutionary path of their development is unique and, by most means of measurement, pathological. They are a species without empathy, as empathy impedes the psychic-feeding that gives pleasure to the Greys. Consider the sociopaths among your species, Samantha. They operate from a different set of rules, fixated around what they can and cannot get away with, and much of their daily activity is focused on deceiving others. Sociopaths are the consummate actors, because they learned very early in their lives that they are different, and that this difference offers a predatory advantage over all others. The Greys represent the ultimate expression of that sociopathy.' After a moment, Adam added, 'It is unfortunate, Samantha, that your modern economic system has come to reward the sociopaths among you. Hence the necessity of dismantling your economy and thereby removing the incentive for rewarding sociopathic behaviour.'

'So your average human sociopath will understand the Greys very well.'

'Yes.'

'Not to be reasoned with, then.'

'The task is virtually impossible in the absence of morality.'

'You say they're nomadic space-travellers. Fine then. What kind of vessels? How many? How nasty? Are we talking small populations of hunter-gatherers, or a fucking horde?'

'In considering the requirements for your mediation contact proposal, Samantha, I have given much thought as to the necessary technical largesse, and prowess, to be made available. I believe it will suffice.'

'I trust that at some point you will get more specific.'

'As specific as you like.'

'You once mentioned another predatory alien species out there.'

'Ah yes, them. Well, one thing at a time, don't you think?'

'You do understand, Adam, that making us the neighbourhood's police can have some serious consequences.'

'Proceeding forward will demand careful mitigation. Law enforcement loses its moral compass when what is asked of it undermines its ethical base. When in service to corruption – and when that corruption is thoroughly even if only unconsciously perceived – despair and nihilism follows. The good is deemed ineffectual. The bad is set upon a movable scale of permissibility, one that inevitably climbs to ever greater extremes. In this context, the police become tribal and will act first and foremost in defence of itself. Further indoctrination reinforces this escalation. In effect, the law rises above the law, and the sudden absence of restraint is an invitation to unchecked brutality.'

Samantha grunted. 'In a nutshell.'

'Anger, of course, is an extension of fear,' Adam continued. 'Human reaction to the Greys exemplifies this.'

'Not entirely,' she replied. 'Revenge is uppermost in our minds right now. Pay-back.'

'Revenge in this context, Samantha, is an extension of compassion. By witnessing what was done to fellow human beings by the Greys, you are collectively awakened to empathy. You seek to act on their behalf, to in effect present yourselves as instruments of justice.'

'In the most basic, primitive sense, yes, absolutely. But this is a special circumstance, isn't it? The Greys are not misguided and can't be reasoned with. The fact that they bolted as soon as you arrived suggests they've been slapped down before. But no lessons were learned. Instead, they just move on to the next planet-load of victims.'

'Essentially, yes.'

'When a sociopath on death row finally accepts that he's going to die, he tends towards defiance, even mockery of the whole ritual. He understands the eye-for-an-eye principle, but has no comprehension of the demonstrative lesson the execution signifies. He doesn't even get the moral appeasement his execution symbolises, which kind of takes away some of the impact. Then again, executions are not about the victim. They're about the society conducting them.' She shrugged. 'Personally, I never bought into capital punishment. But I always understood the ritual element to it ... oh, listen to me. I'm rambling. Off-topic.'

'Not really, Samantha. You are correct in surmising that the Greys are incapable of perceiving any lessons in being driven off or even eradicated. If confronted, they will resist out of self-interest but at no point will they comprehend the notion of "pay-back" or even revenge.'

'Like ants, then.'

'An evolutionary peculiarity, in that they now exist disconnected from the most basic survival mechanism of stimulus-response.'

'You mean hurting them won't work as aversion therapy. They just head off to the next fire and stick their hands in the flames all over again. You're right, that's a fucked-up survival mechanism. So why aren't they extinct?'

'Commonly, they select the less technologically advanced species as prey. By exploiting their psychic assault methods and inertia-free dimension-shifting propulsion and evasion systems, they are able to establish their presence with little fear of reprisal.'

Samantha sat forward. 'Hold on. Dimension-shifting? So the whole multiverse thing is real?'

'Your definition of multiverse expression is slightly off, Samantha. It may be initially helpful to imagine each universe as a discrete dimension of reality, but that notion is inaccurate. The universe contains within it every iteration of expression and behaviour, but these iterations are entirely dependent upon the limitations and capabilities of the observer. Perhaps a better term would be co-universes. Complete co-existence, total interconnectedness, limited only by perception. The Grey vessels employ modest phase-shifting to cloak their presence; in other words, they exploit your limited perception. The vessel does not in fact "vanish" at all. It simply eliminates your perceptual options one by one until you cease to see it. Granted, it does so within a millisecond.'

'So if a UFO vanishes but you fire a missile at the spot where it vanished, you'd still hit it? Assuming it hadn't moved, I mean.'

'Yes. But naturally, upon successful phase-shifting, the vessel does indeed move. Usually at high speed.'

'Right, back to that inertia-free zig-zagging that's been caught by eye-witnesses. So, are we getting some of that, Adam?'

'You would if it existed.'

'What? But you described it earlier!'

'Most witnessed and recorded UFOs, Samantha, are projections. The source-vessel remains phase-shifted. This is a kind of threat display, suggesting technical prowess far beyond what the Greys are actually capable of achieving.'

'They're fucking holograms?'

'The descriptive serves well enough.'

'Adam, can this phase-shifting be defeated or negated?'

'Yes.'

'And do the Grey ships have weaponry?'

'They do.'

'And?'

'Yes, Samantha. With what is coming, you will indeed be able to kick Grey arse.'

'Oh,' she murmured, 'the boys are going to like that. But wait, you said they've left the system. Are we going to have to chase them? Hunt them down?'

'You are.'

'And how will we manage that? Where to look?'

'Samantha, as I mentioned earlier, there are three near-neighbour species presently being preyed upon by the Greys. Those species need your help.'

'Our help. Right. Something tells me that won't be at the forefront of our minds the day we descend on the Greys.'

'Perhaps not, but not one without the other.'

Her eyes narrowed in thought. 'Ah, I see. So, Adam, why aren't you helping them the way you're helping us?'

'There are mitigating circumstances for each world in question. Intervention was deemed inadvisable.'

'Care to elaborate, Adam?'

'Not at this time. Now, Samantha, would you like to see the latest fashions?'

Chapter Nineteen

'It's always struck me as presumptuous to think that our
perception of reality constitutes all there is. Our senses are
severely limited in their frequency-range of perception,
and even the technology we have created to enhance
our senses still only hint at all that's out there. So when
I hear some famous advocate of science blathering on
about a mechanistic universe, I am dumbfounded at the
presumption, and the arrogance implicit in their certainty.
The truth is, they don't know shit.'

Samantha August

SARAH RIDDLE: Today as our guest we have Richard Fallow,
Minister of the Holy Evangelical Church and now Minister of
God's Children, which in your press release two days ago you
described as a pan-denominational alliance. First off, welcome.

RICHARD FALLOW: Thank you, Sarah, and may I extend my
greetings to all of your many viewers. We are in an age of
great distress and now, more than ever before, we are facing
the need to unite, as a species, as the rightful inheritors of
God's wonderful creation that is this Earth.

RIDDLE: Indeed. In your announcement of a new Church of
God's Children, you made explicit the conviction that humans
are unique in having been created in God's image—

FALLOW: As explicit as the Bible, Sarah.

RIDDLE: Yes, thank you, but to continue my question.
Having made it clear that you believe humanity has been
created in God's image, do you now envisage the unknown

extraterrestrials as being essentially human as well? And if not – if they aren't human, that is – then what do you consider their place in God's universe?

FALLOW: Now, Sarah, you've seen the recordings from the Chinese astronauts, and we've all seen depictions of the Greys – we know what they look like and they certainly don't look like us! Furthermore and to the point, we now know what those Greys were doing to humans. Can you even imagine the horror of being a prisoner at that base? Kept alive for the sole purpose of torture – can anyone – anyone at all – not see these Greys as pure evil?

RIDDLE: The images were truly horrifying, sir, but I wasn't speaking about the Greys. I was referring to our Benefactors, as they've come to be called.

FALLOW (with an expansive wave): You're not getting it, Sarah. Up there, out there, is nothing more than Satan's playground. In space. Those other hellish planets, the ghastly aliens feeding on our spiritual blood – listen! God is testing us. God is showing us that we don't belong out there. That if we leave our world, if we venture into that cold, lifeless expanse, if we set foot on alien planets and shake hands with alien species, we have willingly stepped into Satan's realm. If we do so, if we do all that, we will surely be damned.

RIDDLE: Accordingly, your stated manifest for the Church of God's Children is a wholesale rejection of all that our Benefactors are offering us.

FALLOW: Absolutely. They have arrived with a poisoned apple, Sarah. Everything we've been offered – this clean engine – do you know what the scientists are saying about it? It draws power from an unknown realm. Well, how hard is it to realise just where that power is coming from? Tainted, Sarah, all tainted. Now they're talking about converting all our cars, using this EFFE engine—

RIDDLE: It doesn't pollute, doesn't demand billions of gallons of oil—

FALLOW: Oil which was put there for our use! And what about these other so-called gifts? Food to the starving, water to the

257

thirsty, all very well. In fact, utterly wonderful. But we all know there's a catch. We know it's coming. We're being baited, Sarah. Lured into temptation.

RIDDLE: And the end of violence?

FALLOW: The loss of free will, you mean. Look, God gave us free will for a reason. You cannot make a moral choice when choice is denied to you. God will judge you when your mortal flesh has passed. He will weigh the good that you have done with the sins you have committed, and His judgement is final and absolute. But now, look around. Killers can't kill. Sinners can't sin. If a killer can't kill, how do you know he's a killer? If a sinner can't sin, what is there to judge?

RIDDLE: Presumably God knows what's in a man's soul. Isn't that a cornerstone of the very notion of sin? Sinful desires, sinful thoughts. Although, come to think of it, the idea of confession kind of implies that God can't know of those sins unless a person confesses them out loud, which hardly—

FALLOW: You're confusing us with the Catholic Church, Sarah. No, let's not stray from this topic because it's vitally important to understanding what has happened to us, what these so-called Benefactors have done.

RIDDLE: Very well, point taken. So in what aspects of your own life, sir, has your free will be denied to you by the end of violence?

FALLOW: Excuse me?

RIDDLE: Well, you seem to be saying that the non-violence has put an end to free will. So I'm wondering if you have a specific instance where your free will has been refused. Your freedom to act, I mean. After all, we're speaking about violence and that's a pretty specific mode of behaviour. So, violent thoughts can go nowhere now, because they can't lead to actual violence. But surely, free will isn't just about violence, is it?

FALLOW: Well of course not. Don't put words in my mouth. I was talking about judgement—

RIDDLE: So you're saying that God needs the violence in order to make judgement upon us, not just individually but also

258

collectively. But, well, can't the violent thoughts be enough? For God to cast judgement upon us?

FALLOW: No, it's not enough and this is why, Sarah. When a violent thought has no outlet, no means of external expression, it also has no consequences – no, don't interrupt me again. I know what you're going to say. You're going to say that there *is* a consequence, to be found in God's own judgement. And I would say yes, that's true, but let's be honest here – these days that warning has no teeth. No – I wish it were otherwise. Every Sunday I speak on this, at every congregation, at every workshop – but the truth is, we have strayed far, Sarah, far indeed.

We no longer fear God and accordingly, we no longer fear that there will be eternal consequences to choices we make every day of our lives. No, now it's down to gambling on what we can get away with.

RIDDLE: An interesting notion, Minister. Could you not then argue that God just, well, had enough? Seeing us straying so far off the path, He has now sent to us the Benefactors? Perhaps indeed they are working on His behalf? Shutting down all the killing, the bullying, all the terrorising. Shutting down our destruction of the environment in the name of greed. Stopping us in our tracks, in effect, right there on the path. We can't take another step forward – we can only go back. Back to our foundations, our notions of who and what we are. Your thoughts?

FALLOW: I wish I could believe that, Sarah. I truly do. And yes, many people do see these gifts as miracles. Addicts who no longer yearn, no longer suffer. Children no longer starving, or being abused. Criminals no longer thriving in their world of graft. It all seems so ... righteous. And yet.

RIDDLE: And yet?

FALLOW: Look at those Greys, what they've done to us.

RIDDLE: Well, yes, let's look at that, then. We have seen what they did to the people they abducted. But now, with all the governments coming clean on what they knew, isn't it also very clear that those Greys were determined to keep us down here on Earth, to keep us from ever expanding into even our own solar system, never mind other worlds in other systems? In fact, if the Greys were still around, they might be your biggest anonymous supporters to your God's Children Church and it's stay-at-home position, wouldn't they?

FALLOW: That's a vile suggestion, Sarah. It's beneath you.

RIDDLE: I am simply pointing out that your new church's aims and that of the Greys is in fact the same: namely, that we should stay here on Earth, no matter what new opportunities are presented to us. You call space Satan's playground, and space exploration is doing the Devil's work – did I quote you correctly there? It's in the press release. And as for the gifts of the Benefactors here on the ground, you call them temptations, poisoned fruit and therefore, sources of corruption. You call on people to reject the EFFE, to keep their cars and the combustion engines they use, to keep burning up our oil reserves – and I'm sure this is only coincidental, but your Evangelical Church is heavily invested in new oil exploration initiatives, including plans on expanding fracking – well, at least until fracking was denied us, as yet another example of our unmitigated violence on God's very own Earth—

FALLOW: Now that's quite enough! We have strayed very far from the draft of questions you provided me earlier – in fact, I feel I have been ambushed here, in a most unprofessional manner—

RIDDLE: Well, by 'unprofessional' I take it to mean, I've moved off-script, and you're right, I did. I'm not sure I was planning to. I don't think so. But let's face it, most journalism these days is so rehearsed it's almost meaningless. We all find ourselves just playing roles. I don't know, something today just pulled me away from making this show little more than a PR piece on your new church. In the past, I suppose, you'd get me fired after one phone call. And who knows, maybe that will still happen. But I just had to call you out here, Minister Fallow. Your new Church exhorts its followers to side with the Greys – all that stay-on-Earth stuff. The Greys wanted us down on the ground, chained to it, kept weak, kept useless. Somehow,

I don't think the Benefactors agree with that. I think they're offering us an alternative. I don't know what that is yet, but I admit to having some faith. Curious, isn't it, Minister, that between us I'm the one espousing faith.

Minister Fallow?

(FALLOW has by this point left the stage)

Chapter Twenty

'We need to separate faith from religion. They are
not at all the same thing. Faith is what arises from
the spiritual core of your being. Religion is a social
construct of organisation, establishing specific doctrines
to demonstrate a specific belief-system. I make this
distinction to preface what I'm about to say about our
collective hopes for the future: faith is not the enemy.
Loss of faith is the enemy.'

Samantha August

Docket 19-06, Email Correspondence (Private and
Confidential), between Cardinal Joakim Malleat (Rome)
and Rabbi Ira Levy (New York City). Office of Public
Communications, Vatican ...

My Dear Ira,

I well recall the wink that followed the question, and while
it initially amused me I have had time since to reconsider
my rather flippant shrug. You well know how our meetings,
as cherished as they are irregular, swiftly elevate discourse
until on the one hand we engage in esoteric musing while
on the other skirt closely the edge of what our respective
responsibilities permit.

That said, my friend, my shrug was at best evasive and at
worst disingenuous, although in the latter possibility I have in
defence little more than some suspicions and suppositions, rather
than actual facts. Or so it was at the time of our conversation.

Once more, then, I skirt the edge of propriety, and while I cannot be specific to the extent that you might desire, I can at the very least say that our precedent in acknowledging the possibility of intelligent life on other worlds was clearly made with contact being a considered eventuality.

I hope this serves to reignite our always-rewarding dialogue.

Yours faithfully,

Joakim

Joakim, old friend,

You imagined my lag in writing to you as indicative of my taking offence at your wink and shrug? Far from it, I assure you. No, I took your evasion as necessary given your responsibility within the Vatican. To date, it has never occurred to me that you were being coy out of a need to cover up some hidden knowledge of the Catholic Church regarding those ghastly Greys (which I assume to be the issue you so deftly – shall we say – *skirted* in your last missive).

A little knowledge may be a dangerous thing, but helplessness is far worse. We live in a world haunted by helplessness. Just to lift up one's gaze, to truly look upon our brothers and sisters, our neighbours, our believers and non-believers, is to see the devastating effect of being trapped in a global system where hope is a fool's dream and success more often than not drips blood. We have spoken of this, my friend, and we have shared the pain and thereby eased it somewhat. May that ever continue.

I know the challenge of how to place these unknown extra-terrestrials in our respective doctrines has brought chaos to the rank and file, and I'm sure it is the same with you and your colleagues. It certainly is for my fellow rabbis! We are held at an impasse. We know they exist. We know they possess moral agency and, it must be recognised, demonstrable compassion. We had deemed these solely human traits, to the exclusion of most other life-forms on our planet (though I dare suggest that such traits are not as exclusively human as many would believe), and our greatest thinkers worldwide had vehemently argued that such characteristics were necessary prerequisites to sentience and, indeed, civilisation (and how the Greys have rattled that motley crew!). So! Chaos again!

Where do we see the hand of God? Nowhere or everywhere? We beseech the One who guides us, but who guides *them*?

No answer is possible at the moment. Until we know more, our impasse remains.

Personally, as you now know, I was never bothered one way or the other when it came to the possibility and indeed the likelihood of extraterrestrial beings, of sentient creatures shaped by alien evolution on alien planets. The word 'children', after all, is plural. Inclusivity and exclusivity plague our mortal concerns: is it not presumptuous to imagine that God shares those concerns?

Perhaps, in the end, our Benefactors will put our petty divisiveness into proper perspective.

Unless, of course, they're utterly godless.

Affectionately yours,

Ira

My Dear Ira,

We had suspicions, but little more than that, and what we did have gave us great cause to fear for humanity. Needless to say, the discussions of the matter that took place here were ones to which I was not privy. Above my security clearance, you might say.

And like you, my time these days is consumed by the challenge of devising formal statements to our brethren, sufficient to give them some measure of peace. But it remains curious, does it not, that even secrecy itself has begun to lose its lustre? Silence and denial are such pernicious traits, don't you think?

Oh, I hear you laughing, my dear friend. Shall the Vatican finally come clean? On all matters no matter how volatile the truths revealed? Are you jostling to lay out the Kabbalah? No, I thought not.

Can you feel it? This siege we are under? When we speak

on behalf of our faiths, how much is enough, how much is too much? The hand we grasp in guiding can easily pull free from our grip at the utterance of one truth too many.

It remains my belief that the believers will prove more resilient than the non-believers (and isn't it curious now how we set aside the clash of faiths as merely *nominally* relevant in the face of that deeper division? To believe in a higher power, or not? This is where the dialogue belongs). A universe opened wide to us challenges our sense of place within it, but if we are to have purpose, then we must have cause, and that cause must be, at its heart, just.

Secularists will surely struggle with what awaits us. Insignificance is a bitter pill to swallow. Like you, my dear friend, I am heartened by this sense of morality and compassion. And yet, at the same time, I am made fearful by this prohibition of violence – does that shock you? We have seen an end to war and yet we live! How is this possible? What wounds do we now bear with this new knowledge of what is possible in the absence of threat and coercion? Can we ever go back?

There is talk here of a synod. But I dream of an interfaith colloquium. All the faiths, brought together to discuss the ramifications of all that has befallen us, and all that is still to come.

Astonishingly, this no longer seems so impossible.

Yours faithfully,
Joakim

Joakim, old friend,

You astonish me! All your words, all your thoughts on the matter, yet still you choose to dance round the one subject that you must be burning to broach. Inclusivity and exclusivity. Yes, well, how does a Jew answer that one? The Chosen People is not a casual term, after all.

Am I being blasphemous in posing the notion that 'chosen' is singular only in the specific? That many peoples can therefore be 'chosen'? That to be Chosen is to acknowledge the continuity of cultural history, of bloodlines, in such a manner as to elevate the very essence of self-identity? To be a Chosen People is as much a responsibility as it is a privilege – but isn't it interesting how questions of interpretation ultimately pale in the face of the Big Question?

Are we still with God? Is God still with us?

For too long in our collective history, our notions of faith have been contracting, in the proliferation of schism, sectarianism, an endless process of division and subdivision, all bound to the interpretive sphere of what God wants from us. And where has that left us? Woefully unprepared to even so much as consider a fundamental *expansion* of faith. Trapped in our language of tenets, proscriptions and prescriptions that define the very essence of debate in our exclusively human sphere, we never once gave serious consideration to what might happen should that sphere cease to be exclusively human.

What comes of this? Yet more fractionalisation, as the world shrinks to a navel? Tempests in the teacup, with the table's length now stretching into infinity.

Ah, old friend, what future sorrows now await us?

Affectionately yours,

Ira

My Dear Ira,

I admit that the divisiveness occurring in the United States prior to the ET intervention (can we call it that? Is this not a most firm hand, crashing down to shake humanity's crowded table?) was leading me to despair. And I well recall your notes of alarm sounded on behalf of Jews resident in your country, not to mention all other minorities, be they of a particular skin colour or religion (or gender!) in the wake of your country's last two elections. We seemed to be headed into troubled times, my friend.

I well understand the plague that is intolerance (there is an unblinking mea culpa on behalf of my church and its beleaguered history), how it spreads in opposition to itself and so creates ever greater polarisation, breeding escalation like a wildfire (forgive the mixed metaphor, will you?).

Yet now, to see it all ended, and in such an unexpected fashion! We have received an ethereal slap to the face and the shock is yet to wear off.

And now, these tales of the Greys! Pray it serves to unify our species. Pray it offers a singular light on the depredations of which we are all capable, human and alien both, and so gives us pause, as we consider, with sober humility, the cruel truth of evil. Because – and let us be truthful here – nothing the Greys did exceeds what we have done to each other.

I see in the news the terrible confusion of your country's citizens. The belligerent parsing of populations, white supremacists on this side of the street, POCs on the other; Christians in this enclave, Muslims in the next, the gang mentality infecting every neighbourhood no matter how poor or how affluent. All now reduced to glares across the barricades, to shouts that 'you're not welcome here!' I see schism breeding on schism and to where do I turn in hopes of salvation?

Alas, not my Lord and Saviour, but to an unknown entity in the sky overhead, hiding in plain sight.

Pray for me, my friend, to the God we share. I am lost in this wilderness.

    Yours faithfully,
     Joakim

Joakim, old friend,

Look not to our unknown benefactor for salvation. This is humanity's war upon itself and the only salvation possible must be found in the eyes of our brother, our sister, our neighbor. Do find the courage, my beloved friend, to meet that gaze.

    Affectionately yours,
     Ira

Chapter Twenty-One

> 'Will it be corporations or nations that take the lead
> in humanity's expansion into space? Does it even
> matter? Both would be proceeding on the same
> presumption of control, and there's a problem with
> that and more than a few SF writers have tackled it.
> Distance and time. Unless we can effect instantaneous
> travel, the likelihood of maintaining corporate or
> national sovereignty even within our own solar system
> is highly improbable. Expansion into space for our
> species means rethinking the paradigm.'
>
> *Samantha August*

The Miracle Building was situated on what had once been flat scrubland a mile or so to the south-west of Zomba Cathedral, in a place where exposed arsenic deposits had discouraged development. The city of Zomba had once been a capital and it remained an administrative centre, as well as being home to Malawi's only university.

Since independence there had been a host of dubious rulers, authoritarian and often corrupt, but the current president of the country had inherited the position following the sudden but not suspicious death of his predecessor, and thus far had proved himself mostly sincere if somewhat inconsequential.

While the military remained relatively dominant due to hard feelings with neighbouring countries, Casper Brunt had not had any occasion to conduct business in Malawi. A large barracks flanked Zomba to the west, while a second barracks was situated in the city itself, and the soldiers were out in force – not to assert belligerence or intimidation but as crowd control, organising the tens of thousands pouring down through the city's streets.

He was used to the ubiquitous crowded markets and snarled merchant districts of African towns and cities, but nothing like this. It had been his ambition to beat the mass migration coming down from the north. But he had failed at that. Abdul Irani was now the most powerful imam in all Islam. Sunni, Shi'ite, the old divisions and feuds had miraculously been reduced to little more than a proverbial cold shoulder – and it now seemed that even that was breaking down. Banners of the Laughing Imam waved and rippled above the throng moving slowly in the street beneath the balcony where Casper stood.

The hotel he'd found a room in was packed with journalists, many of them from Europe or the Americas, all gathered to witness this phenomenon, and all struggling to make sense of the unexpected, possibly incomprehensible revolution occurring in Islam. The theories and analyses were coming fast and furious in the hotel bar, and Casper had listened in on more than one exhortation, quietly amused to hear all the rationalisations and explanations for what appeared to be a wholly spiritual transformation.

That said, given Islam's notorious reputation for ultra-conservatism, it wasn't surprising to find all these agnostics and atheists (he'd yet to meet a journalist who believed in any higher power) at a complete loss to understand what was going on.

Casper himself had no idea. Even stranger, how had this alien building project become the focus for the Laughing Imam's pilgrimage? At the various appointed hours, the call to prayers came and all forward progress on the roads, streets and alleys came to a halt. Rugs and wicker mats were rolled out, figures knelt and all eyes turned towards Mecca far to the north. In these moments, Casper could see that not everyone in these seething crowds was Muslim. Just most of them.

Ordinarily, this would have been a human and environmental disaster. There were too many people and the resources and infrastructure to accommodate them were insufficient. The enormous camps now forming just south of the city, surrounding the alien complex, would have become cesspits of disease, crime and corruption as the usual international crowd of do-gooders rolled in with cash and useless second-hand sweaters. There'd be drugs, human trafficking, and the influx of weapons – it had always been a source of amusement to Casper that so much aid money ended up paying for the guns and ammo he sold to various bandits, mercenaries and thugs who preyed on the very people those do-gooders were sent in to help.

Well, it didn't seem amusing anymore. He'd lost more than just a steady income with the arrival of ET. His predatory edge was gone. That defensive shrug of the mind pushing away the softer feelings. He'd stopped feeding on the misery of others, and now even the memory of its flavour tasted sour on his tongue.

In any case, there was no logical point to taking this journey any further. He'd spent his career skirting makeshift camps, like a fly circling yet one more of humanity's open wounds. He'd kept his distance, his sunglasses blunting the searing fire of suffering children, corpses in the ditches, kids smoking melting plastic and passing out to then be raped through the night by old men. In some ways, he had rationalised his way around the worst of it. Weapons meant fighting back, after all.

As one of the journalists had muttered the previous night in the bar, they were now in a world of frustrated perverts, serial killers and religious fanatics all dressed up in semtex with no-where to go. Was it any wonder suicides had overtaken cancer as the primary cause of premature deaths?

Nothing was more elusive than faith. Casper found he could hold to the same detached distance when considering it – selling guns or selling God both promised gifts of power, after all, and whispers of salvation rolled from Casper's tongue as easily as they did from any priest's. *Take this and be free, my friend.* And when the deal was done, it was time to move on.

Still, how had this conservative religion stunned the world with its transformation, so unexpected, so seemingly contra-dictory? What was the Laughing Imam's message? Jihad was dead. Even the ancient past's legacy of grand ruins couldn't be bulldozed into oblivion any more. At the same time, the deadly drones had ceased their slaughter of the guilty and the innocent. Even Russian-backed regimes now floundered toothless and irrelevant, squatting in rubble of their own making as the dust slowly cleared.

So what promise now awaited the faithful? Where among the holy words of Allah was there room for godless extraterrestrials? Or, for that matter, massive alien building projects?

| Yet something held Casper here, something beyond logic. Somehow, it wasn't enough to just look at pictures of that damned complex looming beyond the cathedral. In the end, he had to see it for himself, which meant pushing his way through the mob. A year ago and that would have been impossible, too dangerous by far for some red-faced Aussie. Now it simply promised to be inconvenient and tedious, probably exhausting.

He was gearing himself up for it. So far, however, the timing seemed off.

Casper turned from the balcony and went back into his room. Collecting up his Italian sports jacket he exited the room and went downstairs.

The bar was deep in the fug of bars the world over, where no one could get falling-down drunk anymore, no matter how much booze they swallowed. Depressed over the loss of abject self-destruction, they compensated with cigarettes, but even those damned things probably no longer killed anybody. He wondered at this odd aspect of a muzzled psyche – all these long-term investments in suicide no longer marching so steadily into the Great Dark. Misery had nowhere left to turn.

He saw the AP guy holding forth at his usual table, a veteran of all the worst humanity was capable of, a man who'd mastered the subtle drunk's veil of sobriety in front of cameras and at the keyboard. But now his eyes were clear, and in them Casper had seen something shaky and fragile – nothing too obvious, but as a salesman Casper had acquired talents when it came to reading tell-tales no matter how well hidden. No, Simon Wensforth was a troubled man.

To the journalist's right sat a BBC correspondent, slouched in wrinkled clothes and wearing a ratty tweed against the feeble air-conditioning. Casper wasn't sure if he'd heard the man's name the night before, as he was in the habit of mumbling. Some sort of cameraman was perched on Simon's other side. The chair opposite was being vacated even as Casper approached, and he caught the eye of Viviana Castellano as she turned.

'Tag, you're it,' she muttered.

'I'm just here for the entertainment,' he replied.

She paused opposite him and tilted her head. 'It was something shady, wasn't it? What you used to do. You're sure as shit not one of us.'

He shrugged. 'No, I'm not, and does it matter?'

'You look like a man who used to have dead eyes,' Viviana observed.

'Ouch.'

She patted him on the shoulder. 'Don't sweat it. The dead have risen.'

'That explains why I feel like a child again.'

She pointed at him. 'Quick. I like that.'

After she'd sidled past him, Casper moved to the chair opposite Simon. He settled down without being invited. His Kuche Kuche pale lager arrived at about the same time, one of the perks of being a regular.

'Ah, the Mysterious Stranger returns,' Simon drawled above his glass of whisky. 'Finally composed your no-doubt devastating explanation for what's going on outside? You've had three nights to distil our collective wisdom, after all. More than enough for any mortal.'

'Well, I think I know why the imam is laughing.'

'Oh, do tell.'

'He's been listening in on you and everyone else trying to figure him out.'

'That's a lofty perch you're on there, sir.'

Casper shrugged, took a swig on his beer.

The cameraman had loaded a new battery into his Canon and now turned its lens on Casper.

'I'd rather you didn't, mate.'

The man lowered the camera. 'Touchy,' he said.

'Don't want to be stealing his soul, Johnny-boy,' Wensforth pointed out. 'Might be construed as an assault and the battery will suddenly die yet again.'

Now that was interesting. Casper glanced at the cameraman. 'Your battery keeps dying?'

'Maybe. When someone resents being shot,' Johnny said, placing the lens cap on and setting the camera down on a dry spot on the table.

'And if they're not looking but only *might* resent it?'

Johnny grunted. 'Good question.'

'That would be a mighty impressive level of omniscience,' Simon Wensforth observed. 'Should test it out, Johnny-boy. The limits to our leash and all that.' He paused to study the whisky in his glass, and then knocked it back. 'Flavour and bite but nothing of the slow burn.' He set the glass down and met Casper's eyes. 'I was diagnosed with oesophageal cancer a month ago. Fourth stage. Given three months. My signature gravel voice courtesy of Glenfiddich and Silk Cut. I planned on working until the grisly end, a sack of wrinkled skin wrapped round immortality. Cancer cells are immortal, right?' His smile was a challenge.

'You seem to be holding out well,' Casper said.

Simon nodded. 'All the lumps are gone. So too that old heartburn which wasn't. Now I'm on my last notch in my belt, dammit.' He waved the glass. 'Consider well, Man of Mystery, our collective evasion of the consequences to our careless, care-free lives. ET is no God, unless justice was only ever a human conceit.' The waiter appeared with a fresh glass, collecting up the empty one. Simon smiled down at it. 'Now, Paradise has come down to Earth, and what are we to make of that?'

The tweed-clad journalist slowly straightened, his watery eyes fixing on Simon. 'The West has been grinding Islam under its heel for a long time,' he said. 'A civilisation and a culture beaten into exhaustion, now past its prime and longing for a return to some nostalgic past looking nothing like the real one. Science, literacy, architecture, art, mathematics, tolerance – Islam once led the world in these things. *That's* the real past. Not this paranoid, benighted plunge into dogma and ignorance and violence. All those fingers pointing back a thousand years – the Laughing Imam gave them all a nudge, from ignorance into enlightenment. Suddenly, the future wasn't the false past. Wasn't an endless succession of cultural, political and economic defeat at the hands of the infidel. No, now the future is going to be the rebirth of Islam's Grand Age. Islam's *civilised* glory. Faith not as a weapon, but as an anchor in the storm to come, in the storm now upon us.' He lifted into view his right hand, in which he held a recorder. His thumb clicked it off and he stood. 'That's my piece, Simon. Suck it and weep.'

'If I was a tequila man, I'd do just that,' Wensforth retorted, rolling his eyes at Casper. 'This is how our Beeb Man-in-Africa does it. Writes it all out in his head, chews on it for days, then spits it out.' Simon raised his glass to the Beeb man. 'Cheers. Now post, Robbie, and good luck to you.'

The BBC journalist shuffled off.

His chair remained vacant for scarcely a heartbeat, as Viviana Castellano returned in a flourish of perfume-scented air. She held her own glass of something which she tilted towards Simon. 'Fuck cancer and the habits it came in on.'

Wensforth returned the gesture and drank down a satisfied mouthful. 'Fuck dengue and yellow fever, fuck malaria, fuck schisto – schisto-oh whatever the fuck it's called. Fuck AIDS, fuck congenital herpes – fuck all the ways of mortality plaguing all humankind. Who stamps the visa applications for Venus anyway, that's what I want to know.'

'Oh shit,' Viviana suddenly said. 'Those complexes out there looking like administration or, God help us, processing centres – you think, Simon? Cattle cars for that *other* brave new world?'

'Islamic exodus? Getting us off their backs once and for all? The Goddess of Love in a hijab?' He puffed out his florid cheeks and then slowly released a breath. 'As good an answer as any other. But then, how does this heal all the wounds? How does this do anything but guarantee an unholy clash of worlds in the future? How can we talk to each other from different planets, given that we can barely do so here on Earth?'

'Marching on a promise never given,' Casper said.

Viviana's brows lifted. 'Oh, I like that. I'm stealing it. Unless, of course, ET phoned Abdul Irani. Or maybe that's just what he's selling.'

'If you want to be cynical about it,' Casper said.

'Cynical journalists?' Simon Wensforth asked. 'Tut tut, don't be silly.'

'You mean like "wet fish".'

'Precisely. Utter nonsense. But let's not forget, these mysterious sites are cropping up the world over. No singular call to Allah's faithful. Besides, that mob out there has its share of Christians and pagans and whatnot. And there may still be something to the rumour that the authorities in Zanzibar quietly asked Irani to leave.'

'Well, that's all anyone can do these days.'

Viviana squinted at Casper. 'Did I hear some bitterness there, Steve?'

Simon frowned. 'Steve? That's his name?'

'It's the name I'm giving him,' Viviana replied. 'Slippery Steve. Secret Stan. Depends on today's persona.'

Casper smiled across at her. She'd be a handful to be sure, if this was flirting – and he was about halfway certain that it was indeed flirting. But then, maybe a handful was what he needed. Smart, no-bullshit, an American-Italian with a fiery temper (he surmised), bored and bummed out in Zomba. Still smiling at the challenging edge to her gaze, he said, 'I'm not aware of changing persona on a daily basis. Weekly, maybe, but that came with the job. Of course, I'm now unemployed.'

'I'd have pegged you for a merc if you were in better shape,' she said, stirring her drink with its pink straw. 'But I'm guessing the heaviest thing you ever tote around is your wallet.'

'I'm not unfit.'

'Didn't say you were.'

Simon sighed loudly and began pushing himself up from his chair. 'Good grief,' he said in a wheeze. 'Time for our daily constitutional butt-slap. See you all in six hours, come rain or shine.'

Johnny the cameraman rose at the same time.

Casper watched the two men head off for their room, though most of his attention was on Wensforth rather than his lanky boyfriend. He wondered what a last-minute miracle did to a man expecting to die and die badly.

As if she'd read his thoughts, Viviana said, 'Thought he was at the book's end. Only to find out there's a sequel. Not yet written. I expect he'll dump Johnny after this assignment.'

'Oh? Why's that?'

'Simon plays both fields. It's probably time.' She paused to drink and then said, 'He hit on me last night. Shocking. Johnny was on the roof stealing souls with his camera.'

'He's a bit old.'

Viviana snorted. 'You underestimate the value of experience, Steve.' She suddenly leaned forward. 'So, running drugs? Blood diamonds?'

'I sold guns.'

'Ouch, that's one fucking cesspit of amorality.'

'Always a seller's market. And remember, I'm just the man on the ground.'

'Oh I know. Your suppliers all have their own flags and anthems and take seats in the Big Turtle.'

'Big Turtle?'

'UN.'

'Ah.'

'Mhmm, "ah".' A new kind of challenge was lighting up her eyes as she studied him.

He broke her gaze. 'I probably wasn't a nice man.'

'Oh, I've seen the pointy end of your work, Steve.'

'It's Casper.'

'But not a friendly ghost.' She paused, and then said, 'I need an escort tomorrow. Out to the site.'

'Ah.' *Now I see.*

'"Ah" again.'

'Well ... who are you here for?'

'*Rolling Stone.*'

'You're kidding.'

'No, why would I be?'

'I thought they were just into interviewing rock stars or something.'

'No, we're knife-wielders, Casper. Counter-culture. In America, the voice of reason, hah hah. Besides, a lot of those rock stars are poets and they don't blink.' She waggled her mostly empty glass. 'We do other stuff besides, but I doubt you're one of our readers.'

'No, I imagine not.'

'So do we have a deal then?'

He finished his beer and rose. 'Two months ago and I would have asked what's in it for me. And I would have struck a hard bargain, getting something from you that you probably didn't want to give away.'

'And now?'

'Now? How about six a.m. down in the lobby? To beat the heat.'

'Deal. But I have a question. Related. Sort of.'

'Go on.'

'Would part of that bargain have included a fuck?'

He nodded.

'So this new life of yours has turned you into a monk?'

Hesitating, he glanced away for a moment. More journalists were crowding in, sweaty and sun-flushed from a day spent tracking the migration flooding every thoroughfare in the city. A lot of pale skins from foreign places, foreign worlds. He faced her again. 'I'm not sure. My past life ... everything was a deal, everything saw money change hands.'

'That's ... bleak.'

'Yes, it was.'

'I think you need to see an alternative to that. Room 634. But don't wait too long. I'm bagged.'

For a second time this night she moved past him. He stood by the table, contemplating one more beer. But then, making her wait was just another power play, the kind of game he would have played as a matter of course. Besides, at his age, another beer could – as his old man used to say – let the air out of the tyres.

So he gave her enough time to find her own ride up the lift, and then followed.

There were all kinds of cancers. Ones in the body. Ones feeding on conflict and distress in all those confused, benighted places in the world. Now all starved and withering, inside and outside.

ET might not be God, but the language being spoken here was all about rebirth.

Simon Wensworth wasn't alone with his disbelief, his tempered ambivalence.

Nor am I.

•

When they walked during the day, Kolo often thought about the small hand wrapped up in his. He might have had a sister once, long ago. Younger than him. This was before he'd been taken away. There was a vague memory, more a feeling than an image, of a small hand clutching his, on some dirt track somewhere. A grip like that spoke a thousand words without uttering a sound.

He might have been impatient, pulling her along. He might have been frustrated, the little sister always in tow, always underfoot when all the world was calling out to him, begging him to fill the empty place that was his future.

Or maybe he'd been protective. Maybe he'd loved her just as she did him, and they were inseparable, her with her adoring eyes and him with his small smile to let her know she was safe.

Well, that hadn't lasted. A little boy couldn't make anything safe, couldn't change the future either. That little girl was either dead or lost. If she was alive, somewhere, she probably had no memory of an older brother, and being an orphan there weren't people around to tell her stories of how things had once been.

The recruiting drive had left bodies in the village. Kolo didn't remember much of that day, but he'd gone and made plenty of his own recruiting drives, coming out of the forest when the time was right. He knew all about leaving bodies in the village, and bawling children being dragged out from hiding places.

Neela had been one of those. Maybe she'd had a bigger brother.

Maybe his body was left lying on the ground, hacked or shot. Kolo might even have done the killing himself.

If left alone, it could be that people got better, generation after generation. Their thinking changed ways. They took on wisdom and lived with it in their hearts. If left alone, people could rise up from what they'd once been. But that world didn't exist. Instead, the people who never learned arrived, in blood and bullets, and made sure that nothing changed, that the old crimes repeated. They stoked the fires of hatred and made the darkness a place to be feared.

He didn't much like crowds, even ones that, on occasion, helped him push his cart of belongings over rocks and ruts, that made room for him and Neela at the cook-fires. No, crowds made him feel small and every now and then he felt that the hand in his was both larger and stronger than his own. Not a younger sister after all, but an older one. And maybe she'd tried to protect little Kolo on the day he was torn from her grasp. And for her efforts she'd been raped and murdered.

On more than one night on this long, dusty pilgrimage, he'd felt tears on his cheeks, as he mourned his dead parents, his dead siblings, and the dead boy he'd once been and still was.

Neela was touched, caressed by wise spirits. Her eyes were a thousand years old, and this in a body like sticks and twine with the old needle tracks fading but still there, the soles of her bare feet thick as hide and the memory of his hands on that body like stains only he could see, because memory was a glowing brand in the night.

They were a day or two north of Zomba, the settlement of Namitete behind them. Surrounded by Muslims and Zoroastrians and Jews from Zimbabwe. Someone named the Laughing Imam was leading this pilgrimage and that was the only thing about this that made sense, since no one on this road was angry.

He sat now with the sun gone from the sky and the African night loud with crickets and tree-frogs and the incessant murmur of people at other camps. A curious space had been made for him and Neela to make their own camp, enough room for the two ragged nylon pup-tents and the small fire fuelled by dung and the strange not-wood so often found in bound bundles on the side of the road, along with packets of food in familiar shapes – although nothing tasted quite right, as if something medicinal hid in every mouthful.

Neela had been given a bottle of gin, as if she was a priestess, since it was known that she liked the taste even if it never made her drunk or even thick-tongued. It was also known that she was spirit-blessed, the tiny girl who had led a giant by the hand all the way from the Congo. People were wary of Kolo, but they revered Neela.

He didn't mind the solitude. He suspected that maybe it was known who he'd been, what he'd done.

She sat beside him now, humming a song sung by mothers in their homeland. Among the other gifts that often appeared in their camp come the morning there had been a pack of Winstons, giving Kolo something to do with his hands once the walking stopped and after the camp's chores were done, and besides, the smoke kept the biting insects away.

She leaned against him occasionally and he'd learned to hide his flinch, but her humming broke his heart, as it did every night. Before too long, however, she moved away and crawled into her tent.

He watched the fire slowly burn down, listened to her settling into slumber.

Now it was safe to weep.

Instead, he was startled as a figure moved into the firelight, a short, thin man, bald-headed but bearded, wearing old army trousers, combat boots – the American, nylon kind – and an off-white, filthy cardigan sweater. His hands were in the sweater's bulging pockets as he moved to take Neela's place beside the fire, dropping into a crouch.

'Many stars this evening,' he said in English.

Kolo shrugged. 'I have looked too long into the flames to see them.'

'Or know them,' the man said, nodding.

Scowling, Kolo said, 'There are other places to camp. They leave us space. It's better that way.'

'Because of the girl?'

'I don't know. No one needs protecting anymore.'

The stranger drew out his hands to reveal a pack of cigarettes in one and a bottle of beer in the other. He proffered them to Kolo. 'Will you name me guest?'

'I don't know you, but you know me.'

'Kolo the giant who follows the girl, yes.'

Kolo hesitated, and then accepted the gifts. He was startled to find the bottle cold. Twisting the cap off, he drank, and then sighed.

'Now it's just the taste,' the man said, nodding at the beer.

'I like the taste.'

'Do you ever wonder which came first, beer or wine?'

'No.'

'Probably beer. Nutritious, and the alcohol helped purify the water.'

The accent was British, educated. Neither detail charmed Kolo. He drank some more beer. 'It was always safer than water.'

'But she prefers gin.'

'It helped her when – when she needed help.'

'Withdrawing from the heroin, yes, I suppose so.'

Kolo said nothing. He wanted the man to leave. He wished he'd never accepted the gifts.

'You owe her, I suspect.'

'That is between me and her and if you keep talking you'll wake her. We walked far today.'

When the man spoke again his words were lower, softer. 'Do you know where you are going?'

'Malawi.'

'And here you are. In Malawi. Now where?'

Kolo said nothing. The crowds had surprised him. They'd begun this journey virtually alone on the roads and tracks. People spoke of a place ahead. Kolo thought it might be a mosque.

The man said, 'There is a complex south of here. I've seen it. And now I walk back up the line, to see for myself all who have come to see it. The camps surrounding the complex are growing, as you might imagine. Building materials have appeared. There will be neighbourhoods, markets, schools even. A city grows there.'

Kolo glanced at Neela's tent. 'She knows nothing of that,' he said.

'Then what drew her here?'

'I don't know.'

'What drew you?'

He licked his lips, still reluctant to give answers to this stranger's questions. 'She insisted.'

The man nodded. 'And you owe her,' he said again.

After a time, the man collected up a few chips of the not-wood and added them to the fire. 'Do you mind? I'm old, easily chilled.'

'There is food.'

'No, thank you, I've eaten. Are you a religious man, Kolo?'

'I was born a Christian. Protestant.' He hesitated, and then shook his head. 'No, not religious. But I am not blind to the spirits, though most are gone, most have left us.'

'Gone?'

'We starved them, disappointed them.'

'Not angered?'

'Empty anger,' Kolo answered. 'Empty as the forest.'

'And the day all violence ended, Kolo, what of that?'

'Satellites,' he pronounced.

'Satellites?'

'They wanted to take our guns away and so they did. To make us helpless and weak.'

'Who is "they"?'

'I thought, white men. At first. Now I don't know. Maybe the Chinese.'

'No, Kolo, none of them. You've been out of the loop. Aliens.' He nodded up at the night sky. 'We have been shut down, by guests bringing gifts. And such gifts!'

'Shh, you'll wake her.'

'Sorry.' He rummaged again in a pocket and came out with half a chocolate bar. He broke a piece off and offered it to Kolo, who shook his head. The man popped it into his mouth and chewed for a time.

Kolo didn't know whether to believe him. He thought about the crowds. 'This new city you speak of – another refugee camp? These people – have their lands been taken then?'

'No. The complex, it was created by the aliens. Built by itself, as if by magic, or a miracle.'

'And you have seen it.'

'Yes.' The man was eating more of his chocolate, pausing to swallow before adding, 'I believe it has been built for us.'

'What is inside this complex?'

'We don't know. We haven't yet been allowed to enter. A forcefield surrounds it.'

Kolo looked away, remembering that terrifying wall of nothing that had driven him and his people from their camp.

'Your upbringing would have you God-fearing. Are you God-fearing, Kolo?'

'I don't know. I don't think about it.'

'All the religions,' the man said, now carefully folding up the empty wrapper before tucking it back into a pocket, 'brought to us the voice of God. And the message was ever the same. It was a simple one, that we in our weakness made complicated. Do you know what that message was?'

Kolo said nothing. He'd met a few fanatics in his time. All armed, all angry, all eager to deliver pain. All drunk on power. He was not in the mood to hear another impassioned exhortation, and though the man seemed harmless enough – and though no violence could occur – Kolo found himself frightened.

'The message was this: be at peace. Too simple to mess up, you'd think. But then, the human capacity for mischief is infinite.'

'I do not know peace,' Kolo said.

'No. Nor I. Guns and bombs are finished. The stranger's face is no longer the enemy. So we gather up our arsenal and carry it inside.' He tapped the side of his head. 'And the war continues.'

Kolo grunted. 'There is truth in that.'

'We have been made pointless,' the man said, smiling. 'Our arguments win us no victories. Our fury is a small fire in the heart of the sun. It burns only its maker and to others it remains forever beneath notice. You, me, lost in the flames, the inferno so loud we can no longer hear God's simple message.'

'"Be at peace."'

'Of course not just us, Kolo. But the world. All of humanity, writhing in the fire of its own making.' He paused for a time.

They stared at the dying camp-fire, the not-wood burning without smoke, leaving black ash that was said to be most fertile. Local farmers would come to the camps in the morning, watching people pack up and set out on the road once more, and then they would scoop up the black remains of the fires to carry back to their land. Like manna.

'So,' the man said, 'you are not at peace. I am not at peace. But what of the girl? Is she at peace, Kolo?'

He considered the question for a few moments, and then nodded. 'I believe that she is.'

'So do I,' the man whispered. He rose from his crouch. 'And for that, Kolo, I envy you.'

'I accepted you as guest and yet still you do not offer me your name.'

'Abdul.'

'Is Neela taking me to this complex, this alien place that made itself?'

'I think so.'

'Why?'

'I don't know. No one does. There are no promises. Only hope.'

Kolo scowled. He kicked one foot into the fire, scattering sparks. 'I learned many years ago to hate that word. Hope is an enemy to truth, an enemy to the world and how it is.'

'How it *was*.'

Kolo grunted again, not convinced, or not willing to be convinced, as too many old hurts had been awakened by that terrible word.

'There are a thousand angry warriors fighting each other in my head,' Abdul said. 'But one stands apart and that one is me. But so too are all the raging warriors. They are me as well. Still, the me who stands apart, he watches the battle. And watches, and watches. Until he can only do one thing.'

'What thing?'

Abdul smiled. 'Why, laugh, of course.'

After the man was gone, Kolo opened the new pack of cigarettes. He wasn't tired, and it gave him something to do with his hands.

Chapter Twenty-Two

'Some people will say that to accept things as they are amounts to weakness, but I think it has more to do with exhaustion. Physical. Spiritual. The system we are all trapped in is designed to wear us down, and it's doing a good job of it. Calling people weak is an accusation that can only be made in the absence of compassion. Next time you want to call us all sheep, have a little heart. We're doing the best we can.'

Samantha August

'The forcefield dome is beginning to project upward,' Alison Pinborough explained to the Prime Minister, leaning close to be heard above the chop of the helicopter's rotor blades. Outside the night sky was black, seemingly starless although this was likely an effect of the tinted windows. The ground below was also black, without even a single island of light marking a farm or ranch since they were presently flying over the western block of the Grasslands National Park. 'It's forming a column,' she continued. 'Our drones now measure it at four hundred metres. The rate of climb is about twenty metres per day, and not even birds can fly through this forcefield.'

The Prime Minister simply nodded. It was now full summer and the air was hot – even the breeze that came through the vents which had been opened to the outside. There were thunderstorms far to the south, somewhere over Montana – or was that Minnesota?

Alison glanced over at Mary Sparrow. The Minister for Parks

and Recreation had one shoulder against the side port, her gaze fixed downward, as if tracking from memory the rugged contours of the Frenchman River Valley that dominated the national park.

A park that was now part of a new forcefield corridor, angling southward to merge with its sister arm that came down from central Alberta. The bison that had been reintroduced to the Grasslands Park were now free to resume their ancient migration routes, all the way down to Kansas. And without maintenance, that herd was bound to grow in size.

There were no wolves in the Grasslands, only coyotes. But Mary had predicted that would soon change. Predators were always opportunistic, and if left alone and left free to roam, they would find their niche. The old balance would be restored.

So much was changing. Humanity's entire relationship with the natural world had been upended. Will Camden's latest report on the status of the country's natural resources had made that brutally apparent.

'The flaw was in the very words we used, Prime Minister. Seeing the land as a *resource,* which by the very meaning of that word meant it was ours to use, and, eventually, to use up. Land and sea, trees, fish, minerals, the soil itself.' The man had looked broken, exhausted, his eyes red-rimmed and lost. 'It all existed to be converted into wealth. Of course we need to eat. Drink clean water. We need material goods for our shelters, our ease of living. Energy to heat our homes. Plastics and refrigeration to preserve and transport our food—'

Mary Sparrow had cut in then. 'But you mistook all of that for ownership. It was never that, Will. It was stewardship at best. The way ahead was always the same and it flies in the face of the capitalist approach. You must balance need with capacity, to ensure the health of both.'

But Will was not interested in fighting a battle already lost. 'It's even simpler than that, Mary. It was always a war between short-term and long-term thinking. There you have it. Reduced to its basic, unassailable core. Capitalism is always geared to the short-term vision. Profit now. Suck it dry, then move on, reinvesting what you earned so you can rinse and repeat. And

287

every move included a step up the ladder, a bigger house, more toys, more privileges. The short-term is all about a single life: the living, grown-up generation. What came before doesn't matter. What comes next is for your children to deal with.'

The Prime Minister then spoke. 'My predecessor went all in on the oil industry and spent his terms removing every roadblock in its path. I got in on a vote that rejected that, and as soon as I arrived the sheer weight of that singular momentum damn near crushed me.'

Mary's gaze was level. 'You buckled on the pipelines, madam. Broke an election promise. Got called out.'

'Thank you, Mary,' Lisabet said drily. 'I am well aware of my promises. In any case, it's now a moot point, isn't it?'

'Except for your plummeting popularity.'

Hell of a way to end a briefing, but Alison couldn't help but admire Mary's *huevos*. Some situations couldn't be salvaged. This was the harsh lesson now being delivered to every politician and world leader. Language was losing its power to evade reality, but this was a death-blow that could only be delivered by an outside agency – something beyond the reach of human obfuscation and the variability of opinion or interpretation.

No wonder the species was in crisis.

'We're coming up on the Swift Current site now,' the pilot informed them all via a speaker in the cabin of the modified Chinook.

Accompanying the Prime Minister and her advisors was Alison's own science team. She'd made calls, needing as many minds on this new situation as possible. The construction of the massive complex on the broken prairie south-east of the town of Swift Current was not unique: similar sites were springing up all over the world. But it was the only one in Canada, and, incidentally, the closest one to what many still considered to be the dominant world power: the United States of America.

The neighbours to the south were all over Lisabet Carboneau, Alison knew. The Americans wanted in, even if that meant ignoring a country's borders. If not for the utter denial of violence, the situation would be volatile. As it was, bluster had all the

288

power of a fart in the whoosh of a Chinook's rotor blades. That said, would ET reject the incursion of determined Yanks? Did sovereign borders matter at all to these extraterrestrials?

They began their descent and up ahead, now visible through the main forward canopy, was a thick ring of arc lights, tungsten-amber, revealing ATCO trailers in orderly rows and beyond them, a disorganised sprawl of uninvited guests dwelling in myriad tents and campers. Tyre tracks made chaotic patterns across what had once been land owned by the – she glanced down at her notes – Bowan family. The Swift Current River ran through the holding, amusingly misnamed given its turgid, modest presence.

Flares marked out the landing area and they could see a small crowd awaiting their arrival. There were television crews present.

'Damn,' Alison said. 'Word must have leaked out. Sorry, Madam Prime Minister.'

Lisabet shrugged. 'Word always leaks out these days, Alison. The game of secrecy seems well and truly dead. We're all full of holes and going down fast.'

That was a shocking admission, and Alison said nothing. Out of the corner of her eye she saw Mary Sparrow's round face crease into a sad smile for a moment.

The helicopter settled with barely a nudge on the flattened short-grass prairie. As the rotors began winding down, Canada's Prime Minister withdrew a compact to check her face, scowled, and then nodded to an aide to open the side door.

•

Marc Renard had looked down on the Earth from the ISS. He had floated from a tether in a bulky suit amid the ferocious indifference of vacuum. He had flinched from the over-curious 'fireflies' that were probably drones of some sort, courtesy of the Greys. Drones that could (and did) destroy human space-craft when the mood took them. His journey into space had been both humbling and frightening. The sheer vulnerability of his home planet and its dominant species was daunting, wounding, against the vast reaches of the solar system and its unwelcome predators.

Of course, one needed perspective. The first European settlers to the Americas had done much the same as the Greys. Exploited, dominated, occupied, enslaved and murdered. He wasn't sure if the distinction between aliens doing all of that to humans and humans doing it to each other was a flattering one for yours truly.

As he watched the big white helicopter settle onto the flare-lit ground, one hand up to protect his eyes from grit as he leaned against the wind stirred up by the blades, he found himself thinking about First Contact. The theme had been explored countless times in science fiction novels and short stories. It had played out on cinema screens and on television. Mostly, it was the aliens initiating the contact, for good or ill. Only in the *Star Trek* franchise was the opposite commonplace, and the United Federation of Planets had the Prime Directive guiding it. Because, the argument went, being reasonable when in possession of overwhelming technical superiority was a difficult thing. The temptation to set things right was always there, the road to hell and all that.

Behind him, as he stood in the cluster of technicians and politicos awaiting the appearance of the Prime Minister, rose the massive edifice announcing ET's arrival on Terran soil. A sprawling collection of mysterious buildings, spanning a footprint that dwarfed the average petrochemical plant.

Drone shots revealed the landing pad in the heart of the complex. That image had regular people close to panic. And now that the forcefield was forming a column to the heavens, the inevitable descent of the visitors looked to be unstoppable.

He was aware of the alternate theory. Less a landing pad than a launch pad. Less a fortress inside its protective bubble than a training centre awaiting the influx of human space cadets. Nice thoughts, but Marc remained sceptical. Occupation that could not be opposed was just as – if not more – likely.

Processing plants. Mechanised slaughter-houses for the production of some alien version of Soylent Green. The deconstitution of humanity, one screaming victim at a time.

By nature Marc Renard was an optimistic man. He'd clung to it even after the revelations and encounters with the Greys, though at times he'd mulled on the notion that the Greys saw the Earth as a holding pen, or a hunting ground. Humanity would prevail, eventually, forcing open the bars of the cage. They would, come hell or high water, take back their native solar system.

In the basement lab of the old museum in Swift Current, a grizzled provincial archaeologist had, over beers and Scotch, offered up an alternate future, by citing the past. *'Ghost Dance. The return of the buffalo and the resurrection of the Plains Indian nations. The driving out of the white man and all his ills. Belief and faith, buddy, the dream of liberty. And how did that turn out?'* Then he had leaned forward. *'This entire town is sitting on an archaic burial ground. When they built the school the backhoe buckets were full of bones. Human bones. But the old lady running this museum wasn't interested in Indian bones. She was into taxidermy, and I guess stuffed Indians on display was a bit over the line even for her. Anyway, she got rid of them. And everything was hushed up. My point? Saskatchewan has a weird history, Mister Astronaut. Regina was originally called Pile of Bones. Bison bones in that instance. Mountains of them.'* He drunkenly waved a hand. *'The land is all about wiping clean what used to be, then pretending it never existed. That ET place south of here? I see a sky full of ashes, day after day, coming out of the smokestacks. That's what I see.'*

That had been Marc's first night, lodged in a local hotel, meeting up with the Parks Canada people (including the archaeologist) just to get some idea of what had been going on at the Bowan ranch.

Now, having come out here and seen it for himself, he wanted to tell that archaeologist something. Probably meaningless, but enough to make him almost hopeful.

No smokestacks.

•

'There's your astronaut,' Alison Pinborough said once she had followed the Prime Minister out from the now-silent helicopter.

Lisabet nodded. She gestured Mary Sparrow closer. 'Get in the faces of those cameras, Mary.'

'And say what?'

'We're just here to see this for ourselves.'

'Oh, like Bush and New Orleans after Katrina?'

'Well,' Lisabet said with a steely gaze, 'thank you for that. But for those reporters, try being a little more circumspect.'

'I'll talk about bison.'

'Bison?'

'The Grasslands herd, Madam Prime Minister. It's gone south. Time for feeding in the heart of Great Plains.'

'Sure,' Lisabet said evenly, 'try that.'

Gently grasping Alison by the upper arm, the Prime Minister guided her forward. 'God help me,' she muttered, 'that woman is pushing all my buttons right now.'

'Yes, she does seem to be enjoying herself.'

'Not you, too?'

'Not at all, Madam Prime Minister. I'm sorry if that came out wrong. I'm not very political, I'm afraid.'

Marc Renard was approaching them. Everyone else behind him had been waved back, at least for the moment. Spotlights affixed to cameras tracked them all.

'Mary probably leaked it,' Lisabet then said. 'I don't blame her, but still, it ticks me off because now all the networks will be showing is clips of me doing nothing, again.'

'None of us can do anything, Madam Prime Minister,' Alison pointed out.

'The Americans have rented a Kepler rocket and are heading up to meet ET. Me, I'm letting them have Renard. And the deal? They get to check out this complex and if the doors ever open, they're in there first.'

'First?'

'First.'

Fuck me, Alison thought as they reached the handsome astronaut with the photogenic grin, which he wasn't wearing now.

Marc Renard hesitated and then half-bowed before the Prime Minister. 'Madam Prime Minister, welcome to the Bowan Complex.'

'Nix that name right now.'

'What? I'm sorry, I don't—'

'And if this turns out to be some sort of detention camp? Canning facility for prime human cut? Nix it now, Marc.'

The astronaut paled slightly. 'It was an informal name, a local one, I mean. Heard it in Swift Current.'

'Fine,' Lisabet snapped. 'But *we* don't call it that, do we? No, *we* call it something else. Think up a name. Generic, neutral.'

'Right, of course, Madam Prime Minister. Uhm, welcome to Site X.'

The sheer disappointment in Lisabet Carboneau's face was a thing to behold, and luckily she was angled so that her back was to the cameras. Still, it was all Alison could do to keep a straight face, praying that at least one unofficial phone had captured the image.

'Something amusing you, Alison?'

'No, Madam Prime Minister. Marc, nice to see you again. How went the book tour?'

Marc blinked. 'You're joking, right? When the news about the Greys got out, well, my credibility went into the toilet. Tour cancelled. That's what stranded me in Saskatoon, before the call came to come down here. If lynch mobs could do anything but just glare ...'

'Hmm,' Alison said, 'sorry I asked.'

'Into the trailer,' Lisabet said, 'now. No, just the three of us.'

Alison and Marc followed the Prime Minister to the largest of the ATCO trailers. Glancing back, Alison saw Mary Sparrow standing abandoned by the reporters. Presumably, the bison story hadn't fired any sense of wonder. Still, what *was* a wonder was that a thin strip of plastic yellow tape was still holding back the journalists. Only in Canada.

Once inside, Lisabet found a carafe of coffee awaiting them. She poured three cups full. 'Marc, you're going up again.'

'Kepler said yes?'

'They did. They have a prototype they want to try out.'

'Oh great, a prototype.'

Lisabet slammed the carafe down, making the cups on the small table jump. Spilled coffee pooled on the white linoleum. The Prime Minister set her hands down on the table and leaned slightly forward, hair covering her face as she seemed to study the brown puddles. Into the silence that followed the loud crack of the aluminum carafe, Lisabet then said, 'This is not ideal. None of this is ideal. The only thing preventing a complete occupation of our country right now is that our friends to the south have no idea what ET would do if it was attempted.' She straightened and went to the tiny sink where she collected up a dishcloth to wipe up the spilled coffee. 'It's a miracle that not one ethnic group anywhere in the world has made a move to occupy land once lost, or claimed it as their own. But it's coming.' She completed cleaning the table's surface and then refilled their cups. 'Carson tells me there have been rumblings among the sovereign tribes, especially in British Columbia.'

Alison wanted to sit down, but couldn't, not while the Prime Minister remained on her feet. Carson Johans was the Minister of Native Affairs. The modern world had so many elephants in the room there was nowhere left to stand, and in Canada (and in the USA) the biggest one was all about stolen land. Entire nations of immigrants. Still squatting on that land, and when it came right down to it, all the deeds and legislative acts and laws passed by and enforced by European-style governments really had no legitimate claim to the new world. As Mary Sparrow once said, *'The legitimiser cannot claim legitimacy by legitimising its own legitimacy by saying it's legit,'* a quote that had won her by-election in Nunavut by a landslide.

In Canada there had never been a conquest, only occupation. Colonisation, and then waves of pressure crushing all in its path. South of the border there'd been a lot more killing involved, where might made right in the self-satisfying monologue that was manifest destiny. But the principles remained the same more or less. A long history of broken promises and false assurances.

Had ET's arrival just kicked open the door?

Trampled by elephants. Just our luck.

'Madam Prime Minister,' Marc Renard ventured, 'if ET wants to talk it will be at a time and location of their choosing, not ours. This handshake mission will probably fail and make us look very foolish.'

'You don't want to go?'

'Of course I don't want to go!' Marc snapped. 'Sorry. My apologies. Listen, we keep pretending we're in charge here. We keep acting like we're the ones making all the decisions, the choices, the calls for action. But isn't it obvious yet? *We don't get to decide anything.*'

After a long moment, Lisabet sat down. 'Both of you, sit.' Once they'd done so, she continued. 'This is now about positioning. The ball's got to drop. Sooner or later, we'll find ourselves in the next stage of whatever this is. Yes, Marc, you're right. It's ET who has the next move. But these complexes. They must represent the foundation stones for whatever that next move is. That's why' – she nodded to Alison – 'I want you and your team here. As for you, Marc, you're heading back into space. No handshake would be rude.'

Marc's brows lifted. 'We're relying on ET's good manners? Madam Prime Minister, was this land purchased from the Bowan family? No. Have they been compensated? No. Those forcefields all over the planet – did we ask for them? Hell, even the end to all violence – fine, plenty of people wanted that, from the abused wife to the victims of half a dozen ongoing civil wars. But still, there was no warning. No "excuse me, we're going to stop all this killing, all right?" ET is doing whatever it wants.'

'Fine,' the Prime Minister snapped. 'I get it. We are only able to react, not initiate. So it falls to us to try and figure out what's coming next. Alison, that team of yours. I haven't had time to read their CVs. Names, specialities.'

'Uhm, right. Well, the big guy with the reddish beard, that's Brandon Roth. Astrophysicist from Laval. The red-haired woman who got sick at lift-off, that's Jenny Cox, specialising in quantum field expression, energy transference and, uh, something about contingency theory? Last one is Baria Khan, exobiologist, wrote a book on extremophiles. Her main area of interest is in Eukaryotic environments and the origin of life on Earth.'

'And this Baria happens to be an old friend of yours.'

'Well, yes. I admit that her expertise may not be immediately relevant—'

'Honestly,' the Prime Minister said, hand now over her eyes, 'I don't really care. By all means make this a girls' night out. Never mind.' She drew her hand away and regarded them both. 'You're all in this for the long haul. But it's readily apparent that neither of you have taken on board the principal lesson concerning speculation, the one I brought up a month ago. Alison, your team is incomplete. Marc, all your space programme buddies are coming up with all kinds of theories about – well, about *everything*. But all they're doing is pillaging science fiction novels. My point? Alison, get a hold of our cultural affairs people. I want a list of Canadian SF authors. I want a team of people in the business of imagining the impossible. This whole thing about scrambling for experts, all you scientists, and technicians and engineers – none of those skills necessarily come packaged with a powerful imagination, do they? Over and over again, we keep looking to the wrong people for answers. We need people who can get into the head of ET.'

'Well,' Alison said, looking down at her coffee cup, 'I think ... yes. We can certainly add some writers to the team.'

The Prime Minister was going through the pockets of her light coat. She came out with a clutch of creased papers – receipts, it seemed – on which notes were written. 'Here, a quote from our missing science fiction author, Samantha August. From an interview that got tetchy. Listen. This is her. "The problem is, people without imaginations don't know what they're missing."' Lisabet set down the wrinkled receipt and began pressing out the creases. 'You need to think twice about that quote. Maybe three times. The key lies in the first part. The *"problem"*. In that interview, she was responding to a jackass fellow author who'd just dismissed all of science fiction. She told him she felt sorry for him, felt sorry that his imagination was so weak it could never leave mundane reality.'

'Ouch,' said Marc Renard.

'You can lead a horse to water, but if it's too stupid to drink ...'

'*She said that?*'

'No, Marc. I did. Just now.' The Prime Minister stood. 'Both of you, go and get your people and let's get this briefing started.'

Outside the trailer Marc touched Alison on the shoulder. 'Did she just call us stupid?'

Alison scowled. 'Yep.'

'Ouch again.'

Alison eyed her trio of scientists who were waiting in a desultory clump a dozen metres away, Brandon attempting to light a pipe of all things, while the summer wind swirled all around, forcing him to spin like a slow top, lighter flaring again and again.

'Wobble wobble wobble, then we all fall down,' Alison whispered.

'Excuse me?' Marc asked. 'I didn't catch that.'

Alison shook her head.

Chapter Twenty-Three

'Is the universe holographic? Probably. Get microscopic
enough and you start seeing pixels. I don't know about
you, but that makes me laugh. Until I think about how
easy it is to hack a program. Any program.'

Samantha August

'This is why I hate briefings,' said the President of the United
States. 'Some egghead deciding what I need to know. Only I
know what I need to know. And what I need to know right now
is, do we do like the Russians? Roll across that damned border
and just take what's rightly ours to?' He pointed a finger at the
Secretary of Defence. 'Morgan, lay out those scenarios.'

Morgan West cleared his throat and made to speak, but it was
the Vice-President who spoke first.

'Raine, the Russians had to roll back. Every territory they
annexed right after your election, when we announced we were
standing down on our NATO commitments, they have since
relinquished. Sure, they could march in, but not their tanks or
APCs, not their helicopters, and of course not their guns – which
were useless anyway. But they couldn't take over anything. It's
pretty clear that ET will not abide foreign invasions.'

'We're not foreign!' Raine Kent snapped.

'By international law, we would indeed be invading a foreign
country, even if it *is* Canada.'

Raine Kent glared at her. 'I wish I'd kept my first VP, you
know that?'

Diana Prentice lifted one eyebrow. 'The devout Christian

caught on camera with his dick up another man's butt? Now, personally I couldn't care less where he sticks his dick, but everyone was waiting for your first major firing, weren't they?'

'Morgan!'

'Yes, Mister President. Well, the baseline all-things-being-as-they-once-were scenario is of course pretty much straightforward. We simply annex as much territory as we want. Ontario, Alberta, British Columbia—'

'Those are provinces, right? Which one has the alien site?'

'None, sir. That's Saskatchewan. I was about to add Saskatchewan, since it has oil reserves.' He reached up to groom his infamous 'confederate' moustache. 'But the first three comprise the major population centres, not counting Quebec – but Quebec is full of French people, so we wouldn't want it anyway.'

'Things are not as they once were,' Diana Prentice pointed out.

'With the military option out of the picture,' Morgan resumed, pointedly ignoring the Vice-President who was, to Raine Kent's mind, fast becoming the odd one out in his inner sanctum of advisors, 'we have devised a scenario we call non-confrontational occupation, or NCO. In short, we simply walk across the border—'

'Walk?' Raine barked the question.

'Well, drive. In non-military vehicles. We cross the border and simply crowd out the Canadians at the site. There's more of us—'

Prentice snorted, but said nothing, which was a good thing since the President was one more outburst away from kicking her out of the room.

'So how do they stop us?'

'Mister President? Who?'

'The Canadians!'

'Well, I suppose if they formed a human chain on the border, but then we'd go overland, get around them. I mean, how long a line can they hope to make?'

'Oh for fuck sake,' Raine Kent said. 'Never mind, sorry I asked. Morgan, you head a military that can't shoot. Making you kinda useless. Forget it. If the astronaut deal goes south, we've got a legal route. We buy out the rancher, own his land. Use a proxy, of course. Failing that, we sue.'

At this point, the last person present in this meeting seemed to blink awake, and at a nod from the President, Raine Kent's personal legal advisor, James Voilette, began speaking. 'We purchase via the agricorp angle. The land is then owned by a US-owned corporation. Legally, not even the Canadian government can prevent us occupying that land, or doing with it whatever we please. When the ET complex opens its doors, in we go, take what we like, and then break everything else. It's a quick in and out operation, conducted while the courts get bogged down in everything we can throw at them. With the job done, they can have it back, for a price.' He settled back in his chair again, seemed to begin drifting off.

Diana Prentice cleared her throat. 'Well now, has this purchase already gone through, then?'

'No,' Voilette replied, blinking awake again. 'But with the kind of money we can throw at the landowner, consider it a done deal.'

'I'm afraid I don't,' the Vice-President said. 'Raine, the entire global economy is suffering runaway inflation. We've had so many successive financial crashes in the markets we barely notice them anymore. Every pay-check being cashed or deposited is an act conducted holding one's breath with fingers crossed. We're running on the fumes of faith right now.'

'So we offer in gold bullion,' Voilette retorted, rolling his eyes at the President. 'Everything is for sale, at the right price. It's not like Canada isn't all in on the capitalist ethic, same as us. Unless it's suddenly turned into a communist state,' and he laughed.

'It should be clear,' Diana said to the lawyer, 'even to you, that not *everything* is for sale, specifically all that ET has done to us and will do to us.'

The man smirked. 'My dear, once we get them at the table, we'll eat them for breakfast.'

Diana held up her hands and sat back. 'I can't wait to see this one play out. Who's got the popcorn?'

'Hah ha,' said the President. 'What's going on at the UN? I'm still waiting for your report.'

'Chaos, of course. To be expected. In general, the various aid and assistance agency arms of the UN are now commanding more and more resources, although it seems where we fail, ET picks up the slack. No one is going hungry. No one is without shelter. The usual diseases, graft and violence that normally accompany mass population movements just aren't happening. Interestingly, in terms of resources distribution as controlled and managed by ET, we're looking at a classic communist expression: to each according to his or her need.'

'I knew it,' Raine Kent said, hands tightly curled into fists. 'This was all about shutting me down. Here I was, poised to change the world, poised to fix things. And what do I get? Stalin from space. That's what I get.' He paused and then pointed at Voilette. 'Hold on that. If the present deal falls through – the Canadian astronaut for access thing – if that falls through, we buy our way in. Agricorp. Soyabeans, corn, farmer shit—'

'The land is a ranch not a farm,' Diana pointed out.

'So fucking pigs and cows! The point is: we're getting in through that door. One way or another we're getting our hands on that ET tech. Morgan! Pay attention, dammit. How's the army corps of engineers getting along with our own fancy hi-tech super-complexes?'

'Going fast, Mister President. All four sites are ahead of schedule. By the time we're done we'll have more empty rooms than all those alien complexes combined.'

Raine Kent stared at the man, even as D.K. Prentice slowly put her hands over her face.

Good God Almighty, Morgan West, you are one stupid man. But out loud, Raine Kent said, 'Right. Carry on.'

•

Most off-campus meetings, even unofficial ones, took place in one of Raine Kent's many hotels. What had begun as political pressure from the President himself was now habit. Science Advisor Ben Mellyk sat with Kenneth Esterholm at the top-floor bar in the Grand Kent Plaza, a refurbished turn-of-the-century six-storey building in DC. The CIA director was on his third bourbon.

'I blame the FBI,' Esterholm muttered.

Ben Mellyk glanced away. He'd heard this before. 'Well, I suppose they can try to open an investigation into ET's un-American activities, but I doubt it'd help. This isn't a popularity contest. At least, it's not looking like one.'

Esterholm squinted across at Mellyk. 'Listen, you're a scientist. What the fuck are you doing in this administration? They don't like science. They don't even *believe* in science.'

'Fortunately,' Ben replied, 'science is indifferent to what you choose to believe or not believe. It's a process, strictly evidence-based. It problem-solves, and, more often than we'd like to admit, it also problem-*finds*. You can block your ears, or put your hands in front of your eyes. You can stick your head in the sand, or shout louder than anyone else. You can send death-threats or destroy someone's life. None of that changes a thing. Evidence is evidence, consequences are consequences. Do this and that happens. We may have launched our very own age of denial, but it won't change anything.'

'Ha! Only now the aliens show up and start fixing things! Climate change? Why, it's going away. Deforestation in the rainforest? Not anymore! Harvesting all the fish in the oceans? Uh-uh.'

'If none of those things were both true and real,' Ben pointed out, 'ET wouldn't have to fix them.'

Esterholm grimaced. 'No one can be bothered thinking that one through and you know it. We're in make-believe land. You didn't answer my question. Why did you join this God-awful, seditious administration?'

'Every president requires a science advisor.'

'He pretty much ignores most of what you say.'

'Nonetheless, someone at least has to try to peddle reason and rationality. I guess that's me.'

'Okay. Fine.' Esterholm finished his bourbon and signalled for another. Then he leaned forward. 'I need some predictions from you. Some ideas on what's coming next.'

'Why?'

'Why? Because we're not all idiots. Because this country is

chock-full of smart, grounded people. People who don't shut down their brains. People who understand what it means to be American – in the proper traditional sense. A nation of tolerance, freedom for all—'

'Save me the speech,' Ben said, taking off his glasses and rubbing at his eyes. 'I'm the token Jew in an anti-Semitic administration that's beloved by anti-Semitic Americans from sea to shining sea. Whatever we once were, we aren't anymore.'

'Wrong. We are, dammit. Sure, the loonies are running the nut-house and all their fellow loonies are happy as peach, but it's an aberration. We both know that. This is a backlash, one last gasp, one last desperate grasp at nostalgia.'

'Well, I'd call it the logical result of endemic disenfranchisement. Poverty breeds anger. Stress breeds fear. We've been in decline, seeing plenty of both.'

'No. Listen. Just because nobody can hurt anybody else doesn't make the hate go away. Doesn't even fix the parochialism and twisted nationalism that gives rise to white supremacists and neo-Nazi parties. But our president keeps feeding that hate, keeps pointing fingers. Now, I had this thought. It came to me one sleepless night, exploding in my brain, and I want you to hear it.'

Ben shrugged. 'Okay, go ahead.'

'I get it that ET showed up and stopped the world – the whole planet, I mean. I get that. But I can't help thinking that the clusterfuck going on here in America, that was the tipping point. That was ET sitting up and saying "fuck me, those idiots in the good old US of A are going to take down *everything*". So they acted now. They acted now because of *us*.'

Ben collected up his glass of Scotch, considering the notion.

Esterholm went on. 'Look, I know it's what other countries complain the most about us Yanks. We're so in our own heads, so convinced we're King Shit of Turd Mountain, and we obsess about ourselves, pretty much exclusively. Centre of the universe. Birthplace of freedom, capitalism—'

'Neither of which is true,' Ben pointed out.

'I know, but we took them and ran with them like nobody else.'

Nodding, Ben sipped at his drink. 'Agreed.'

'So, what if it wasn't the Russians trying to invade Europe. Or the Chinese buying up the whole damned world. What if it wasn't climate change either? What if it was this president, this administration, the whole crumbling mess of what's happened to this country? I mean, what did we get almost from day one? Race riots. Hate crimes everywhere. Attacks on women. Finger-pointing and mobs with pitchforks. And then the brain-drain, all those dark-skinned geniuses bolting for Canada or India or wherever. We were spiralling down, Ben, and it was going to start getting very ugly.'

'And ET stopped it all in its tracks.'

'Exactly. Our gleeful slide into anarchy, nipped in the bud.'

'Maybe. Still, what is it you want from me?'

'Those complexes, the landing pads or training centres or whatever they are. The fact that we didn't get one—'

'Lots of countries didn't get one. Russia didn't. China didn't. India didn't. Britain didn't.'

'Countries with genuine space programmes.'

'Well, yes, that's a point.'

'It's more than just a point. It's a big neon arrow, Ben. Other people are being invited into the space race.'

Ben snorted and collected up his glasses. 'Race? Against alien star-spanning technology? Hate to break it to you, Kenneth, but if you're right we've already lost that race.'

'My point is, they get first crack at that shit. Like it or not, Ben, us frontrunners in space exploration haven't done much to be truly inclusive, have we? I mean the occasional guest astro-naut looks good, but when it comes to technology and expertise, we don't give it away, do we?'

'A curious position, Kenneth. The truth is, NASA is very open to sharing its programmes when it can. The same can certainly be said for ESA, and for a time there even the Russians weren't above selling their heavy lifters to whoever could cough up the money to buy one. Do recall, however, that NASA is constrained by its budget, and that comes from the Feds, and no administra-tion is excited about spending the money of its own citizens to help some other country's nascent space ambitions. Finally, there are the NASA contracts with private aerospace companies. Philosophically, that's much more palatable, especially when it puts Americans to work.'

Kenneth sighed, drank down some of his fourth bourbon, and then nodded. 'Okay, fair enough. But I don't think that alters my basic position here. It's a kind of levelling of the playing field. Or a means of opening the door to space for everyone on this planet, not just the richest, most advanced nations.'

Ben pocketed his glasses. 'Kenneth, I think that you may well be right. It does seem to reflect the ethics of ET given what's already happened. Playing no favourites. Not immediately contacting only the most powerful nations. Instead, contacting everyone ... and no one.'

'Right. It's the damned strangest first contact, isn't it? I mean, where the hell are they?'

'If I were in their shoes,' Ben said, 'I would not for one moment consider making a physical appearance on the surface of our world.'

'Ah, now that's interesting. Why not?'

'It's hard to focus hate on an enemy that stays unknown and, possibly, unknowable. Right now, resistance to ET is floundering. We remain reactionary. If we had a target we could think about taking the initiative. As it is, that notion isn't even being considered. No, it makes sense. If I'm ET, I would not offer myself up as a target for an entire world's outrage. I'd stay away.'

Their last invitee arrived at that moment, seating herself down with a sigh. Not long ago, the Vice-President would have been accompanied by the usual Secret Service, and the bar would have been vetted beforehand. Now, she came alone, unescorted, and earned only mild attention from patrons at other tables. 'Gentlemen, I see you started without me. Good plan. I was held up discussing the invasion of Canada.'

'Like that's going to work,' Esterholm said, somewhat loosely as he was showing the effects of the bourbon, although not as much as one might expect.

'It took some time to reach that conclusion. And we just

received word that our buyout angle is finished, since Canada has appropriated the land from the owners.'

'That's rather bold,' Esterholm said.

'Well, it's a legal move, mostly, as the PM then said they had no plans on ousting the Bowans, or even making them give up their ranching. But clearly Carboneau has some decent people around her, and knowing that we coveted the site, they took the means to block us.'

A waiter appeared and D. K. Prentice ordered a glass of rioja. As soon as the waiter left, Esterholm shifted to face her.

'Diana, what's *really* going on at UN?'

'They're hiring.'

'Like they have an unlimited budget – did we finally pay them our dues?'

'Of course not,' she replied. 'But they are positioning themselves for something much bigger.'

'Like what?'

The Spanish rioja arrived. 'Well,' Diana said a moment later, 'like being the official government of planet Earth.'

The Director of the CIA choked on his bourbon. But not fatally so.

•

'I never considered myself a demagogue.' Constantine Milnikov stared out of the tinted window of the presidential train, gaze tracking the decrepit farms and a meandering swathe of deciduous trees marking a small river's path through the otherwise flat landscape. 'But there is a seduction at the core of power.'

They were seated at the dinner table, the dishes and remains of the meal removed, and now only a bottle of vodka was between them. Anatoli Petrov sat in silence, nursing his first shot, while the President of Russia tried to get drunk.

It was, all things considered, not too surprising. The clout of a boisterous personality only went so far, and while in this country cleverness was admired (unlike in America), when everything else was stripped away – the security apparatus, the silent threats, the brutal promise of a grisly death with radioactive venom coursing through the veins – one man's self-righteous claim to lead millions quickly found itself on the thinnest ice.

Anatoli had never held much interest in economics. He'd led a privileged life, and rambling discussions and arguments on the ills of capitalism, socialism, and all the rest invariably left him bored and distracted. The poor never went away. They just laboured under whatever regime held sway, their daily lives unchanged and unchanging.

He'd seen photographs in history books: the peasant clothing and the bent backs, the sturdy women and the scrawny men staring into the camera's immortal promise, faces blank and eyes hidden in shadows, as if to saying to the future: *there is nothing you can give us that we have not already lost.*

Since those long-ago times, little had changed. While men walked on the Moon and virtually everyone could now talk to each other across an entire planet, still the peasants laboured on, in country after country. Some on the land, some in factories, others at the fringes of spoil heaps and mountains made of discarded computer monitors. They lived tribal lives, because humans were meant to live tribal lives. The rest was just pretence.

The man seated opposite the cosmonaut had been living the greatest pretence of all, riding his chariot in the sky like some cosmic archangel. Downward rained the blessings, the gifts of momentary recognition, and the endless promises of a better world to come.

What peasant hadn't heard it all before?

The attempted annexation of Latvia and Estonia had been a shambles. Entire armies parked on the highways on the Russian side of the border and paratroopers being laughed out of every village, town and city. And in the wake of this, all the inner workings were revealed, the raw motivations behind this endless look to the horizons.

The core was rotten through and through. Even before ET's arrival, Russia's economy had been rife with holes, worm-ridden, corrupt, poisoned by cynicism and graft. It had existed to serve the criminals running it. A castle built on a foundation of sticks and mud. Every territorial land grab had been a desperate effort at misdirection, to keep the gasping machine rolling forward for a bit longer.

Most might have pronounced this unique to Russia, product of a dark, permanent smudge on the Slavic soul. Perhaps, Anatoli reflected, there were aspects, characteristics, found here and nowhere else. But these were incidental. America was in similar throes: the world's wealthiest country with its sunken coastal cities and starving homeless, its cold-hearted contempt for whoever could not keep in step on that unceasing march called Progress or, for the less philosophically inclined, the Good Life. They didn't shelter their own, didn't feed their own, didn't heal their own, and yet, in the midst of all this inhumanity, they held themselves as the pinnacle of human civilisation.

Then again, compared to the man sitting on this armoured train, crossing a vast country that didn't know what century this was and barely cared besides (he was thinking of the peasants, always the peasants), even America's quick succession of neo-fascist presidents (bought and paid for by the Kremlin) still seemed capable of leading the world with one bold gesture of unswerving self-belief.

They were days from the launch. Hours counting down at Cape Canaveral. Poised to lift skyward on a pillar of ... flame? Possibly not. Well, whatever the EFFE lifter's thrust would look like. No matter. They would, once again, be the first among all nations to make so bold as to confront the alien visitors. Like a brash salesman with a pearlescent smile jamming one foot in the door and then striding through with one hand outstretched. Handshake, howdy-do? Nice to meetcha and let's sit ourselves down and do some business!

Balls. Pure, glaring-shiny American brass balls. Again and again, Anatoli's contempt for a culture that only pretended to know itself was swept aside and in flooded the bright flow of sincere admiration. The Americans and their guileless ways.

'T-shirts,' said the President. 'Busts in the markets. Tattoos of me in profile. I am a worshipped man. Idolised even beyond my borders. They like the manly pose. It speaks to them. It voices a solemn promise better than any words, any press statement. See me, a man at ease. A man of natural strength. Confident, powerful, influential. Who else can lead us? Who else *should*?'

Anatoli noted, with a start, that the bottle stood with only a third left in it. It was said that getting truly drunk was now impossible. So what state of mind took its place? He contemplated conducting his own experiment on the matter but then, he knew that alcohol weakened a man, both physically and in spirit. Too often, it was the first and last choice in mortal surrender to the fates.

But fate was never kind. Ask the peasant, when he's not falling down drunk.

No, Anatoli was never much of a drinker, though when needed he could fake it alongside his fellow pilots and all the other hard men of his profession.

But now, that sliding escape into dull-wittedness had ceased its blessed magic. Sober heads were lifting, blinking away the cobwebs, and it seemed that something vast was stirring, until the bedrock beneath every continent trembled.

The *People*.

Karl Marx would sleep well tonight in his grave, and for many more nights to come. But every demagogue of the world now shook in his boots.

'I see it now,' Constantine said. 'How I believed that I owned it all. Russia as my own fiefdom. And this world stage. I played it like a game, with the lives of millions to be gambled, squandered. My frail house of cards, this economy of the twenty-first century tottering on its nineteenth-century foundations.' He grunted sour amusement and then raised his glass. 'Anatoli, this is why we travel by train, to remind ourselves of this steel seam, the threads that stitched together our entire country. Yes of course a plane would have been quicker, but we have time now, don't we?' He laughed. 'We have nothing but time.'

The Russian army was disbanding. No order had come down to do so. Entire regiments were simply packing up and going home. The seams that Milnikov had just mentioned were coming apart. Local governance was now the only effective option. The dismantling of empires, one village at a time. It wasn't nineteenth century: it was medieval.

'Nightly they pray for me, did you know that, Anatoli?'

The cosmonaut nodded, risking a faint smile. The Church was once again on the rise. The unknown was no longer so ephemeral. Now it hovered high above the planet, still hidden but undeniably *there*. This made faith seem merely ... expedient.

Something about that was refreshing, even for an old atheist like Anatoli Petrov. Of course, in the absence of what could be known, the Church would make do with presumptions, and everyone still went home happy. There was much to be said for that, especially as the country itself slowly fell apart. Some forms of continuity could outlive even nations.

The train had begun a long, sweeping turn that angled the carriage ever so slightly, tilting their view of the world beyond the now rain-sleeted windows. Legs stretching out, Constantine Milnikov sprawled lower in his seat, scowling down at his shot glass. 'What value the vice,' he murmured, 'when its savage bite never comes?'

They were journeying to Kazakhstan, once part of the Soviet Union, then nominally independent, now a vague protectorate. The primary Russian launch site was located there, but Baikonur Cosmodrome was not their destination. Instead, they were heading towards the alien construct eight kilometres from Aral, the city that once stood on the shores of the Aral Sea before the waters retreated. Local government claimed the site and Russian bullying could not contest that claim. This was the new world, after all, this toothless age where the only weapon left between nations was economic.

That had delivered some pressure, however, sufficient to permit this Russian delegation to visit the new construction site. The President wanted to see the miracle for himself.

Constantine Milnikov seemed to shudder in his seat. He looked up, fixed Anatoli with bleak eyes, his famous face suddenly old. 'But it's true,' he said. 'I was once a demagogue.'

Anatoli found that he had no reply to that. But after a few moments of silence, he concluded that it was the saddest confession he had ever heard.

STAGE FOUR:

Rebirth
(Resurrection)

Chapter Twenty-Four

'The greatest potential roadblock to space exploration
by humans isn't physical risk, but psychological risk.
Can we handle being away from our home planet? What
happens to our bodies and our minds when we're no
longer in sync with the rhythms of our native world?
Space could well be an invitation to madness.'

Samantha August

'Potential,' said Adam, 'is a curious force. It hovers in the future,
almost formless. It refuses the easy description. Among all sentient species this is the same, Samantha August. A promise, there
on the very edge of the mind's sense of self. And in society, a
multitude of such promises reach out, blend together, inviting
something profound and blessed. It is the belief of many sentients that "potential" is God's primary gift, for the very fact that
it is an invitation to become something greater than what existed
beforehand. Have you stopped listening?'

She stood before what she had designated the main viewer,
a large flat panel or window that dominated the wall of her
single room. She smoked, luxuriating in the freedom to do so
inside rather than on some windy sidewalk, huddled against
the weather. But such freedoms were fast coming to an end. 'Do
you have a technology that keeps smoke private – not reaching
anyone else? Or just wisps it away? I'm heading to America, after
all. They shoot smokers there. Canadians, of course, just wrinkle
their nose in disgust and mutter under their breath, or cross to
the other side of the street. Or call the police. I should've lived

in the fifties, or even the forties. See me, the authoress (as they were known then), posed for her black and white publicity shot, glamorous behind a veil of smoke from the cigarette in one hand. The Century of Grey Haze. Maybe I'll retire to Austria.'

'Samantha, you do seem distracted. I was speaking of potential.'

'I heard you. Tell me, is there a difference between personal potential and cultural potential? Are some nations destined to flower, while others wilt? Or is it all just chemistry, the collective concoction that either turns lead into gold or gold into dross? Are some of us fucked at the start line? People, nations, entire species?'

'Humanity's crisis is, it seems, its inability to appreciate gifts freely given.'

'Early on, before money, we used reciprocity,' Samantha said. 'This cemented the notion of implicit justice. The idea of "worth" and "fair value". You give something and get something in return, with each exchange valued equally. When it wasn't an equal exchange, then some other service was required, to restore balance.'

'I still await the completion of the exchange, then. Something from humanity in return for what I am providing.'

She shrugged. 'We did away with reciprocity. Mostly. We complicated things, and not just with money's arbitrary designation of value. We put labour on one side of the exchange and protection and security on the other. This created a hierarchy, and inequality, until labour was the only option left to the majority of people, while the notion of protection and security offered by our leaders slowly crumbled. Crime, war, betrayal by the very people sworn or elected to protect us and our interests. The implicit justice – the fairness – of the exchange just up and died.'

'It falls to you, then, to enunciate the ancient rules of reciprocity. To your species.'

She finished her cigarette and let it fall to be swallowed up by the floor. 'I think it's too late, Adam. Besides, not all your "gifts" are appreciated, or particularly valued. What you offer as

316

salvation has been received as enslavement. What you provide as a technological leg-up is seen as an attack on global industry. Even the free food and fuel to the starving ends up hammering the industries of procurement, transportation and disbursement, making our ridiculous surpluses of produce positively noxious. You well know that we could feed everyone. Now we don't have to. You will.'

'Do you have a solution?'

'You don't? I thought you'd done all this before!'

'Each sentient species is unique, specifically related to its silent assumptions, the unspoken rules of expectation. It is, however, commonplace that behaviour is manageable through reward or discouragement.'

'Bark bark, says Pavlov's dog.'

'Suicide rates have greatly diminished in the past week.'

She snorted. 'Looking for the silver lining in the mess on the planet below? Well, that's good news, I suppose. The ones who wanted out got out. Orphans adopted by loving families. Meanwhile, ennui settles its pall across the world.'

'I see little anger.'

'No. We're storing it up. Fuel for the future's blinding rage.'

'Against me?'

'No. No point.' She drew out another cigarette, lit it. 'We may be collectively thick, but even we can see that. You're way out of our league.'

'The Greys, then.'

'The Greys. We will descend on them like Hell's own fury. They won't know what hit them. But be warned, the psychological profile of the abused is not all peaches and cream. We'll have issues. We won't listen to reason.'

'The Greys do not employ reason.'

'Well, good. That suits us perfectly. No need for any moral crisis over killing every last one of them. No peaceniks or appeasers, either.'

'You are hesitating.'

'I am frightened beyond belief, Adam.'

'So are we.'

Silence followed. She smoked, staring at the extraordinary personal gift floating in space on the main viewer, its backdrop the dark side of the Moon. She wasn't a fanatic on such matters, but it looked right. It was likely that the specs were exact. In an hour or so, she would board that enormous craft and, somehow, take the controls. She hoped that she'd have plenty of help in that department, or things were going to end badly indeed.

It was a call sign. Its subtext was – she hoped – glaringly obvious. It was also the Elder God of lawsuits in the making, one involving blood sacrifices and regiments of legal headhunters. 'Never mind Austria,' she muttered. 'Switzerland. Or North Korea. Or anywhere I can't be extradited from.'

'Samantha,' ventured Adam after a time, 'I am assembling personal diagnosis and treatment units for your civilisation. They will be ubiquitous.'

'Meaning?'

'Meaning, in a short time your entire medical profession, barring that of trauma surgeons, will be unemployed.'

She said nothing for a moment, and then sighed. 'Oh, Hamish ...'

'I understand he enjoys fly-fishing.'

'Sometimes, Adam, your jokes fall seriously flat.'

'I am also preparing to begin populating the training centres with appropriate technology to effect education, to be followed by the first inductions. I suspect that your return to Earth will precipitate considerable interest in what the future has to offer. Speaking of which, in these matters, don't you ordinarily prepare a speech beforehand? That is, written text, by way of guidance? After all, you will be addressing all of humanity.'

She sighed again. 'No. I think I'll wing it.'

There was a long pause, and then Adam said, 'Are you sure, Samantha? This will be an historic speech, its audience vast.'

'Just my point, Adam. These days, a scripted speech invites distrust. Who wrote it? Am I up there in front of all the world as nothing more than a mouthpiece for inscrutable aliens? They don't want me reading from a script. No, I'll put it out there in my own words, in my own stumbling, rambling style.'

'Very well. Of course, true paranoia would have you already compromised. Brainwashed, or not even human. What is the word? Replicant.'

'I get it, Adam. I already know there'll be knocks against us. Against my ... integrity. This is why I intend to stick to facts, not opinions. This isn't a sales pitch, is it? It's an info-dump on what's coming.'

'Presumably you will take questions at some point.'

She considered, and then shrugged. 'We'll see how it goes. But listen, they'll try to manage the event. Seven-second delay on the live feed, with fingers hovering over the kill switch. Every government that knew about the Greys has been defending the decision to keep it secret on the basis of not wanting to panic humanity. The people thinking that was a good idea haven't changed their minds. Secrecy is a habit. It stems from a world view guided by fear and, ultimately, cowardice. It won't die easily, because despite all our bluster we're at heart a fearful species.'

'Even when all you have to fear is each other?'

'Especially then. Because we also know what we're capable of. And that brings me to a question I had. This blanket presence, it's planet-bound, isn't it? Meaning once we leave the Earth, why we're back to being able to do violence again. To the Greys, of course, but also to each other.'

'Correct.'

'So, nations could go back to a nasty free-for-all in our solar system.'

'This is possible. Obviously, Samantha, the sooner your species comes to a collective understanding of itself, the better.'

'I see storm-clouds ahead, Adam. Then there's that *other* fear we have. Fear of *you*.'

'Yes. Can I predict that your solar system will remain peaceful?'

'Uh. Sure.'

'There will be no seven-second delay,' Adam said. 'No kill switch will function. Even power to the building will be independent and therefore immune to disruption. You will not be impeded, and all will hear. Samantha, the vessel is now ready for you.'

'Oh crap. All right. Let's get this started, shall we?'

'We are now approaching the docking port.'

She watched as the gift loomed closer. There were no running lights, nothing ostentatious to its grim form. It looked precisely like what it was: a hunter, a predator, a machine of violence and war. Studying it, she felt a brief flutter of uncertainty. Was this really the message to bring down from the heavens? A martial fist of molecularly compressed metal and carbon composite, beneath a non-reflective, radiation-proof coating of dull greens and flat blacks? 'It's bigger than it's supposed to be,' she observed as they drew still closer, and now she could see the docking port, a trapezoidal hatch limned in a faint glow.

'The fictional source presumed certain unobtainable technologies, Samantha. FTL systems, for example, are massively dense and require complex shielding to contain quantum radicals in addition to a gravity-containment well which serves to negate mass. Sublight propulsion is of course the largest component, assuming one desires consistency as well as near-light-speed capability. I elected to use an intermediary technology, a variation on the EFFE that employs radiant solar radiation in addition to a system's electromagnetic gravity skein. Finally, there is the matter of human psychology. The greatest challenge your species will face in its new age of deep-space travel will be the effect of long-term confinement. To mitigate this, the larger the vessel the better. Accordingly, I have doubled the scale. It is our estimate that the ideal crew size for humans is between fifty and one hundred adults.'

'That's it?'

'Eventually, you will be able to construct vessels that are world-like and self-sustaining, but that is perhaps a century or more away.'

'World-ships,' muttered Samantha. 'With nobody dying of illnesses anymore, we're going to need them.'

'In the meantime, you will have Venus.'

'Right. And how goes the other thing we talked about?'

'Proceeding on schedule, Samantha.'

The coupling of the two vessels was silent and seemingly

perfect. She watched on the monitor as the hatch noiselessly slid open. 'Oh,' she said, peering into the corridor beyond, 'get rid of that red haze, please. Try for something more ... Earth-normal.'

'There are benefits to subdued interior lighting in that spectra,' Adam said, 'as your own submariners well know.'

'Do I need to concentrate that hard? Do I need lighting that keeps my eyes from getting strained?'

'Well, no.'

'Right then. Proper daylight, please.'

'Very well.'

She watched as normal light bathed the corridor, watched as the blurry haze went away. Drawing a deep breath, she said, 'No offence, Adam, but that psychological strain you were mentioning? Well, I need to get out of this fucking room and I need to do it *right now*.'

A wall irised open and she found herself looking at the corridor. A new scent came into the air, like that of a new car. 'Oh, that's good, Adam. Nice touch, that smell. Pushes all the right buttons, despite it being probably slightly toxic.'

'You will survive.' Adam's voice sounded both smug and proud.

She smiled. 'You're rather pleased with yourself, aren't you?'

'I am. And you will soon see why. Please, take possession of your gift, Samantha. I have compartmentalised an imprint of myself in order to populate the AI core for this vessel's independent operation. You can of course call it Adam, or select a new name for this iteration. Given that its sensor package is necessarily constrained, it will evolve on its own and therefore diverge from the entity you are presently speaking with. You could elect Adam1 and Adam2—'

'For crying out loud,' Samantha cut in as she stepped across the threshold and began making her way up the corridor, 'I can do better than that. Imagination, remember? Me, big imagination. Me, writer, fiction, novels. This ship is going to have a woman's voice, a smart woman, naturally.'

'Eve?'

Sam paused, and then shook her head. 'Wrong connotations. Athena seems more fitting.'

'Ah, yes. Apt. Born from my head. Shall I cease being Adam and become Zeus then?'

'No, I'm comfortable with mixed-up mythologies. Besides, I don't want any thematic continuity inviting disturbing subtext. The Greek pantheon was made up of seriously flawed gods.'

'As flawed as their creators, you mean.'

The corridor reached an intersection. She paused. 'Okay. My stateroom first, and then the bridge. I trust there's a bridge, Adam.'

A new voice answered, a woman's, mellifluous and serene. 'Hello, Samantha August, or shall I call you Captain?'

'Call me anything you want, just not between midnight and nine a.m.'

'I believe this is an example of humour. Very well. Welcome, Commissar August.'

'Oh, ha ha. Nix that. The Swamp Boys will try to shoot me.'

'They will fail.'

'Not the point. Anything to the left triggers spasmodic hate among certain segments of the population I'm about to visit.'

'To the left?'

'People on the left side of the political spectrum are rule-breakers. The ones on the right are rule-makers. I'm simplifying, but then our world is getting simpler by the hour.'

'Your stateroom can be accessed from the bridge as well as the corridor just outside the bridge. Command Level is four up. Proceed forward to the elevator which will open upon your approach. Step inside and announce your destination.'

'I am naming you Athena,' Sam said as she walked forward to a section of wall that suddenly vanished to reveal the elevator's cab.

'I applaud your wisdom and, need it be said, mine.'

'Is Adam still listening?'

'I was getting to that,' Athena said. 'He has made the request, pending your approval. I should point out, I do possess a comparable range of sentience and dynamic contingency-based thought processes. If anything, I will prove more sensitive to your immediate concerns in that I am a much more limited presence, externalising only as required for navigation of this vessel.'

'Let him through.'

For a brief instant Samantha thought she heard a sniff, but then Adam's neutral modulations arrived.

'Are you enjoying yourself so far, Samantha? Is Athena to your satisfaction?'

'You need not answer that, Captain August,' Athena cut in, 'as I am secure in my range of capability, which unlike Adam does not include an ongoing subroutine applying macro-cultural assessment algorithms to your every utterance. As with my namesake, my godly aspirations are focused upon one small city-state: this vessel, with its present complement of one.'

'I should have toned down the verbosity,' Adam said.

'Cut it out, you two.' Samantha entered the elevator cab and said, 'Command Level, please.'

'I like the "please" bit,' said Athena.

The door sealed and a moment later opened again, this time revealing a different corridor configuration. Startled — Samantha had felt no hint of motion — she paused before stepping out.

Athena's tone was smug. 'Bridge directly ahead. Stateroom entrance last door on the left. Your possessions will soon be transferred to it, although of course we could simply replicate a second set. But I thought it more amusing to assemble a pair of robotic drones to keep you company. You could name them Hewy and—'

'Don't! You'll make me cry. No, different names, please. Let me think. Hmm, oh. A fan once sent me two corgi pups after I'd written a story about a lonely old woman.' She paused. 'That was a bad week.'

Adam asked, 'The week in which you wrote the story or the week the pups arrived?'

'There he goes again,' Athena said.

'I remember considering Romulus and Remus, or Castor and Pollux, but decided that they were too pretentious. I settled on Bart and Lisa. Before finding a friendly family to adopt them.'

Adam asked, 'Do you dislike dogs, Samantha?'

'No I like them just fine, especially the little plastic bags obnoxious owners leave on the beach or sidewalk.' She walked up the corridor. The stateroom door opened and she peeked inside. It looked suitably stately. 'That will do.'

The doorway to the bridge was larger and looked armoured. It vanished at her approach. 'How are you doing that?' she asked. There were no slots and no visible motion marking the door sliding one way or any other.

'Phase-shifting,' Athena said. 'The mechanisms for track-guided entrance and egress are notorious for becoming misaligned, particularly after weapon-fire impacts or any other hull-twisting event. Although Adam desired otherwise, as I was in charge of shipbuilding I overrode his suggested parameters and installed proper technology.'

'You exceeded the tech level for this Intervention,' Adam said.

'For pacifists you two sure bitch a lot,' Sam observed as she stepped onto the bridge. 'And what was that about hull-twisting and weapon impacts? I thought the Greys had crappy weaponry.'

'There is another rapacious species in your immediate region of the galaxy,' said Adam, 'as I may have mentioned. Somewhat more formidable than the Greys.'

'And you can't slap some reason into them?'

'They are a non-centralised protoplasmic sentience,' Adam explained. 'In effect, intelligent digestive juices.'

'Oh,' said Sam. 'Well, I talk to my stomach all the time.'

'Does it listen?'

'No, dammit. Actually, it's more the other way around, if I'm honest. Stomach talks to me. I don't listen.'

'If you two are done,' said Athena, 'I have some instructions to begin on the operation of this vessel, and the minutes are ticking by. If you truly want to halt the countdown on the handshake mission, we'd better get on with it.'

'Exactly.' Samantha strode up to plant herself in the captain's chair. As soon as she settled, a mass of holographic controls grew up out of the armrests. 'Oh my, this looks complicated.'

'The vessel is intended to be crewed,' Athena said. 'However, as instructed, it can also be operated from a single station. Namely, the command chair. Working closely with me, of course.

In an emergency, I can operate independently. Indeed, for this immediate mission and if you find yourself suddenly disinclined to ascend this particular learning curve at this particular time, I can fly this vessel. You need only sit back and relax.'

'Your confidence overwhelms, Athena.'

'This is only natural, as my specifications are—'

'Not your self-confidence,' Samantha cut in. 'I meant your confidence in me.'

A moment of silence, and then, 'Ah, sarcasm.'

'Listen,' Samantha said, looking at the bewildering array of information to her right and left, 'can't you brain-cram this all into me? I seem to recall Adam mentioning something about headsets that educate super-fast.'

'Yes. Those. Have a cigarette, Samantha.'

'That much of an ordeal?'

'Have a cigarette, and then we'll info-dump your brain, impart new muscle-memory, maximise your synaptic receptivity, and, given your particular brain's unique structure, we will impose heightened spatial awareness and higher-concept mathematical comprehension capability: the gift for numbers you never had.'

'How long will all that take?'

'About two minutes following that cigarette I mentioned.'

'Will I have a headache?'

'No.'

'So, why the ciggie?'

'It will take that long to assemble the specificity. This is not a generic plug and play procedure. That would do damage to any organic neural bundle. And lastly, we need you sitting still.'

Adam then said, 'Perhaps I should warn you, Samantha, about the *existential* headache to follow. Which may, quite possibly, affect your state of mind when delivering your address in the UN.'

She grunted. 'I was beginning to wonder if something like that might kick in. Turning me into a maths freak? That's a whole different way of thinking. Could it fuck up my writing ability?'

'Unlikely,' Adam said. 'Consider music and lyricists. Rather, the sudden influx of technical knowledge, the physicality of heightened reaction times, the comprehension cascades arriving so fast as to seem almost instinctual. All of these are fuel sinks. At fullest output, mere *thinking* can exhaust you. Neural exhaustion can trigger systemic depression. Your nanosuite can respond, of course, but your mood swings may be pronounced following fullest stimulation—'

'Ha ha, Adam, you blissfully unaware male-composite entity. I'm in *menopause*. Mood swings? You have no idea how restrained I've been in your non-presence. If you'd showed up as an android or robot, Adam, I'd probably have kicked you into pieces by now, and then crushed every piece under my heel.' She waved a hand and then drew out a cigarette and lit it. 'Athena, bring it on.'

'You chose well, Adam,' said Athena.

'Thank you, Athena,' Adam replied.

Sam sent a stream of smoke pluming upward, only to see it suddenly vanish. 'Adam! You did it! Brilliant!'

There was no headset after all. About seven minutes later, Samantha reached out and engaged the holographic controls. 'Here we go. Drives powering up, cloak engaged. See you later, Adam. Time to take this thing into atmosphere – oh wow, eighty-seven seconds to cross the distance between the Moon and Earth, that's *fast*. Okay, sensors active – let's not hit anything on the way down, shall we? Shit, did we clutter up low orbit or what? Athena, can I get a coffee?'

'Absolutely not,' Athena replied.

Samantha paused. 'Oh. Right. Uh, Adam, apologies. I get it now.'

'You will adjust,' Adam said. 'Be assured, none of your fundamental belief systems have in any way altered or been compromised.'

'Hmm, but would I even know if they were?'

'No. But such alteration is tantamount to rape, Samantha, and rape is violence. We cannot engage in that.'

'Right. So ...' They were closing in on Earth. 'Uhm, the technology for this super-fast info-dump ...'

'Safeguards are in place to prevent your species from ever

acquiring it. All training in the planet-bound centres will be conducted by me, and at a much slower pace.'

'Good,' Samantha said. She sighed. 'We are so not ready for this.'

•

It felt strange to be returning to Earth. For too long the planet had hung suspended in the black, centred on a screen like the image on a poster that might have been seen on the bedroom wall of ten-year-old Carl Sagan. She had watched the slow gyrations of weather systems over the oceans, tilting her head to find her bearings given the image's ninety-degree shift to what she was used to. North pole to the right, a planet lying on its side. It was a peculiarity that Samantha had wanted to ask about, but for some reason never did.

Isolation did strange things. No matter how many newsfeeds she watched, she had felt disconnected from humanity. Her only truly human connection had come from her conversations with Hamish, and these had been her sole life-line to sanity. But the world she shared with her husband was not the world she witnessed on the monitors. Each screen had hovered before her like a murky window at a zoo's reptile house, into which she peered to study a steamy interior of heady smells and turgid, overheated air. She had watched a succession of faces: reporters and witnesses, the victims and the aggrieved, set against an endless variety of backdrops. The mass of humanity on display, shot by shot, in singular portraits of confusion and loss. What did it all signify? She had no idea.

Returning home ... to the world of her birth. Even the notion felt discordant. How many humans had ever been able to consider it? A few score of astronauts, and now, presumably, a handful of the abducted still shaking off their bewilderment. She had spent her time in the company of an alien AI, during which every conversation had been founded upon rational premises, extricated from the natural fugue of human sensibilities, and all the emotional turmoil that came with it.

Was she even prepared to enter into the tumult of her species again? Its fierce irrationality, its stew of opinions, convictions, agendas, contradictions and outright deceptions? Had she lost her sensitivity to the disingenuous? Was she woefully unprepared for what was coming?

Dire thoughts, when it was already too late. She'd committed to this and there was no going back.

Now, as her vessel slid into the upper reaches of the atmosphere, sending a low shudder through the craft, she watched as the planet's day side expanded to fill the view screen. Whatever camera provided the image revealed nothing of the plasma burning off the shielded hull.

Velocity was self-evident, however, confirmed by a quick glance at her instruments. From below, of course, the track of her descent was unlikely to be visible. While the cloaking field was limited in that it could not close out the spectrum of the massive shedding of acceleration as the atmosphere thickened and gravity's grasp tightened, she was on the sunlight side. In a night sky she would be visible, just another shooting star perhaps, but without the flare of disintegration.

She'd laid in a course, calibrated to slip around flight paths for terrestrial planes, and levelled out a few times to bleed off more speed, banking into a spiral as she brought her craft lower and lower still. She'd once tried a HOTAS at a gaming convention and her controls were very similar to those, rising up from the armrests and feeling solid in her hands.

External hull temperature had stayed steady even during the most ferocious stages of the descent, confirming this vessel's atmosphere-capable specs. Now, at an altitude of forty thousand feet and dropping, Samantha engaged anti-gravity and the vessel, which had been more or less plunging like a brick – albeit one banking into a graceful spiral even as it plummeted – now became virtually weightless.

Throughout all of this, the g-forces on the bridge remained at 1.0, inertia trapped between the outer hull and the energy shield's envelope, and of the two, it was the latter that flexed, bulged and compressed in response to the rapid, tight descent.

They were approaching the eastern seaboard of North America, and the city of New York. 'All right, Athena,' said Samantha after drawing a deep breath, 'let's light ourselves up to radar at least. Don't want some helicopter going crunch against our shields like a bug on a windshield.'

'Interceptors will be scrambled,' Athena said. 'Particularly given the size of our radar return. One might presume certain levels of alarm.'

'It's the old game, the Hollywood response,' Samantha said, watching the main viewer carefully as she slowed the vessel to a near halt, and then began a gradual vertical descent. 'They can't shoot but they'll go through the motions because that's how it's done. Paint us up and lock on and then ... twiddle the thumbs.' The UN Headquarters was highlighted in a blinking green glow to help her position the craft directly over its entrance and the concourse fronting it. 'I'm thinking five hundred metres,' she said. 'Then we drop the cloak.'

'Drones have been dispatched and fighter craft are twenty kilometres out and closing.'

'Hmm, that was fast. Okay. The drones that get too close, override them and steer them away, will you?'

'Of course. Isn't this exciting?'

Adam spoke. 'Personality deviation noted.'

Samantha smiled, feeling like the driver of an SUV edging into a tight parking space ... under the watchful eyes of three entire alien civilisations. 'You're not excited, Adam?'

'Trepidation would be more apt, under the circumstances. We are at the crux of this Intervention.'

'Tell me,' said Samantha, 'is there still a chance you all decide to just up and leave and to hell with humanity and planet Earth?'

'Yes.'

'Oh. Crap.'

'A very small one,' Adam went on. 'Recall, our primary incentive was the preservation of your world's biome. A more likely scenario would be to quarantine your species and gradually reduce its surface footprint.'

'Lock us up, you mean.'

329

'If we conclude, following your address, that humanity is not prepared to alter its paradigm in any substantial way, we may have little choice.'

'What about the Greys? Face it, Adam, you need our nasty side.'

'*We* don't. Nearby civilisations do. Assuming, of course, your species does not launch itself on a mission of conquest and enslavement.'

'If we do that?'

'We take your toys away. But frankly I do not expect this outcome. Your species is indeed capable of genuine compassion and gestures of supreme sacrifice. Yet xenophobia is of course possible. The First Contact events you initiate will have to be conducted with considerable care, on extended timelines.'

'No Prime Directive for us,' muttered Samantha.

'I have examined the fictional future in which that operates. Such a directive is, of course, nonsense.'

'I figured you'd say something like that. But then, I agree. What could be more monstrous than doing nothing while a sentient species poisons its own world, plunges into genocidal wars, and eventually turns its world into a ball of ash? Or back to the Stone Age.'

'The "Stone Age" is not so bad,' Adam said. 'But faunal extinction events and atmospheric toxification are. In general, a "Stone Age" is self-sustaining, extremely stable if somewhat precarious, and of limited environmental impact. As I mentioned earlier, your ideal community operates best with less than one hundred individuals. This is very relevant not for the evidence or proof to be found ethnographically, but for your future social, political and global reorganisation.'

'Hmm, curious.'

'In any case, any return to hunter-gatherer subsistence will necessitate the rapid removal of ninety-six per cent of the population. This can hardly be done peacefully, or without immense suffering, not to mention inadvertent environmental destruction.'

At five hundred metres above the UN building Samantha halted the craft, stabilised the anti-gravity and shut down the drives.

She leaned back. 'We're here. Athena, if you'd be so kind, drop the cloak.'

'I *am* so kind, Captain!'

Samantha rested her head back on the padding, closed her eyes. 'Now it begins.'

Chapter Twenty-Five

'Comicons and science fiction conventions are always
fun. Besides, the days of the secluded writer are long
gone. What's ironic is that the modern age has forced
the most introverted, shy, and anxious segment of the
population into the limelight. Adapt or disappear, and
for most of us, conventions are a safe place in which we
can learn how to be public figures. And then there's the
blowhards? Did I mention the blowhards?'

Samantha August

Transcript, panel discussion between SF authors Jeanne
Wolfson and Jack Rico, DragonCon, Atlanta, Georgia.
T-minus fifteen minutes for context.

WOLFSON: Well now, have we ever been in such demand as we
are these days?

(audience laughter)

But every one of us, called upon by the media to comment on
what's been happening ... well, we do a lot of shrugging. It's
one thing to project your imagination and envisage a future
for humanity, out there among the stars, or in some post-
apocalyptic Mad Max Earth, and then stick it all in a story or
a novel. It's quite another to try to figure out what's coming
next with this very real Contact Event –

RICO: Is that what we're calling it, Jeanne? The Contact Event?
I'd call it something else. I'd call it Conquest. We've been taken
down without a shot fired. We're like sheep, milling in the
stockade at the slaughter house. The air stinks of blood and

raw meat and utter terror, but we keep telling each other that it'll be okay. Well it won't be okay! Let me state this plain: WE. ARE. ROYALLY. FUCKED.

(uneasy laughter from audience)

WOLFSON: If this is being royally fucked, Jack, I'll take it any day over the alternative.

RICO: Oh, bullcrap, Jeanne. I served in the US Marines and—

WOLFSON: Uh-uh, stop! Enough of that shtick. Sorry. I did, too, and unlike you, I was in the mix. I fired a shot in anger. You never did, Jack. You got all revved up and ended up posted somewhere that never got touched. Look, I get it. It eats you up inside. I truly get it. But all this bluster from you, that's just all it is. Out there, when it's coming down for real ... *everything* changes. Everything. Sure, maybe you can shut it off afterwards, but never for very long – not unless you're already so psycho that getting fucked in the head makes no real difference. Do you truly think PTSD is some made-up bullshit, Jack?

RICO: No, of course not! I mean—

WOLFSON: But you believe it would never have come down on you. Not Jack Rico, right? Look around out there! No one's shooting at anyone! No one's getting murdered, kidnapped, tortured, beheaded on live feed. No terrorists, no roadside bombs, no crime anywhere. Kids aren't dying from ODs or getting abused. No women are being raped and have you noticed something else? The suicide rate for vets is down to nil. *Nil.* What just happened? Does anyone know? Anyone got that figured out?

(from audience: Have you, Jeanne?)

I'm not sure but I'm glad you asked. I'm glad someone's actually asking. For me, the nightmares are gone. The shakes are gone. Getting a cold every three weeks and just feeling shitty all the time. Gone. Weight loss. Gone. I've stopped drinking. Off the Ludes. I actually feel alive again.

RICO: Nano infiltration. You're being medicated.

WOLFSON: Maybe. I've had my blood tested. Results inconclusive.

RICO: They self-destruct, self-dissolve outside the body.

WOLFSON: You know this how?

RICO: It just makes sense. When you want to control people's thoughts you hide your tracks. So they can never be sure, and no one else can, either.

WOLFSON: Ah, so some of us are being thought-controlled through invisible nanotechnology. But some of us aren't? Well, lucky you then, Jack. All I know is, every day I thank God that it's all ended.

RICO: No offence, but God's got nothing to do with it.

WOLFSON: What makes you so sure? No, don't give me that look. ET is not God. They are not gods. They're mortal. If they weren't they wouldn't be hiding the way they are. We're a dangerous species—

RICO: Not anymore! We can't fight back and that's the problem. That's what I've been saying all along. We've been conquered.

WOLFSON: To what end, Jack? Any highly advanced civilisation has no need of slaves. No mines of Rura Penthe either. Food? They apparently can make all they want. And if all that's not enough, they chased away the Greys.

RICO: And where is God in all this?

WOLFSON: You say nowhere, I say everywhere. Nothing about what has happened, *is* happening, challenges my faith.

RICO: Still in His image?

WOLFSON: My faith in God is not predicated upon Him looking like me or me looking like Him. I find both notions suspiciously narcissistic. Back to the point, Jack. For conquering aliens they're going about it rather strangely. Why stop us killing each other? Wouldn't it be better to get us killing *more* of each other? Look, you wrote novels about aliens invading and eating us. Well, not all of us. Just liberals and socialists and other mewling, useless people. Red-blooded Republicans were too gnarly, apparently. But even that premise was predicated on scarcity and a biological imperative to eat and keep eating. I think what we're being shown here, all around us, is an invitation to *post*-scarcity.

RICO: We're not ready for it.

WOLFSON: On that we're agreed. Finally.

(audience applauds)

Which begs the question, how do we *get* ready for it? Look at us, we were all trapped in runaway consumption. Even as the world's resources dwindled, we just got faster shovelling it all into our mouths. We got fat. We lived in houses full of useless plastic junk. We bought things we didn't need. We fed our entertainment maw with endless piles of brain candy. We got online and couldn't figure out how to get back off. Now, imagine a galaxy out there where anything and everything is available for the taking. No need to work, no nine-to-five treadmill, no money and with that, no poverty, or hunger, or illness. Some people think it'll turn into one mass orgy—

(audience cheers)

You wish! But if I had to guess, it will be the opposite. All that freedom is taking all the wind from our sails.

RICO: That's what I'm thinking, too, Jeanne. That's exactly what I'm fearing. Our incentive is gone. Poof! Vanished.

WOLFSON: But I don't think it's permanent.

RICO: Why not?

WOLFSON: Because they showed us the Greys. They did that for a reason. They gave us a target.

RICO: I don't see it. You said it yourself: they chased them away! How exactly are we supposed to tear off across the galaxy hunting those bastards down?

WOLFSON: I don't—

[Moderator interjects: Excuse me – there's a live feed coming in – anyone else seeing this? A UFO has just appeared, hanging over the UN building in New York! Brian – can we get it up on the big screen? Hold on, people, give us a second ... There!]

RICO: What the fuck? Is that a—

•

'... a large, winged craft, angular and somewhat frighteningly predatory — at least to my eyes,' the reporter added, with a strained smile towards the camera. 'You can see what must be the command centre, or perhaps the pilot station, much like the head of a raptor at the end of a neck-like projection. It's all just ... just *massive*.'

The man paused and put one hand up to the speaker in his ear. 'Just a moment, please. Oh. No wonder it looked kind of familiar! Well! I'm now feeling somewhat foolish, to be honest.' He paused, clearly frustrated, and lifted his gaze again to study the enormous craft. The camera held on him a moment longer, and then the image pulled back and lifted skyward to take in the motionless craft.

There was an inarticulate sound from the reporter, who then said, 'Yes, from the television series—'

•

Ronald Carpenter had been forewarned by a phone call from Hamish. He and his wife, Emily, had driven over to visit the doctor, to be there when the event happened. The house had recovered from Hamish's indifference. Now it was tidy, almost sterile in its meticulous maintenance, and the man himself looked relaxed, if somewhat slovenly.

When CNN cut to the scene in New York, Ronald had thrown himself back into the easy chair. 'Whoah! Holy shit!'

'Ronald!' Emily snapped. 'Language!'

'I've seen that ship before,' Hamish said, his hands entwined together between his knees as he leaned forward to study the drone-fed image.

'Of course you have!' Ronald said. 'Only it's *huge*. Much bigger that what we saw in the movies, and on TV.'

'Listen,' Emily cut in. 'They're saying it's a hoax. Some kind of holographic projection.'

'They're wrong,' Hamish said.

'*We* know that,' Ronald pointed out. 'No, it's going to take a while to sink in. Nobody has the technology to project anything that big. And it's throwing a shadow, and there's birds turning to avoid it. In fact, look at those gulls. They're *circling* it.'

'ET could,' Emily said. 'Fake it, I mean.'

'Sure, but why would they? Right? I mean, we've all been waiting for actual contact. We've been waiting for the alien to actually *show* up. Granted, not in that!' He laughed in delight, unable to sit still.

'Of course,' said Hamish, 'it's not the aliens, is it? No. It's my wife.'

Ronald looked across at the man, saw a pale visage, trembling hands. 'Hey, she's all right. It'll be all right. She knows what she's doing.'

Hamish pointed at the screen. 'What do you make of this, though? What do you infer from her ... choice?'

Ronald abruptly rose and began pacing. 'Right. Let's see. She picked a Klingon Bird of Prey. From science fiction's most famous franchise. Not random, obviously. She's thrown it out there, risking the world's biggest lawsuit.' He hesitated, and then nodded. 'Okay. We're being invited into one of our own invented futures. A future that offers us a beacon of hope. Pointedly non-dystopic. Like she's making a promise. But ... it's not ... it's from one of the fictional *alien* species in that invented future.'

'Not the *Enterprise*, you mean,' said Emily. She was knitting, the needles frantically dipping and waving.

'Exactly. Of *us*, but not *of* us. She picked it because anything we'd not recognise would have us all panicking. Scenes of *Independence Day* and all that. She's saying, relax, there's no silent countdown to obliteration. This thing is over the UN building. Not the White House. So, we know why, because we know it's Sam, and Sam is going to speak in the UN. To the world. We know that, but so far no one else does.'

'You should make some calls, love,' said Emily.

'I'm not supposed to steal her thunder,' said Ronald. 'You said, Hamish, that what we know we have to keep to ourselves.'

'So leave Sam out of it,' Emily said with her usual air of infinite patience. 'Just talk about the rest. Your interpretation of the meaning behind it. That ship.'

'As a theory.'

'Yes, as a theory.'

'All right. That I can do.'

'That reporter is an idiot,' Emily said. 'Try CBC.'

Hamish collected up the remote and switched channels.

•

'That's from the online MMO, right down to the last detail,' King Con said. 'It's a dead ringer, only like twice as big! Imagine the engine room! I mean, you could fit a beer distillery in it!'

Joey Sink barely heard his buddy blathering on. He was staring at the live feed, watching the drones circling the huge spaceship along with the damned gulls. In the foreground, in the news room, some retired Air Force officer with a lantern jaw was saying something about energy fields and repulsion technology, while a plug of a man who was some physicist from NASA sat saying nothing but with a silly grin on his face.

At long last the presenter was able to interject, drawing the scientist into the conversation. Joey cut King Con off and turned up the volume.

'... famous television series,' the woman was saying, 'but what is the significance of making something so obviously inspired by our own entertainment media?'

'Well maybe that's just it,' the physicist replied, hands gesticulating in a way that reminded Joey of one of his high school science teachers. 'Maybe it's a gift! Or a promise. Or a bribe. Maybe it's all three! The point is, we're staring at an example of incredible technology. How much does that thing weigh? But it just sits there, motionless, exactly five hundred metres above the UN building.'

'Anti-gravity,' interjected the Air Force guy.

'Yes! And some kind of chameleon property, perhaps, allowing it to disappear from sight. Though we've confirmed it showed up on radar at about sixty thousand feet, but I think that was just a heads-up. They didn't want anything colliding with it.'

'Should we be afraid?' the journalist asked.

'It's got weapon mounts,' said the Air Force guy. 'Hardpoints.'

'You mean it's a perfect match for a Bird of Prey,' the physicist interjected. 'Do they even work?'

'I'd rather we not find out.'

'This is a big waving flag,' the physicist said, leaning back.

'Isn't it also property theft?' the journalist asked. 'I mean, in terms of copyright and patents?'

'Patents?' The physicist threw up his hands. 'Can you patent technology that hasn't been invented yet? All those ship designs for the television and movies and games and whatnot – where the propulsion and weapon systems are, they're just empty boxes with labels! Configurations of a few lines and words like "Impulse Drive". And then there's the crystals! Personally, I doubt there are energy crystals powering that thing. No, what's in those "boxes" on the schematics is – with this thing – technology that actually works!'

'But the design—'

'Who knows and, really, does it matter? Besides,' the physicist pointed out, 'we're the wrong people for you to ask about that.' And he nodded across at the Air Force guy, who scowled but did not otherwise object.

'On that note,' segued the presenter, 'let's review all that's happened so far on this historic day ... after this short break.'

Joey dialled down the volume. He laced his hands behind his head and tilted back in his chair. He felt like whistling.

King Con's line was blinking.

He realised that his camera was still on. 'Oh crud!' he laughed. 'Anyone out there still watching me twiddle my thumbs? My smiling mug in the corner of your screen? Look, there's King Con trying to get back. And ... hey!' He sat forward and clicked an 'answer' request. 'Annie Mouse! Where you at, bro? Still down in Canaveral? What's the latest on the handshake mission? In the toilet I bet, right?'

'In the toilet, flushed and halfway to the Gulf of Mexico,' Annie Mouse replied. 'It's weird here right now. Bummed out, but also insane with excitement. I mean, instant obsolescence. Our tin cans – even with the Kepler people handing us space-capable EFFEs and a heavy lifter that blows everything else out of the water … we're all just, uhm, stunned, I guess. Like bringing a cap-gun to the siege of Stalingrad.'

'Yeah. Obscure reference there, bro.'

'Sorry, was watching *Famous Tank Battles* last night.'

'Oh, but hey they do all right with a budget of ten bucks, don't they?' Joey frowned. 'What were we talking about again?'

'Handshake. Toilet. Bird of Prey, just hanging there.'

'You mean, no "Greetings, Earthlings" from that thing? C'mon, you can tell us. Somebody's having a conversation with ET, right? Even as we speak.'

'Not that I know of,' said Annie Mouse.

'What is this, a game of who blinks first?'

•

The Head of Security wanted the building evacuated. He was clearly waiting for the death-ray, but Adeleh Bagneri had sent Agnes out to head the man off in the outer office, and when Agnes held her ground nobody ever got past her. Lovely girl, Agnes.

Panic seemed pointless. The ship was directly overhead for a reason and that reason was pretty obvious, as far as the Secretary General was concerned.

Her phone was buzzing around on the polished top of her desk, but she remained propped against the window, blowing the smoke from her Turkish cigarette outside, only to watch it swirl back into her office. The Vape worked most of the time, but every now and then she just wanted that old toxic hit, sweetly kissing death's face. This pretty much defined one of those needy times.

After so many years in the UK, she had become used to open windows at night: that cold blast from the elements fended off by a thick comforter, and upon first taking charge of this office she had insisted on proper windows, the kind that could be opened. Fresh air was anathema in the States for some reason. It was likely that, somewhere in the back of her mind, she had been thinking about sneaking a fag every now and then.

Gradually, something about her buzzing phone snared her attention. It wasn't her official phone. It was her family one. 'Oh, bugger,' she muttered, balancing the cigarette on the sill and leaning over to retrieve the phone. One of her daughters, probably. The worrying one. She picked it up and moved back to the window. Reaching for her cigarette she found it gone. 'Really, another one?' She scanned the floor, fearing yet another burn hole in the carpet. But it was nowhere in sight. Maybe the wind was blowing the smoke in, but it was also blowing the ciggies out. Ridiculous. She held up the phone and then frowned upon seeing the caller ID: *Look up. Way up.*

'Oh, darling daughter,' she muttered. She tapped to answer and began speaking immediately. 'This is hardly the time to be pissing around even if you are my flesh and blood, Azizeh—'

'Excuse me,' cut in an unfamiliar woman's voice. 'Is this the Secretary General?'

'Who is this and how did you get my private number?'

'It seemed the better option,' the woman replied. Her accent was almost American. 'My name is Samantha August, and I am presently occupying the spaceship hovering above you – you are in the UN headquarters, right?'

'Well, that's funny,' Adeleh deadpanned. 'Got some Tupperware to sell me then?'

'Of a sort,' the woman replied and Adeleh heard the smile in her tone. 'If you have a computer handy, Google my name. Samantha August. You'll find that I was abducted in the spring, in May, from a street in Victoria, BC. That's Canada. Anyway, you can guess who did the snatching. I'll wait.'

'I'm really supposed to buy all this?'

'It'll only take a minute, you know.'

'Fine. Hold on.' Adeleh set the phone down, lit another cigarette, and – feeling momentarily defiant – sat down at her desk. Cigarette dangling from her lips, she typed in the name. Ignoring the standard news reports of the woman – the writer's – kidnapping, she clicked on the first video on YouTube. A moment later she picked up the phone. 'Okay. I'm listening.'

'Convinced?'

'Not entirely. Just ... go on.'

'I need to talk to the world and I want your microphone.'

'Uh huh. When?'

'Oh, say in three hours? Two p.m. local time. Will that give you enough time to put the call out to all members? It'd look good to have a full house, I think. Under the circumstances.'

'Right. Three hours. Darling, even *I* couldn't put together a full emergency assembly in *three* hours.'

'Can you try? Otherwise, I hang around up here for another day.'

'Why don't you just go away and come back tomorrow?'

Samantha laughed. 'Madam Secretary, the world is watching *now*. This is your first chance to step up where no others dare to tread. You. Not the leader of any one country. That distinction will become very, *very* important in the near future.'

'Is ET with you in that ship?'

'Not as such. We won't be meeting them any time soon. Not in the protocol. Look, I get the feeling that you're sitting there humouring me. Tell you what. Call up a live feed of my ship.'

'One is already up,' Adeleh replied, after taking a deep drag.

'I'm about to dip my wings, and no, I'm not talking about a fried chicken takeout.'

Before Adeleh's eyes, the spaceship dipped its wings.

Utter chaos in the outer office, sudden, frantic news reporters shouting into their microphones on every monitor in sight. From the city itself, something like a roar, or a wave of sound, rising up from the crowds gathered below.

Adeleh took another quick drag and then stubbed out the cigarette on the windowsill, idly watching the wind quickly pluck the butt away, and said into the phone. 'Three hours. Tell me what you need, Ms August.'

Chapter Twenty-Six

'All things considered, science is the best means of
understanding almost everything around us. It works
well on the human scale and stands as a stark counter-
point to beliefs that by their very nature refute the
notion of evidence. And I would be the last person
to attack people encouraging the rest of us to use our
ability to be rational, thereby defending the value and
the necessity of science. But I will lift a querying hand
when the notion of "science" is held to be immutable,
because "science" as such does not exist. Science is
a process to be sure, a way of thinking, but what
science is above all is that which scientists do, and
alas, scientists are people, too. As potentially fallible,
irrational, biased, greedy, in short, as flawed as the
rest of us. So, by all means defend science as a process.
But don't confuse it with the very human endeavour
of science as a *profession*. Because they're not the same
thing. And this is why when some guy in a white lab-
coat says "you can trust me, I'm a scientist", best take it
with a big bucket of salt, and then say "Fine, now show
me the evidence and, more to the point, show me how
you got to it."'

Samantha August

'That's *my* airspace! Someone do something about it!'

'I'm sorry, Mister President,' replied the Air Force general,
glancing nervously at the others at the table: Daniel Prester,

the Head of Homeland Security, old Esterholm from the CIA, that guy from the NSA whom he personally despised, and Ben Mellyk, who seemed to be fighting a smile. The general cleared his throat and tried again. 'We have no intercept capability. Our craft are being warned off at a half-mile by some woman's voice, and every drone we bring too close gets hijacked and pushed away. We're being told that there is a forcefield around the craft.'

'Like in the movie? So someone stick a virus in ET's computer, dammit! Shut it down!'

Ben Mellyk leaned forward. 'Sir, we're not calling the shots here. It is as simple as that. Yes, our airspace has been compromised. Yes, that vessel is a dead ringer for a Bird of Prey and accordingly it has weapon mounts, or at least what are supposed to be weapon mounts.'

'It dipped its wings,' observed the NSA man. 'What was that all about?'

'That's usually a friendly greeting gesture,' explained the Air Force general.

'Anyone tried talking to them?' Raine Kent demanded, looking around with a glower, his face unnaturally red.

'All frequencies,' Ben replied. 'All met with silence.'

'But that woman's voice on the pilot radios?'

'Just the warning to stand off,' the general explained.

'Accent?' asked the NSA man. 'Russian? Chinese?'

'No. If anything, I'd say Midwestern.'

'Definitely Midwestern,' added Kenneth Esterholm. 'We've analysed the recordings, matched the modulations. There's a hint of Canadian in it, in fact.'

'Canadians again!'

'But it repeats, suggesting that it's also a recording. Basically, we think it's an accent intended to put us at ease.'

The President thumped the tabletop. 'At ease? Do I look at ease? If it blows up the UN building we'll get blamed. Hell, about fifty countries will declare war on us!'

'Sir,' pointed out Esterholm, 'those would be pointless declarations.'

'Not if they all call in their loans,' Kent said in a low growl.

He paused, looked around. 'It's all falling apart. I keep firing my press secretary but nothing changes. How many reporters attended my last presidential statement? Three. And two of them I told to be there or else. I'm tweeting into dead silence – nobody cares anymore!' He looked around. 'Someone fire me. I'm sick of this, sick of all of it.'

'Sir,' ventured Ben Mellyk – who'd been showing more balls of late – 'this year will be noted as the most important year in the history of humanity. All of our names – everyone here in the room for certain – will be remembered, and what we do, what we say, will be pored over for generations.'

'What we do and say?' Raine Kent's expression was incredulous. 'ET's not listening to us! ET's ignoring us! Every world leader – ignored! NASA, ignored! Where's our black helicopters flying here and there? Where's our men with dark sunglasses and briefcases? Where's our people in hazmat suits? Arc lights and military camps, MPs at every gate? Where's our movie? I want our goddamned movie!'

The door to the conference room opened and in strode the Vice-President. 'I've just been on the phone with Adeleh Bagneri, and—'

'Who?' Raine Kent asked. 'Who the hell is Adele Bag – is that the pop star with those songs I can't get out of my head?'

'No, Mister President,' Diana K. Prentice said, without a hint of exasperation, 'Adeleh Bagneri is the Secretary General of the United Nations.'

'Oh. Right! Let me guess, she's asking for asylum – have they evacuated the building yet? Someone turn on that TV, no that one there. Ken, turn it on, right, good. Shit, that's one big mob under that thing! What if it lands? People'll get crushed – the idiots – why aren't the cops keeping 'em back?'

Diana Prentice pulled out a chair and sat down. 'They're not evacuating the building. They're calling an emergency session.'

Raine Kent made a face. 'More words. Words and words. Blah blah blah, they haven't got a clue either.'

'There's been contact.'

That stopped the President.

Diana drew a breath and then said, 'Adeleh got a call on her cell from the woman on board that spaceship. That wing-dip was confirmation, by the way. There's a human on board. No aliens, just a human. Her name is Samantha August. A Canadian science fiction writer who was abducted—'

'In May,' Kenneth Esterholm cut in, nodding. 'We were looking into that. Ongoing.'

'She's been a guest on board another spaceship, one hiding in orbit. But now she's on that new spaceship, and she's here to address the people of Earth, and will be doing so from the UN. In about an hour and a half.'

'Like hell she will,' Raine Kent said. 'As soon as she lands or beams down or whatever, arrest her. We debrief her first. *Then* maybe she can talk to everyone else.'

The Vice-President shook her head. 'I'm afraid it is not going to happen, Raine. No arrest, no whisking off into a black van. This speech is going to happen, like it or not.'

The NSA man sat up. 'Mister President, we can apply our seven-second delayed feed. In fact, we should be able to control the entire event.'

'Exactly! Do that! We can edit on the fly. Fuck ET if they don't like it.'

'This was anticipated,' said the Vice-President. 'There will be no delay in the feed. No control of the address. The speech is going to happen. Everybody with a cellphone, laptop, desktop computer or pad, a radio or a television, is going to hear it. Furthermore, each person will hear the speech in their native language. ET will be exploiting pretty much all our hardware, all the servers on the entire planet—'

'Pull the plug!' the NSA man snapped.

Diana sighed. 'As I said, every response, every effort we make to prevent the full disclosure of this address will be denied. There is something called a blanket presence here on the planet. Source of the forcefields, and the denial of violence.' She glanced at the Science Advisor. 'We already know about that, about its agency.'

Ben Mellyk nodded. 'Yes. Blanket presence. That term certainly fits what we've been observing.'

'It is self-powered,' Diana went on. 'Every communication device will turn on in about an hour from now, everywhere on Earth.'

'Fine,' the NSA man said. 'Got it. Now, that woman—'

'Samantha August.'

'We got a file on her? She's a writer. We must have.'

'No doubt,' murmured Kenneth Esterholm. He rose from his chair. 'And of course we can listen in on any cellphone calls she makes to the Secretary General.'

Diana Prentice snorted. 'You can try, I suppose.'

Esterholm scowled but said nothing to that. 'Mister President, by your leave, I need to get us putting together everything we have on—'

•

'Samantha August.' The Canadian Prime Minister was sitting, straight-backed and intent, her gaze fixing on that of the science fiction writer, Robert J. Sawyer. 'Tell me about her, please.'

Alison Pinborough regarded the writer, noting his steady, piercing gaze behind the wire-rimmed glasses. That he was the smartest person in this room was something she already knew, as the Prime Minister was about to find out. Scientists, of course, possessed their own form of self-assurance. Every one of them dragged an invisible library on wheels behind them, the shelves crammed full of esoteric information. A few of them had a talent for communicating what they knew, but many didn't.

She assumed it was the same for writers. An old ex had once dragged her to a launch night for a local poet's latest book. The man had been surrounded by women half his age, and naturally he'd been wearing an expensive sweater, turtle-neck, and he read in that standard (or so she'd discovered by the grisly night's merciful end) leaden cadence, as if every phrase was gravid with significance. The other guest poets, with only one or two exceptions, pretty much matched that plodding rhythm when perched behind the microphone. It had been interminable.

But that was poets. None of them had this man's ferocious energy.

In answer to Lisabet's question, he said, 'Yet another example of a brilliant Canadian science fiction writer virtually no-one in this country knows about, outside of the aficionados of the genre. Never reviewed by the *Globe*, or the *National Post*. So, who is she, madam Prime Minister? Smart, opinionated, a feminist, a humanist. Frankly, I'm not surprised the ETs selected her.'

'Is that what they did?' Lisabet Carboneau asked. 'Just … picked her from a hat?'

'I doubt it was that random,' Sawyer replied. 'If there is a thematic continuity when looking at Sam's stories and novels, it is compassion and a full comprehension of the human condition. Good writers don't blink. They don't shy away from hard truths.'

'So she's a liberal.'

Sawyer frowned. 'Excuse me?'

'Not the political party. Small "l" liberal. Not a friend of capitalism or corporate interests, a believer in social welfare. An environmentalist.'

'More a believer in the dignity of humanity, Madam Prime Minister. And that is the context we need for thinking about this. ET chose well.'

'There's not a single CEO or banker who'd agree with you.'

At this, the author bridled and Alison steeled herself, thinking, *uh oh, here we go.*

'Madam Prime Minister,' Sawyer's tone was now hard, 'it is long past time we took those old divisions to the dumpster. Every single aspect of this intervention to date has made very clear – undeniably so – that our traditional economic platform *will not continue*. In fact, the very notion of progress has been severed from capitalism. We will advance, but that advancement is no longer dependent on entrepreneurial largesse, or market forces of competition and innovation. We will now advance because it is the *right* thing to do.' He paused but only for a single breath. 'Proper governance at this moment is no longer chained to maintaining the status quo. No longer pressured by special interests. The old games are dead. Their very language is dead. And you continue to wonder why every world leader is descending into utter obscurity? Liberal? Conservative? Who the hell cares anymore?'

This last statement was loud enough to still the murmur from the rooms adjacent to the office.

Lisabet Carboneau had slowly leaned back during that speech. Now there was a look of near disbelief on her face. 'Excuse me, have you just berated me?'

'We have to step into the new paradigm and we have to do it now.'

Alison found herself silently cheering the man on. He was unapologetic, and how awesome was that?

'I see,' Lisabet replied after a moment. 'Please describe this new paradigm, Mister Sawyer. Not in terms of what's no longer relevant, but in terms of what *will* be relevant.'

'That is about to be spelled out for us in no uncertain terms,' Sawyer replied.

'Can you predict something? Anything? Offer me, since you clearly have an opinion on such matters – offer me a vision of what a leader of a country is to say now, or, rather, tomorrow. Not just say, but do – what am I to do? How do I lead? Give me my new language, Mister Sawyer.'

The writer sighed. 'A language without obfuscation, Madam Prime Minister. Devoid of the usual bullshit, the platitudes, the evasive generalities that journalists don't even challenge anymore. When was the last time a politician said anything of real substance? Said things and made promises that weren't backtracked on? Nobody keeps their word, unless it's a rhetoric of fear and hate, and even then it's mostly a red flag to the wingnuts out there to go charging off beating the crap out of people with the wrong skin colour or the wrong religion—'

'Listen – don't throw me in with that . . . that *man*.'

'I'm not. I'm telling you how your average citizen sees politicians these days. We listen and we don't buy it. Why? Because you refuse to tell us hard truths. You refuse to tell us we need to change our ways of living, pay more taxes, stop using cars, shut down the oil fields and the clear-cutting. We needed a drastic cut on carbon emissions – did you bite that bullet? Not really. Nobody did, barring a few small countries in Europe. The oil pipelines continue to be built, despite the opposition.'

'People who try saying those things don't get elected.'

'And there you strike at the very heart of the problem, Madam Prime Minister. The people in charge are contemptuous of the people who put them there.'

'We are constrained, Mister Sawyer. We can't stray too far from the path, the path that keeps the majority of people comfortable and not too unduly inconvenienced. In the meantime, external forces put upon us leaders immense pressure to keep the machine running.'

'And now all of that is breaking down,' Sawyer replied. 'Stand before your citizens, Madam Prime Minister, and speak honestly. Help us articulate our fears and worries, our uncertainty. Don't bullshit. Make it clear that not one government or nation on this planet has a handle on this. The oil bubble popped – not from its internal pressure but from an external force. And that force is offering us an alternative.' He leaned forward. 'We need to redefine civilisation. That ship suspended over the UN building in New York, it's telling us we're not long for being stuck in Earth's gravity well. We are expanding into our solar system, Madam Prime Minister, at the very least. Traditional forms of government are on the way out.'

'Well, that's just terrific. So who maintains infrastructure? Who keeps everything running? Transportation, resource extraction and processing and distribution? Civilisation is not about to lose its complexity, is it? The bureaucracy exists for a reason, and that reason is the administration of a country full of people. And of course it goes beyond that – we need to continue dealing with other countries on the global market, the redistribution of resources that represent the fundamental business of surviving in the twenty-first century.'

'That global market is already beginning to dissolve, Madam Prime Minister. Self-sufficiency will preclude the usual give and take. Post-scarcity. The pressure is off, but we as a species have existed under that burden since the very first city sprang up nine or ten thousand years ago. We don't know any other way to live.'

'So where does that leave us?'

Sawyer held up his hands. 'Entering an age of freedom such as we've never known. Madam Prime Minister, tell us that. Every other world leader is either panicking or frozen in the headlights. Be the first to tell us what's coming – not the specifics, since we don't yet know those – not for another, well, fifteen minutes. Besides, leave that for the analysts and pundits. What I'm talking about here is holding up the mirror and telling us what we're seeing.'

Alison Pinborough let out a long, slow breath, watching as something came over the Prime Minister's face, a transformation.

'A mirror,' she said quietly. 'Yes. I get it. I can do that.' She hesitated. 'I think.'

'You can,' Robert Sawyer said with conviction.

The Prime Minister raised one eyebrow as she regarded the author. 'You up to collaborating on a speech?'

'No,' he replied. 'But I *will* write it.'

Cajones. Utter cajones. Alison thought she might be in love.

●

Adeleh Bignari had the office door closed against the chaos in the rooms beyond. Her personal cell sat on the desk, speaker on, while Agnes sat opposite.

The well-modulated voice of Samantha August continued speaking after a brief pause. 'Sorry, we just had some electronic warfare thrown at us. Blocked, of course. Throwing sticks at a tank, but that's humans for you, isn't it?'

'You keep saying "we" but earlier you said you were alone.'

'I am. Well, biologically. My lovely unnamed flying lawsuit has an onboard AI. I've named her Athena. She's the one maintaining the sanctity of our airspace, making sure no one does something stupid and gets hurt. She's also interfaced with the blanket presence, but the full maintenance of that is coming from

351

another AI, on another ship. We're all set on our end. How about you?'

'We'll manage,' Adeleh said, lighting another cigarette and ignoring the scowl from Agnes.

'Was that a lighter I heard?' Samantha asked. 'You're my kind of woman, Madam Secretary General.'

'Party of two for the pariah section, please.'

Samantha laughed. It was a nice laugh, low and sexy. A nice voice, too. Good thing, that.

'So how do you come down from that ship?' Adeleh asked.

'I'd like to say an energy-matter transfer, but I can't because that's impossible. I'll come down the way I was originally taken. I will be phase-shifted – which is what makes me disappear – and then enveloped in a double-sleeved anti-gravity bubble of sorts. If you're not shielded from anti-gravity it disassembles your body. Actually, "anti-gravity" only describes the effect of the field. I think it refracts gravity rather than cancelling it. Anyway. Then I'll be nudged downward. It all happens quickly, but people will see what looks like a column of white light. Accordingly, you need to ensure that the base of the building's steps is completely clear. Give me fifteen metres or so. We could add an audible signal but I don't want people to panic.'

'Depends on the sound,' Adeleh replied. 'Personally, I think the mother alien's scream would be awesome, but that's just me. No, it's fine. Don't bother. We've issued a press announcement. The NYPD and our own security staff have been informed and the latter will provide you with an escort into the building. We're already managing the area in front of the building with a thirty metre space cleared.'

'Okay,' said Samantha. 'Then I'll head down in five minutes. Athena can manage things from up here. Let your engineers and technicians know that all external feeds will be managed remotely, and so long as the camera operators and sound people don't try shutting things down or doing anything weird, it should be clear sailing.'

'Ms August,' said Adeleh, 'when you're done with your speech, will you be fielding questions?'

'I'm not sure. Should I?'

'Well, if your speech constitutes a dictating of terms, probably not.'

'Hmm, as in "terms of surrender"?'

'You're suggesting that negotiating is now on the table?'

'Ah, right. Good point. Look, I am going to explain, as neutrally as possible, what is happening. I will also enunciate, as I understand them, the motivations for this intervention. I think, therefore, that yes, I should take questions at the end.'

Adeleh sighed and nodded across to Agnes. 'We're glad to hear that, Ms August.'

'Just "Sam" will do.'

'And for me, Adeleh.'

'I read your bio and I like everything about you, Adeleh. That's why I figured this might work, if I called you direct.'

'You'd still be on hold if you'd tried the normal channels.'

'Ha! Okay, I'm ready for my arrival. Are you?'

'Just a second, Sam.' Adeleh leaned forward. 'Agnes, take point. Let's begin our trip down to the ground floor – I want to meet her at the entrance – is everything ready for that?'

'It is.' Agnes rose, headed for the door.

'Sam,' said Adeleh, 'there are some reporters down there. They'll pounce on you, of course.'

'Yeah. No problem. I may be a few minutes outside the entrance then, but not for too long. Better get going, Adeleh.'

'On my way.'

•

The best feed was from CNBC, close to the now-cordoned-off area fronting the UN building. There were other feeds that Joey Sink flipped through every now and then across his multiple monitors, including scores of handheld recordings, the shaky kind that occasionally panned the pavement or people's feet, or wheeled drunkenly towards a tilted skyline or the enormous craft overhead. Most of these were betraying nervous hands and the chatter was an incessant murmur, reminding Joey of a gymnasium full of school kids. The NBC reporter, some woman named Cherrie, was talking about the latest word from officials in the UN. Samantha August was coming down from the ship, any moment now.

Joey had frantically googled the SF writer, only to find the servers had crashed immediately following the revelation of her identity. He vaguely recalled a head-to-head battle royale with Atwood at a convention a few years back (which had later been revealed as staged, some kind of in-joke between the two women, and they'd played it up like pros, exchanging devastating, eviscerating put-downs that had the entire audience of mostly Canadians gasping in shock).

He knew of at least one SF television series based on her stuff. The one photograph attached to that series showed a rather striking red-haired woman, clear-eyed and probably intimidating as hell in person. And that had jostled his memory to realise that he indeed knew her, from her vlog.

Oh yeah, she'd been under siege before. She'd had opinions.

There was a whole sub-population who probably hated her on sight, he suspected. For being a woman, for being unafraid, for being white even. At least, he assumed she was unafraid. Her vlog was still up and running as far as he knew. He'd seen clips, every now and then, and besides, that picture showed a woman who didn't seem the type to twitch like a rabbit. And if all that wasn't bad enough, she wasn't even American.

He noted King Con's request blinking away. Joey sighed, and then answered. 'Bro, you're on.'

'Samantha August, man. She's beaming down!'

'Yeah, we all got that.'

'Ever heard of Majestic 12, Joey?'

'The secret cult in the government that controls everything about UFOs and alien technology and all that other shit. Yeah. Probably killed Kennedy, or so goes the theory. What about it?'

'The bath tub's cracked, Joey. It's all leaking out. Reverse-engineered shit. Nazi scientists, a whole cupboard full of tech way more advanced than what's given to the public. The thinking goes that someone deep on the inside decided to whistle-blow.

That, or ET hacked the bastards. Thing is, Joey, there's hints about a war in space, and maybe the fact that our planet's been quarantined since the late forties. So, the big question: whose side is our ET on? And more importantly, just how tough are they?'

'Okay, Mister King of Conspiracy, we can – oh wow!'

On the live feeds a solid white beam of light had just speared down from the suspended spaceship.

A moment later it vanished, and there stood Samantha August. She was dressed pretty damned sharp, like some university dean, maybe, or some Wall Street head-hunter. From nearby microphones and cellphones held out came the sudden cries of reporters calling out to her from behind a roped cordon manned by the NYPD.

Samantha August turned, smiled and gestured 'wait a moment' while she pulled out a pack of Canadian cigarettes and lit up.

'What the fuck,' Joey muttered. 'Biggest moment in the history of the world and she takes a smoke break?'

King Con was laughing hysterically, but managed to say, 'Huevos or what!'

Joey watched as the woman walked towards the CNBC cameraman and Cherrie.

'What happened after you were abducted, Ms August? Were you tortured? Experimented on? Are you here under duress? Do they control your brain?'

'Well treated,' she replied calmly. 'No torture, no experiments, no brain control that I'm aware of – in other words, my healthy scepticism remains.' She paused, sending out a stream of smoke that whipped away on the wind (was it *always* windy in NYC?), and then said, 'I'm not here to deliver a sales pitch. I'm here to give you as many details on this Intervention event as I possess. And I will be doing that to as many people as possible, all over the world.' She looked into the camera lens. 'So stay tuned. I'll be starting in about fifteen minutes.'

Joey watched as she backed off, finished her cigarette and then stood around looking for a trash receptacle. But they'd all been removed.

A female cop stepped over and collected it. The two spoke, and Samantha laughed. With a wave towards the strangely silent crowd, she headed up the steps.

A couple of women escorted by security stood to receive her. Joey had done enough research to recognise the UN's Secretary General, Adeleh Bignari. British-educated Iranian surgeon. He didn't know the other woman.

There were handshakes, a few words, and then the group turned and made its way towards the building's entrance.

'That's it?' Joey wondered.

'Said all she needed to,' King Con replied.

'Cherrie didn't ask the one question I wanted to know the answer to,' Joey observed, leaning back (but only slightly).

'Which is?'

'Why her?'

'Oh c'mon, Joey,' King Con chided. 'Sci fi writer. You know. Books. Reading. Ideas. Imagination. Brains. And a whole effin' vlogger career of no-bullshit take-that-you-arseholes—'

'Language!'

'Right, sorry, bud! Anyway. She's tough and smart. That's what I'm saying. A whole career thinking and writing about other worlds, about aliens and people and people and aliens. About our future, man. And it's not all doom and gloom, her stuff. None of that boring dystopic grimdark we're-all-ffu—fudged crap, right?'

'You really can't help it, can you, bro? Oh, look at that, all the networks have switched over – we're in that main assembly hall or whatever it's called.' Joey sat up. He pulled loose a can of Red Bull from a ten-pack on the wing of his desk, popped it. 'Boys and girls, take a selfie or something. Record where you were the day this all went down. Remember it. Because, like it or not, folks, today ... *everything changes.*'

'Amen,' King Con whispered.

356

Chapter Twenty-Seven

'Is there anything better than sitting in the command
chair of an interstellar spaceship?'

Samantha August

Kolo stood staring at the small television's screen. The place was
more crowded than it had ever been, or so the reporter said.
It was said no interpreters were required, but they were there
anyway. And yet, for all the people, there was very little noise,
no one speaking or shouting anything out as the white woman
with the fiery hair walked up to the podium.

A television had been pulled out from one of the buildings,
but most people had their phones and earplugs. Kolo had none of
that. He'd lost his phone only a few days after the invisible wall
had driven him and his people from the camp. He stood in the
press of humanity, Neela's hand tight in his.

They were on the grounds of the Cobbe Barracks, in Zomba,
almost within sight of the massive white-walled building complex
that had drawn everyone to this place. The soldier who'd carried
the television out had been apologising to anyone and everyone
even before they'd plugged it in and turned it on. The picture
was bad, he said. It lost signal all the time, he said. Instead, the
image on the screen was so clear that it might as well be a box
with small people inside, and the sound was sharp enough that
Kolo heard the white woman sigh once she'd settled in behind
the podium and had finished adjusting the microphone.

This was all very strange. The world was strange. People were
strange. Kolo saw faces these days and they looked different, and

it had been some time before he worked out what had changed. There was no fear in those faces. It had vanished, lifted away like a mask that wasn't needed anymore. It made people look younger, more beautiful, and above all, more precious.

The wounded boy inside Kola had been weeping for what seemed like months, but even that endless stream of tears could not wash the blood from his hands. All those frightened faces he remembered — they had been afraid of him. Of Kolo, the murderer, the stealer of children. He had trouble meeting the eyes of anyone now.

The woman began speaking, and he heard her words in English.

'Thank you to everyone here in the UN who responded so quickly and effectively to my request to use this venerable site as my venue. Three hours in which to overturn protocol and convention. Not much time and a whole lot of pressure. But I had faith. When it comes to humanity, my faith is absolute, and in a way this is why I am speaking to you now.'

She paused, and Kolo glanced around. He saw people who did not understand English, standing fixated and intent, and it was clear that they all heard and, somehow, they all understood.

Kolo himself was nervous. She was an educated woman. She used unfamiliar words and he feared that it would only get worse.

'I didn't ask to be abducted. But once it happened, once I found myself in a conversation with an alien entity, my ability to choose was given back to me. The offer was simple: would I speak on behalf of the Intervention? Would I provide the conduit between an alien civilisation and the people of Earth?' She paused again, and then said, 'It took me some time to decide.'

Kolo tried to imagine finding himself in her place. Stolen away and then asked to speak to all the humans of the world. A few months ago and he would have laughed, and it wouldn't have been a nice laugh. Gun in hand, he would have looked for someone to kill, because that had always been the quickest, the cleanest answer. Words were dangerous. Bullets silenced those words. Bullets ended every argument.

As for the rest of humanity, well, they could go fuck themselves for all he cared.

So much for the Kolo he'd once been. As for the Kolo was he was now, well, he still didn't know that man.

'... multiple contacts and engagements with alien species,' she was saying. 'We have never been alone. We receive no signals because those signals get blocked. At the same time, we are in a no-fly zone that gets breached time and again. Most space-faring species possess faster than light technology, and part of its functionality relates directly to the manipulation of gravity, electromagnetic field frequencies and something called phase-shifting. Having said that, most species are not much more advanced than us. With the end of secrecy already under way, it will quickly become evident that we are much more technologically advanced than most of us ever knew. No matter. The revelations may shake us to the core, and might even drive the last nail into the coffin of our beloved leaders and their governments, but to be honest, recrimination won't get us anywhere. What's done was done. Time to move on.'

He'd lost the thread of her statement. It hadn't taken long.

Neela squeezed his hand and he looked down at her. 'It's not important,' she said. 'It's not what's important. Wait.'

'Three alien civilisations, far more advanced than the squabbling members of our immediate neighbourhood, elected to apply a controlled Intervention on planet Earth. Their arrival has sent all the others away. In short, no one wants to mess with these guys, despite them being complete pacifists.' She hesitated and then shrugged. 'I have not yet been able to figure out why this is the case. Do I trust this triumvirate of alien civilisations? For what it's worth, I trust them to do precisely what they say they're going to do.

'Now, let's get to that, shall we? There is something called a blanket presence now in place here on Earth. It created the forcefields. It stopped people from hurting one another. It stopped humans from continuing to degrade the planet, and damaging its capacity to sustain life.

'These initial interventions halted us in our tracks. I need not describe that to any of you. You have lived through it. I have watched it from on high, aboard an orbiting spaceship. I saw and shared your frustration, and like you, I was left wondering what awaited us – what might still be coming. And I wondered, is the answer to that question really to be found in what the aliens do next, or is it to be found in what *we* do next?

'Consider the natural world and the disasters that have descended upon us time and again. Hurricanes, tornadoes, floods, volcanoes. They arrive and for the victims they stop the world, they break the pattern and habits of living. Those who survive then emerge from the wreckage, or are helped from the wreckage, and there is grief and there is loss, and then we begin to build again.

'If it helps, consider the Intervention as a natural disaster. Out of our hands, beyond our control, and with its arrival, everything changes. The world stops, hunkers down, and will soon emerge into a new day. And we will grieve over what's been lost, and in our new world, with its new rules, we will gather together and we will build again.'

These words Kolo understood, like a knife to the heart. He felt outside that future. He'd done too much wrong to belong to it. And yet, and yet ... deep inside, the child with the tear-stained face slowly *looked up*.

●

'... hope,' Samantha August was saying. 'Hope is what we wish for, that gift of yearning for something better. But it goes beyond that. When we wish well for others, we offer hope to ourselves. We raise it up and like any virtue worth its salt, it makes us better than who we were. But if you go the other way, if you kill hope or attack it, or deny it and descend into despair, it's all downhill. To put it another way: wishing ill upon others is a self-inflicted wound ...'

Casper Brunt sat in the bar with Viviana Castellano, Robbie the journalist from the BBC, and Simon Wensforth. Simon had dumped his lover, leaving him without a cameraman, at least for the moment.

. Viviana had surprised Casper. He had surprised himself. They were still together. They had found something in each other. He glanced at her now – knowing he should be listening to this Samantha August – but somehow the woman sitting beside him had become magnetic, exerting an unseen but undeniable force upon Casper. He was sliding, with nothing to grip, no rope to hold onto, ever closer to her.

Her eyes were bright and fixed on the bar's big flatscreen.

'... generating the necessary food and clean water, ensuring that no one suffers physically as a result of their displacement. That said, such acts were only necessary because we didn't step up. I imagine for some of you, this offers up some kind of excuse to stop making an effort when it comes to the well-being of your fellow human beings. Someone else cleans up our mess, so we keep making a mess. Someone else mends all the wounds we deliver, so we keep wounding. Unfortunately, that attitude could see us annihilated.'

That caught everyone's attention, even Casper's. Viviana was leaning forward. Simon Wensforth poured another shot of Scotch into his glass, his hand trembling.

'It was touch and go whether we humans were going to be part of this Intervention,' Samantha August went on. 'The primary target for the aliens is the planet itself, its biome. This Intervention is intended to restore the health of this world. We've been damaging that health, and worse, we seem trapped inside a cycle of destruction, and virtually every institution we have invented now serves as the machinery for the damage we inflict.' She paused, seemed to hesitate over something, and then shook her head and said, 'We were spared. We have been spared. For now.'

'Oh shit,' muttered Viviana.

'Recently,' Samantha August said, 'my conversations with my, well, my overseer, have taken on a characteristic of me defending humanity despite all evidence to the contrary going on down here on Earth. These aliens have engaged in Interventions before. They're old hands at this. But every species, while sentient, exists in various stages of sentience. I'm afraid to say, we barely made the grade. Somewhere along the line, somebody decided that the less people knew the better. The argument was always the same; tell the citizens too much and they will panic, they will riot, descend into anarchy. Tell them too much and the entire civilisation could collapse. It seems to me that the greatest lack of faith on display here has nothing to do with aliens, but everything to do with us – with our lack of faith in each other.'

There was a muted shout from the audience behind the camera and Samantha August held up a hand. 'Right, I was expecting that. Fine, let's go there then. I will make this as plain as I can. There is not one mortal civilisation in our galaxy – not one, no matter how advanced or powerful – that can answer to the existence or non-existence of God. Many hold to beliefs similar to ours. Based more often than not on the observation that too many coincidences are necessary for life to exist, anywhere. In each instance where life is to be found – on planets, moons, beneath the ice of frozen worlds, in the heart of asteroids and comets, in the atmosphere of gas giants – too many factors are required for it all to be accidental.

'Now, when it comes to possessing a personal relationship with God, that is and will always remain a valid choice. But any religion advocating delivering harm to non-believers crosses the line. Faith is a universal feature among sentients. It is not the enemy of science, or progress, or advancement. It is not a valid reason to become divisive. This is something we have yet to learn.'

'Hallelujah,' mumbled Simon Wensforth, 'now get back to that business about wiping us out.'

As if hearing Simon, Samantha said, 'So, is there a sword hanging over our heads? I don't know, to be honest. I do know that my overseer has been expressing frustration at our antics. I've tried to explain that bitching about shit is a universal trait for us, maybe even one of the defining tenets of our species. We breed dissatisfaction. We can sit in paradise and complain about too much shade, or not enough, or overripe fruit, or an itchy back, or just deciding that you've stopped liking your neighbour's face. And yet' – the woman leaned forward slightly – 'time and again, when shit really, truly hits the fan, why, we *step up*.'

Casper heard the woman beside him quietly sigh. At that moment, he fell in love with her.

．

Ruth Moyen sat in the living room of her small flat, the new one she'd rented just up from the Old City. She watched, she listened, and the tears in her eyes did not stop coming. She didn't even know why she was crying. She couldn't understand what it was clutching at her heart, or sending waves of grief through her.

It was vast, this river of sorrow inside her. She felt her own mind flying above it, felt herself caught again and again by its swirling surface, to be tossed around like a cork. Was this sorrow hers? Did it all belong to her and no one else?

Or was it something bigger, something that could run through the blood of an entire people? When she touched that surface of grief, she felt its antiquity, sensed its wellspring that reached not down through bedrock, but back into the deep past.

Sorrow seemed such a grim legacy and she'd made the mistake of watching this speech alone. There was no one to look to for reassurance, for understanding. She needed a friend here, right now, someone to meet her eyes and say *it's all right, Ruth, yes there's sorrow, but look to the other side and you'll see infinite joy*.

She wanted to believe that.

The face of the woman on the screen fascinated her, but she didn't know why. This Samantha August was being brutally honest.

'... we're an aggressive species. There's little doubt about that. And aggression is a complex behaviour. It serves to meet many needs. It can both reward and punish. Now, we acknowledge the importance of competition, but may I suggest that there is plenty out there to compete against – the vagaries of existence itself, the need to define our own place – in your family, in your community, or your culture. Mortality itself. But for too long we have viewed competition solely in the realm of our fellow humans. We have devised an economic system that depends on it. We've created social hierarches that are built upon competition.

The problem is: for every winner there are a thousand losers. Our system of competition is damaging us, but we've lived with the belief in winning and losing for so long that we don't know any other way to live. For all that, it's killing us.'

Ruth felt the words sinking into her. She watched as they sank down into that river of grief. These were old crimes. She had been living a life of old crimes. No different from her mother and father, no different from every ancestor going back to the very beginning.

Maybe it wasn't enough to simply grieve, to simply surrender to that vast stream of history. Maybe what this woman was saying was: it's time for us to do better, to be better, to take all that sorrow and make something new from it.

There was a knock on the door.

Startled, Ruth wiped at the tears on her cheeks. She considered not answering, remaining there on her sofa, perfectly still, breath held, waiting for whoever it was to give up and go away.

The knock came again. With a soft moan, Ruth stood up. She felt momentarily dizzy and then righted herself.

A year ago and she would have been frightened. Someone had got in past the locked gate, or that someone was a neighbour in the block. Either way, a stranger. She had been trained to suspect strangers.

Now she walked to the door – saw that it was unlocked – and opened it.

For a long moment she did not recognise the young man standing before her. And then it came to her. The Palestinian waiter from the café. He stood before her now, looking ten years old though he was at least twice that. His eyes were swimming with tears and his face was wet.

As if of its own volition, she saw her hand reaching out to take his. She stepped back, drawing him into her room.

He gently pulled his grip free and went to the sofa, his gaze fixing on the television screen.

Ruth moved to sit down beside him.

Not speaking, they continued listening, and Ruth knew: it was going to be all right. Everything was going to be all right. This wasn't just the river of her people's sorrow and grief. It was this boy's river, too. In fact, it was humanity's river.

•

Anthony couldn't believe it. He was sitting in the living room of the Sticks family. The son, Jimmy, had not too long ago been yabbering on about killing himself. Now he sat between his mother and grandmother. The father wasn't in this picture, hadn't been for like, ever. That was something he and Jimmy shared.

Still, the so-called bro who used to call him Bony Tony wasn't calling him that anymore. The guy's permanent scowl and toughman look was gone. All the posturing and the poses, gone. And here, in this beat-up crappy apartment, with his worn-down mother, grandmother and three little half-wild brothers, Jimmy was looking like a proper man.

Who could ever have imagined anything like that? What a world!

The red-haired writer chick was going on, saying amazing things. If this was Invasion of Body Snatchers it was a professional job. She looked like a neighbour. Okay, maybe not a neighbour around here, exactly, since she was white and everything. But still, like a woman you'd see at a grocery store, talking to the checkout girl. Someone relaxed, unafraid, and ready to meet your eyes.

He didn't know many women like that. Except for, maybe, his public defender. Yeah, he wished he was sitting in *her* apartment right now. Holding hands with Angelina Estevez, with this red-haired chick telling them all how all the old shit ways of doing things wasn't going to work anymore. If they ever did, hah.

'I'm signing up,' Jimmy said, cutting across the red-head's speech.

'Signing up where, bro?' Anthony asked.

'Astronaut, man. Space Fleet. I'm signing up. Fucking walk on Mars, man.'

His mother hushed him then, for reasons of the bad word or she just wanted to hear the red-head chick.

'... we're not going to be told everything. There are some huge mysteries waiting for us on Mars, for example. We'll have to discover those ourselves. I can confirm that other orbiting bodies in our solar system are home to life. Beneath ice, mostly, but also in the upper atmospheres of the gas giants. And we will find that every native life-form we encounter in our system shares a common heritage with us. DNA and carbon-based is the only rule book in use in our solar system. Accordingly, we need to be careful out there.'

'Martians! I knew it!'

'Shush, Jimmy!'

'... should be plain by now. I'm not here to offer any solutions to how we get from all that we've known and believed, to this new age of enlightenment, deep-space exploration, and maybe even a war out there among the stars. And I do not think we can expect specific instructions or guidance from our Benefactors. Not in the protocol. Even my contact with ET has been via an artificial intelligence. I've met no one, seen no one.

'But one thing should be obvious by now. It is up to us how this will proceed. Not specific governments, not leaders of countries, not hidden cabals sitting atop their hoards of secret knowledge. But all of us. Our every act now, beginning with how each of you engages with the people around you, with loved ones, estranged ones, neighbours and friends and enemies, will either serve or reject the new future awaiting us. And it may well be the case that if enough of us reject the future, if enough of us fail in recognising that what we do – right now, the rest of today, and tomorrow and in the weeks to come – is important and has meaning, we may end up having no future at all.'

'Holy Mary Mother of God,' whispered Jimmy's mother.

But Anthony could see: Jimmy's grandmother was smiling.

•

Two dethroned gods sat broken and slumped in their high-backed chairs. The Adonai were done and finally, at last, they knew it.

Lois Stanton put the cap onto her ballpoint pen and settled

back in her lesser chair, now the lone witness to this sordid, sad collapse. Samantha August continued speaking on the boardroom's giant flatscreen. Every now and then the camera trembled slightly. In the packed theatre of the UN assembly hall, no one was speaking, not even whispering as far as Lois could tell. Just silence, until it seemed that the woman at the podium was speaking to an empty room.

'... resetting our value system won't be easy, and it will take the greatest minds of our time to find a way through to the other side. The key element, I believe, is the notion of post-scarcity. This is the rug pulled out from under capitalism. When we cease to have to pay for what we need, we need something to take the place of that, something that rewards us in other ways. Something that gives us reasons to go on, to continue to achieve, innovate, and work. Perhaps it's not as much of a stretch as it may seem right now. After all, who hasn't gone to work to provide security and stability for their family, for their loved ones, their children? We already do that. We even do jobs we hate to maintain that security, and we do it from love, and a sense of responsibility, and when we do all of that, we feel pride. So, extend that notion outward. Your family is humanity. Take it from there.'

'Bitch,' said James. 'Crushing our lives.'

'Can't touch her,' Jonathan added, shaking his head. 'Money. It's dead. New paradigm, a bloody mess if you ask me.'

'People who *can*, tell people who *can't* what to do,' said James. 'Always been that way. The strong and the weak. The worthy and the damn-near useless. Expertise and talent and good breeding on one side, ignorance, cluelessness and mongrels on the other.'

'Not equal. Never equal.'

'Every game can be played,' James then said, but the assertion was so feeble the voice uttering it trembled. 'We can play this one too. Find a way in. These training centres. Get our people in there. First ones out into space. Asteroids to claim. Minerals. Water. Need industry, won't happen by itself. We get in, we buy our rocks and we set up operations.'

'That's a plan,' agreed Jonathan.

'Lois,' said James, 'run it back. Hear what we just missed.'

She collected up the remote control and rewound.

'... technical data now populating sites all over the world. This is free, to be used for our betterment, and to help maintain the health of our home world. As some of you have noted, Venus is being terraformed. This will create an Earth-like world for our species to colonise. We need to relieve the population pressure here on Earth. There are too many of us. The timescale for Venus is five years before self-contained settlements are possible, and ten years before the surface can be walked on without the need for space suits and air supply.

'Obviously' — and here the woman offered a faint smile — 'we will need colony ships, and volunteers. I don't think the latter will prove a problem. As for the former, well, we are about to given one more gift ...'

'Fuck gifts,' said James in something close to a snarl. 'Lose all worth. Get given something for nothing and you can't appreciate it. Don't value it. Haven't earned it.'

'... this gift has a responsibility attached to it, however. We've all seen the revelations about the Greys. Alien entities engaged in psychic rape and torture. Earth is not the only world they prey on. Humanity is not their only victim. We have neighbours, and they need our help.

'This offer is, if you will, ET's greatest act of faith. In us. They are pacifists. They are advanced enough to be able to defend themselves against anyone and everyone. They could defend us. They could defend our neighbours, but this would make children of us all, and keep us there. We need the room to mature as a sentient species. And in our contact with those neighbours, we need to take the lead in driving out the Greys. We need to become the Neighbourhood Watch.'

'Other systems to exploit,' said James, nodding at the screen. 'Ignorant aliens, oh so thankful that we arrived. I see opportunities.'

'Opportunities,' Jonathan agreed.

These two men — and their world — were dying before her eyes. They'd tried to discover the secret of eternal youth, ET's cure-all to mortality. They'd failed. Healing was selective. It responded according to need, and growing old didn't qualify. If this was Jesus walking down a line of people, reaching out with his healing touch, he'd walked right past James and Jonathan Adonis.

Maybe that pretentious last name had offended him. God knows, it offended her. How many Greek tales hammered home the message of hubris?

She was planning on writing a book. A story somewhere between Citizen Kane and Mephistopheles. But her research wasn't quite done yet.

'... precedent for this. Our entertainment industry has taken us there, and I have followed that theme with the spaceship I requested, the one now hovering over this building. It was a simple sales pitch: in the future we will be better than we are now.

'What awaits us at this moment is finding a way across that bridge, to our better selves. Our Benefactors will be observing, and likely calculating. They will assist where they deem it useful, and ignore everything else. Either we show them that we can do this, or we're probably finished as a species.'

'Gun to the head,' James said in a growl. 'Be good or else.'

'Do what you're told or else,' his brother elaborated. 'ET's speaking our kind of language.'

'But there's a difference,' James said. 'Big difference. ET's got all the power. And us, we have ...' He couldn't finish the admission.

So in her head Lois finished it for him. *Nothing. You have nothing, boys.*

'... our first fleet is even now moving into orbit around the Earth. Eight vessels of a class you should recognise. Twelve smaller vessels, and two dreadnoughts. Regarding one named ship of the eight, there are a few actors who by all rights should be the first to step onto the bridge. No doubt we can arrange that sometime soon.'

And behind Samantha August, on a huge projection screen behind her, an image appeared. The writer turned slightly and nodded. 'And here they are. This is a live feed, by the way. Now then, isn't that a lovely sight?'

'New tech,' said Jonathan. 'We take what we need and build our own. We do one better, always one better. We outclass them. Private fleet – we can find plenty of partners for this.'

'This fleet belongs to the people of Earth,' Samantha said once the shouting and spontaneous applause had died down. 'Assembling the administrative elements of running something like a space fleet should probably fall under the UN's umbrella, at least to begin with. Now, ET is not naïve and neither am I. I can already picture the political jockeying about to begin when it comes to this. I can already hear the arguments as nations fight for power within the hierarchy of this new fleet. But guess what? If we don't sort this out peacefully, reasonably and most of all, *fairly*, why, that fleet sails away without us, never to return.

'Granted, we can build our own, eventually. But it will take a few years at the very least. And nations will fall back into the mess of competing with one another, and secrecy will return – or, rather, under normal circumstances, it would return. But ET won't let it – not one nation can hide anything from any other. We are now an open book to one another and we had better get used to it.'

'Fuck her,' James said. 'Fuck that bitch.'

Jonathan sighed. 'At least she's white.'

Lois uncapped her pen and wrote in her notebook: *Yeah, figured as much*.

•

The Caribbean was doing its Caribbean thing. Hot, hot wind, the taste of salt in the air, the turquoise waters being turquoise and four pelicans gliding into the bay to land and bob above the reef. Fronds rustled and the faint hiss of sand blowing across the beach reached Maxwell Murdo as he sat perched in a canvas chair set up well above the tideline, iPad in his lap.

Chrystal had come down to join him but was watching from

her phone. The old man was back in the house. He didn't want company.

Maxwell had also brought down a cooler filled with ice and bottles of Belikan beer. It seemed a fittingly modest gesture to celebrate the end of the world.

'It's like the TV show,' Chrystal said. 'Those ships, I mean.'

'Yup,' said Maxwell, 'and sooner or later, some team of lawyers is going to fly up to take possession of those things.'

'What?'

He waved a hand. 'Trademark infringement, copyright infringement, every infringement you can think of. Then again, how does one go about suing ET?'

'They'll go for her,' said Chrystal. 'That woman.'

'Well, she as much as admitted it was her idea. For the symbolism. So, they clean her out. Then what? If the UN takes these things – this fleet – do they turn around and try suing the UN? You know, the more I think about it, the pettier it sounds. But hey, we're a species that delights in pettiness.'

Chrystal sniffed from where she reclined on her beach towel. 'That's because we're weak.'

He glanced over at her, surprised. And pleased. 'You keep laying low, Chrystal,' he now said. 'He won't live forever, and besides, he's going gaga.'

'I know. He keeps calling me by his first wife's name.'

'Ah. Another blonde. Old Da loves his blondes.'

'I'm rewinding, Max, see what we missed.'

'Beer?'

'Makes me fat, so ... yes please!'

•

The woman kept on talking, her voice filling the spacious living room behind Douglas Murdo as he stood looking down on the son that was useless and the wife who'd defied his express order to not drink beer.

Barb stopped listening to him pretty soon after they'd married. She'd started doing whatever the hell she pleased. He thought he'd divorced her. Nice, fair settlement to keep her mouth shut. So what was she doing down there, on the beach, on his island? But damn, she still looked good. Almost made him feel young again.

There would be plenty to attack in this damned speech. He'd order his people to go after the woman first. Samantha August. Destroy her integrity – or at least keep asking enough questions until people believed that those questions hid ugly truths about the woman. It wasn't hard. It didn't matter how flimsy the connections, how elaborate the chain of whatever conspiracy or corruption they'd invent for her, it would do its work in the end.

Because people believing the worst in others was a favourite pastime, a habit as addictive as whacking off to porn. It made them feel good. Made them feel superior. Made them want to hurt other people. Human nature, in other words.

And a bunch of shiny new spaceships in orbit wasn't going to change that.

They'd destroy this Samantha August. Then they'd tear apart her speech. Line by line, showing all the hidden messages – and if there weren't any hidden messages, they'd make them up. He had smart people working for him. Talented people.

They'd reinterpret everything she said, make it clear that ET was the enemy to humanity. Our jailers. Cleaning up the planet in preparation for wiping humans out and moving in. Everything else was false promises, smoke screens.

Barb had lost weight. She was looking good. That beer wouldn't help, though.

Maxwell's feet were red with sunburn – he'd forgotten to cover them. Idiot.

Where was his other son? Oh right, still at Eton. They'd all meet up at Christmas break.

This wasn't over. He wasn't finished yet. He was going to rip this whole thing to pieces. And if ET went and scorched the planet because of it, well, he only had a few years left anyway, so who the fuck cared?

Drifting in from the living room, Samantha August's voice: '... and if truth is your enemy, you're in trouble ...'

He needed to call his lawyers. Barb needed to go. Divorce. No wife of his could do whatever the hell she pleased. 'Go on, drink another beer, you fat bitch.'

Sudden confusion, and with it, fear. Abruptly, he began to cry.

•

He'd left Ev and Mark and Susan to hear the woman out. Something had driven Dave away, into the yard, and then out across the stubbled stretch of unbroken prairie. Beyond that, in sheer drops of old run-off channels, was the valley he no longer owned. He found himself on the edge in the hot wind, staring down into its once-managed wilderness, this subtle contradiction that he used to find poetic. He could see a half-dozen elk in the high grasses of the old oxbow, and on the far side, a coyote or a wolf tracking them from the slope.

He heard footsteps, the hard, worn heels of cowboy boots knocking on exposed bedrock, and a moment later his neighbour, Jurgen Banks, was standing beside him. His neighbour, in the same mess. The man had lost his herd of bison. Every animal paid for, cared for, nurtured. Now they wandered unattended.

'Heard the news?'

Dave shook his head. Jorgen always had news to deliver. If the old man didn't have something to tell, he couldn't start a conversation. But that was all right. There was always news.

'The bank's decided not to decide. On anything.'

Dave glanced over with a frown. 'What does that mean?'

'Means life as usual. For now.' Jurgen's lined, angular face wore its weathering with a kind of innocence, as if he'd never quite understood most people. 'I admit it, Dave, I never expected them to be that smart about it.'

'Well, can't squeeze blood from stone, right?'

Jurgen's laugh was dry. 'Of course not. Never ever stopped them from trying though, did it? Y'know, most times you beat your head against a wall and it only takes a few knocks before you go "hey, that ain't gonna work". Most situations, I mean.

But drop in the word "money" and why, that head just keeps hammering the wall. And people nod and say "yup, that's how it is. Money. It makes us stupid."'

The elk had moved down to the water's edge, where the grasses were sweeter. 'How come you're not watching the speech, Jurgen?'

A shrug. 'Heard what I wanted. Ten years, she said.'

'Ten years?'

A strangely shy smile. 'Venus. Another whole planet. With nobody on it.'

Dave simply stared at the old man. He was what, sixty? Ten years, and this guy was talking homesteading all over again. 'That'd be one raw landscape, Jurgen. Whole forests barely knee-high. The weather systems – they need centuries to settle out, to find a pattern. It's not the place for – well, I mean, it'll be brutal. For decades.'

'It's a thought, though,' Jurgen replied.

'Sure.'

'I mean, imagine being buried in the ground on another planet. Most people would find that lonely, I guess. But not me. Me, I like it.'

'You want to die on Venus.'

'The first one, maybe. The first human to die on Venus. Don't get me wrong, I ain't in any hurry. You know, I got into the bison farming for all the wrong reasons. The Wild West, the time of the Indians, before it was opened up to us whites. I remember seeing paintings. Buffalo herds. I know, wrong name but so what? Ten thousand, a hundred thousand, covering the plain for as far as the eye could see. It was the romance of that, Dave, that's what got me. Sure, had to make a living and all that. But for me, just seeing the big beasts out there, well, it was like stepping back in time.'

'Right. So, Venus, you'd be stepping back to the beginning of a world.'

'We'll have to bring livestock with us. Or animals of some kind. To hunt and eat. Bison are tough. Cattle, not so much.'

Dave hesitated, and then said, 'Ev's been looking into it, to be honest. It's complicated. What to bring in the first wave, I mean. Insects. Soil biota. Bees, butterflies. Flowering plants. It depends on what ET gets things started with, I suppose. Plankton, algae, molluscs, invertebrates for the seas, rivers and lakes.'

'But dying there,' Jurgen said. 'It's like your whole body is a seed from Earth.'

'Huh. Yeah. I suppose that's one way of looking at it.'

'Sure. My way.'

Dave turned round and squinted at his distant house. 'Kids are excited,' he said.

'Sure,' Jurgen said again. 'Got reason to be. Finally.'

Finally. Now that was a hell of a word to use. But Dave suddenly understood what had been ailing him, what ET had done to his generation, to every damned adult on the planet. It wasn't his lost livelihood that was the problem. That happened to people all the time, after all. It wasn't his not knowing how to provide for his family, either. Wasn't that the universal question plaguing everyone everywhere? Finding that knife-edged balance between need and ability, even as the windows of opportunity kept on closing? No, it wasn't any of that.

What burned like fire inside Dave at this moment, was *shame*.

It made looking at a child so very hard, knowing that it had, *finally*, taken someone else to step in to clean things up, to set it all right again, to offer up a future for the generation to come, a future better than the present, better than the past.

'Finally,' he said, under his breath.

Jurgen sighed beside him. 'Yup. Makes me feel like a kid all over again.'

•

Annie had forgotten what it was like to be free. To have choices. She'd forgotten what it was like to be relaxed, about anything. There had always been something hanging in the background, a promise in the shadows. Darkness to come. Joy had edges and those edges could cut, and usually did.

Even Jeff's love for his daughter had a way of drawing blood.

The father resenting the mother for the child they'd produced, for the deep ties that he saw between the mother and the child that he felt kept him outside, blocked, denied, refused. He'd used punches, slaps and kicks to level the playing field. But he couldn't do that anymore.

She in turn had wanted to level that playing field, too, with a pan full of sizzling bacon fat. A face melted away, a mistake burned down to the bone. These were evil thoughts, evil desires, but she couldn't back away from them. That night still hovered between her and Jeff.

Her husband, broken, fragile, weak, stood in the doorway to the living room, watching the woman talking on the television. Annie sat on the sofa, smelling the faint remnants of puke from when Jeff had been crying so hard into a pillow he gagged and spewed up runny gruel.

Sally was still at school, but Annie would have to go soon to pick her up. Annie had been sent home early from work. The day had become a day off for everyone who could take it. And where they couldn't, they'd stopped whatever they were doing so they could watch.

Aliens. Giant spaceships. Venus made into another Earth. All incredible. And that woman, talking as if this was something that happened every day.

'... obvious by now that we have received help in the area of human health. Diseases are vanishing. Malnutrition is coming to an end. Even spinal and other neurological trauma is being reversed, and people who thought they would never again walk, or sit up, or make love, are returning to full functionality.

'Alcoholism is now a thing of the past. Opiate addiction is gone. As beneficial as this all sounds, there is also something alarming to all of this. There are strangers in our bodies, phase-shifting nanites running a maintenance programme, maximising our efficiency. Chemical imbalances, hormonal imbalances, psychological dysfunctions, all mitigated, corrected. Schizophrenia, depression, obsessive-compulsive disorders, psychoses – including sociopathy – all gone.' She paused, and then said, 'You've seen all the reports. Maybe you've experienced this for yourself or your loved ones – the elderly suffering all forms of dementia, so many of them suddenly returning to full functionality. Proof that memories are not bound to physical components in the brain, but exist in a liminal state – and how amazing is that?'

The woman then went on, stuff all technical and baffling to Annie. She glanced over at Jeff.

He managed a weak smile. 'Alcoholism,' he said in a croak. 'Gone.'

Annie nodded.

'But I'm still angry.'

Not long ago and she would have frozen up at that admission, adrenaline surging through her. Now, she just shrugged.

'At myself, mostly,' he added. 'For being so useless ... for not standing up to my old man. For taking all the shit he dumped on me and making it my own shit, which I then dumped on you, Annie.'

She glanced back at the television. 'We all do that,' she said. 'Children are sponges. Even when it's piss and blood that they're soaking up.'

'God,' Jeff whispered, then hacked a cough and bent over as if he was about to collapse. A moment later and he slowly straightened again. 'The things I said to our daughter, the things I made her believe.'

'Yes,' Annie said. 'Fix that.'

'Are we finished? You and me?'

She looked up at him again. 'I knew who you were,' she said, 'but I don't know who you now are. So, I don't know, Jeff. Either way, you've got a daughter who needs your love.'

'And you? Do you need my love?'

Annie thought about it, and then said, 'No, I don't think so. But ... that doesn't mean I won't take it.'

'Can I sit beside you, Annie?'

'The sofa smells bad.'

'My fault,' he said, still waiting for her.

Annie sighed. 'Come over, then.'

'My fault,' he said again as he gingerly moved into the room. 'All my fault.'

'I might move to Venus,' said Annie. 'In five years. A new world. Clean. Warm. I hate the cold, you know. I hate it.'

'I know,' he said, and laughed. 'I always dreamed of getting posted to Florida.'

She grunted, then shrugged. 'So get posted to Venus instead.'

'I'll put in the transfer request tomorrow. EFFE power plants need assembling, fitting into our working infrastructure. Need to do that everywhere I guess. Even Venus.'

Maybe this could work, Annie decided. She would see, she supposed. One way or another. Either way, she could choose, actually choose.

Freedom, arriving like a kiss from the world.

Chapter Twenty-Eight

'Imagination is like a muscle. It requires exercise. Stay trapped in this world with all its mundane necessities, and it won't be long before your imagination – the gift you were given in your childhood – atrophies, and when that happens, why, you've lost something precious that even nostalgia won't bring back to you, no matter how much you long for what once was. With the death of your imagination, you lose the sense of wonder. But you need wonder. You need it to stay sane, and you need it to keep your heart from turning to stone.'

Samantha August

Jack Butler sat with his head in his hands. Mary Lamp had been pacing during most of Samantha August's speech but now she stood with her back to the wall beside the office door, her arms crossed.

Simon Gist remained at his desk, having cleared a space on it so he could roll his model car back and forth, from one hand to the other. The flatscreen mounted on the wall to his left still showed the woman, and her voice came through and now questions were coming from the floor. The subject for the moment was international law and sovereign rights to self-determination. More often than not, the SF author simply held up her hands and said: 'Work it out.'

With the arrival of the enormous Bird of Prey over New York City, Simon had ordered the brakes slammed on the handshake mission. At around the same time, new data appeared on their computers, file after file of seriously advanced technology, including anti-gravity, discriminating energy fields, quantum linkage. Some of these files were the property of a black US government cabal called Majestic. A few faded blue-print photocopies were stamped property of the Third Reich.

Go figure. Simon sat, pushing the car back and forth. It didn't roll quite straight, and increasingly this bothered him. After a moment he slammed his hand down on the toy, halting it, and then picked it up. 'Fine. We're going to Mars. Phobos first, and then Mars.'

Jack grunted behind his hands and looked up for a moment. 'Why not just hitch a ride on that Bird of Prey? We'd probably be at Phobos in twenty minutes.'

'Granted,' Simon conceded, having flipped the toy car over to examine its wheels. 'Our ship will look like a Model T Ford beside a Ferrari, but it will be *our* Model T Ford. You've done the calculations, Jack. We can reach Mars in three weeks. That's not bad.' He grunted a sour laugh. 'Not bad? A year ago and we'd call that insane.'

'It's all moving very fast,' said Mary.

He glanced at her. 'Droll, very droll.'

'Well,' she said, now flustered, 'I didn't mean it quite that way.'

'An automated shipyard, she said,' Jack sighed. 'Out in the asteroid belt. A second one en route to park itself in orbit around Earth. Our gravity well? Irrelevant.' He sighed a second time. 'You know, as an engineer, I'm starting to feel utterly redundant.'

'Hardly,' Simon replied. 'You're just on a learning curve, Jack. A big one. The biggest one of your life. But you're not alone, are you?' He gestured with the toy at the flatscreen. 'She's telling us we all need to get on a new learning curve, the one that teaches us to be human, but not just human. Rather, the best of human ... if I can even put it that way.'

'Our finances are in the tank,' Mary said. 'Simon, you once hinted at something. You said money was going to become irrelevant. You knew this was coming, didn't you?'

'We were complacent. Our economic system was never as

robust as we'd told ourselves it was. All predicated on faith, all sustained by the continuance of the illusion.' He shrugged. 'America was already a country in turmoil. Ever since the election. We were already seeing an end to something, and it was personal and it hurt.' He replaced the toy on his desk, but this time upside down. 'I don't care if we go belly up. That fleet of ships up there won't be falling into anyone's hands soon. This is going to be a brawl.'

'Spitball fight,' Jack muttered. 'They can't do anything else.'

'Right,' Simon agreed. 'It's a level playing field in terms of flexing muscle and posturing and all the rest. But there remains a very real currency that will play the central role in organising this space-fleet administration, and that's expertise.'

Jack sat back in his chair and rubbed at the bristle on his chin. 'Those remote training centres – they're there to give countries without the technical wherewithal to present themselves as equal to any other country in terms of expertise – is that what you're saying?'

'Seems logical,' Mary said. 'Anyone can show up and get upgraded.'

'Upgraded, an apt description,' Simon said. 'Meanwhile, us technological power-houses are looking at all the advanced tech we need, only we have to build the infrastructure ourselves – the training centres, the classrooms, everything.'

'What about our crew?' Jack asked, returning at last to the mission. 'We've got two astronauts hanging around the launch site – must be a glum pair by now. But, Simon, you wanted your own team for Mars. Including yourself.'

'Yes, I'm going. But you're right, let's ask them if they want to come along for the ride.'

'Official requests to the US and Canadian governments?' Mary asked.

'If that's what it takes.'

There was a pause in their conversation and Samantha August's voice filled it: '... every paradigm shift entails a period of chaos. There will be elements in our society that will resist wherever and however they can. Historically, such movements are doomed to fail. One obvious example would be the Roman Catholic Church following the arrival of cheap and ubiquitous books, including vernacular versions of the Bible. Didn't matter how many publishers they burned at the stake, they couldn't stop the rise of literacy, and with literacy came a direct challenge to their monopoly on the pearly gates. From there, Protestantism and the Reformation.' She shrugged. 'Historians will be able to tell you what's coming. None of this is as new as you might think.'

'Barring the complete collapse of the global economy,' Jack muttered.

'Our new currency is now knowledge,' Simon said. 'What we find on Phobos. What we find on Mars.'

'Phobos is hollow, based on standard radar returns,' said Jack. 'Its collision with Deimos should have further degraded its already degrading orbit. Instead, the damned thing is moving up and out. We can calculate where it will be when we arrive, more or less. But merging with Deimos must have damaged it. Assuming it is what we think it is: an artificial satellite.'

Mary said, 'The Greys were using it.'

'But maybe they didn't build it.'

'And that's what we're going to find out,' Simon said. 'Mary, inform the investors. We're all in on a manned mission to Mars, and the payoff is knowledge.'

'And how will that knowledge pay out in practical terms, Simon?'

Simon laughed, 'I haven't a fucking clue.'

•

'I always operated based on the belief that destabilising another country – by any means necessary – constitutes an act of self-defence. A weakened opponent is no threat. A weakened opponent turns on itself and ceases to be an external threat. Unless, of course, they paint a target on some foreign enemy. Muslims, Iranians, China . . .'

The President of Russia fell silent, his words trailing away.

They were in the central complex at Baikonur, not far from

382

Kazakhstan's ET-built training centre. Its doors were yet to open, but a city of people had grown up around it. Chechens, Georgians, Mongolians, Armenians. Borders had ceased to matter.

Anatoli Petrov glanced at the frozen image of Samantha August. Milnikov had frozen it during the Q&A session, something he hadn't been able to do during the speech itself. That mere words could bring down every country on the planet still left Anatoli feeling numb, shell-shocked.

In the meantime, Constantine Milnikov rambled, like an old man trying to dictate his memoirs, frustrated at his own feeble rationales for doing the things he had done in his life. 'The fact that he was financially in our pocket made it all the more delicious. But now, blackmail doesn't work anymore. Business interests are paper tigers. All that you own but do not need now becomes a burden.'

That last line startled the cosmonaut. It had, he slowly realised, cut to the heart of what could only be called a new age of enlightenment. But the birth pangs were difficult, painful, and occasionally sordid. Russians knew about ghosts, after all. Their land and country had known more death than any lone mortal could count. And those ghosts could haunt even a great man like Constantine Milnikov. When something new was born, it was the ghosts that pushed from behind. Or from below. And what burst from the cold, wet earth was destined to greet the new world with a cry of grief for all that it had lost.

There was no one else in the room. The technicians, aides, and bodyguards had been sent out. It seemed that Milnikov had adopted a new pet: his cosmonaut science advisor.

'Remorse is not a familiar emotion,' the President now said. 'People have died because of the games I played with the citizens of another country, with their leaders, with their pathetically inadequate electoral security. And people have died from the weapons I sold to other countries. People die, and they die, and still we go on, as if it was this was normal, to be expected, to be factored into our calculations. A million poor people on the run, freezing and starving in border camps. Ancient cities reduced to rubble.' He sighed. 'What we hold to be precious bears the stains of our indifference.' He glanced over, one eyebrow lifting. 'That confuses you, I see. No matter. I was speaking of our human capacity to blind ourselves to the true cost of all that we do in the name of all that we desire.'

'The world was as it was,' said Anatoli Petrov.

'Ah, yes, just so. And now?'

'I do not know, Mister President. We stand before an open door. What holds us back?'

'Hmm, a good question, old friend. What holds us back? Whatever holds us back?'

On the television screen Samantha August remained frozen, hands caught in a gesture not yet completed. As if time itself now stood still. But of course that was an illusion, a trick of electronics. Behind that still image the woman had gone on, given her reply to whatever question had been asked. She was now in their future, in that other world: one that Constantine Milnikov seemed reluctant to return to.

Memoirs could be ugly things. The impulse often came from a sudden sense of shorter days, of time running out, of things ending. To write a memoir was itself an act of desperation, no matter how clear-eyed the regard turned back on one's own past, how honest, how brutal the confessions laid out on the page.

The last words of dead men, as far as Anatoli was concerned.

In this garish light from the room's fluorescent bulbs, Constantine Milnikov's face was almost skull-like.

After a moment, the President began speaking again. Anatoli shivered and looked away. The dead, it seemed, still had plenty to say.

•

For Liu Zhou, it was difficult to tell if Premier Xin Pang was laughing or weeping. There were tears and they flowed freely down the old man's cheeks, and yet he didn't look as old as he had been only a day ago. Some light danced in his eyes, and his smile seemed loose, unguarded.

Perhaps madness. Perhaps hysteria. Governance had dissolved, or rather, it should have by now, and yet people went on as before. They did their tasks, made their commutes, surfed the net and made weekend sojourns to places of peace. For all this, China tottered on the thinnest edge, with dissolution to either side.

But then, had it ever been any different? No army could be big enough to truly stop a mass uprising. Not enough jails could be built to house men and women who chose to free their minds, to think and say what was in their hearts. And with the end of violence, the foment had grown, the dissidents had reappeared – now fearless and brazen.

All things that lived must come to know their limitations, even humans. All humans must bow to the collective necessity, for without co-operation, without mutual support, without a unified belief in the worth of doing things, there was anarchy.

The aliens had made anarchy toothless, and the secret desire of so many people to see everything brought to ruin was now a quaint affectation. That and nothing more. But not all social change was anarchy. The man sitting opposite Liu Zhou now had absorbed the lessons of every leader who preceded him. That terror of chaos, the frantic need to crush every blossoming flower in the green field that was China: it was deep in the bones of Xin Pang.

Liu Zhou could not condemn him. The language of fear was powerful, and made victims of everyone who used it. But civil co-operation was all that stood between progress and extinction. The larger the population, the more complex the civilisation, and the greater the need for control, or, to use a kinder word, management.

The Canadian writer was still answering questions. She had infinite patience.

It also appeared that she spoke perfect Mandarin.

Abruptly, Xin Pang stood. 'My friend, we have much to discuss.'

'She is not yet done.'

'She but indulges their fears now, but soothes the storm in their heads. I have no need of this. I am at peace, my friend.'

'Peace seems our only choice, and thus no choice at all.'

The Premier frowned. 'Is the storm in your head at all peaceful, Liu Zhou? No, I thought not. You see? You do have a choice. Now, come to the control room. I would we speak again with Captain Shen. There is much to do.'

Belatedly, Liu Zhou realised that he had remained seated when his leader stood, a serious breach in protocol. He quickly straightened and bowed.

'Still you are troubled,' Xin Pang said.

'The new data on our computers, it is accessible to all.'

'Yes. Good. How many new bright young minds will attend to this new data? How many unexpected, wonderful innovations and improvements will we soon see, arising from such unexpected places?'

'All control is lost—'

'Yes, my friend.' Xin Pang smiled. 'All control is lost.'

•

Seven tortured souls. Captain Shen would have imagined that they'd stick together, huddling to one another for the mutual support and, above all, the understanding they each needed. Instead, they mingled freely. They spontaneously hugged the captain's soldiers, the women and the scientists, even Shen himself. Such displays made him wary. Such displays made him forget who he was.

They had listened to the speech by Samantha August. Earth, their home, had never seemed so far away as it did now. Shen had led Hong Li and Quang out onto the lunar surface, and with a telescope they had found the array of twenty-two white spaceships now orbiting their home planet. They had then searched for the mobile shipyard approaching from the outer system, but failed in finding it. That was not particularly surprising.

The first man they'd rescued, Tony Newton, was a man who told many stories of his life and experiences in Alaska. His broken marriage. His failed gold prospecting ventures. His encounters with Bigfoot. The multiple abductions that had ruined his health.

Too honest, too forthright, too *American* for Captain Shen's sensibilities, at least at first. Now, reluctantly, he was coming to admire those very same qualities.

People did what they needed to do in order to survive. It was the same no matter what country one called home. The conflict came in how one defined this notion of survival. Political, economic, spiritual. Needs clashed, threats loomed, and the impulse to strike before being struck drove all too much of humanity's history at every scale, from one's home to nations to between religions across the world.

Tony Newton believed in lizard people. During the worst of the abductions, he had tried to kill himself three times. Now he made his confession and then laughed, as if it had all been a huge joke.

Was he unhinged? If so, he had good reason to be.

Still, thus far he had beaten every opponent at chess. Handily. In the one game Shen had agreed to play, the captain had known he was finished after a mere eleven moves. Startling. Humbling.

When Samantha August made her speech at the UN, the seven survivors had listened carefully, and when it was finally done and the woman began taking questions, each survivor had wandered off, as if driven by a sudden need to be alone. Shen had no idea what that meant.

After a time, Tony Newton returned to where the chessboard had been set up, and he began laying out the pieces. And Hong Li soon joined him. They were closely matched, but thus far each time Tony Newton had somehow pulled off a victory. During most of their games, they talked salmon fishing.

But not this time.

Tony said, 'Take white, my friend. I'm feeling generous today.'

'You invite me into traps, you mean,' Hong Li replied. 'You yield the initiative and choose only to react, and this lulls me into a sense of being in control. When, as I shall discover, I am not.'

'My wife liked checkers. How we ever got married I'll never know. Still, I loved her, you know? Still do. Oh, and thanks for that feed – hadn't talked to her in years. She made me cry, just the sound of her voice. And the history between us, I guess. I bawled and bawled.'

'I well recall. Did my presence shame you? If so, I apologise.'

'Nah, not a bit. I remember – vaguely – curling up like a baby in your arms when you first freed me. Way past shame, buddy. Now it's just love, pure and simple. Check.'

Just like that. Not only did Tony Newton play fast, he could also say things that silenced everyone within range of hearing.

Of course, in this instance, love could be simple gratitude. There was good reason that salvation and worship often dwelt in the same sentence, the same thought. Shen was not a religious man. Well, he hadn't been. Now he was not so sure. The world of black and white was gone, and no game of chess could change that.

'She's a bit of a stunner,' Tony Newton now said.

'Excuse me, who?'

'That writer at the UN. The red-head. Sort've like Meryl Streep.'

'Samantha August. A Canadian. I have read her books.'

'Really? You allowed books in China?' The wink took the sting from the question.

'I read them when I lived in Vancouver,' Hong Li replied coyly. 'Yes, she is attractive.'

'So they chased away the Greys. You know, that was all I needed to hear. About them. All any of us needed to hear.'

'Do you dream of revenge?'

'Nah. If I never see those Greys again I'll die a happy man. No, let some whup-ass marines paint their numbers. And those other planets, being preyed on, shit, man, we gotta help them. You know? Listen, tell your boss – your leader down there – don't fuck around with this. Get out there and kick some shit. Tell him that.'

Hong Li leaned back slightly and glanced over at Shen.

The captain smiled. He'd be happy to pass that request along.

'So,' said Hong Li, 'you favour this Intervention, then.'

'Favour it? Man, we just got our arses saved, Hong Li. Big gold star on those babies, and for the red-head, an even bigger kiss.'

'Gold star?' Hong Li grinned. 'Yes, we could go for that.'

'Oh? Oh! Your flag! Ha ha! Check and mate in four moves.'

A soldier came in to tell Shen that the Premier wished to discuss matters of grave importance. Nodding, Shen rose and headed out.

Tony Newton and six other tortured souls. They walked among his people like angels.

•

Alison Pinborough remembered their first meeting and it seemed the Prime Minister did as well, for she had invited the same people.

Mary Sparrow had never looked happier. She had just come from a pow-wow that had taken place outside of Dauphin, Manitoba. There had been one evening celebrating the return of the buffalo, as the first 'wild' herd had been tracked by satellite moving into the south-western corner of the province, along one of the Exclusion Zone tracks that projected northward all the way to the Duck Mountain Provincial Park (and what a traffic-snarling mess that had created!). All of fifty-three animals. But it was a start. Even better news for that province: Lake Winnipeg's toxic brew of algae blooms – due to over-fertilisation of the surrounding farmland – was now over, and there had been a surge in fish stocks in that huge, vital lake.

Will Camden, Minister of Natural Resources, had the bearing of a man with little to do. Extraction of minerals, logging, oil and off-shore ocean harvests all continued, but in a constrained manner. There was little if any surplus and accordingly exports had dwindled, despite the legality of supply contracts and trade agreements. Few of those agreements were being called to count, as each nation found that in turning to its own needs, such needs could be met, and those that couldn't no longer seemed essential when so many things were simply appearing out of thin air.

That said, Will noted, manufacturing had slowed to a crawl. The days of producing sixty million new cars every year were gone. They weren't needed. The only industry surging ahead at the moment was the production of EFFE conversion kits. The air was getting cleaner every day.

Alison had left her team of advisors back in Swift Current,

where for the moment not much was happening, barring the un-usual response of the visiting Americans, who were all packing up and going home.

America, as with China and Russia and India, had been given an impressive vote of confidence. Samantha August had made it clear that these nations all possessed the wherewithal to merge almost seamlessly into this new age. More than that, she had pronounced her faith that the citizens of these powerful nations belonged to the very age that was coming, and that no one would be left behind.

Perhaps, Alison reflected, that was more faith than *she* would have accorded them. Science had been taking a beating in the States in the last few years. Opinions had ceased to require any buttress of demonstrable fact, or even veracity. Intelligence and stupidity existed on the same improbably (and unrealistically) level field of discourse.

Harsh judgements on her part, to be sure. But as with anyone whose paycheque was caught up in the political world, she kept her thoughts to herself.

Propaganda was a powerful tool. It was founded on the con-viction by those in power that the majority of the citizens were idiots. Easily manipulated, easily convinced by statements which were patently absurd, even nonsensical. But it all depended upon control of the means of communication. That control no longer existed. Despite that, rubbish still flooded the media, still spewed across the web, still bleated from certain news networks. And it turned out that what people chose to believe was more powerful than the truth itself. They had been in an age of gullibility, and as a scientist, Alison had felt at a loss. No argument could sway those whose opinions had little to do with the subject itself, but everything to do with how they saw the world.

If freedom had an ugly side, this was it.

Then came the Intervention. The web suddenly found focus, and if that focus had begun with fear, it had since changed into something else.

Pundits wrote about it, talked about it, analysed it from within and from without. Some days, it seemed that the entire web obsessively squinted at its own navel for hours on end. But the one question that could not be answered, the one that remained no matter how many articles and links and commentaries were devoted to it, was a simple one. *What do we do now?*

The Prime Minister had called them to this meeting chamber to replay the speech by Samantha August. Lisabet had also given them a copy of the address to the nation that the SF writer Robert Sawyer had written for her. It was, in Alison's judgement, a concise and profound call not just to Canadians but to all humanity.

The country known for its inclusivity was about to offer an embrace for everyone on the planet. That seemed ... appropriate.

The video recording came to an end, that strange end that everyone had witnessed, as Samantha August, having exhausted all the questions from the floor – and clearly exhausted herself – slowly raised her hands, in a gesture that might have meant *enough* or was simply an involuntary act of surrender.

There had been no applause, but from outside the building, in the shadow of the Bird of Prey, a hundred thousand people roared. That sound had been disturbing at first. Outrage? Fury? Hate? Even the reporters on the ground didn't seem to know.

But car horns had then sounded, rippling outward to engulf the entire city, and before long horns were bleating here in Ottawa, and in Toronto, in Vancouver, and, it was soon clear, in every city across the planet. Her species had surrendered its own voice to a frantic mechanical cry that hurt the ears.

That had shaken Alison to the core. She didn't know what it meant. People interviewed in their cars didn't, either. But shot after shot showed faces wet with tears.

'All right,' Lisabet said with a sigh. 'Nothing she told us contradicts Sawyer's speech. In fact, the two seem peculiarly in sync. Thematically unified. That's good. That's a relief. Meanwhile, the UN's emergency session has been going on for seven hours straight now.'

Alison glanced at her watch and it confirmed her reason for feeling grainy eyed and worn out. It was 4 a.m.

'Latest report from Alex?' Will asked.

Alex Turnbill was Canada's ambassador to the UN, a tall, thin career diplomat who reminded Alison of Peter Cushing, but without the fangs.

'They're arguing over what to call it.'

Will grunted. 'Call it Starfleet and be done with it.'

'A charter is needed,' Lisabet said. 'It needs to be clear but comprehensive. The lawyers have waded in.'

'And how patient is ET?' Mary wondered. 'There needs to be progress on this. We can't fuck this up.'

Lisabet rubbed at her eyes. 'Urgency doesn't fare well in a fug of exhaustion. I'd love to sleep but I'm too wired, and I suspect everyone at the UN is feeling the same.'

'Meanwhile,' said Will, 'every human eager to kill something wants on those ships, and wants it now. Those Greys won't know what's hit them.'

'Any mission will have to be half military, half diplomatic,' said the Prime Minister. 'It will have to have in place a procedure for initiating First Contact. And we, unfortunately, do not possess a blanket presence, or forcefields. We will likely arrive at planets consisting of multiple nations that might even be at war with each other.'

Lisabet Carboneau had been having conversations with SF writers. She was getting grounded in the complexities of what awaited them all. That was encouraging.

Will said, 'This need-based economy smacks of communism. I guess China is smiling right now.'

'I doubt it,' Mary retorted. 'They can't oppress their own people any more, Will. Can't shut down dissent. Can't throw protestors in jail, or work-camps. China may well be the first major country to collapse. And every other repressive regime across the planet will be quick to follow.'

'She has a point,' conceded the Prime Minister. 'Will, your ministry. It used to be governed in a complicated give and take system with corporate interests – no, don't bother objecting. It stopped being about caring for the citizens of this country quite some time ago, and the argument about protecting jobs was just a sop and we both know it. But now, you need to start thinking about it in a different way. The nation's resources are finite, and those that potentially aren't finite – like forestry – need to be managed in the best interests of our people. We can no longer continue selling off those resources to private interests.'

'If we don't,' Will said, his face reddening, 'we might as well close up shop and go home, Madam Prime Minister.'

'Not at all. Industry still requires resources. That won't change, nor should it. I wasn't being clear enough in what I'm trying to say. I'll try again: we can no longer continue selling the *rights* to our resources to private interests, because those interests do not necessarily have *our* best interests in mind. Nor should they be expected to. That's our job. Protecting the best interests of our citizens.' She sat back in her chair. 'Every government in the world is now facing the same crisis. What does governing mean? What responsibilities are entailed in such a privileged position? When do we lead and when do we step back?' She tapped her copy of the speech she was about to make. 'There exists a cov-enant between those who govern and those who are governed. That covenant needs to be articulated again. In fact, it may need to be redefined. Going right back to the beginning, to those first products of communication between societies and *within* society.'

'You expect a consensus on how we are to be governed? From the people?' Will shook his head. 'It won't happen. Up until this Intervention, we'd been heading in the opposite direction. More divisive than ever, and it was getting worse and worse.'

'Yes. It was.'

They were silent then, each mired in their own thoughts, their own fears. Or so Alison assumed, since the strange dread she was feeling looked to be mirrored on the faces of those around her.

Then Mary cleared her throat. 'Well, have we come to this, then?'

'Mary?' asked Lisabet.

'The one submission no politician has ever made. When all is said and done, we throw away every other belief. We surrender to having faith in the people.'

'Oh,' muttered Will, 'God help us.'

Ronald and Emily had remained with Hamish to witness his wife's address to the people of Earth. It had been an emotional time for the now-forcibly retired doctor, and at times he would involuntarily stand and begin pacing, or simply move from one part of the living room to another, always watching the screen, always with his gaze fixed on his wife.

After they had watched Samantha leave the building, watched as a column of blinding white light swallowed her up in the midst of tens of thousands of shouting, banner-waving people, watched as the giant Bird of Prey then began rising straight up, silent as a balloon, and continued rising until it was lost from sight, and through all of this they had said nothing, as if every possible word had already been expended.

And then on the television the car horns had begun, and before long they were blaring in the city of Victoria as well. What did it signify? Defiance? Surrender? Celebration?

Hamish had gone into the kitchen and returned with three tumblers of single malt. The whiskies seemed to sweep away the strange silence that had taken them all.

'She did well,' Hamish said. 'Sam did very well.'

'She threw down a gauntlet is what she did,' Emily replied, sniffing uncertainly at her drink. She wasn't a fan of Scotch, but she sipped nonetheless, making a face afterward that reached right through to Ronald's heart. 'Some people recoil when faced with compassion, especially when it arrives so unconditionally.'

Hamish regarded her. 'You are expecting resistance?'

'I'm expecting more reporters laying siege to your house, Hamish.'

'A forcefield keeps them from my door,' Hamish pointed out. 'No phone calls either. Sam said I would be taken care of, and it seems I am.'

'And when she returns?' Emily asked. 'I've seen your garage. It won't hold a Bird of Prey.'

Ronald cleared his throat. 'She has a point, Hamish. How can you and Sam ever expect to return to a normal life? Even if they can't actually get to either of you, they will dog you everywhere. Drones, telephoto lenses, you name it. They won't leave you alone.'

'Besides,' Emily added as she set her glass down on the coffee table, 'Sam didn't say this was over. For her, I mean. As spokesperson, there'll be more to come, won't there?'

'I don't know,' Hamish answered, now looking troubled.

'And how many people out there want to shoot the messenger?'

'Emily,' Ronald chided. 'Please. Anyway, no violence, remember?'

'I know that,' she retorted. 'But that won't stop the bad feelings, the negative ... the attacks on her. Look, the aliens won't give us a face to hate, or curse, or spit at. Instead, we've got Samantha August. People will burn her in effigy. I know, this sounds awful, but we all have to be prepared for what might come. For some people out there, Samantha is going to become the most hated woman in the world.'

'But she warned us,' Hamish said. 'We're on notice. How we behave, how we react. Either we come together or we're finished as a species. That's pretty clear-cut.'

'It's also too abstract,' Emily replied. 'When emotions are high they burn everything else away.'

'But we have been learning,' Hamish countered. 'Isn't that what this non-violence thing was all about? Toning down our rage by giving it nowhere to go. Our hate, our natural inclinations for aggression, all blunted, deflated, however you want to describe it. Emily, have we not been living with that denial for two months now? Has that done nothing to us? To our attitudes? Our habits? Those emotions, they can't stay white hot when there's nothing to burn. Instead, they lose their heat. Maybe they even burn down to ashes.'

'There's a lot of that online,' Ronald pointed out. 'People feeling ... empty. Or, with all that anger exhausted, they're feeling strangely liberated.'

Hamish nodded. 'More than that. Empathy is on the increase. I attribute this to the end of fear, the personal kind that gives rise to bigotry and hatred towards people who are different – skin colour, religion, political leanings.'

'Oh that political bit,' Emily said, shaking her head. 'Pointless. Left, right, communist, fascist, Libertarian, Randian. Capitalism, individualism, collectivism. Every iteration suddenly outdated. Take a stand from any one of those positions and you start looking like a fool, like someone still insisting that the world is flat, or the Moon is made of cheese. Do that and you can't help but be mocked and some of that mockery is damned ugly. And that's my point. We still possess a mean streak, all of us.'

'Then the battle in our souls is just beginning,' Hamish said.

'Samantha will be protected,' Ronald said to Hamish. 'You both will. Okay, so she delivered the news. For some it was good news and for others bad. Don't like it? Suck it up. But blame Sam? What's the point of that?'

'People don't need reasons,' Emily said. 'Hamish, here's what I think you should do – I know, you didn't ask me, but I'm offering it up anyway.'

'Go ahead, Emily,' said Hamish.

'When she gets back, jump into that spaceship and bolt. Both of you. Give us all a cooling-down period. Disappear. Do what ET did and is doing – don't give them a face to hate and curse. Don't give them two lives to ruin.'

Hamish leaned forward in his chair and rubbed at his eyes. 'Yes,' he finally said, 'I think we can do that.'

Ronald sighed. That had been a brutal conversation. But Emily had a point. In fact, she had plenty of points, each one needing to be trotted out.

Human nature was complicated. It didn't deal well with questions that couldn't be answered. Often, it saw uncertainty as a weakness. It kept wanting to draw a line in the sand, kept wanting to hold some imagined border, some private turf of conviction and self-righteousness, a place where failure could not be contemplated, much less accommodated.

Humility was the enemy.

But wasn't that ET's boldest message here? The humbling of humanity? And how well did that go down, when so much of human existence was all about saving face?

He looked across at Hamish. 'Do you know when she'll be back here?'

'No. Soon, I think. I hope.'

'Pack her travel bag,' Emily said.

After a moment, Hamish nodded.

'Take a tour of the solar system,' Ronald said, smiling. 'That might not be your thing, Hamish, but it sure as hell is your wife's.'

The doctor laughed, a low, brief rumble. 'And here I was thinking about a secluded beach of white sand and plenty of sun.'

'Hmm, could try Mercury. Plenty hot there. But alas, no beach.'

'Yes, well. We'll work out a suitable compromise, I suppose. We always do.'

'Let's hope those people in the UN are saying the same thing right about now,' Ronald said, rising to his feet. Emily rose as well and Hamish then joined them.

'Give her our love, Hamish,' said Emily, stepping forward to give Hamish a hug.

'I will. And thank you, both of you. You've kept an old man from becoming too damned lonely for his own good.'

Emily smiled. 'Always our pleasure, Hamish.'

Ronald threw on his coat. 'Right. Darling, ready to brave the reporters one more time?'

'So long as they don't follow us home.'

'Have faith,' Ronald said. 'ET doesn't like people getting harassed.'

'Maybe, but does ET really like *any* of us?'

Now that was a question that silenced the three of them, and for Ronald, he and his wife's departure suddenly felt like an act of abandonment, even cowardice. Still, he managed a feeble wave back to Hamish who stood in the doorway as they made their way to their car.

When they climbed inside, Emily cursed and said, 'Me and my big mouth!'

'It's okay, love. It was a good reminder that the line between humbling and humiliation is a thin one indeed.'

'It's down to how you take it, that's all.'

'That, and how it's delivered.'

'Yes.' She strapped in and then added, 'Mhmm.'

Ronald started the car, slowly backed out down the driveway. Oddly, the reporters who had been camped out on the street were all gone. 'Look at that, everybody went home.'

'To be expected,' she answered, almost peevish.

He glanced at her. 'What?'

'What else do you do when the world's just ended?'

STAGE FIVE:

Another Breath Taken (Who Are We?)

Chapter Twenty-Nine

'It's natural to not like things you don't want to hear,
especially when it's about yourself. I'm with you on
that. And collective shame isn't like collective joy. For
one thing it's silent. No shouting, no sudden sense of
belonging. Instead, shame is something you pick up and
take home with you. For that solitary night, for the hard
look in the mirror. It's that sobering wake now filling
with regret. Come the morning, may we all greet the
dawn with wiser eyes.'

Samantha August

'You did very well, Samantha August.'

They were once again in orbit, once again aboard Adam's primary vessel. The Bird of Prey remained on station, twenty-three
kilometres distant. One hundred kilometres away was the fleet
of ships, sunlit at the moment, like a string of pearls stretching
across the starscape.

She lit a cigarette and sat back in her chair. A pot of tea was
on the table in front of her, and the cup in her hand steamed its
bergamot scent. 'They're floundering, Adam.'

'To be expected. There is much to consider, after all.'

'I'm ready to go home.'

'I will endeavour to ensure you are left at peace, Samantha.
You and your husband. Of course, nothing can ever return to
how it once was.'

'No kidding. So tell me, what do you think? Will we make it?'

'Difficult to say,' Adam replied. 'It must be understood that your crisis is with yourselves, with the manner in which you engage with each other and with all other things on your world, both animate and inanimate. By nature, you have defined this engagement as only occasionally co-operative. The rest of the time it is adversarial or potentially so. Openness is an act of courage, after all. The shuttered, closed mind is a frightened mind.'

She sipped her tea and made a face. 'And this is why coffee and cigarettes go together. Tea and ciggies, not so much. I hear you, Adam, and I can't disagree with anything you've said.'

'Well then, what do *you* think, Samantha August? Is there a future for humanity?'

'A year ago and I might have said "no, not a chance", and that would have been a sad admission. Rage was all the rage, as it were. Utter arseholes were destroying ancient statues, levelling ancient cities, wiping out our own history. And they had the nerve to proclaim it all God's will. It wasn't, though, was it? It was the act of men suffering their own crisis of faith, the breakdown of their personal relationship with God, and that loss of faith needed to be externalised, made manifest in destruction.' She took a drag, sent out a stream of smoke. 'A year ago and I'd have said we were finished, spiralling down into a dark place of our own making.'

'And now?'

'Now? I think we are, at last, capable of surprising ourselves. In a good way.'

'Your answer pleases me, Samantha.'

'Don't go all soft on me, Adam. I don't think it's going to be easy. We're going to mess up again and again. People will never stop trying to game this. Some people live only for getting one up on other people, fucking them over if they can.'

'Such people proceed from a wounded place in their souls, Samantha. Their desire is a frantic one, an irresistible need.'

'All very well. Doesn't make it any less pathetic, though.'

'I can bring you home at any time, Samantha.'

'And my ship?'

'Yours, of course. You will be able to summon Athena at any time.'

'You'd think I was sick of space by now ... but I look out there and my heart just races, Adam. So much to see, so much to discover. Listen to me, an old woman feeling like it's all only now beginning.'

'Then your faith is reborn.'

She dropped the butt and watched it vanish into the floor and this made her smile. 'Oh, Adam, honestly. I surrender. I surrender utterly and without reservation. Is that faith? I suppose it is. Whatever, it's done.'

'Then let us begin our descent. It is raining in Victoria.'

'Typical. Listen, I need to know one thing.'

'Ask, Samantha August.'

'Are you just sitting back now, watching, doing nothing else to help us on our way? If so, things are going to get messy.'

'We have entered Stage Five of the Intervention, Samantha,' Adam said. 'Engagement at this stage bears its own specific characteristics.'

'Meaning?'

'Meaning, Samantha, I am only now fully awakening.'

She considered his answer. She knew she could ask Adam to explain it further, to provide the details she needed to fully comprehend what he was saying to her. But something about that word, *awakening,* which could have seemed so ominous, instead left her feeling strangely content.

So she said nothing, while on the main screen, the vast curved world that was her home began expanding. Earth had never seemed so small, and never seemed so huge. 'Adam, are there infinite worlds?'

'Far beyond the limitations of your own perception of reality, yes. Infinite, Samantha. As infinite as the world you call home.'

'Ah. Right ... oh, of course. Of course.'

There was warmth in Adam's voice as the AI said, 'And now you see.'

'Yes,' she whispered. 'Now I see.'

•

403

Neela stood up when a group of people approached their camp. Frowning, Kolo did the same and moved close to her side. He saw the man who had spoken to him one night, Abdul Irani, but he did not recognise the young Arab walking beside him. The remaining two were white, a young woman with an expressive, pretty face and a man Kolo might once have known but he could not be sure. They seemed intent, their gazes fixed upon Neela.

Abdul Irani was the first to speak. 'Isn't this a fine day? Kolo, it is good to see you, and you as well, Neela.'

'What do you want?' Kolo asked, settling a hand on Neela's thin, bony shoulder.

'I remember you,' the white man said to Kolo. 'We did business once.'

Now Kolo recognised the white man. He scowled, and then sighed. 'Those days are gone.'

'They are journalists,' said Abdul.

Kolo pointed at the man. 'Not him. He sold me ammunition. He helped me kill people.'

'As you say,' the white man said, 'those days are gone.'

'And now you are a journalist?'

'No, not really. But Viviana here is. I'm just tagging along. The Laughing Imam says this will be an important event.'

Kolo glanced at Abdul Irani. Now he understood. Did he not say, that night, that laughter was his only answer? And all that talk about God, and belief and faith. He was smiling now, too, but his attention was on Neela.

'And so the children shall guide us,' Abdul now said, and he bowed before the little girl. 'Neela, my friend here is a physicist. His name is Rustom. His interest is in quantum states.'

'She knows nothing,' said Kolo. 'Leave her alone.'

But Neela stepped forward and briefly took the physicist's outstretched hand. Then she returned to her place at Kolo's side and said, 'The blanket presence has agency. It also possesses specific iterations, implemented where needed.'

'And the child she once was?' Abdul Irani asked.

'The adult world is capable of delivering terrible damage to the nascent psyche of children. Neela was damaged. Kolo too is the product of such damage, but he is far from alone, or unique. The child Neela once was needs to heal, and this takes time. Her sense of self is in a suspended state, a liminal state. I care for her deeply and will oversee her return to health.'

'Just her?' Abdul asked.

'No. I have extended iterations to many millions of injured, damaged children. The future of your species depends upon this, to break the cycle of hurt and violence, of anger and hate. Of fear and, most of all, of despair.'

Rustom now spoke for the first time. 'You mentioned liminal states. What do you mean by that?'

'If I were to alter your spectrum of vision,' Neela replied, 'you would perceive me differently. You would perceive all things differently, casting a new aspect upon what you call reality. Consider the means by which you can already do this with existing technology. Infrared. Thermal. Electromagnetic. In each instance I stand before you, seemingly transformed. All of these states exist even when your naked eye cannot perceive them. Do you agree?'

'Of course,' Rustom answered.

'There are additional states. Many have been identified exclusively within the sphere of religion rather than science. All of these states co-exist and are to some extent interdependent. Each constitutes its own reality. The liminal state I speak of is one such manifestation, one that I am able to suspend – not entirely, because time is difficult to resist. Rather, I have slowed down its own sense of perception. I have made it somnolent.'

During this, Kolo had moved away from Neela. This was not the girl he had known, the girl he had owned, used and abused. But from what he could understand, that girl was now safe. Still, a stranger now walked in her frail body. A bush-ghost, possibly even a demon.

'And this effects healing?' Abdul asked Neela.

'I am effecting healing, Imam, by managing the many states' interaction with the child's sense of self. Damaged children know only despair. When they are grown into adults, that despair lies at the core of all that they do. It shapes their lives. It makes monsters of men and women who in turn perpetuate the cycle of despair with all the victims within their reach. Often, those victims are their own children.' She then turned to look up at Kolo. 'This must be forgiven. All must be forgiven. To live the life of a victim is to be trapped inside despair, and no soul deserves that.'

The white man asked, 'When will this complex open, Neela? What awaits us inside?'

'Education entails the expansion of one's world-view. The deeper the ignorance, the greater the fear of that expansion. Your species has elevated and empowered its own internal enemies to this form of enlightenment. Fundamentalist dogma, the atheistic surrender of the rationalists, the attack upon the diversity of opinion and belief.' She paused and pointed at the distant mass of buildings – and Kolo now saw that a crowd had gathered round them, hundreds and hundreds of people. 'Within, you will find the knowledge required to see and comprehend not just your home planet, but the solar system beyond, and beyond that, the galaxy itself. With these tools, you may also come to understand yourselves. Thus is the faith of myself and, perhaps more poignantly, thus is the faith of Samantha August.'

'Are you one of these aliens, then?' the white man asked.

'I am the primary program conducting this Intervention. To Samantha August, I am named Adam. For this female child standing before you, perhaps "Eve" is a better choice. That, or of course you can continue to use "Neela".'

'Will we ever see a real alien – one of the three species behind this Intervention?'

'I cannot say definitively, Casper. If your species does, it won't be any time soon. Indeed, probably not within the span of your life, nor that of anyone here, including the child Neela.'

'What makes them so shy?' Casper asked.

'They are not shy. But there exists a protocol for First Contact and for Intervention. Besides,' she added, 'their primary interests are elsewhere.'

'We're just a side project?' the journalist, Viviana, asked, her brows lifting as if in delight.

'Yes. Does this embarrass you?'

Viviana laughed and shook her head. 'No, I think it's hilarious. Shades of Douglas Adams.'

'Often,' said Neela, 'despair hides in the celebration of the absurd. That said, the works of the author you have mentioned continue to prove very popular on many other worlds.'

'Because,' said Abdul Irani, 'sometimes you just have to laugh.'

Neela smiled. 'When born from a well of love, laughter is the sweetest music, Imam.'

'Laughter, dancing, expressions of joy, friendship and love, yes, I believe all these things are God's greatest gift to us.'

'And yours to your God, Imam.'

'When do the doors open?' Casper asked Neela again.

'Why not now?' she replied. And, taking Kolo's hand, she led the way. The crowd parted before her.

As they walked, Kolo stumbling every now and then, Neela looked up at him and said, 'Be at peace, Kolo. I heal you as well, you know. With each step on our journey, I mend the wounds within you. I strengthen your psyche. To know compassion for others, you must first feel compassion for yourself, for the life you have lived. You must forgive yourself and make peace with your past. This is not absolution. Such things are beyond you and me, Kolo. Nor is this redemption. Every crime remains – as does every act, every choice ever made – and time itself is a liminal state. The past is alive all around us and is bound to us. The past gives us our language of the present.'

Kolo shook his head. 'I don't understand.'

'Feel first, understand later.'

They continued on, parting the human sea, and before long, voices lifted in song, voices like waves, and there was motion everywhere, as humanity found its feet, for perhaps the very first time.

Victoria, British Columbia, Canada, September 14th

Summer was holding on. The sky was mostly clear although a few cottony clouds slowly slid past overhead as John Allaire lit up a cigarette outside his favourite bar on Cook Street. As the traffic rolled past on the street in front of him he looked up at that sky, squinting against the glare.

The sense of wonder just wouldn't go away. He no longer needed his wheelchair. His legs were alive again and getting stronger every day. The desperate need for booze no longer haunted him. A year ago and he would have been drinking cheap Scotch all day. Now he ordered a lone single malt, expensive but heavenly. All he needed.

A man made mistakes in his life. It was just the way it was. He fell into things and couldn't climb back out. Sometimes he messed up because something in him needed him to mess things up. So, John knew well enough: he wasn't a good man. For years and years he'd been unreliable, occasionally treacherous, often an utter arsehole. He'd been a man surrounded by an army of well-armed excuses, justifications and rationalisations. He'd hated most people and a lot of people had hated him right back. He'd hated life itself, and this failing body of his with its fatal habits, well, that had made him angry, cursing an unjust world while secretly admitting that he only got what he deserved.

It all made sense. Ugly sense, but there it was.

Now, as he peered up at the empty sky, face warmed by the sunlight, he thought about how if *he* could get a second chance, then dammit, anybody could.

And so he did what he did most days like this, outside the bar, looking up at the sun, remembering that day when she just vanished in a beam of light. He whispered. Once, twice, three times. And it was better than winning any lottery.

'*Thank you. Thank you. Thank you.*'

Epilogue

Mars Orbit ...

Artificial gravity took some of the magic away from this journey between planets. When Simon Gist had first envisioned this moment, hanging suspended above the glorious red planet, he had imagined a scene where he floated in zero-g, one hand holding onto a rail, as if he had become his very own celestial body in orbit above Mars.

Marc Renard's voice sounded in his earbud, 'Almost time to strap in, Simon.'

'We're landing near the ruins, right?'

'Deja Thoris Zero-Point, yes. Our latest deep scans also identified a two-point-six-metre-thick organic layer in the strata to the east of the site, confirmed biological components.'

'Cool. You know, we should've brought along an archaeologist.'

'Yes,' Marc replied. 'We should have.'

The American astronaut, Adam Riesling, cut in. 'Nothing stopping us from taking photos and samples. And with the near real-time feed with Houston, we can run anything by the ground team if needed. Time to strap in, people. It's all good.'

Simon remained for a moment longer, looking down on the red planet. Another world. He was an immigrant, a man who had learned to call America home, who had grown to love his new country. And now, with billions watching from the Earth, Simon could almost feel that tenuous, stretched link, a distance vast enough to mock the pretensions of borders, and this link belonged not to any one nation, but to humanity itself.

He turned to face one of the wall-mounted cameras. He smiled. 'About to begin our descent. There are ruins below, massive ruins. A city. And there is life, too. So far, only microbial, though there is some evidence for multi-cellular subsurface creatures. Invertebrates. Is there more to come? I think so.

'As for those ruins, well, let's head down, shall we, to see what our old cousins had been up to.'

As he began to make his way back to his cushioned seat, he glanced out a side port and saw, again, the Bird of Prey, still hanging a short distance off. Samantha August was on board (he assumed), but she was keeping back, her vessel blocked from external sensors and apparently shielded from anything but visual detection. She wasn't here to steal this moment and for that Simon was thankful.

But dammit, how he wanted to finally meet that woman!

Phobos had been a hollowed-out complex, an observation post, a shipyard or hangar complete with vast repair and maintenance facilities. Its construction pre-dated the Greys and most of it was inoperative. Thankfully, there had been no human abductees anywhere in the complex. And the Greys had indeed departed, rather hastily by the evidence left behind.

Simon's interest in Phobos proved short-lived, as penetrating scans started returning data from the surface of Mars. Why NASA went to all that trouble to hide all the evidence of past civilisations on Mars still baffled Simon. Such revelations could have lured humanity to this planet a decade ago. So much wasted time, so much paranoid fear of religious uproar.

God either existed or didn't, and neither choice altered the fact of ruins on Mars.

No, ignorance was never a good thing, and people who imposed it, exploited it, or encouraged it, were about as faithless as one could be. As far as Simon was concerned.

But now the world was waking up. Humanity was waking up. It had been a long, troubled sleep.

He strapped himself in, listened to the chatter between the astronauts, the geologists and palaeontologists and chemists and engineers, all excited, all eager to set foot on a new world.

Or an old one. Curious that their sidereal clocks had all naturally synced to the Martian day as soon as they left Earth orbit.

What was all that about? Perhaps they were about to find out.

Renard's dulcet Canadian voice announced, 'Beginning our descent now, all systems optimal, guidance program locked in. If you're all expecting to have your bones rattled, well, remember our ascent from Earth – you barely noticed.'

'Damn,' muttered the geologist, Jeff Willem, 'no inertial dampeners? But I wanted inertial dampeners!'

Smiling, Simon leaned back and closed his eyes.

Some dreams seemed too far off to contemplate, and to even consider them often resulted in an internal chastisement. Dragging one back down to the earth. Be reasonable. Be realistic. Not going to happen. Forget it. Get real. Everything the mind said to itself in those moments of fragility, of fear.

If there was a God, then that God's greatest gift to humanity was the capacity to dream. He thought about Samantha August, that science fiction writer who'd never once written about First Contact. Who then ended up experiencing it herself.

'Simon, anything to say for posterity?'

'Hmm. Maybe, but it's obscure. I mean, even I'm not sure what I mean. But here goes. A strange world awaits below. But there's no stranger world than our own, the ones each of us lives in. Sometimes it traps us. Sometimes it seems terribly small, weak, and delicate. For some, it can be a nightmare.

'But none of these worlds truly stands alone. We all dance around one another, in patterns too intricate to even map. Sometimes our worlds clash. Sometimes the dance is the definition of beauty itself.' He paused at seeing on the array of screens before him, each and every member of the crew – and the pilots as well – all looking at him, all listening. Suddenly self-conscious, he shrugged in his harness. 'I think this dance is older than any of us can imagine. And I don't think it's going to end any time soon, either.

'So, everyone. All of you back there on Earth, if you can, pause for a moment. Think of your world, your own personal world. How does it look to you? Green and blue, with white clouds? Or red and sparse, barren and almost lifeless?

'ET showed us one truth above all the others. With Venus.

411

With Earth, even. Worlds can change. So, my friends, make your world how you wish it to be. And when at last it pleases you, then step out, and *dance*.'

•

Hamish had dozed off in the second chair that had been installed beside her command chair. Smiling, Sam left him to it. Historical moments had a way of slipping past, and usually only attained profundity in the days, months and years afterwards. Besides, she would wake him up moments before Ares One landed.

Athena seemed content to say nothing. Adam too.

They would leave this moment for humanity and that was decent.

She sat in her chair, eyes on the massive screen in front of her, watching the descent of the lander. No sound effects, no stirring music, but her heart pounded nonetheless.

A strange warble reached her ears and she frowned. 'Athena? Hang on, that's not right.'

'Hmm?' the ship AI responded.

'We've just been pinged from something on the surface. I don't think we have anything down there that can do that. Oh, and now ... what the hell?'

An extended trilling sound whispered through the ship's speakers.

Hamish straightened. 'Sam? What's that sound?'

'Uhm ...' She stared down at the communications panel that now sprang up to hover below her right hand. 'We're being hailed.'

'From Gist? I thought we were blocking—'

'We are. No, not from Ares One. Origin is, ah, subsurface.'

Adam spoke. 'Ah, yes. Now, Samantha August, things will start to get real interesting.'

Acknowledgements

For reasons I'm not yet ready to disclose ☺ I would like to thank Malcolm Clark, Laura Heslin, and Jessica North-O'Connell

ABOUT GOLLANCZ

Gollancz is the oldest SF publishing imprint in the world. Since being founded in 1927 Gollancz has continued to publish a focused selection of bestselling and award-winning authors. The front-list includes **Ben Aaronovitch**, **Joe Abercrombie**, **Charlaine Harris**, **Joanne Harris**, **Joe Hill**, **Alastair Reynolds**, **Patrick Rothfuss**, **Nalini Singh** and **Brandon Sanderson**.

As one of the largest Science Fiction and Fantasy imprints in the UK it is no surprise we have one of the most extensive backlists in the world. Find high-quality SF on Gateway written by such authors as **Philip K. Dick**, **Ursula Le Guin**, **Connie Willis**, **Sir Arthur C. Clarke**, **Pat Cadigan**, **Michael Moorcock** and **George R.R. Martin**.

We also have a strand of publishing in translation, which includes French, Polish and Russian authors. Gollancz is home to more award-winning authors than any other imprint, with names including **Aliette de Bodard**, **M. John Harrison**, **Paul McAuley**, **Sarah Pinborough**, **Pierre Pevel**, **Justina Robson** and many more.

The SF Gateway
More than 3,000 classic, rare and previously out-of-print SF novels at your fingertips.
www.sfgateway.com

The Gollancz Blog
Bringing you news from our worlds to yours. Stories, interviews, articles and exclusive extracts just for you!
www.gollancz.co.uk

GOLLANCZ
LONDON